The Bad Luck Spirits'

Social Aid

and Pleasure Club

Andrew Fox

MonstraCity Press

Manassas, Virginia

MonstraCity Press

Manassas, Virginia

www.monstracitypress.com

Books by Andrew Fox

Fat White Vampire Series

Fat White Vampire Blues (Del Rey Books)

Bride of the Fat White Vampire (Del Rey Books)

The Bad Luck Spirits' Social Aid and Pleasure Club (tie-in)

Fat White Vampire Otaku (ebook available; print edition available April 2021)

Hunt the Fat White Vampire (available June 2021)

The Good Humor Man, or, Calorie 3501 (Tachyon Publications)

The August Micholson Chronicles

Fire on Iron

Hellfire and Damnation (available August 2021)

Collections

Hazardous Imaginings: The Mondo Book of Politically Incorrect Science Fiction

Edited by Andrew Fox

Again, Hazardous Imaginings: More Politically Incorrect Science Fiction (available December 2020)

For Dara and the kids, who endured their Katrina exile with humor and grace;

For the dozens of friends who offered refuge and support;

And for the men and women of the U.S. Coast Guard and the Louisiana Department of Wildlife and Fisheries

"As long as we are lucky we attribute it to our smartness; our bad luck we give the gods credit for."

Josh Billings, nineteenth century
American humorist

"New Orleans... the city that *never* shoulda been."

refrain repeated every few blocks by
Gray Line Tours bus driver on
Crescent City route, circa 1982

Cast of Characters...2

Part I: The Gathering Storm.. 5

Part II: Ain't Got No Home... 157

Part III: No Joy in Mudville?... 271

Cast of Characters

Members of the Miasma Club

Kay Rosenblatt, Ashkenazic Jewish bad luck spirit, or *ayin hora* ("Evil Eye")

Owl Lookingback, Houma Indian trickster

Pandora, Greek bad luck spirit

Ti Malice, Dahomean-Haitian trickster spirit

Eleggua-Eshu, Yoruban trickster spirit

Reynard the Fox, French trickster spirit

Balor the Fomorian, Irish bad luck spirit (and Faebar, the trickster leprechaun who lives inside Balor's tear duct)

Fortuna Discordia, Italian Evil Eye spirit

Na Ba and Na Ong, married Vietnamese bad luck spirits

Glenn the Gremlin, bad luck gremlin to all things mechanical

The Triumvirate:

    Mephistopheles, Spanish bad luck spirit

    Old Scratch, English bad luck spirit

    Krampus, German bad luck spirit

Mortals

Roy Rio, mayor of New Orleans

Daniel Weintraub, Kay Rosenblatt's mortal boyfriend

Lily Weintraub, David's sister, head nurse at Baptist Hospital, Roy Rio's high school sweetheart

Amos Weintraub, David's and Lily's father

2

Councilwoman Cynthia Belvedere Hotchkiss, Roy Rio's ex-wife

Nicole Rio, Roy's and Cynthia's teenaged daughter

Sergeant Quincy Cochrane, Cynthia's uncle, officer in the New Orleans Police Department

Bruno Galliano, Mayor Rio's Special Assistant for Homeland Security, former U.S. Marine

Bob Marino, former head of FEBO, the Federal Emergency Backstop Organization

William "Duckie" Duckswitt, current head of FEBO

Walter Johnson, Mayor Rio's chief of staff and Roy's oldest friend

Merle Morehouse, former mayor of New Orleans, Mayor Rio's cousin and political rival

Annalee Jones, executive partner, MuckGen Energy Solutions

Amitri "Mike" Zoukeni, co-founder/chief researcher, MuckGen Energy Solutions

The Muses

Euterpe ("Felicia"), Muse of Music, the Giver of Pleasure, the Mother of the Double Flute

Calliope, Muse of lyric poetry, eldest of the Muses

Terpsichore the Whirler, Muse of the dance

Urania the Heavenly, Muse of astronomy

Polyhymnia, Muse of sacred hymns and geometry

Erato the Lovely, Muse of love poetry

Thalia, Muse of comedy

Melpomene, Muse of tragedy

Clio, Muse of history

Part I
The Gathering Storm

Chapter 1

Kay Rosenblatt. *Ayin hora.* Embodiment of the Evil Eye. Bad luck spirit.

Is that all I am? she asked herself.

Was that truly her *essence?* Something she could never, ever rise above?

She refused to believe it. Her endless life would be intolerable if she ever allowed herself to admit it. If the thing inside her, her aura, ever convinced her that *it* was truly Kay, all that Kay truly was, and that what she had come to think of as her personality was nothing more than a disguise to fool the mortals who surrounded her, a layer of pancake makeup that the aura could wipe away at will... well, she would have to find some way to do away with herself.

If doing away with herself was even possible. She wasn't sure it was.

Today was Friday the Thirteenth. The semi-annual meeting of the Miasma Club would be held tonight. The Triumvirate had assigned prework: each of the members had to review the others' progress reports online prior to the meeting. Normally, the members gave verbal reports to the assembled group. But tonight would be different, for some reason. The Triumvirate had decided they could not spare the time for bureaucratic routine.

Shuddering with anticipative dread, she sat herself down at the rolltop desk near the bay window of her cottage off Elysian Fields Avenue. She turned her computer on. Of her dozen fellow Miasma Club members, she felt flashes of simpatico with only four — Owl Lookingback, Pandora, and two of the club's most recent additions, the

Vietnamese couple, Na Ong and Na Ba. But even that simpatico was merely relative; their bad luck auras or trickster natures still made the part of her she had come to think of as her own true self feel a queasy aversion.

She forced herself to read. The Triumvirate would probably quiz them on their knowledge of each other's activities. Ti Malice's report appeared first. His braggadocio came through loud and clear as he described his successful efforts to induce corruption among the members of the Orleans Parish School Board, teachers, and contractors, helping to keep the New Orleans public school system one of the nation's worst. His fellow African spirit, Eleggua-Eshu, reported next, gleefully describing how he had kept the violent turf battles between the St. Bernard Project and St. Thomas Project drug gangs on the boil.

Fortuna Discordia, Kay's personal *bete noir*, snidely wrote of slowing the inadequate maintenance efforts of the Streets Department into somnolent lethargy, allowing potholes on many streets to grow to the size of small lakes. The French spirit Reynard the Fox's area of specialization was culture; he had influenced the musical director of the Louisiana Philharmonic Orchestra to program an entire season of mid-twentieth century avant-garde symphonies by Communist Bloc composers, which had come within a hair of forcing the orchestra into bankruptcy. Balor the Fomorian and Faebar, the evil leprechaun who lived inside the tear ducts of Balor's single eye, wrote of inciting police officers of Irish ancestry to engage in on-the-job brutality so blatant as to fall outside the pale of even the NOPD's notoriously lax standards. It was obvious to Kay that Faebar had composed the progress report; Balor, the dumb brute, was borderline illiterate.

Glenn the Gremlin rattled off a laundry list of infrastructure and technology projects he'd managed to snafu, including the external fuel tanks for the space shuttles being maintained at the Lockheed Martin plant on the east side of town. Then came the turns of Kay's friends. Pandora had little new to report; she meekly apologized to the Triumvirate that her Ills had been unusually quiescent over much of the past half year. She had been able to convince Pestilence to spread an outbreak of strep throat among the nursery school students enrolled at the Greek Orthodox Cathedral's educational center, but that had been the extent of things.

Empty as Pandora's account was, Kay shook her head in silent wonder at Owl Lookingback's report. His sole accomplishment in the last six months had been to induce a homeless man with faint American Indian ancestry to spit a loogie onto the sidewalk outside Rubensteins Haberdashery on Canal Street. He might as well have spat a loogie into the faces of the Triumvirate themselves. How did he manage to get away with such open insolence?

Na Ba and Na Ong complained, as they usually did, about the difficulties inherent in blighting the lives of a group of people as diligent, disciplined, and resilient as New Orleans' Vietnamese community. She could hear their gently bickering voices in her head:

"We have hard job," Na Ba would say flatly, crossing her arms in front of her petite breasts.

"No complaining, wife," Na Ong would insist.

"No, it *true*. Our people come from Vietnam with good, strong values. Hard work. Hard study. Support family. Go to church. Honor the elders—"

"The young ones," Na Ong would insist. "I tell you again and again, wife — forget about ones who come from Vietnam. Focus on next generation, ones born in Village L'Est and Marrero. Ones who go to public school with American youngster and absorb American way. Look at bright side, focus on positive. Did I not give you gang fight in Village de L'Est for our wedding anniversary? Is not fighting between Vietnamese gang and black gang in high school a bright and promising thing?"

"Yes, husband," Na Ba would say with a notable lack of enthusiasm.

Who was left...? Kay realized with a sinking feeling that she was the only Miasma Club member who hadn't yet reported on her progress, apart from the Triumvirate, who exempted themselves from the requirement. And she hadn't yet written a word.

She cast her mind back over the past six months. What did she have to report? There'd been that trio of Tulane med students who'd botched their end-of-semester exams thanks to their adventure in that Bienville Street massage parlor she'd led them to. And the scandal at Dorignac's Supermarket's kosher bakery department, when she had caused *traife* beef lard to be mixed into the icing for Sylvia Mintz's wedding cake, which had then been eaten by over two hundred Orthodox guests. Pretty picayune stuff; she could imagine each of the members of the Triumvirate rolling their eyes as they read her words.

She hadn't been able to accomplish much new, either, with Lieutenant Colonel Branson Schwartz, commander of the South Louisiana District of the Army Corps of Engineers, despite being his personal administrative assistant. Oh, she'd done the usual, encouraging his bulldog-stubborn refusal to accept any criticism of the engineering work he oversaw on the South Louisiana flood protection and levee system. But degrading the flood control system had always been a long-term play; she didn't have anything solid to show for herself in that area for the past six months.

She couldn't just make stuff up, much as she wanted to. The Triumvirate would know, somehow. Or her aura would find a way to force her to reveal her falsehood, taking revenge on her for her efforts to avoid seeding misfortune among the Jewish community. She'd just have to be honest and go with the (thankfully few) scraps of bad luck work her aura had managed to squeeze out of her during the past half year. She cobbled together her report as best she could, took a deep breath, and hit the Send button.

The meeting. It was only two hours away now. The thought of attending made her want to crawl out of her own skin. Why couldn't she be like a snake and shed her skin, leaving her aura behind, trapped in a pile of flaky, dead scales?

She hadn't always felt this way about her aura. There had been a time, she remembered, when she hadn't even thought of it as something separate from her own self at all. It had simply been a part of her, as harmonious and dependable in its workings as her heart or lungs, and just as unremarkable. How many persons raged against their lungs, or even thought about them much? Who wished they could expel their heart from their chest?

When had all that begun to change? She knew the day. She knew the exact moment. She could recite the events of that day, that hour, that moment like a litany of horror, the way penitents on Yom Kippur would recite the Martyrology, the long list of disasters which had struck the Jewish people because of their turnings away from God.

She needed to remind herself yet again. She could never allow herself to stop thinking of that day.

She rose from her desk and went into her bedroom. She sat on the edge of her bed, in front of her mirror, where she would be forced to look at herself. Staring back at her from the glass was a seemingly unremarkable woman in her late thirties, of Ashkenazic Jewish heritage, barely five feet tall, thicker around the middle than she would prefer, sporting sturdy peasant feet and unruly, frizzy black hair. No one looking at her would guess she hid a demon inside her, a malevolent aura which could twist the fortune of any person with so much as a drop of Ashkenazic Jewish blood in their veins.

Could she ever manage to exorcise that demon? She knew she would be irrevocably evil if she failed to try. Once, to her everlasting mortification, she had laughed at the tragedies she and her aura had caused.

That had ended with the Weintraubs. That had ended with Daniel.

She stared at herself in the mirror as she recited, like she would a confessional prayer, the story of the worst day in her long, long existence. The part of her capable of being hopeful hoped against hope that confronting her aura with the pain of this story enough times would eventually reduce it to nothingness, the way repeated applications of acid could gradually dissolve away a hideous wart.

She knew her lines by heart. If she could be said to possess a heart.

"The Weintraubs came to New Orleans from Europe after World War Two, part of a group of a dozen young Jewish refugee families. The Displaced Persons came here with lots of the Old Country still in them, old superstitions and *bubba meisters*. After decades of my unsatisfied feedings on the fading superstitions of Americanized Jews, being around the DPs... it was like main-lining heroin. My aura and I couldn't get enough of them.

"Amos Weintraub was a favorite. By the time he and his wife Miriam had their children, I'd already been influencing him in half a dozen different ways, in half a dozen different guises. I'd been a business partner named Avram, a poker buddy named Yankel, a synagogue secretary named Hannah. I'd encouraged him to invest his meager savings in bum deals, coaxed him into late night poker marathons and gambling debts, gotten him to cheat on his wife.

"Yet despite it all, they were blessed with children. Lily Weintraub was born first, Daniel six years later. The children's natural fear of the dark and innocent belief in a world of elves and spirits were raw meat for me and my aura. I settled into one main guise as far as the Weintraubs were concerned — Lily's eight-year-old girlfriend Hilda. I played with them, my aura causing far more than the usual childhood quota of chipped teeth, spider bites, and roller skating expeditions that ended in the Emergency Room.

"But the more time I spent with them, the more my amoral destructiveness shaded into something approaching fondness. My aura must've sensed that. It must've detected the hesitancy growing in my heart. So it took control. For the first time ever, I caused something base and evil to happen without consciously willing it to occur. That was the beginning of the schism between us, between my aura and me. The start of the horror I now live with every waking moment and in all of my dreams.

"It happened on a Sunday. The Weintraubs and I were all in Amos's Buick, heading to Pontchartrain Beach Amusement Park. Amos was driving, Miriam was in the front passenger seat with Daniel on her lap, and Lily and I were playing in the back seat. Everyone was happy and excited, except Amos. He seemed melancholy, lost in thought. Then he started humming a song I'd heard other immigrants sing, an old Polish lullaby..."

Her voice trailed off into silence, but the story continued in her head. In the back seat of the Buick, she'd felt her face grow itchy and hot. Without intending to, she'd started singing the lullaby, in a different voice than her own — in Polish, a language she'd never learned. Leaning forward, she'd seen her face in the rearview mirror — a stranger's face. She'd then seen Amos's hands tremble on the steering wheel and heard him say, in a choked voice, '*Rachel?*' And he'd turned around to look at her. And even though she'd never heard him speak her name before, she realized he had called out for his baby sister, the one who hadn't survived the war.

Amos lost control of the car. The Buick swerved off the road at the intersection of Robert E. Lee and Marconi Drive. It surged up the slope of the levee, hurled over the top, and plunged into Bayou St. John. The windows were open; the impact with the levee threw baby Daniel out of the Buick before the car went into the water. Miriam's head hit the windshield. Kay heard screams... not Miriam's, but Lily's and her own. Her door opened before the Buick went entirely underwater. She swam the few yards to the levee's edge and crawled up onto the grass, near where baby Daniel lay, very still.

Amos pulled Lily free of the car, pushed her onto the mud, and leaped back into the water to rescue his wife. He didn't reach her before the car went under.

"I... snuck away before the ambulances came," Kay heard herself say aloud. She couldn't see herself in the mirror any longer; her vision had grown cloudy, suffused with hot tears. "After that, I managed to stay clear of the Weintraub family for almost thirty years. Maybe my aura figured I'd hurt them all as much as I could. But then I went to that damned Hanukkah party at Spanish Plaza, prospecting for fresh marks... and there he was. Daniel Weintraub, baby Daniel, all grown up and handsome. Daniel Weintraub, flashing an eager, overly friendly smile at everyone. I knew who he was as soon as I saw him holding Amos's hand.

"I tried to leave before he noticed me. I had an inkling of what was about to happen. But I didn't get away in time. My aura didn't let me escape. Daniel saw me. His whole demeanor changed — he stared at me like I was the shiniest, most exciting toy in the world's greatest toy store. He broke away from his father and followed me from booth to booth, lingering thirty feet away, watching me with a look of delight so radiant and childlike it broke my heart. There was no sense in my leaving at that point; I knew he would've just followed me to my car.

"Finally, he gathered enough courage to approach me. He told me his name, and then, in a breathless rush, he asked for my phone number.

"And I gave it to him.

"We've been a couple ever since. For six years now we've been an odd match, the pair that gets gossiped about at synagogue — the sad little woman on the cusp of middle age and the younger, mentally challenged man. And each day we've been together, every damn *day* he's with me, I pull bad luck whammies on him, without meaning to, without wanting to. I hex the beautiful young man I love, the beautiful, sweet young man whose brain I made swell up three decades ago, as surely as I make his heart swell now.

"And if I ever lose all control — if I ever give in and let him make love to me — my aura will own him, body and spirit, for the rest of his mortal life."

Chapter 2

KAY parked her ancient AMC Gremlin in the virtually empty parking lot of the defunct River City gambling casino complex. It was nearly seven P.M. She was almost a half-hour late for tonight's meeting of the Miasma Club.

A familiar, raspy voice reached her before she could finish exiting the car. "Kay! Where the hell have you been, young lady?"

The voice, rutted as a dirt road in the Bayou Sauvage wildlife preserve, belonged to Owl Lookingback. She couldn't help but stare at him slack-jawed — in the six months since she'd seen him, he'd *changed*.

"Owl, are you — are you *all right?* Friday the Thirteenth's done a real number on you. You look—"

"Don't matter none what I look like," he said, pulling her across the parking lot. "All that matters is that we get your pretty ass into that building, the quicker the better. Could be you're in a heap of trouble, girl."

He'd lost more teeth since she'd seen him last, and the fringe of gray hair that fell to his shoulders from his yellowed, flaking scalp looked like barbed wire trampled into the dust by a thousand head of cattle. He looked a century old. Of course, he was at least three hundred years old, Kay reminded herself, but members of the Miasma Club could look any way they chose to look... except on days like today, Friday the Thirteenth, when the members' bad luck auras turned potent enough to affect even the members themselves.

"Owl," Kay asked, "why do you say I'm in trouble? It's not like I haven't ever been late to these shindigs before—"

"Something's up, babe," he said, pulling her more quickly toward the entrance. "The Three Stooges don't want us working as independent agents no more. They want results — *big* results — and anybody who don't toe their line this time is gonna get voted off the island. No more Club membership. Which, for us, means no more nothing."

Kay forced herself to smile. "Oh, we've all heard those threats before..."

"It's different this time. Pay me mind. I'm not saying you actually gotta buy into whatever scheme they're gonna cook up tonight. But you gotta at least *look* and *sound* like you do."

Kay smirked. "Hey, *I'm* not the one who calls the Triumvirate 'the Three Stooges.' "

Owl let himself smile. "Seniority's got its privileges. I can get away with stuff you can't."

As soon as Kay and Owl reached the entrance, three catering staff shoved past them from inside. They stumbled outside blindly like World War One doughboys who'd just suffered a gassing. One retched onto a patch of dead grass. *Poor things*, Kay thought... with almost the entire Miasma Club having congregated inside, the stench of fermenting cabbage must be unbearable.

As soon as she entered the shuttered casino, she doubled over with pain. "*Shit*," she hissed from between clenched teeth. "Oh god, I should've *known* this would happen..."

Owl steadied her on the stairs. "You okay, girl?"

She pushed his helping hand away and forced herself to stand up straight. "It's... all right. It's just the effects of Friday the Thirteenth. I'll be fine. Just *fine*."

Suddenly, her slinky black cocktail dress didn't fit right anymore. All her strenuous efforts to rearrange her figure, all her primping to look presentable for this damned meeting... *wasted*. The curse of Friday the Thirteenth. Her lacy bra barely contained newly stretch-marked breasts, which now drooped to her belly. That belly, flat as the Nebraska plains just seconds before, oozed over her low-rise panties and threatened to split her dress's seams. Kay didn't need a mirror to know she now sported a Ukrainian peasant woman's figure. She could hear Fortuna's jibes already.

Friday the Thirteenth! Thanks to the mortal population's universal, if subconscious, dread anticipation of misfortune on this day, her bad luck aura was more potent and wide-reaching than at almost any other time. But so were the bad luck auras of the other twelve members of the Miasma Club... and on Friday the Thirteenth, Kay found herself as vulnerable as any mortal to the others' baleful influences.

Her one consolation was that *they* were vulnerable to *her* aura, too.

They entered. She sucked in her gut and pulled down the edges of her too-tight dress. As cruel fate would have it, Fortuna lounged on a cushioned bench near the door, plucking mini-muffuletta *hors d'oeuvres* from a tray held by a young waiter, who valiantly tried not to sneeze. Unctuous satisfaction dripped from Fortuna's cow-like eyes as she watched Kay approach.

Fortuna struggled to sit up, using her generous hips, thighs and bottom as ballast. "Barefoot *and* pregnant, my dear?" she sniggered. "Aren't we just a *vision* of Hebrew femininity? Has that retarded boyfriend of yours finally gotten into your panties?"

Owl tried to insert himself between the two. "Ladies, let's keep the evening civil, shall we?"

Kay pushed Owl aside. "Daniel is *not* retarded." She unclenched her fists, deciding she wouldn't give Fortuna the satisfaction of a physical tussle. "He suffered a head injury as a little boy, which is more excuse for a dulled intelligence than you'll ever have." She noted with no small glee that the Club's massed bad luck auras had taken their toll on Fortuna, as well. Her oily olive skin was dotted with raised red blemishes, as though she'd stuck her face into a mound of fire ants.

"Those look like delicious *hors d'oeuvres* you're eating," Kay said. "Do they also have mini pizzas? Ones covered with *pepperoni*, perhaps?"

Fortuna wasn't the swiftest wit in the Miasma Club. So it took a few seconds before Kay's jab registered. Her fingers, animated by dawning mortification, fluttered to her face. "You... you—"

Kay pressed her advantage. "Don't worry, dear. I hear Walgreens is running a two-for-one special on Clearasil and Oxy Deep Cleansing Pads."

Fortuna's face turned lupine. "*Whore*, I'll split you open like a wormy apple—"

She grabbed for Kay's throat. Kay sensed her rival's bad luck aura crackle like a live wire.

But before Fortuna's talons could connect, they were batted aside by a bouncing ball of purple protoplasm. The thing screeched and gibbered as it careened off Fortuna's arms, the floor, a table, and then the ceiling. Chasing the purple thing was an equally agile green lizard-man who bounced on cloven hooves and impaled a sofa with his goatish horns, hissing and snickering with delight.

Poor Pandora, Kay thought, ducking behind the bar. The purple ball-thing was one of Pandora's Ills — either Mania or Incoherence. Some of the other club members had apparently tricked Pandora into sliding open the latch on her box. And now Krampus, the most animalistic and exuberant member of the Triumvirate, was working off his excess energy by terrifying the almost mindless escapee.

Kay heard a thundering belch, then drunken laughter.

"Please! Please stop frightening them!" Pandora cried. "They mustn't get away! They *mustn't!*" Her soft, high voice was obliterated by sadistic guffaws which could only come from the misshapen maw of Balor the Fomorian, the Irish cyclops infamous for his magically evil eye. Seconds later, a brown cloud the size of a bed pillow, but with the fins, tail, and whiskers of a catfish, floated past the bar, propelled by a *putt-*

putt-putt exhaust. A foot-tall human skeleton scurried by next, holding a tiny scythe and glancing fearfully over its shoulder.

Then Kay felt the pavilion's floor shake. Balor thundered past. The hairy, long-bearded giant ran flat-out after the fleeing ills, but he was running blind — his single, immense eye was covered by a swollen, purple-veined eyelid. He wielded a gnarled stick as both cane and weapon, batting obstacles out of the way and swatting at the Ills as he sensed their nearness.

"Stop it! Stop it!" Pandora ran after Balor, her box hugged tightly against her small bosom, her eyes wild with fear. Barely five feet tall, with a sylph-like figure Kay couldn't help but envy, she caught up to Balor and, failing to restrain him, began beating his broad back with her box. Her puny blows only made him laugh all the harder. Fortuna joined in the teasing, laughing her ample ass off.

Kay wasn't about to try messing with Krampus, one of the Triumvirate. But fouling Balor up didn't carry nearly the same risk; he was a doofus without much stroke in the Club. And Fortuna appeared to be enjoying this childish display of cruelty *way* too much. Enough was enough.

The brown cloud and the tiny skeleton circled back. Before Balor could get past, Kay darted out from behind the bar and grabbed a sturdy chair. Then she focused her bad luck aura on Balor's knees and swung the chair as hard as she could.

The chair shattered against Balor's legs. The giant pitched forward and toppled in a hairy heap, roaring a litany of Gaelic curses.

The casino's public announcement system crackled. *"Attention all Miasma Club members, attention."*

Kay shivered; the amplified voice of Mephistopheles somehow combined the rich, unctuous tones of a Southern Baptist preacher with the abattoir sounds of cattle entrails being rendered into dog food. *"Report immediately to your assigned seats in the main dining hall,"*

Mephistopheles said. *"Krampus, your presence is required behind the podium."*

Kay followed the others toward the dining hall. She passed a pair of white-faced waiters and wondered what they had witnessed since the Miasma Club's arrival. Had Krampus appeared to them as a hyperactive frat boy? Balor as some kind of overgrown jock? And what about the Ills? Potbellied pigs let loose as a Club prank?

She entered the main hall. During the six scant weeks the River City Casino had been open for business before gross mismanagement and political chicanery had resulted in bankruptcy, this hall had been the Captain's Buffet, a round-the-clock, all-you-can-eat saturnalia loosely patterned after Disneyland's Pirates of the Caribbean ride. Now it operated as a rental party hall and special events club.

Na Ba waited for Kay, apparently eager to chat. The Vietnamese spirit, whose outward appearance was that of a kindly middle-aged woman, embraced her colleague with honest affection. "Kay! So good see you! How your boyfriend? You get married soon, hah, like me and Na Ong? Be old married lady? You kiss your happy days goodbye, then!"

Kay gratefully accepted Na Ba's embrace, even though the nearness of the other woman's bad luck aura caused Kay's stomach to pooch out half an inch further. Apart from Glenn the Gremlin, Na Ba and Na Ong were the newest members of the Miasma Club, having appeared and petitioned for membership just a few years after the great Vietnamese wave of emigration to New Orleans following the fall of Saigon in 1975. Had they replaced anyone in the club's ranks? A chill ran down Kay's back as she realized she couldn't remember. If two other spirits had been cast out of the club, they had been equally cast out of her memory.

"Don't plan on buying a bride's maid's dress anytime soon, Na Ba," Kay said, managing a smile. "Daniel deals with enough troubles without having a manifestation of the Evil Eye for his wife."

Na Ba poked her in the ribs. "Yeah, bad enough you his hoochy-sweetie, hah?"

Kay's smile froze lifeless on her face. Although Na Ba had been joking, her remark hit too close to the truth.

"Kay, *ma chere*, you suddenly look so forlorn, so terribly, terribly sad." Kay found her right hand silkily clasped by two manicured paws. When she looked up, she met the intense black eyes of Reynard the Fox. His long snout quivered with a precise evocation of concern. "Tell me, is there anything I might do to ease your woes?"

A natural quadruped, Reynard somehow pulled off both bipedalism and sporting a seersucker suit, porkpie hat, and monocle with insouciant grace. Kay extracted her hand. Two meetings back he'd cornered her and whispered hotly in her ear, *"Once you've tried canine, the rest go to the back of the line."* Smoo-oo-ooth. Plus, he was a total politician. Whereas Na Ba and Na Ong couldn't give a crap about Club intrigues, Reynard lived for that shit.

"I'm fine, Reynard, thank you," Kay said coldly. "Shall we take our places at the table?"

Walking behind him, Kay was pleased to see he was suffering from mange.

Kay sensed waves of animosity and anger flowing from the end of the dining table closest to the podium. It was time for Ti Malice's semiannual hissy fit. Seven feet of indignant, seething maleness, ebony as the heart of a collapsed sun, with fury arcing like lightning from his eyes, Ti Malice pointed at the place cards sitting at the head of the dining table, the position of prominence and favor.

"I demand my rightful place! I demand *justice!*" His volcanic gaze would've eviscerated anyone sitting behind the podium... anyone, that is, except for Mephistopheles, Old Scratch, and Krampus, all of whom appeared utterly unfazed. Old Scratch glanced up briefly from his ledger book, sighed, pushed his spectacles to a more comfortable position on his bewarted nose, then returned to his calculations. Krampus's obscenely long tongue unspooled and followed the rounded rump of a buxom young waitress as she passed by the podium. Only Mephistopheles, seated between his two fellow Triumver-*istas*, deigned to offer Ti Malice his undivided attention.

"Really, Mr. Malice," Mephistopheles said, resting his scarlet quarter-moon chin on braided fingers, "haven't we heard this all before? Over and over and over again? We have vital matters to discuss this evening."

Ti Malice failed to take the broad hint. "Injustice remains *injustice*, no matter how many times one's nose is ground into its bitter putrescence. Why are my esteemed brother and I denied our rightful places at the head of this table? Do not Eleggua-Eshu and I represent the largest of the Club's constituencies?"

"Do take your seat, Mr. Malice," Mephistopheles said, frowning, his yellowed fangs poking briefly over his lower lip. "Thanks to a certain member's tardiness," — Kay's heart stutter-stumbled — "our proceedings are running late this evening. This is a pointless complaint. You know well our traditions. And you know they carry the force of law."

Eleggua-Eshu stepped forward. He stood before Mephistopheles and doffed his brown felt derby hat in deference to the Triumvirate. "But, y'know, boss, laws, they get amended or abolished all the time, *all* the time." He ran his large, tender-skinned brown hands with their golden fingernails across his clean shaven pate, as though to buff it. "I mean, I know T.M. may get a little 'uppity' at times, but that don't mean he don't have a point. Between him and me, we're responsible for hexin' or trickin' near *seventy percent* of the folks that live in New Orleans. Now, you got to admit, that is quite a *load* for just two fellers outta thirteen to carry between them—"

"*Racism!*" Ti Malice thundered. His gaunt ebony form grew taller as Kay watched, seeming to suck fresh substance from all the shadows in the room. "This is nothing more than a base *conspiracy* to keep the deities of those who once were slaves permanently stuck in humiliating servitude—"

Mephistopheles's moon-face turned a livid scarlet. "I will tolerate *no more* of this *insolence!*" His torso expanded like a giant jack-o-lantern made of smoke and octopus ink, until the top of his pointed head scraped the twenty-foot-high ceiling and he dwarfed even the augmented Ti Malice. "You will all take your seats in the places which you have been assigned, and you will do so *NOW.*"

Kay hurried to the seat by her place card. Owl and Reynard, the two most senior non-Triumvirate members, sat opposite each other closest to the head of the table, followed by Ti Malice and Eleggua-Eshu, then Balor and Pandora, Kay and Fortuna, and Na Ong and Na Ba (who, being a husband and wife team "servicing" the Vietnamese community, were generally considered a single member, although that point was open to dispute). At the far end of the table, grumping there like an unruly, rebellious adolescent n'er-do-well whom none of the adults wanted to sit near, slouched Glenn the Gremlin, the youngest member.

Old Scratch banged the podium with his little hammer. "Attend ye, attend ye," he said. "Due to a vitally important matter, we will omit the customary readings of members' reports on their activities, as well as the treasurer's report."

"I have taken the time to carefully review your most recent reports," Mephistopheles grumbled. "All of them, are... underwhelming. Your imaginations, your methods, your scope of operations... sadly, sorely lacking. We cannot continue to proceed on this same path. There is only so much bad luck energy to be divided among us, and too many of you squander your portions on parochial or trivial projects. While you waste the Miasma Club's precious resources on petty foolishnesses, our enemies, the Muses, grow ever stronger, ever more bold, audacious, and ambitious."

Ti Malice's hand shot up like an ebony rocket. "Has it ever been proven beyond the shadow of a doubt that these so-called 'Muses' even *exist?* I myself have never seen—"

"Of *COURSE* they *EXIST!*" Orange steam shot from Mephistopheles's ears. "Fool! How dare you question me?" He paused for a moment to wipe flecks of black, steaming spittle from his lips. "The Muses... are the greatest challenge we as an organization face in our struggle to dissolve this city. Where we tear down, they build up. Where we corrupt, they ennoble. Our grand vision is an abandoned necropolis sinking into the mud. Theirs is of a shining city, a temple of human self-actualization and accomplishment, of scientific, moral, and artistic achievement."

He shivered before continuing. "I have heard rumors of their most audacious, most potentially dangerous assault yet. The mortals, unsatisfied with their current theft of the substrata of oil and gas which underlay the Mother, have taken notice of the Mother's own abundant reservoirs of miasmatic energy. Our foes, the Muses, have inspired mortal geologists and chemists to begin exploiting that energy for foul human purposes. If we do not act quickly and decisively, we face a future in which the mortals become leeches on our holy Mother's energy. With their unquenchable appetites, they will suck up the miasmatic fields which sustain us, which provide us with our very forms, our beings! My colleagues, if we do not take drastic action, concerted, unprecedented, action, and soon, we face utter *disaster!*"

He smashed his scarlet fist onto the lectern. "No more dividing of our efforts! We cannot afford to act like hobbyists and amateurs! We are *professionals*. And true professionals work as a *team*. From this night forward, each of you shall abandon your separate pursuits and shall dedicate every conscious moment to a joint goal, a glorious, shared victory over the abysmal Muses. Together, united, we shall—"

"Incite the inferno of a race war!" Ti Malice thundered, thrusting high a Black Power salute.

"Breed armies of vermin and mosquitos!" Fortuna demanded.

"Make gang fighting spread from public school into Catholic school!" Na Ba screeched.

"Drown dis town with pure, cool, *sweet* heroin," Eleggua-Eshu suggested with a dreamy smile.

More orange steam spurted from Mephistopheles's ears. "No, no, *no!* This is *precisely* the sort of division of effort which threatens to defeat us—"

"Info-apocalypse!" Glenn shouted joyfully. "We'll make every server within a fifty mile radius eat-eat-eat its own data!"

"If I may be so bold," Reynard purred, "I do think that motivating every musician in town to relocate to Austin or Nashville would be a delightful coup..."

"Race war, I say!"

"Flood o' heroin, man."

"Mosquitos and vermin!"

"Make all priest in all parish lust for little boy!"

"*SILENCE, YOU CRETINS!*" Mephistopheles thrust his arms beseechingly toward his two partners — the signal for them to merge together into their Combined and Terrible Aspect. Kay, who had wisely kept her mouth shut during the preceding brouhaha, knew the Triumvirate meant serious business. They didn't pull this trick too often.

The air within the room shimmered, its molecules driven into a frenzy by the sudden avalanche of arcane geo-energy. Mephistopheles's outstretched hands melted into Krampus's and Old Scratch's linked paws. Krampus bounded up and down like a Labrador retriever anticipating a sirloin dinner. But Old Scratch appeared to be suffering from the kind of intestinal flu which threatened to send unspeakable substances shooting out both ends.

Suddenly, the remainder of Krampus's and Old Scratch's substance was sucked into Mephistopheles's arms. Gross protrusions funneled their way up his wrists, forearms, and then biceps as the other two bad luck spirits were seemingly digested. When those swellings passed through his shoulder blades and collided with Mephistopheles's neck, his moon-shaped head exploded.

Kay shielded her face from waves of fierce heat. A column of flame erupted from his head's shattered top, hit the ceiling, and spread to every high corner of the room, a tidal surge of weightless lava. The fire raced down the walls' velvet draperies without scorching them. Then it crossed the carpeting back to the podium without leaving so much as a soot mark.

Mingled scents of brimstone, charred flesh, and fermenting cabbage filled the hall. The streams of fire reunited in the spot where the shattered husk of Mephistopheles's body quivered. The husk crumbled like a cigarette ash grown too unwieldy. The flames then took on the shape of a fifteen-foot-high jester — but a jester with curved horns of seething magma; the body of a praying mantis, dressed in glowing brimstone, bubbling pus, and writhing scorpions; and eyes that could seemingly freeze the heart of the sun.

"We will control the remainder of tonight's agenda," the merged entity insisted with a voice like crows being electrocuted on a power line. "You will listen, and you will *obey*. Thralls!" he called to mortal attendants in the adjoining room. "Bring forth the Great Wheel of Misfortune."

Three waiters, eyes glazed, rolled in a giant upright roulette wheel. Kay hadn't thought any of the Triumvirate gifted with even a smidgeon of a sense of humor, but their contraption resembled nothing so much as the main prop from the *Wheel of Fortune* TV game show. Long chrome strips divided the roulette wheel into eight pie-shaped segments, each slice containing words spelled out in light emitting diodes.

"Turn it on," the Triumvirate's Combined and Terrible Aspect said. Hundreds of electronic filaments burst into sudden illumination. Kay craned her neck to read the contents of each pie-shaped segment:

TSUNAMI OF POLITICAL SCANDAL

ACCELERATED DECAY OF MAJOR INFRASTRUCTURE

DEADLY EPIDEMIC OF COMMUNICABLE DISEASE

CROSS-RACIAL CRIME WAVE IGNITING HATE STORM

POLICE DEPARTMENT MELTDOWN

MAXIMIZING DESTRUCTIVE POTENTIAL OF HURRICANE

PLAGUE OF ARSON IN FRENCH QUARTER & GARDEN DISTRICT

MARDI GRAS MAYHEM

The fiery joker gestured proudly at the Wheel with a sweep of his mantis foreclaws. "We of the Triumvirate debated long and hard to determine the eight potential disasters of greatest systemic impact, all capable of pounding Greater New Orleans back into the muck it was spawned from. Working as separate fingers, any of us, given the right circumstances, may poke out one of the city's eyes. But curled together, unified as a single mighty fist, we thirteen will smash its skull, shatter its bones, bludgeon its lungs, crush its heart. We will push the Muses aside like straw before a hurricane. But only if we strike a united blow."

"And that there Wheel is gonna tell us which disaster we all gonna be workin' on?" Eleggua-Eshu asked, cocking his derby with a manicured index finger.

"Yes. The Great Wheel of Misfortune will be spun this night, and whichever segment is stopped by the clapper at spinning's end, those words written within will foretell the city's doom. All of you will share the honor of setting the Wheel to spinning. By placing your hand upon it, each of you makes a sacred pledge to work exclusively toward the achievement of whichever goal the Wheel commands. Any member who dares pursue his or her own parochial objectives after this night will face expulsion from the Club. Be warned — *none* of you are irreplaceable. Now step forward, each of you, and take hold of the Great Wheel."

"Wait!" Ti Malice said. "How can we trust that one of us, or some conspiracy of a few, hasn't jimmied the Great Wheel's clapper to land upon their favored disaster?" He pointed to Glenn at the opposite end of the table. "I propose that, due to his knowledge of all things mechanical and electrical, Glenn the Gremlin be permitted to examine the mechanism. Only Glenn is qualified to certify the Wheel free of chicanery. And because he does not represent any particular ethnic population, he is the least likely among us to be biased."

"Insolent ignoramus!" A fiery mantis claw splintered the banquet table inches from where Ti Malice's hand rested. "Look around you! Can you not see the maladies which afflict every member here? Today is Friday the Thirteenth, fool! One of the only days of the year when you all fall prey to each other's bad luck auras. No 'jimmying device' which has been secretly installed by any of us — not even us of the Triumvirate — can withstand the combined hexing touch of all of us. *There* is your safeguard against treachery. No more hesitation — come forward, all of you!"

Kay rose unwillingly from her seat. Na Ong and Na Ba both looked mildly intrigued. Opposite them, Fortuna and Glenn nearly fell over each other in their eagerness to reach the Wheel first.

Kay found herself pressed between Reynard's plush shoulders and the edge of the Wheel, the top of both of their heads squeezed within Balor's gargantuan armpit. Hovering above them all, the Triumvirate, too, grasped the rim. "Upon our mark, spin the Wheel clockwise as though you are all limbs of the same body — which you indeed are. Five, four—"

Rivulets of sweat ran down Kay's sides. Only now did the enormity of what she was about to do hit her. She loved New Orleans, and in a few seconds, she would help drive a stake through its heart.

"—two, one, *SPIN!*"

She tried to command her arm to freeze. But her forearm had a will of its own — she felt her wrist spasm with a sudden upward jerk before her fingers lost their hold. Powered primarily by Balor's monstrous strength and the Triumvirate's arcane kinetic energy, the Great Wheel of Misfortune spun with the velocity of a jet turbine. As they all stepped back, hundreds of glowing red L.E.D.s spun so fast they formed a solid disk of scarlet.

The clapper wailed a continuous roar. As the velocity of the Wheel's spin began falling off, the glowing red disk devolved into the segmented blurs of hundreds of separate lights. After a few seconds, Kay could differentiate various segments as they raced past the stopping point.

"Mardi Gras Mayhem"? How bad could that be? she thought. *Even if we had a few terrible Carnival seasons and the tourists stopped coming, that wouldn't mean the end of New Orleans. Let it stop on that.*

Her eyes crossed as she attempted to read every segment. *"Tsunami of Political Corruption"? Been there, done that. "Police Department Meltdown"? It happened back in the early nineties, and somehow the city bounced back. I could live with either of those...*

Slower, slower, the Great Wheel spun. Infrastructure, Disease, Inter-Ethnic Hate. Police Meltdown; Hurricane; Arson; Mardi Gras. Infrastructure... Disease... (*depends on WHICH disease; whew!*)... Inter-Ethnic Hate... Police Meltdown (*come on, clapper, come on, you've almost stopped, almost almost...*)

oh, no

please, please, no

oh no oh no oh no no no

The Great Wheel of Misfortune stopped spinning. The clapper bounced back and forth between pegs. Heart throbbing in her throat, Kay forced herself to read the evil words which glowed within that segment:

MAXIMIZING DESTRUCTIVE POTENTIAL OF HURRICANE

A doomsday scenario for a bowl-shaped city whose lowest neighborhoods sat twelve feet below sea level.

And, as fate would cruelly have it, Kay's area of expertise, due to her malign influence at the Army Corps of Engineers.

She was now the point of the spear. Her spine turned to ice as each of her fellow members of the Miasma Club turned their pestilent gazes upon her.

Chapter 3

"**L**ADIES and gentlemen of the press, distinguished guests, I am delighted to announce a new chapter in the economic history of New Orleans, the dawning of a bright new day for this city we all love."

Mayor Roy Rio's smile shined even brighter than his cleanly shaven head. Standing at this podium at the edge of the swamplands of New Orleans East, about to cut the ribbon for the MuckGen Consortium's pilot demonstration project, represented the culmination of a dream he had cherished since his teen days — that he could rise above his family's reputation for political corruption and lead his city, blinkered, backwards, stuck-in-the-past New Orleans, out of the musty nineteenth century and boldly into the twenty-first.

"It's not very often that a major metropolis gets the opportunity to completely reinvent itself," he continued. *And it's not very often that a major political family gets the opportunity to completely reinvent itself, to scrub itself clean*, he thought. He glanced at one of the dignitaries in the front row, his great-uncle Charleton Morehouse, the city's first African-American mayor, elected a quarter century earlier. "For too long, our city has been content to rest on its past glories, to depend upon its great port and the generosity of millions of tourists to see it through. A hundred years ago, New Orleans was the Queen City of the South. Today, we've been surpassed by Houston, Dallas, Atlanta, and Miami, and even Birmingham and Mobile are nipping at our worn-down heels. But no decline needs ever be permanent — not here in America, where our talent for invention is matched only by our genius for renewal. And today, the Crescent City begins her renewal. Today, our beloved home turns away from the polluting industries of the past and turns toward the clean, green, sustainable industries of the future."

That's an applause line, Uncle Charleton, Roy thought. But his great-uncle sat with his hands stolidly in his lap, a morose, somewhat pained expression on his lined face. Charleton's son, Merle Morehouse, Roy's immediate predecessor as mayor, also looked out of sorts, as though he'd just eaten bad oysters. But the two men's discomfort paled next to that of Roy's ex-wife, Cynthia Belvedere Hotchkiss. She sat amidst her fellow city councilpersons and openly glared at him, detesting him all the more strongly for this very public triumph.

If looks could kill, I'd be laid out in a crypt in St. Louis Cemetery, Roy thought. *I know none of them can stand me. But can't they at least be happy for their city? Don't they realize what MuckGen means for this town?* "Thirty-five years ago, we experienced our Oil Boom. This very area we visit this morning, this desolate stretch of wetlands, was intended to be developed into sprawling new suburbs. But then, in the 'eighties, our Oil Boom went bust, and the oil and gas industry retreated to Houston. An industry which we had counted on to be our bread and butter left us high and dry, and much of New Orleans East remained swampland.

"What is different about MuckGen? Why can we rely on them in ways we could never rely on the oil companies? We can rely on them because their whole purpose is to develop a renewable, potentially inexhaustible energy source which is unique to our area — the tiny, organic powerhouses which reside beneath our feet. Naysayers have complained for years that these wetlands of New Orleans East are useless. But today, we can say 'nay' to the naysayers. Not only do these wetlands provide essential protection against hurricanes and irreplaceable habitats for our seafood industry, but we now have learned they can provide energy to light our homes, to heat and cool our office buildings, and someday soon to power our vehicles.

"Think about the paradigm shift! For decades, these wetlands have been looked at as a nuisance. The oil companies cut hundreds of canals through them so they could get their heavy equipment to deep water more easily. This short-sightedness resulted in massive salt water intrusion, which in turn has caused the ongoing loss to the Gulf of a football field's expanse of wetlands each hour that passes. But now, we have every incentive in the world to conserve those wetlands and turn back the northward march of the Gulf of Mexico. I'm talking *bucks*, people. *Big* bucks. I'm talking wealth creation on a scale this city hasn't seen since the inventions of the steamboat and the cotton gin. Wealth that can rebuild our schools. Wealth that can provide opportunities for the most disadvantaged among us. Wealth that can attract the best and the brightest to New Orleans, and help us keep our most talented kids right here at home. And best of all, it's wealth from an industry that won't despoil our environment.

"Thus, I consider myself the luckiest mayor in America this morning. Because I'm the mayor who gets to cut the ribbon on the MuckGen Consortium's very first dedicated field research facility. Thanks are due to the U.S. Department of Energy for their technology demonstration grant and to the Louisiana Office of Economic Development for their support. Thanks also go to the public-spirited elders of the Holy Tabernacle Maximum Gospel Church, who agreed to lease this land to MuckGen." *Have to give Cynthia and her people some of the credit... although to judge from that sour look on her face, I'd have done as well to spit in her eye.*

"My friends in the press," he continued, "I want you to remember how to get out here, because I expect you'll be coming back frequently. And the next time you come out, I want you to bring your journalist friends from around the world. Because this is a major, *major* story. I want the whole *world* to know that the Crescent City is back, and she's headed straight for the top!"

He cut the ribbon to mixed applause: tepid on the part of the Morehouses and their political allies; heartfelt on the part of the other political figures; and near ecstatic on the part of the MuckGen Consortium partners.

Annalee Jones, one of those partners, a statuesque, exquisitely dressed African-American woman, was the first to pump Roy's hand after he handed over the podium to MuckGen's CEO, Arthur Li. "Mayor Rio," she said, "I've got to say, you're as big a booster of MuckGen as the most passionate member of our board. That was one hell of an introduction."

"It was easy. I'm a believer."

"Well, you talk like you've got skin in the game..." She smiled. "Are you planning to invest when we go public?"

Roy's smile faded. "That would be unethical, not to mention illegal. My only interest is the benefit to my city."

"Oh, of course, of course. I was only joking."

"Of course, Ms. Jones."

She glanced quickly at the Morehouses and Cynthia Belvedere Hotchkiss. "Look, Mr. Mayor, I know you have a packed schedule, but do you have a minute to troubleshoot some concerns of ours, before they get out of hand?"

Roy caught the significance of her glance. "Certainly. You want to walk over to my car with me?"

"That would be best, yes."

He opened the rear door of his Lincoln limousine for her. "Okay," he said as they sat down. "I was hoping this morning could be problem-free, but that never seems to be the case when you're the mayor of New Orleans. What's up?"

"It's the Holy Tabernacle Maximum Gospel Church. More specifically, their Associate Pastor, Councilwoman Belvedere Hotchkiss, who's been their primary negotiator. She's stonewalling on the land."

He smiled grimly. "What a surprise."

"You know we wanted to do a straight purchase. Or, at least sign a ninety-nine year lease. The church has title to vast tracts out here—"

33

"They bought it cheap during the Oil Bust, when everybody figured New Orleans East would dry up and blow away."

"Right. We want to buy two thousand acres out here, and we've offered more than fair market prices. Our technology is still speculative, so there's no guarantee our research will pan out into anything of economic value. But the best Councilwoman Belvedere Hotchkiss will do is advise her elders to approve a two-year lease on twenty acres, and at a rate that, honestly, is completely unrealistic. The only reason my board went for it was this competitive, time-limited grant from the Department of Energy, and..."

"And Cynthia's got you over a barrel."

"For now, at least. Another thing. Did you know that the terms of the D.O.E. grant stipulate collaboration with local public research universities?"

"I wasn't aware of that."

"I didn't expect it would pose any sort of a problem. Both the University of New Orleans and Southern University have perfectly adequate research facilities and qualified faculty. We figured working out cooperative agreements would be easy. But we've run into roadblock after roadblock. From what we've been able to discern, the source of the bureaucratic delays is very disturbing."

Roy frowned again. "Let me guess. It's the Morehouse family and friends. They've honeycombed the administrative staffs of U.N.O. and Southern like a swarm of bumblebees."

"Exactly."

"Christ..."

"Look, I didn't just fall off the pickle truck. I know how the game is played, especially here. But we're not a wealthy firm. Not yet, anyway. These people are your family, aren't they? Can't you make them see reason? Explain to them that if they help us now, the payoffs in the long term are potentially *huge*? We've offered the church elders a percentage of net future profits in exchange for land, but that's been a non-starter. We don't want to rip anybody off. That's not what we're about. But we don't want to get ripped off ourselves, either."

"So you want me to talk with Cynthia and the Morehouses?"

"Anything to get matters moving forward."

"I wish it were that easy. Look, you're not from around here, are you?"

"I grew up in Dallas."

"Different world. Even the black community in Dallas that you grew up in, it's a whole different universe from the black community here. The Morehouses, they're Creole royalty. Uncle Charleton's family on both sides were all freemen fifty years before the Civil War. He was one of New Orleans' leading civil rights lawyers during the sixties, then went on to get elected twice as mayor, the city's first black chief executive. He couldn't get the voters to change the city charter to allow him to run for a third term, but he had enough influence to ensure that his son Merle, my cousin, followed his footsteps into the mayor's office."

"Very impressive. But what does this have to do with them standing in our way?"

"It's not about you. It's about *me*. In their eyes, I'm not a Morehouse, not in name or though ties of blood or loyalty. Cynthia, my ex-wife, who isn't even legally related to them anymore, is more of a Morehouse than I am. You can sort of call me the 'white sheep' of the family."

"'White sheep'?"

"My mother married a poor Dominican carpenter, not of African heritage. For that sin, she was pretty much drummed out of the family. My cousins grew up in Pontchartrain Park and went to the best Catholic schools. I grew up not too far from here, in a little shotgun shack in the Lower Ninth Ward, and went to the crummy public schools in the neighborhood. Even after my father died, the family still refused to have anything to do with my mother. They could've helped her; they had the means. But they let her struggle on her own. And they let me struggle on my own. The only way I made it into college was through scholarships."

"But still, you managed to found your own software company, at, what? Twenty-four? And you managed to get yourself elected mayor. Not too shabby for a boy from a shotgun shack."

Roy shook his head. "Maybe. But sometimes I think I got elected more for who I *wasn't* than who I was. The fact that I'm a pariah with the Morehouses actually helped me, at least with those voters who had gotten sick and tired of the Morehouse dynasty. It was a nasty election. I ran against the family's handpicked successor. I had to exhume a whole lot of the Morehouse's dirty laundry to help make a case for myself. The Morehouses and Cynthia know MuckGen's success is incredibly important to me. So in their eyes, you've got to fail."

Her face fell. "Oh..."

"Don't let yourself get discouraged, though. There are ways around them. I can call in favors with the governor's office, get her staffers to clear up some of those roadblocks you've been running into with the universities. And if the Holy Tabernacle Church stonewalls y'all for too long, I'll have the city's lawyers look into declaring eminent domain over their land out here. Cynthia's folks aren't doing a thing to develop it or improve it. I think we could make a strong case."

"That could get ugly, though, couldn't it? A mayor facing reelection, trying to appropriate land from a church?"

"I'll cross that bridge if and when we get to it." He noticed the small crowd outside beginning to break up. "Looks like the press conference is over. You'd better go join your partners. I've got a hurricane preparedness exercise to get back to."

He opened the door for her. She got out, then turned and shook his hand again. "Roy... I appreciate your being so candid. And I really appreciate the offer of help."

"Keep your chin up, Annalee. I won't let the Morehouses railroad me on this. They won't deny this city the renaissance it deserves, especially not out of sheer spite. We're going to win. You know why? Because I'm better than they are, and I'm smarter than they are. And I'm damn well gonna show them."

Chapter 4

ONE of the aspects of life in New Orleans Kay had come to love was its festivals. The city never passed up an excuse to throw itself a party. St. Patrick's Day was no exception to this rule. Over the past few years, the St. Paddy's Day observances had grown into a mini-Mardi Gras, complete with parades, dances, and public concerts.

Hurricane season was still months away, she reminded herself. Not even the Triumvirate could make a hurricane roar into the Gulf of Mexico in February. She consoled herself with that thought. There was still time. Time to figure out a way for her to wiggle out of whatever part in the conspiracy they planned for her. Time for her to snatch whatever fleeting pleasures she could.

Like spending time with Daniel. Like hearing music in a park. Like going to the French Quarter on St. Patrick's Day, when the neighborhood would be crowded with people of Irish descent, people her aura had no power over. Like enjoying a day in which she could pretend to be an ordinary mortal, not a bad luck spirit.

They followed their ears to a small stage in a pocket park off Decatur Street, near the entrance to the fresh produce market. A Cajun band played a raucous French-language waltz. It wasn't Irish music, but it would do, certainly.

They found seating on a broad set of steps. As Kay scooted over to make room for Daniel, she experienced an unsettling tingling in the small of her back. It wasn't her bad luck aura about to burst into bloom — thank heavens. But someone in this crowd wasn't the ordinary mortal they appeared to be.

She scanned the faces of the people sitting near her. She wondered whether Reynard the Fox was here, cooking up some Gallic mischief. He was every bit the virtuoso at conjuring various guises as Kay was — perhaps more so — but his enormous vanity generally led him to stick to one of half a dozen Continental faces of extraordinary handsomeness. Kay knew these guises all too well; she didn't see any of them here. Could it be Balor? This was an Irish celebration, after all. But she would recognize any of his guises, too, and she didn't see any of them.

Why, then, did she so strongly sense the presence of an alien yet somehow kindred spirit — a hidden power so much like her own?

The waltz ended. The band's leader, a diminutive accordionist with a drooping black mustache and protruding eyes, walked to the microphone. He nodded proudly, acknowledging the crowd's applause. "T'ank you, t'ank you, ladies and gentlemen. But the best, it is yet to come. I am t'rilled to introduce my very talented niece, Miss Evangeline Bonnet, all of eleven years old, who will sing for you a very lovely ballad called '*Le Femme D'un Petrolier*.' Or, *en Anglais*, 'The Oil Worker's Wife.' Please give Miss Evangeline your most kind attentions."

The girl who now approached the microphone looked like a very ordinary eleven year old girl; a pretty one, to be sure, with long, silky brown hair tied back in ribbons, but otherwise a typically shy, slightly awkward child in a modest white dress. She waited for the accordionist, fiddler, wash board player, and drummer to play the introductory bars, then pulled the microphone from its stand and began swaying in time with the strong beat, a little girl pretending to be a *chanteuse*.

And then she started singing.

No eleven year old girl has any business singing like that, Kay thought. *She's a sexpot, a little Brigitte Bardot!* She sensed the electric response from the crowd — even passers-by stopped to gawk. Kay could only translate a few stray words, and she doubted that many in the crowd could do much better. Yet the song's story came through, loud and in-your-face clear, all due to Evangeline's seductive, knowing phrasing, combined with sultry body language that the girl shouldn't have mastered until well past the age of thirty.

Kay looked around her. The women in the audience appeared bewildered and disturbed by the erotic heat this seemingly mousey little girl cast. The men, however, (if they weren't cringing with acute embarrassment at their own responses) were amazed, delighted, entranced, and aroused. Daniel definitely fell into the latter category, and she couldn't much blame him.

The song approached its finale. Evangeline, her face damp with sweat, her small, unwomanly body seeming to make love to an invisible partner, stiffened as she hit grace notes so pure and piercing that Kay felt shivers cascade down her back.

And then she saw it. For just a fraction of a second, a sparkling corona surrounded Evangeline. Then it swirled above her head to form the ghostly pattern of a face, so bright that it lingered on Kay's retinas as an after-image long after the crowd erupted into cheers and passionate applause. The face was that of another woman, much older than Evangeline. Her joyous phantom essence promised something Kay needed so much it hurt... water for her parched spirit.

"*Muse*," Kay whispered to herself. Swelling with awe and hope, her arcane imitation of a human heart beat as fast as a hummingbird's wings.

"'*Moose*'?" Daniel said, looking around. "Where's a moose?"

"Never mind," Kay said, springing back to an awareness of her mundane surroundings. A woman had just risen from the blanket she'd been sitting on directly in front of the stage. Her long, strawberry blonde hair was plaited in loose braids, and her arms, neck, and bare midriff were decorated with a fabulous profusion of tattoos. Before the illustrated lady turned to leave, Kay caught the briefest glimpse of her face.

The face I saw in the corona! she thought. *The Muse! I'm not letting her get away before I talk with her!*

She grabbed Daniel's hand and pulled him from his seat. "Come on," she said. "We're going."

"But I thought you said you wanted to hear music—"

"I changed my mind. A woman's allowed to do that, Daniel."

Not letting the woman out of her sight, but staying half a block behind her, Kay pulled Daniel through the crowds thronging the French Market's stalls, then past the curio shops and coffee houses along lower Decatur Street. Daniel asked several times where they were going, only to be met with an exasperated silence. He finally gave up asking and allowed himself to be dragged along.

They left the Quarter and crossed into the Faubourg Marigny neighborhood. Kay's quarry paused by the open doorways of Café Brasil and the Spotted Cat, smiling as she listened briefly to the Afro-Caribbean music and blues that drifted outside. Both times, Kay yanked Daniel into the entrance alcoves of neighboring stores.

The woman crossed the grassy Elysian Fields Avenue neutral ground and headed into an antebellum Creole neighborhood. Shotgun doubles, ancient mansions divided into tiny apartments, and corner groceries and bars sat nearly atop one another, separated by alleys barely an arm's span wide.

The tattooed woman entered the Royal Roost Cafe. The little bar, a ramshackle tacked-on afterthought, clung to the front of an imposing three-story Spanish townhouse like a barnacle on the prow of a high-masted galleon.

"Let's go in," Kay said to Daniel.

"Huh? A *bar?* But you don't drink—"

"So buy me a lemonade, all right?"

The Royal Roost was dim inside. Kay's eyes adjusted to the gloom just in time for her to see the woman leave the bar through a door next to the kitchen.

41

As soon as the door swung shut, Kay caught the attention of a bartender. "Excuse me," she said, pointing toward the door. "Is the ladies' room through there?"

He shook his head. "Nope. Bathrooms're over there. That door's a side entrance to the courtyard for the apartments behind this place."

"A courtyard? Really? Is it okay if I take a quick peek?"

"Suit yourself. But if Mrs. Gruenwald's Doberman is roaming around back there, I'd advise making it a *really* quick peek."

Kay pushed the door open. The courtyard was lush with potted trees and vines crawling up rusting iron filigree and cracked peach stucco. No sign of any dog. The distant sound of a key unbolting a lock made Kay look up. High above, on the third story balcony, the tattooed woman walked inside the corner apartment.

"Hey, Kay, come on out of there," Daniel said behind her.

"I'm coming." But before she turned around, she memorized the number on the third story apartment door. "I know where you live now, Muse," she whispered to herself. "I'll be in touch. You can bet your enchanted harp on it."

It gave Kay an enormous sense of relief to know where she could find a Muse. If things got really bad, if it looked as though the Triumvirate's scheme might actually come to full fruition, she would switch sides, no matter how dire the consequences might be for her. She'd tell the Muses all about the Miasma Club's destructive intentions for the upcoming hurricane season. If anyone could derail the Miasma Club's plans, it would be the Muses.

Or so she hoped...

On their walk back through the Quarter to Daniel's truck, Kay experienced a repetition of the uncanny, clammy tingling across the small of her back that the Muse's presence at the outdoor concert had conjured. *Could it be another Muse?* she asked herself, glancing all around her. She didn't think so. This tingling felt much more familiar. In fact, she'd felt precisely the same sensation, akin to an allergic reaction, a few nights earlier, at the meeting of the Miasma Club.

The crowds lining the Royal Street sidewalks grew thicker the closer they came to Canal Street. Throngs of tourists and locals awaited the passing of the St. Patrick's Day parade, hoping to catch cabbages or potatoes tossed by revelers riding on the Irish-themed floats.

The tingling grew stronger and more noxious. Kay scanned the faces surrounding her for a familiar guise. *There!* She spotted Pandora pushing her way through packs of parade goers, carrying her wooden box of Ills. The petite Greek spirit was followed closely behind by a tall, ponderously built blind man, wearing dark glasses, sweeping his cane before him. That could be no one but Balor. They appeared to be following a short, olive skinned man with wire-rimmed glasses and a salt and pepper Van Dyke beard. He headed determinedly in the direction of Canal Street, carrying a briefcase that he transferred incessantly from hand to hand.

"Hey, Kay," Daniel said, "my truck is over on St. Peter Street, remember? Slow down — we've gotta turn that-a-way..."

Kay wanted desperately to see what Pandora and Balor were up to. But she didn't want to get Daniel involved. "Daniel, hon, there's something I've got to do. You go back to the truck. I'll take the Elysian Fields bus home."

"You want to watch the parade? We don't have to go home yet. If you want to watch the parade, I'll be *glad* to watch it with you—"

"No, sweetie, it's just, uh, I spotted a couple of people from work, and there's a big project we're working on that I've got to discuss with them." The crowds were slowing Pandora and Balor down; otherwise, they would already have escaped Kay's sight. "Hon, you'd be really bored — we'll be talking about political and engineering stuff—"

"You're sure? You really want to take the bus home?"

"I'm sure, I'm sure. Look, I'll call you as soon as I get home, okay?"

"Well, okay, I guess..."

She hurried after her two fellow bad luck spirits and their quarry, pushing her way through the milling crowds. She hated ditching Daniel; he'd looked hurt. But she simply had to spy on Pandora and Balor. Ordinarily, she'd avoid the doings of her fellow Miasma Club members like she would an outbreak of hoof and mouth disease, but Project Big Blow had forced her to take an active interest.

From across Royal Street, she saw Pandora briefly open her box. One of her Ills — Hunger, it looked like (Kay recognized him by his grotesquely protruding ribs) — slipped back inside before Pandora hurriedly relatched the lid. The man she and Balor had been following, the bearded man with the briefcase, entered a tiny Greek restaurant, little more than a kitchen with a service counter and two petite tables. Pandora and Balor waited outside on the sidewalk.

What were they up to? Kay heard the parade drawing closer, descending from Canal Street into the Quarter, its marching bands blaring big brassy versions of sentimental Irish tunes. The man Pandora and Balor had been following must be Greek, or have Greek ancestry, Kay told herself. Otherwise, Pandora's Hunger would have had no effect upon him, and, judging by the alacrity with which he'd ducked into the restaurant, he had been ravenous. But why drive him into a Greek restaurant in the midst of an Irish parade? Did Pandora hope to give him a fatal case of food poisoning, utilizing another of her Ills? Yet if that were her plan, why had she brought Balor along? It's not as though they were friends; Kay knew for a fact that Pandora despised Balor for all the teasing he subjected her Ills to.

A police car, one of the parade's escorts, rolled slowly down Royal Street and passed Kay, its blue lights flashing, its siren emitting honks like an enraged, giant goose. It was followed by the first of the bands, a group of middle-aged men wearing metallic green tuxedos and carrying a banner which identified them as the Knights of Hibernia. Kay saw the man with the briefcase emerge from the tiny restaurant, his arms laden with bags of carry-out food. He tried turning back in the direction from which he'd come, but the crowd had grown thicker during the few minutes he'd spent inside, and its impenetrability held him fast near the restaurant's front windows.

Kay saw the "blind man," the disguised Balor, remove his glasses. He then punched himself in the nose with great force; blood trickled from his nostrils down his chin. The effort he'd put into savaging himself and the pain he'd inflicted caused Balor to momentarily lose his concentration; his guise flickered, revealing the cyclopean giant, but everyone else's attention was riveted on the parade. In any case, no eyes other than those belonging to bad luck spirits or possibly Muses could have detected the quick shimmering in his form. Kay had seen Balor punch himself this way many times before — in order to release Faebar from his tear ducts, it was necessary to force himself to cry.

Fearsome as Balor was, Faebar was far, far worse. Kay watched with queasy trepidation as the little leprechaun with the face of a rabid goat crawled out of the corner of Balor's eye. Something truly awful was about to happen.

The float that followed the Knights of Hibernia was a green medieval Irish castle mounted on the back of a flatbed truck. Most of the masked riders threw shiny green beads to the crowds, but a few others tossed cabbages. The vegetables flew about like volleyballs, bouncing from one pair of upraised hands to the next, getting hurled from one side of Royal Street to the other.

A Tulane University student standing across the street from Kay caught one of the cabbages. Before he could throw it across Royal Street to some of his fellow students, Faebar leaped from Balor's shoulder and landed atop the cabbage.

What is he going to do? Kay asked herself with mounting dread.

The next float featured a fiberglass statue of Saint Patrick driving the serpents from the Emerald Isle, wielding a giant green cross like a pitchfork. Mounted on the roof of the truck's cab was a fiberglass snake the size of an anaconda. The Tulane student threw his cabbage. But with Faebar aboard, it veered off its intended course, gaining velocity like a rocket. Visible only to Kay and the other two bad luck spirits, the leprechaun waved his hat and cried out, "Yee-*haww!* Yip, yip, *yipeee!*"

The cabbage soared through the open window of the flatbed truck, smashing into the left side of the slightly inebriated driver's head and then splattering against the inside of the windshield. The truck float immediately veered to the left — directly toward where the man with the briefcase and the bags of take-out Greek food stood. Caught in the midst of the crowd, he was unable to flee.

What happened next hit Kay's eyes like a series of incandescent flashes. The truck leaped the curb. Its front bumper smashed into his chest as the truck's brakes screeched. The man flew backward and landed against the door of the restaurant, his arms splayed wide. The truck crashed into an iron lamp post. The sudden, brutal deceleration tore the fiberglass serpent from its moorings atop the truck's cab. Airborne, with Faebar aboard to control its trajectory like an inertial guidance system, it soared straight for the stunned man's midsection.

Kay managed to look away a split second before the fiberglass snake impaled him.

She heard Faebar's goatish laughter even above the screams of injured parade-goers and the rending of metal as the damaged lamp post collapsed onto the truck. She saw Pandora and Balor flee down Royal and turn onto a side street. She heard the dying man gasping, his struggles for breath fatally compromised by effusions of blood that spilled from his mouth.

Who was he? she thought. *Why did Balor and Faebar kill him?* Taking advantage of the chaos which had halted the parade, she ran across the street, dodging around the damaged truck and jackknifed float and ducking between members of the panicked crowd. Incredibly, the impaled man's open eyes still held a glimmer of life, even though the snake's snout had penetrated both his lower chest and the restaurant's door, pinning him like a bug on a corkboard. "Won't... get to eat that moussaka," he said faintly as Kay approached. "Never find out now... why the bacteria engine... wouldn't work... *why...*"

"Help will be here soon," Kay said. "Just hang on..." But she knew the reassurance she provided was useless, and that she'd mouthed the words out of a lack of anything else to say. The man groaned a final time. His arms spasmed and his eyes turned upward, as though looking to heaven for relief. Then his head drooped low enough to bang against the snake's fiberglass scales.

"Who were you?" Kay asked aloud. Too late.

Backing away from him, she stumbled over something on the sidewalk. His briefcase. The truck's impact had torn its clasps partially open and caused a profusion of business cards to spill out. Kay picked one up and read it:

Amitri "Mike" Zoukeni, PhD

Professor of Biochemistry

Louisiana Technical University

Senior Research Biochemist / Founding Consortium Member

MuckGen Energy Solutions

A researcher for MuckGen! So that's why the Miasma Club wanted you dead, she thought. *You're one of the men who want to leech away the Mother's energy.* She eyed the briefcase with intensified interest and knelt down to examine it. She could see that it held a laptop computer and bunches of papers covered with graphs and columns of figures. *His last words were that he couldn't make the bacteria engine work.* What did that mean? Who did she know who could make sense of all this stuff...?

She started to gather up the briefcase and its papers when she felt a dissuading hand on her shoulder. "Don't touch that," a man's voice said. "That's evidence at a possible crime scene."

Kay turned around. A tall, slender black man stood over her. He wore a checkered gray sport coat whose color neatly matched the closely cropped hair at his temples. "Are you a police officer?" Kay asked.

"Sergeant Quincy Cochrane, NOPD. Off-duty, but duty schedules don't mean anything when something like this happens." He jerked his thumb at the dead man. "You see what happened?"

She briefly considered telling him the entire truth, but she knew her aura would never allow it. "It was... a horrible accident. People on the previous float, the one before the one that crashed, threw cabbages into the crowd. Some students started throwing them back and forth. One of them hit the driver of that truck—"

The sergeant took a few steps towards the damaged truck and its unconscious driver. "You mean that guy there? That unlucky son of a bitch better hope he can pass an Intoxalyzer test when he wakes up. If he flunks, there's gonna be hell to pay." He knelt by the briefcase, shoved the loose papers back inside, then placed it under his arm. He glanced at the impaled man and whistled mournfully. "That poor sucker must've pissed the devil off something awful," he said.

When he went to take a closer look at the dangling corpse, Kay slipped into the crowd and hurried around the corner before the sergeant could ask her for an official statement. She'd had a second reason for not trying to tell him the full truth of what had happened.

Sergeant Quincy Cochrane had the stench of Ti Malice's touch all over him.

Chapter 5

MAYOR Roy Rio leaned wearily against the edge of his desk. The afternoon's conclusion to the hurricane response simulation had been messy, divisive, and disheartening. Now only the grim postmortem remained. Bob Marino, Director of the Federal Emergency Backstop Organization, looked like a man attending his best friend's funeral.

"So, Bob, how'd we do?" It was a nearly useless question. They both knew the answer without anyone saying a word.

"I guess you know, Mr. Mayor."

"Yeah," Roy said. "I guess I do." He rubbed his tired hands and glanced down briefly at his long, slender fingers. His mama, who'd cooed over her child's elegant hands, had wanted him to be a concert pianist. But his fingers had gravitated to a computer keyboard, instead. In light of evenings like this, maybe his mama'd had the right notion after all.

"Let's hear the bad news," Roy said. "I've got thirty big kahunas from twenty-two different agencies and parish governments waiting in my conference room to learn their grade."

"I can give it to you in one word. Dreadful." The bags beneath Bob Marino's eyes looked big enough to pack two weeks' worth of luggage. The last three days had been hard. Most of the key participants had been getting by on four hours of sleep, with the notable exception of FEBO's second-in-command, William "Duckie" Duckswitt, who'd snuck off every chance he could to sample local cuisine in the French Quarter. Bob, however, had taken this simulation as seriously as he would a real catastrophe. Roy had to give the man credit for caring, *really* caring, a rare attribute in a fed. "In terms of a grade, I would have to give you all an F."

"Now wait a minute, wait just a damn minute," Sergeant Bruno Galliano interjected. Mayor Rio's Special Assistant for Homeland Security looked as ready to burst as an artillery shell. Maybe it hadn't been such a wise decision to include the ex-Army sergeant in this informal post-exercise consultation. "Let's be fair here," he said. "This city's only had an Office of Homeland Security for two years. Our learning curve's been steep, but we've been making progress like nobody's business—"

"Bruno, let the man talk," Roy said, placing his hands on the smaller man's shoulders. "Bob's not here to condemn you or to condemn us. He's here to point out the weaknesses in our system, to help us get better." He steered Bruno into one of the leather chairs in front of his desk, then hovered by his side. "Go on, Bob."

"If Hurricane Patty had been an actual storm, rather than a nasty figment of our computer's imagination, right now we'd be living through the aftermath of the worst natural disaster in the nation's history. According to the simulation, your city just suffered thirty thousand casualties, lost ninety percent of its housing stock, and pumping systems in the urban core were completely disabled. Some neighborhoods will retain as much as fourteen feet of water for six months."

Mayor Rio hadn't heard a word past *thirty thousand casualties*. The rest of Bob's litany of destruction had been blocked by images of Roy's aunties, friends, and neighbors in his childhood Ninth Ward neighborhood floating face down in murky, black water.

"But, but," Bruno stammered, "but those outcomes, they're for the worst possible scenario."

Bob nodded. "That's exactly right, Mr. Galliano. That was the whole purpose of this exercise. To role play our response to the worst possible scenario... direct hit by a Cat Five hurricane on the City of New Orleans, with the heart of the city falling within the northeast quadrant of the eye's track, and Lake Pontchartrain being pushed over the levees."

"But thirty *thousand*..." Mayor Rio shook his head with stunned disbelief. "Not that I distrust your simulation program... it's just that, casualties on that *scale*—" Roy felt sick to his stomach. "What can my people do better?"

Bob sighed. "I wish I could offer you a magic bullet, Mr. Mayor. But I can't. Based on what I've seen the past three days, you've got a major systemic problem in this region and this state. Too many chiefs, too many competing tribes, and not enough Indians. One example — public safety personnel. In just your parish alone, you've got the New Orleans Police Department, Criminal Sheriff's deputies, Civil Sheriff's deputies, Levee Board Police, Harbor Police, and Crescent City Connection Bridge Police. The only one directly accountable to you, Mr. Mayor, is the NOPD. The rest of them are little independent political fiefdoms.

"Take that situation and multiply it by the eight civil parishes in this metro region. We're talking an administrative and logistical Tower of Babel. No logical manager would've set up a system like this. The devil himself could hardly have done a worse job."

Roy nodded. "I get you. But untangling all the knots in our local political system could take twenty years or more. The best we can do in the meantime is hammer out the most effective evacuation plan we can, figure out ways to get the folks without cars the heck out of Dodge, and do whatever possible to keep the stay-behinds alive for a couple of days until the cavalry rides in. By 'cavalry' I mean you guys — FEBO, the Army, the Navy, the National Guard, Red Cross, Salvation Army. We locals have just got to hold down the fort a couple days, right?"

Bob failed to give Mayor Rio the encouraging nod he'd hoped for. "Maybe that was a reasonably accurate statement during the last administration," Bob said grimly. "FEBO was the best it's ever been. But then FEBO found itself absorbed into the Department of Homeland Security, downgraded from direct cabinet access to one of a dozen or so subagencies. Morale went into the crapper, especially when the current administration started using FEBO as a dumping ground for big campaign contributors." He made a face like he'd just swallowed a wad of chewing tobacco. "You've met Duckie. Enough said."

"William Duckswitt," Bruno said with barely concealed contempt. "Where'd that joker come from? Wasn't he managing spa memberships for the Four Seasons hotel chain?"

Bob shook his head. "That was earlier. He came to us direct from a short stint with the American Association of Arabian Horse Breeders. But don't get me started on that guy... I'm already crossing a bunch of red lines here without bad-mouthing my second in command. The reason I went into any of this is to warn you not to count on the cavalry charging into town by Day Two or Three. Maybe not by Day Four or Five, either. We lost a hell of a lot of our experienced people after the reorganization. And their replacements have been—"

A knock on the mayor's office door cut Bob short. Mayor Rio nodded for Bruno to open it. Walter Johnson, Roy's chief of staff and one of his oldest friends, stuck his head in. He looked stressed.

"What's up, Walt?" Roy asked.

"The natives are getting restless, Mr. Mayor," Walter said. He massaged the tensions out of his dark hands. "Rabineaux and Maestri are making noises like they want to cut out for the night, and I saw lots of nods from the other bigs. You guys gonna be much longer in here? Should I order in some food?"

"Don't bother, Walt," Roy said. "We're done." He turned to Bruno and Bob. "Fellow Christians, let's go face the lions."

Bob Marino's summation went over even more poorly with the gathered participants than it had with Bruno Galliano. Cynthia Belvedere Hotchkiss almost immediately attacked Lieutenant Colonel Branson Schwartz, commanding officer of the U.S. Army Corps of Engineers'

South Louisiana District. "Colonel, how can you sit there and tell me your levees performed within '*design specifications*'?" she spat. "To *hell* with your 'design specifications'! My entire New Orleans East district just got wiped out by a wall of water twenty feet high that tore through the Industrial Canal's levees like they was made of *tissue paper—*"

Colonel Schwartz's self-satisfied expression remained unfazed, his tone forcefully civil. "With all due respect, Councilwoman Hotchkiss, I must take issue with Mr. Marino's computerized projections. I personally oversaw the design specs and construction of the Industrial Canal's levee system. While I agree that a twenty-foot high surge would overtop the levees, causing isolated pockets of deep floodwaters within your district, to suggest that these levees would catastrophically fail is simply fear-mongering—"

"*Ten thousand casualties!*" Cynthia shot back. "Ten *thousand!* Just within my district alone!"

"According to a computer simulation which rests on a number of questionable assumptions."

"Colonel, are you saying that you're smarter than Bob Marino's supercomputer?"

"No, ma'am. But are you familiar with the acronym GIGO? 'Garbage In, Garbage Out.' The data that Mr. Marino's team fed their computer is highly speculative."

"But even if the computer models were off by fifty percent — that's still five thousand drowning deaths in New Orleans East alone! How can I trust you and your agency?"

What made her think she could ever be an effective politician? Roy asked himself. Already an associate pastor at one of the city's largest, most influential churches, Cynthia had gotten herself elected district councilwoman not more than eighteen months after their divorce and his inauguration. Nothing anyone could say would convince him she hadn't done it just to spite him.

Colonel Schwartz's expression remained deadpan. "Councilwoman, did you personally oversee the building of the Industrial Canal levee system?"

"No, but that's beside the point—"

"Did you personally examine the soil substrata? Did you approve the design specs? Did you specify the grades of clay and interior fill that were used in the levees' construction? Did you watch them being built? If so, how long did you spend? A month? A week? A day?"

Cynthia started to say something, but she swallowed whatever it was. After a few long, bitter seconds, she said, "No, Colonel. I didn't spend one day watching those levees getting built."

Roy didn't like Schwartz, not at all. But as of this moment, he respected the hell out of him. If Roy had ever figured out how to shut down Cynthia's righteous tirades like Schwartz had just done, maybe their daughter Nicole wouldn't now be dealing with the aftermath of an ugly, highly public divorce.

Sheriff Herman Chin, the chief law enforcement officer for Jefferson Parish (and the self-advertised "one and only Chinese-Cajun sheriff in the U.S.A."), held up his beefy hand. "Colonel Schwartz, how come, if the last storm to hit St. Bernard and Plaquemines, I mean Betsy in '65, was a Category Four storm, you guys built us a bunch of levees over the past thirty years designed only to stand up against a Category Three storm surge? What kinda sense does that make?"

Mayor Rio didn't see the colonel actually roll his eyes at the question, but the man's body language epitomized disdainful impatience. He turned to his aide, a slightly stocky woman with dark, shoulder length curly hair, not unattractive, whom Roy remembered from earlier meetings. "Ms. Rosenblatt, would you mind fielding the sheriff's question? My aide, Kay Rosenblatt, is an expert on the history of Congressional authorizations and appropriations as pertains to the Corps' flood control work in Louisiana."

Roy took a second look at Kay, who'd been mostly mute throughout the three-day simulation exercise. He realized that if she were thinner and taller, she could easily pass as a sister to Lily Weintraub, Roy's high school sweetheart.

He confirmed his observation by staring across the room at Lily, now the nursing supervisor for Baptist Hospital. Prior to three days ago, when she'd arrived to provide her emergency medical expertise to the exercise, Roy hadn't seen her in fifteen years. In the months following his divorce, he'd occasionally called her during long, lonely nights at City Hall. He'd managed to reach her only once. She hadn't returned any of his other calls.

Lily caught him looking at her. She glanced away quickly. It was hard for him to tell for certain, but he thought he'd caught her blushing.

"Sheriff," Kay Rosenblatt began, "the Corps of Engineers can only perform work that has been authorized by Congress, at a pace strictly limited by the annual appropriations process. The Corps recommended that Congress authorize a levee system adequate to protect against another Betsy-sized hurricane. But instead, Congress authorized construction of a protection system designed to hold against what was then termed a 'hundred year storm,' or one which statistically has a one percent chance of hitting New Orleans in any given year. Since the 1970s, this authorization language has been interpreted by the Corps to mean providing protection against the surge produced by a fast-moving Category Three hurricane."

Sheriff Chin frowned. "So you're sayin' it's *Congress's* fault, not the Corps', that we got stuck with what we're stuck with?"

"Uh... yes, sir."

The Chinese-Cajun sheriff scowled at Schwartz. "That sounds like passin' the buck to me, Colonel. I don't think Harry Truman would've liked that none. Sounds like y'all shoulda done a much better job of yankin' those politicos' ears until they gave us what we damn well need—"

Colonel Schwartz rose abruptly from his seat. "Mr. Mayor, Mr. Marino, I refuse to sit at this table any longer and suffer insults from this ignorant, backwoods sheriff."

"'*Backwoods*'?!" Sheriff Chin also rose from his seat, although with much less grace and alacrity than Colonel Schwartz had. "Mister, I'll have you know that Jefferson Parish is the second most populous parish in the great State of Louisiana. You're callin' *me* 'ignorant,' you ignorant sonofabitch—??"

"Stop it! All of you! This stupid name calling is just making it worse!"

Mayor Rio stared with amazement at Kay Rosenblatt, who'd just grabbed her much bigger boss and pushed him back down into his seat. Roy hadn't thought this seemingly mousey aide had that much gumption in her. Colonel Schwartz looked shocked, too.

"Don't you all realize there are forces out there that *want* you to fail?" Kay said. Despite the energy she'd just shown, the woman didn't look well, Roy thought; she'd turned white as chalk. "Don't make it easier for them! Sheriff Chin is right. We *don't* have the storm protection we need. But instead of fighting each other, you need to work *together*. The South Louisiana wetlands are eroding at a catastrophic pace — you need — you *must*—"

Sounds akin to overripe grapefruit being pulped in a juicing machine gurgled up from her stomach. Roy had never heard anything like it emerge from a human being's mouth. The poor woman stared wildly around the room, as if invisible forces were assaulting her. Was she suffering some kind of a fit?

"You must — must—" She clung to the edge of the table for support. Roy saw that Lily had begun elbowing her way through the crowded room to come to Kay's aid. "You must — never stop pushing — gaahhh-aaaahhh—"

Mayor Rio never would've imagined that Sheriff Chin could move so quickly. The obese lawman shoved a waste basket onto the table beneath

Kay's face just in time to prevent a score of major dry cleaning bills. Before Roy allowed himself the mercy of averting his eyes, he could've sworn he saw an entire kidney slither out of her distended mouth and plunge into the trash pail, propelled by a jetstream of steaming gastric juices.

Loud gagging issued from several regional emergency management personnel around the table. Roy feared the meeting would end in a spasm of chain-reaction vomiting. But Sheriff Chin once again saved the day by grabbing the perilously full trash can and hustling it outside into the hallway. Lily gently escorted the gasping woman toward the ladies' room.

As Lily and Kay made their awkward exit, William "Ducky" Duckswitt, FEBO's second in command, squeezed past them into the room. Roy noticed he was wearing a brand new Giorgio Armani suit that still had a Rubensteins tag dangling from the vest. Ducky used a toothpick to dislodge a bit of food stuck between his lower front teeth. "Did I miss something?" he said. "My apologies to all — I had to take a very important call from the President. Some dam situation in Wisconsin — a dam is threatening to give way, and four ranchers stand to lose about a thousand head of cattle apiece. I've been personally overseeing the crisis. Anybody care to give me a quick update on the exercise?"

This was both a dam lie and a damn lie. Mayor Rio knew it. Bob Marino knew it. Everyone in the room knew it. But politically, the man was untouchable; he'd been a close high school chum of the President's brother.

Ducky *tut-tutted* and shook his head as he listened to Bob Marino's brief recap. "To borrow a felicitous turn of phrase from Rodney King," he said, "'Can't we all just get along?' How can you people be expected to run a Wee Willies Day Care center, much less a shelter of last resort for twenty thousand people? You can't agree who's responsible for provisioning the Superdome. Or which agency will provide inside security. Did I board the wrong plane? Is this Port au Prince, Haiti, or a major metropolitan center in the good ol' U.S. of A.?"

Ducky's impolitic remarks set off a fresh round of arguments and recriminations. After ten minutes, Mayor Rio called a halt to the proceedings. Nothing was getting accomplished — if anything, the longer the meeting lasted, the farther they all seemed to be getting from fixing matters.

Roy was collecting his papers when Lily Weintraub poked her head into the emptied conference room. "Everyone gone already?" she asked, sounding a little lost.

Roy hadn't expected she would've hung around. Especially not given the pains she'd taken to avoid any one-on-one time with him these past three days. "Gone, and good riddance," he said, smiling. "Hey, how's that lady from the Corps of Engineers doing?"

"Kay Rosenblatt? She's an odd bird, that one." Lily frowned, then shook her head. "I offered to drive her over to Baptist and have some of my docs check her out. But she wouldn't budge from the ladies' room. And wouldn't you know it, within ten minutes she looked as though nothing had ever happened. The only thing that worried her was that I might tell Daniel about what had happened; she didn't want to scare him."

"Daniel? As in, Daniel, your little brother?"

"Unfortunately, yes. They've been dating for the past five or six years."

Now *that* was interesting, given what Roy remembered of Lily's brain-damaged brother. He motioned for her to sit down, then sat down himself. "Uh... how is Daniel doing these days? Is he, y'know, working at anything?"

"Daniel's trimming lawns for the Orleans Parish Levee Board. He even started his own business on the side."

"His *own* business? That's impressive."

She shrugged her shoulders. "I mean, it's nothing too impressive, basically just an old pickup truck that he uses to haul away people's debris on weekends. My dad helped him get all the permits."

Roy was pleased; so long as they stuck to the subject of her brother, she didn't display any of the skittishness she'd shown around him in recent days. Talking about Daniel, they were just a pair of old high school buds reminiscing.

"So what's the story with Daniel and this Kay?" he asked.

She pursed her lips. Roy remembered those lips, and that pale, flawless skin, framed by raven black hair, soft, curly, and bountiful. Their four years together at Ben Franklin High School, where they'd both been honor students, certainly didn't feel like twenty-five years gone.

"I honestly can't recall how they first got together," she said. "It just seemed like, one day, she was *there*. And the weirdest thing, looking back now, is that it felt like she'd *always* been there. As though he'd known her since he'd been a child, before his accident, even. I can't explain it; it's just the strangest feeling."

"What does Amos think of her?"

Lily smiled ruefully. "Oh, you know my dad. *Nobody* is good enough for his precious progeny. He's suspicious of her. He can't figure out what a seemingly normal woman like Kay sees in Daniel. She's a few years older than he is, and she's never been married. So I guess Dad thinks she's an old maid using Daniel for sex. Or maybe he thinks — he's told me this, actually — that she figures Daniel stands to inherit a wad when Dad passes away. The only reason Dad puts up with her at all is she's Jewish."

There. She'd gone and done it — she'd mentioned the elephant sitting in the middle of the room, the one both of them had been trying to pretend wasn't there anymore. Roy could feel their friendly intimacy quickly evaporating. He tried to rescue the dying warmth. "Look, how about I order in some food? You've gotta be famished; I know I am."

She cast her eyes downward. "No, Roy, I... I really should be leaving."

He impulsively reached for her hand. "Come on, Lily. You've got to eat sometime. Might as well be with me."

She pulled away from him and stood. "Really, no..." Sadness haloed her face. "This was a mistake. I never should've agreed to be part of the disaster prep exercise. Not with the messages you've left for me."

"Lily, please don't go. Not like this." He felt his stomach tie itself back into knots. "Can't you give me a chance? People start over again all the time. Why can't we at least *try?* We've been done with high school a long, long time. We're grown up people now, with our own lives."

She shook her head. "I passed Cynthia in the hall just before I came in here. She hasn't let go of you, Roy. Legally, yes, but not emotionally. She stared at me like she wanted to tear me into pieces."

Roy's face tightened. "Cynthia Belvedere Hotchkiss is my *ex*-wife. She's the one who walked out on *me*. She's a non-factor in my life. A *zero*."

"She's still the mother of your daughter, Roy. You just went through a bruising, very public divorce. I've counseled enough men whose wives have left them to have some idea of what you're going through. It's still raw. It has to be. And on top of all that, you're the mayor of New Orleans. You've got the well-being of nearly half a million people weighing on you. You're reaching out to me because you need comfort. There's nothing wrong with that. But... the time just isn't right. Maybe not for you. Certainly not for me."

"So what's the problem?"

"Same as it's always been." She looked away.

"Does it start with 'A', end in 'S', and have an 'MO' in the middle?"

She wouldn't meet his eyes. "My father's feelings are extremely important to me. You know that. Nothing's changed in the past twenty-five years."

"Nothing's *changed?* Lily, we're both on the downslope of forty. You aren't Daddy's little girl anymore. I know how responsible you've felt for your father ever since your mom died. I respect that; in fact, it's one of the things I've always loved about you. But you aren't Amos's wife — you're his *daughter*. You've got a right to live your own life."

She turned toward the door. "I have to go. I just — I have to go, Roy."

Damn. This had turned into an ugly flashback of his most excruciating moments at Ben Franklin High School. Being rejected out of hand because of race and religion, even if by a stubborn old man... he thought he was past that. "Look — before you go, just answer me one question. Give me the right answer, and I promise I'll never call you or bother you again."

"All — all right."

"How come you came back in here? The meeting was over. Everybody else left."

She waited half a second before replying. "I — I came back for my purse."

Inwardly, he breathed a sigh of relief. *Wrong answer.* "No, hon," he said softly. "You had your purse with you when you came in just now."

She clutched her purse to her side and walked silently out the door.

He resisted an urge to chase after her. Let her come back of her own volition, in her own time. After all, she'd just proven she would.

He waited a couple of minutes, then stepped out into the hall. His foot banged into something. It clanged and tipped over with a metallic crash. He'd knocked over a small trash can. The same trash can that Sheriff Chin had shoved across the table for Kay Rosenblatt to vomit into — Roy remembered the stenciled *fleur de lis* on the can's side, the symbol faded and scratched with a big gouge.

But nothing had spilled out. Gingerly, he turned the can upright and peered inside. He didn't see (or smell) any vomit, not even a speck. The tissues and wadded-up stationary at the bottom of the can were dry and unstained.

I'm tired, he told himself. *I'm remembering things wrong.* The only possible explanation was that a janitor had carted away the vomit-filled can and replaced it with a different one.

The hell with this snafued exercise, he told himself as he walked to the elevators. *Think about the MuckGen groundbreaking. Think about the day when this city becomes the Silicon Valley of the energy world, and all our picayune, piddly problems — lousy levees, hurricane evacuations, schools without toilet paper — become yesterday's bad news.*

Chapter 6

FORTUNA Discordia had never tried pulling a job like this one before. Spreading bad fortune was her stock-in-trade — not standing around a downtown Time Saver and sprinkling *good* fortune, like some goddamn tooth fairy.

She wasn't even sure this was going to work. But she'd done the metaphysical calculus. Good fortune for Bob Marino and his top lieutenants potentially meant infinitely greater misfortune for the population of New Orleans. The big pitfall was wrapped up in that word *"potentially."* Fortuna knew this would be a gamble. And she didn't like gambles. She liked sure things. But since that hebe bitch Kay seemed to have the Corps of Engineers angle of Project Big Blow tied up tight, Fortuna had been forced to be improvisational, to go for the long shot.

She ducked behind the snack food aisle when she saw Bob Marino and his little entourage approaching along Baronne Street. She checked her watch — 10:23 P.M. Mortals were such creatures of habit.

She pulled her Nokia deluxe photo phone out of her purse and speed-dialed Glenn the Gremlin. "Glenn, you in position yet?" she whispered.

Glenn's high pitched voice, tinged with electronic distortion, blared back at her. "Of cuh-*course* I'm in position!" She quickly turned down the volume — that *idiot*. "Getting through the suh-security gate at the Fairgrounds was easy. All I had to do was dih-dih-*disguise* myself as a spare buh-Betacam unit, and I got carried inside by a cameraman. I'm maybe ten feet away from the mechanical horse racing gizmo, huh-hiding behind a curtain."

"Are you sure you'll be able to jimmy it?"

Now he sounded insulted. "There isn't a mechanical or electronic doohickey on this whole puh-*planet* that I can't jimmy. This little toy is pra-practically beneath my contempt."

Fortuna squirmed with impatience as she saw Bob and his coworkers get in line at the counter. "All right, I trust you! Set your phone to conference call. I'm gonna get Eleggua-Eshu on the other line."

Eleggua picked up. "'Leg, the mayor get home yet?" Fortuna whispered, frantic that Marino and his pals would purchase their Louisiana Lucky Loot ticket before she'd had a chance to work her reverse-whammy.

"Yeah, his limo pulled up ten minutes ago. He's in the kitchen, makin' himself a chicken salad sandwich. I can see him through the window. I got a real good fix on him—"

The elderly lady in front of Marino's group finished buying her Powerball lottery ticket and pack of Camel Lights. "Great," Fortuna said, "stay on the line, gotta go." She hurried around the corner of the snack food aisle to the front counter area, trying to look nonchalant as she pretended to glance through a copy of *Auto Trader*. She stood within six feet of Bob Marino and his coworkers, close enough to taste their ethnicities. Marino himself was full-bore Italian; hence the origin of her audacious plan. But she was lucking out with the other three, as well — the taller man's mother was Italian, the shorter one had two Italian grandparents, one on each side, and the woman was another full-blooded wop.

Marino turned back to his friends. "Guys, the usual? One Powerball and one Louisiana Lucky Loot?"

"Oh, I don't know," the taller coworker said, "maybe we ought to go with two Powerball tickets instead. The Powerball payoff's reached ninety-six million."

Fortuna wanted to strangle the man. If they didn't buy a Louisiana Lucky Loot ticket tonight, her plan was *fucked*. Neither she nor her associates could affect the outcome of a multi-state Powerball drawing, headquartered in Louisville, Kentucky.

"Yeah, but our chances are better with Louisiana Lucky Loot," the woman coworker said. "Besides, it's a lot more fun. That clunky old horse racing gizmo is so hokey, it's worth spending a dollar just to watch it go."

The Middle Eastern clerk spoke up from behind his register. "If you want to play Louisiana Lucky Loot, you give me your numbers and money now. My machine cuts off all entries for tonight in two minutes."

"All right," Bob Marino said. "I'm making an executive decision. We'll do both, just like we've done the last four nights. Same numbers as we've been playing — our four scheduled retirement days and our four wedding anniversary days."

Showtime. Fortuna wished she'd had an opportunity to practice this maneuver. It was like taking a shit in reverse. Metaphorically speaking, she'd have to force her bad luck muscles to pull, rather than push, sucking all bad luck out of these four feds, leaving only good luck behind.

"Quick, quick," the clerk said. He turned on the TV above the counter and tuned it to Channel Four.

"Here goes," Bob Marino said, pulling a rumpled piece of paper from his pocket.

Fortuna emptied her lungs, willed all of her pores and assorted orifices to open, and began to slowly, slowly pull in a breath.

"Seven, thirty-one," Bob Marino said.

Fortuna willed herself an invisible, ectoplasmic third eye, then made it tiny as a flea's scat and extended it on a tendril one-tenth as slender as a human hair. She used it to burrow inside Bob Marino's abdomen. She found the black blob of bad luck energy encasing his liver like a ravenous squid — it was a safe bet Bob Marino drowned his sorrows in copious adult beverages. She tried snaring the black blob with her tendril, but it was like trying to grab a shadow.

"Twenty-two, seventeen..."

Only when she willed her tendril to become a hydra-headed, sucker-mouthed lamprey did she sense the beginnings of progress. At first, the sensation reminded her of eating imported Italian bon-bons, each sinfully rich chocolate morsel infusing her with shivery pleasure. But then it was as though some brute was stuffing her cheeks with the entire box at once and forcing her to swallow. The damned bon-bons still tasted good, but she nearly gagged. She felt herself bloat like a Goodyear blimp afflicted with PMS.

"Four, eleven..."

Fortuna belched. Most unladylike. She hid her mouth with her *Auto Trader*, then saw Bob Marino staring at her breasts in the convex security mirror above the counter. Yup, her underwire Wondrous Bra had gotten cramped, all right. Let him ogle her. She'd been ogled by experts.

"Uh, thirty, and, oh, thirteen. Got that?"

"Got it," the clerk said.

Fortuna licked her lips. Even they felt swollen. She'd finished with Marino. Now that she'd figured out the process, she'd be able to suck the other three clean of bad luck in a jiffy. She just hoped her Wondrous Bra and Spanx Supreme Support Girdle could handle the strain. She repeated her mental exercises of a moment before, but much quicker this time, working over the other three bureaucrats. The woman really lucked out — Fortuna felt herself vacuum up a black bad luck stain that had been about to metastasize into ovarian cancer.

Sheesh... she was bloated almost to bursting now. If she tried holding onto this much bad luck energy for too long, she might literally explode. As soon as she was through here, all this stored up miasmatic energy would have to get dumped on somebody, and damn fast. The first poor sucker she'd stumble across with a drop of wop blood in him was gonna end up sorry he'd ever been born.

The clerk handed Bob Marino his Louisiana Lucky Loot ticket, and Bob handed him four quarters, one from each member of the group. As discretely as she could manage in her swollen state, Fortuna, having wrapped her Nokia inside the curled-up *Auto Trader*, leaned over and took a picture of the numbers on the ticket, which she then transmitted to both Glenn and Eleggua-Eshu.

She crept back behind the snack food aisle so she could whisper again into her phone. "'Leg, you got the photo?"

"Check."

"Glenn, you got it?"

"Yuh-yup."

An Alka-Seltzer commercial wound down. The Louisiana Lucky Loot spot would be next. The circuit between Bob Marino and his pals, the lottery machine, and Mayor Roy Rio was open and live, throbbing with the possibility of major mischief. All Fortuna had to do now was hang on to the collected bad luck energy with all her strength, not allow even a smidgeon of it to seep back into its former hosts.

Green, purple, and gold galloping horses burst onto the TV screen to the fanfare of racing music. "Welcome to the Thursday night edition of Louisiana Lucky Loot," an off-camera announcer said, "the televised racing game where your eight numbers can win you up to eight million dollars! So, without further ado, let's pay a visit to our fabulous mechanical fillies inside the grandstand of the New Orleans Fairgrounds..."

The animated intro dissolved, replaced by a live shot of what looked like a toy version of a carnival's Giant Slide. The mechanism was divided into eight lanes, with four drops undulating into brief straightaways. At the top of the slide, eight tin horses waited behind miniature paddock gates. At the finish line at the bottom, eight separate tumblers marked with all numbers from zero to forty spun continuously, one for each lane.

Recorded trumpets sounded a racing fanfare. One by one, about a second apart, the little paddock gates sprang open, releasing their eight horses to the pull of gravity. Even Fortuna had to admit she got a childlike thrill watching the toy stallions hurl down the dips and glide swiftly across the straightaways.

The leftmost horse hit the finish line, triggering a halt to the first tumbler's spinning. The resulting number was digitally projected at the bottom of the TV screen. Then the second horse hit the finish line, then the third, then the fourth, until all eight had completed the course and eight numbers flashed at the bottom of the screen.

Fortuna held her breath as Bob Marino glanced down at his Louisiana Lucky Loot ticket.

He stared at the TV, then back at his ticket, then back at the screen again.

"Well, I'll be damned," he said.

The following morning, Mayor Rio was mildly surprised when his secretary told him the head of FEBO was waiting for him in the reception area. But when Bob entered his office, Roy found himself far more surprised to see the guilt-ridden expression on the man's face.

"Hi, Bob," Roy said. "Weren't you and your crew scheduled to fly back to Washington?"

"We had to change our flight," Bob said. "Something... well, something entirely unexpected came up. That's why I had to see you one last time before we left."

Roy took another look at Bob's expression. What could have the man looking so incredibly guilt-stricken? Sure, he'd been rough on Roy and Roy's people, but it's not like his sternness had been without reason. "What's wrong, Bob?"

"It's just the weirdest thing," Bob said, his voice uncharacteristically subdued. "My three top aides and I — Sal, Maria, and Ben — we've been playing Louisiana Lucky Loot all week, just for kicks. Last night... we won six million dollars."

Roy grinned. "You're shitting me, right?"

"No, I'm not."

Roy got up and vigorously shook his visitor's hand. "Then why the glum face? That's great!"

"The four of us... we're planning to retire from FEBO."

Suddenly, Bob's expression made a little more sense. "What?"

"I've worked at the agency since the Nixon Administration. The other three have been in almost as long. I used to love my work. But not anymore, not in years." He sighed, then tried massaging the tension out of his hands. "My wife's been bugging me to get out for what feels like forever. And now... this falls into our laps. Like magic. I already gave my notice, called it in this morning."

"The others, too?"

"Yeah. Three more weeks and we're all gone."

A capsule of concentrated acid burst in the pit of Roy's stomach. "What about Duckie?"

Bob's hands clenched into fists. "Duckie's staying. He'll likely move up into my slot." He looked Roy straight in the eyes. "Are you a praying man?"

"This job has made me one, yeah."

"Then pray every single night that no storm remotely like Patty hits anywhere near here for the remainder of this President's term."

Chapter 7

D ANIEL Weintraub let go of his ride-on mower's throttle and let the machine coast to a halt. He squinted hard at the section of sloping levee grass just ahead of him, with its concrete flood wall thrusting from the hilltop like a bony fin on the back of a dinosaur. He tried to make certain he was seeing what he *thought* he was seeing.

He'd mowed more than a mile of Levee Board property along the Seventeenth Street Canal levee and flood wall since this morning, starting at the Lake Pontchartrain end of the canal. An unusual early spring dry spell had made his mowing more efficient. Yet, unless he was staring at a heat mirage, the slanting strip of levee grass just ahead of him was sodden. A shimmering rivulet about thirty feet wide slowly flowed down the levee's slope from the lower edge of the concrete flood wall, forming muddy pools where the grass leveled off in the back yards of homes along Bellaire Drive.

Daniel walked over to the wet grass. It had begun turning a sickly yellow color. "That... that just isn't *right*," he said to himself. "When was the last time it rained? Wasn't it, like, uh, weeks ago?"

Where was all that water ending up? Daniel walked to a wooden fence, its lower edge now coated with black mold, and peered over its top. The house and property surrounded by the fence looked abandoned, a rarity in Lakeview. Much of the back yard had been transformed into a swamp. A drained in-ground swimming pool had begun to fill with a murky, brownish soup.

He returned to his mower and sat on it until his supervisor, Tran Ho, caught up to him. Tran's job was to follow behind Daniel with an edger and trim the borders Daniel's machine failed to reach. Daniel watched Tran, sheltered from the sun beneath his umbrella-like hat, slowly approach. Tran looked displeased. "Why you stop, Daniel? Lots more to do today. Lunch break over."

Daniel pointed ahead of him. "The grass is wet."

"Wet? It no rain."

Daniel nodded. "I know. Something's wrong. You think maybe the canal wall has, like, a crack in it, or something?"

"'Crack'? What you talking about..." Tran's rebuke faded when he saw the extent of the inundation. He immediately approached the flood wall and began inspecting its lower reaches, running his hands over the seams between concrete slabs.

"You want me to help you search for cracks?" Daniel called after him. The idea seemed exciting, a welcome break from the monotony of mowing.

"No, you stay there," Tran shouted back. A few minutes later, he returned to the mower. "I no find nothing. Seams all dry. Water look like it come up from ground. Not through wall, but from *beneath*."

"What should we do?"

"I call supervisor. Lee Hwang. He know what to do." He pulled out his cell phone and called the Levee Board's main office. After identifying himself in English, Tran carried on the rest of the brief conversation in Vietnamese, a language Daniel couldn't understand a word of. Tran shoved the phone back in his pocket. "Hwang no there. Someone else on way to take a look. New supervisors. Don't know them."

Twenty minutes later, Daniel saw a Levee Board pickup truck park in front of the abandoned house on Bellaire Drive. The driver and his passenger walked back to the levee along an access path between properties. Daniel didn't recognize the middle-aged Vietnamese man and woman. But they seemed to recognize *him* — the woman stared openly at him, then said something in Vietnamese to her companion while pointing at him. Maybe they were business owners who'd once had him cart away trash or used cooking oil? He didn't always remember all of his customers' faces.

They walked over to Tran. The woman continued staring at Daniel. "We Na Ong and Na Ba," the man said to Tran, "new maintenance supervisors. Show us problem, please?"

Tran walked them over to the stretch of soggy grass. The three of them spoke rapidly in Vietnamese. Tran gestured with great urgency at the flood wall and the drowned grass. Daniel thought he saw the male supervisor shrug.

Tran surprised Daniel by suddenly switching to English. "What you *mean*, this not a *problem?* How say you that?"

"It not a problem," the male supervisor said. "Everything fine."

The woman nodded in agreement. "Yes, it not a problem," she said. "Meant to be like that. Special irrigation project. Big experiment, you know?"

Tran didn't appear convinced. "Never heard of this," he said flatly. "If experiment, going very, very *wrong*. Look over fence there — whole yard filling with water. Will spread to other yards soon. Needs to be *fixed*."

"Everything fine," the male supervisor repeated.

"No — *not* 'fine'!" Tran pointed furiously at the flood wall. "Dangerous bad! Canal water seeping up through the ground! Whole wall could fall down, any time now!"

The male supervisor pointed lazily at Tran. "Go, wife," he said. "Do your business."

The woman *tsk-tsk*'ed. "Must do *everything* in this family," she said. She approached Tran and cradled his face between her hands, the way a mother might gently but firmly correct a wayward child. Then she began to chant in Vietnamese. Daniel waited for Tran to pull away, or at least object to this sudden, strange invasion of his personal space. Yet his supervisor stood stock still, his expression vacant, his mouth slightly agape.

The woman's chant took on a hypnotic, sing-song quality. Daniel felt its tones lulling him towards sleep. His head nodded, and he had to grab for the steering wheel to keep himself from falling off the slanting mower. He recovered in time to see Tran slump to his knees in the wet grass.

"All done," the woman said. She walked to her husband's side, then glanced back at Tran. "He all fixed now." As she walked by Daniel, her smile appeared warm and genuine. "Bye now, Daniel Weintraub. Good meeting you. Have nice day!"

She and her husband drove off.

Daniel helped Tran up from the sodden ground. "What... what just happened?" Daniel asked.

His supervisor didn't answer. Daniel offered him some cool water from his canteen. "Mr. Tran, what did those people say to you?"

Tran blinked rapidly in the bright sunlight. "What?"

"What did the lady do that made you fall in the water?"

Tran stared wide-eyed at Daniel, as though he were seeing his employee for the first time. Then his expression turned harsh. "None of your business," he said.

His supervisor's dismissive tone made Daniel afraid. But he had to know what had happened. "Are they going to do anything about the water? You told them it's dangerous. I heard you."

"None of your business, I said! No problem here. *None.* Is irrigation project."

"But — but you said the flood wall could break any time—"

Tran seized Daniel's Saints cap from his head and hurled it to the ground. "Daniel Weintraub! Do not argue!" Daniel had never seen Tran this furious before. "You are mental defective! Foolish man! Belong in mental hospital, not working for Levee Board! You know how many time my supervisor want to fire you? But I stick up for you, all the time. And you repay me this way? With argue and question?"

Daniel felt ready to cry. "I was just — I wanted to do the right thing—"

"You want to do right thing? Then get back on mower. Do job you get paid for. Mowing, not asking question."

Daniel felt his face burn. The sun was hot, but not this hot. He climbed onto the mower and started the engine.

"Daniel Weintraub!" Tran ran in front of him and pointed to the area of wet grass. "You no mention this to *anyone*. You understand? Not *anyone*. I find out you open your stupid mouth, I fire you from job. Right away. You understand, Daniel Weintraub?"

Daniel nodded. Not even his father had ever reprimanded him so cruelly. His heart beat so fast it hurt. "Yes, sir," he said.

* * * * *

"Daniel, are you all right?" Kay asked.

Daniel didn't say anything. He kept staring blankly at the Adam Sandler movie on his TV. He'd been seemingly afraid to look at her ever since Kay had arrived for their at-home movie date.

"Sweetie, what's wrong? Please tell me." Kay had rarely seen him like this. Usually Daniel's outlook on life was that of a happy Irish setter. In her experience, only a bad argument with his father Amos or his idolized sister Lily could drive Daniel into a withdrawn funk like this one. Normally Kay could jolly him out of these moods with just a bit of teasing or a hug. She'd tried those things repeatedly tonight, to no effect.

Impulsively, she scooted closer to him on the couch and began kneading his shoulders. He turned to look at her, eyes wide with surprise — she'd rarely touched him this way. *This is really playing with fire*, Kay told herself as her fingers moved down his spine and massaged the muscles beneath his shoulder blades. She found herself momentarily afraid that her hands had gone on auto pilot, commandeered by her aura. But she sensed she still retained control, that she could pull back if she deemed it absolutely necessary. *Thank God for that.* If she ever lost control of herself with Daniel, if she ever let their mutual attraction segue into sex, he would become her aura's creature forever.

Kay felt him tremble. She stopped her massage, and his trembling gathered into a barely suppressed sob. When he turned to look at her again, he was crying.

"I — I — I don't want to lose my job," he said. "Dad would, would *hate* me if I lost my job."

Kay shook her head. "No, he wouldn't, no, sweetie. Trust me. He knows how hard you work, how hard you try. But what's going on? I thought everybody at the Levee Board was really happy with you. You're one of the most reliable workers they've got."

"I saw something bad today," Daniel said. "But Mr. Tran... Mr. Tran said that if I open my stupid mouth, I'll lose my job. But... but if I *don't* open my stupid mouth, lots of people might get hurt."

Kay's chest tightened. This reeked with the rotting cabbage stink of the Miasma Club. "Daniel, you've got to tell me what you saw."

He shook his head. "I — I'm *scared*. What if Mr. Tran finds out—?"

"The only way Mr. Tran would find out would be if I were to tell him. And that won't happen. You can't keep this bottled up inside you, honey. Please. Please tell me."

Daniel looked deeply into Kay's face. She was both humbled and shamed by the trust she saw reflected in his eyes. He began telling her his story. The more she heard, the angrier she grew.

Upon hearing the names of her Miasma Club peers, Kay rose from the sofa. Her fury grew hotter by the second. "I've got to go, Daniel," she said.

"Are — are you mad at me?"

"Not at you," she said.

"Stay away from my boyfriend," Kay said, "or I'll make you both regret it."

Na Ba pursed her lips, although her eyes still sparkled with friendly amusement. "Thank you for nice greeting, Kay," she said. "Always good to get big hello from friend. You want sit down? Na Ong order *café au lait* for you?"

"I don't want any coffee." Kay made no effort to sit at the little table tucked beneath the rear of Café du Monde's awning. "What I want is for you to take your hex off Daniel's boss."

Na Ba nodded with comprehension. "Ahh, so *that* what got your panties all in a bunch." Her husband Na Ong motioned impatiently for one of the Vietnamese wait staff, all dressed in white uniforms and wearing Café du Monde paper caps, to come take his order. "You know," Na Ba continued, "I no put no hex on Daniel himself. Could not, even if I wanted to. He just happen to be there, mowing near leak. Just doing my job, Kay. Working on Project Big Blow. Nothing personal, swee-tie."

Nothing personal. That wasn't good enough for her, not by a long shot. "Na Ba, it doesn't matter to me that you didn't put the hex on Daniel directly. What you've done is probably *worse*. You've made his life *hell*. Daniel loves his job, but he's also got an ironclad sense of what's right and what's wrong. You've set up a terrible ethical conflict for him, and it's tearing him apart."

She heard a sudden clatter a few tables behind her, followed by gasps, objections, and hurried apologies. The waiter who had been heading for Na Ong had tripped over a tourist's cane, jostling a table loaded with cups of coffee and plates of sugar-covered *beignets*.

"I very sorry to hear that, Kay," Na Ba said. "Truly, truly. But you get attached to mortal pet, that invitation for hurt, you know? Your heart too soft, swee-tie. I always think that. Big problem for you."

"But you're my *friend*, Na Ba. Can't you undo this one thing?"

Na Ong motioned for Kay and Na Ba to be silent. The waiter arrived at their table, looking more than a little flustered. Na Ong ordered *café au lait* and *beignets* for himself and his wife. Then he looked up at Kay. "For you, too?"

Kay shook her head. The waiter left. Kay stared beseechingly at Na Ba. "So you'll do this for me? You'll take your hex off Daniel's boss?"

Na Ba shrugged sadly and shook her head. "No can do, swee-tie. I *love* give you this one, do favor for good friend. But hex already on record, swee-tie, with Big Three. I get in, how you say, 'hot water' if undo it now."

Somewhere near the kitchen, a tray laden with cups and saucers and plates of *beignets* crashed to the floor. The clatter of breaking and rolling crockery was punctuated with a fusillade of Vietnamese curses. The noise made Kay jump, but Na Ba or Na Ong stared lovingly into each other's eyes with fond, satisfied smiles. The pleasure they obviously took in ruining the evenings of a host of Vietnamese wait staff made Kay angry all over again.

"Don't you ever step back and really *look* at what we're all doing?" she asked. "I used to think it was fun to cause pratfalls, too. But now I realize we're not just nuisances — we're poisoning people's *lives*. Don't you understand what will happen if Project Big Blow succeeds? This city will become a ghost town. Maybe you don't care about your people, but I know you care about each other. What will happen to you — what will happen to *all* of us — if we chase all of our people away?"

Na Ba stared at Kay with what appeared to be honest pity. "Swee-tie, you no should worry. New Orleans is like, what you call it? Palmetto bug. Big flying cockroach." She made scurrying bug motions with her hands. "You stomp it, you stomp it more, it still crawl away and hide. Then it show up in living room again. You agree? New Orleans been around for, what — three hundred years, right? And all that time, there been a Miasma Club. City been through floods, Civil War, civil rights, civil unrest, civil *everything*, you know? And still here. Still this Café du Monde making *café au lait*, still big Saint Louis church on Jackson Square. Not going anywhere, swee-tie. *We* die before *it* die."

This unexpected statement of faith failed to comfort Kay. "How can you be so sure, Na Ba? How can you be so confident the Miasma Club's plans will come to nothing?"

"Never said Miasma Club's plans will come to *nothing*. All things that we do, they make good challenge, strong contest for strong people. Like big football game where *everybody* play, not just Saints in Superdome."

The coffee and *beignets* arrived. "Na Ba, I don't get what you're saying..."

Another cascading crash interrupted the conversation. "Kay Rosenblatt, look there," Na Ong said. He pointed across the café to where a young, very pretty, and very tired-looking Vietnamese waitress knelt on the dirty floor, picking up pieces of broken crockery. "You think us mean, Na Ba and me?" he asked. "You think we make trouble for fun, for laugh? Maybe you think we no love our people like *you* love *your* people. You wrong, Kay Rosenblatt. We love our people, too. We help them."

"You *help* them?"

"We do. Make them strong. They need to be strong."

Na Ba nodded approvingly. "Our people, it like they come to different planet when they come here," she added. "Not like Vietnam *at all*. Many choices here. Many, many temptation. Weak ones, they lose way, get lost. We give tough love. Girl over there, you feel bad for her, maybe, but she no serve coffee and *beignets* forever. She move on to better job, maybe — but only if she *strong*. She need remember what it is to work hard, get through bad, bad shift. That way, she move up ladder, 'cause she no want come back to this."

"So you — you *test* them?" Kay asked.

Na Ba smiled brightly. "Yes! That right." She stuffed an entire *beignet* in her mouth and swallowed it.

"But... but what if you test them so hard that they *break?*"

"No problem, that," Na Ong said. "In Vietnam, are tigers. Tigers eat sick, weak cattle, kill foolish men who wander in forest alone. Good for both herd and tribe. But no tigers in city. Here, *we* the tigers."

Na Ba finished her coffee. "You tiger, too, Kay," she said, reaching over to pat her hand. "You no want that, maybe, but that what *yin* and *yang* give you, so you stuck. Make peace with tiger inside you. All work out for best." She and Na Ong stood. Then, with a deftness which could not be matched by any mortal thieves, they scooped all the tips off the nearby tables. Then Na Ba planted a quick kiss on Kay's forehead and, hand in hand with her husband, took a circuitous route out of the cafe, pilfering any tips within reach.

Something warm and wet sloshed against Kay's foot. She looked down. A puddle of filthy coffee had flowed into one of her open-toed shoes, propelled by a mop wielded by an over-zealous waiter.

"So sorry," the man said sheepishly. "Big, big mess tonight. I get you towel."

"It's all right," Kay said, wincing at the clamminess between her toes. "It's not your fault."

She rubbed her tired eyes with her palms as she thought about Daniel's dilemma. Would it help him to become stronger? She couldn't see how.

The reluctant tigress crept out of the café on paws that went *squish, squish.*

Chapter 8

AYOR Roy Rio rubbed the back of his neck, wincing at the tightness there. Despite it being seven in the evening, he figured quitting time was still two hours away. The shit hit the fan so often around here, he couldn't buy fresh fans fast enough... The public safety unions were threatening job actions during Jazz Fest unless the administration granted four percent cost-of-living raises retroactively for the past three years. Cynthia and the Morehouses were still stonewalling on the MuckGen deal. Speaking of MuckGen, they'd lost one of their key researchers due to that incredibly bizarre accidental death at the Saint Patrick's Day Parade. What next? King Kong climbing the Superdome?

Alberta, his administrative assistant, knocked, then stuck her head through the door. "Roy? You got time for a visitor?"

Roy frowned. "Unless it's the budget fairy flying in with fifteen million new dollars, I don't have time. Squeeze whoever it is into my calendar somewhere."

"But you've still got to eat, don't you?"

"If it's Sidney Fouchet from the police union trying to bribe me with some take-out fried catfish, tell him I'm not that cheap a date. If I accept so much as a single hush puppy from him, the editorial staff of the *Times-Picayune* will roast my sorry behind."

"It's not Sidney Fouchet. It's Lily Weintraub. She called ahead to ask if you'd eaten anything yet, and I told her you hadn't. I hope I haven't spoken out of turn."

Roy saw Alberta try to hide a smile. She knew all about Roy's teenaged infatuation with Lily. So now she was trying to play matchmaker for her divorced boss? "You didn't make a boo-boo, Alberta," he said. "Please send her in."

A moment later, there Lily was, standing in his doorway holding a big paper sack. Her demeanor seemed entirely different from a few weeks ago. Then, she'd been guarded, on edge, almost skittish. Not that she didn't seem tentative now — she hovered on his office's threshold like a butterfly trying to decide whether a particular sunflower's nectar would prove delectable or poisonous. But it was a hopeful sort of tentativeness. And for Roy, that made all the difference in the world.

"Hi," she said. "I hope I'm not interrupting anything too important." She held up the bag as though it were a peace offering. "I brought two dinners from the Redfish Grill. Thought I'd make up for turning down your invitation last month."

He walked over to take the bag. "There's nothing to make up for. I'm really glad to see you. And I'm hungry as a grizzly. Thank you." He set the bag down on a table in front of his sofa and began removing its contents. "So... so was this a spur of the minute thing, or...?"

Lily helped him arrange the food. "No. I... I've been thinking some, Roy. Maybe I've been too... risk averse."

Roy allowed himself an arch smile. "Is getting involved with me really such a risk? Unless my ex-wife organizes a successful recall petition, I'm gainfully employed for at least another year."

"Roy, please don't kid... you know what I'm talking about."

His smile faded. Lily, beautiful and conflicted... it felt like old times. "Your dad," he said. Amos Weintraub, who had always stood between them, stern and unyielding as the Old Testament prophet he'd been named after. "So what's going to be different this time? Has Amos finally decided to let you live your own life?"

She fussed with the napkins and plastic utensils. Roy watched her long, slender fingers glide across the table. They were mesmerizing.

81

"Last Saturday," she said, "at the kiddish lunch after services, Dad tried fixing me up with another one of his 'finds.' This particular guy wasn't an ogre. But for the first time, I didn't make even a token effort to make Dad happy. Right in front of Dad, my brother, and Kay, I turned the guy down flat. In a nice way, of course. My father refused to speak with me for the rest of the weekend. Aside from asking me to pass the brisket, he hasn't more than nodded in my direction all week."

Roy whistled softly. "So how does that make you feel, hon?"

"*Angry*. Really, really *mad*."

He bit his lower lip. He really, *really* didn't want to ask this next question, but avoiding it invited disaster. "Uh, your coming here tonight... are you sure this isn't just your wanting to kick your dad in the shins?"

She looked stunned. "Roy, I — *no!* Of course not! How could... do you really think I'm the kind of woman who would use one of the dearest people I know as a, a *blunt instrument* to beat my father with?"

Shit. "Lily, that's not what I meant. But all of us, at some time, have done things for hidden reasons, hidden even from ourselves. I had to ask. Honey, right now, my dearest wish, aside from the health and happiness of my daughter, is that you and I find some way to make things work between us. But if we're going to make that effort, I want us to make it for only the right reasons. Are we on the same page?"

She nodded. "Roy, what I was trying to tell you is this. I love my father. He awes me with his strength, and he always has. He deserves to be honored, and with all my heart I *want* to honor him. But I can't honor him anymore by surrendering my life to his wishes."

She took a deep breath, as though she were steeling herself for her first-ever sky dive. "I want a chance to create my own happiness. I want a loving husband and life partner. I want to start my own family, build my own home. I want to raise children—" Her voice caught in her throat. "*Jewish* children."

His heart stopped. He had no idea where she was heading with this.

She took his hands, and her eyes filled with a kind of pleading. "Roy, this isn't about my father. This is about what *I* want. I want my kids to grow up celebrating Shabbat every week. I want to hear them reciting the Four Questions at the *seder* table. I want to see them lighting candles on Fridays and for Hanukkah, and dipping apples in honey for Rosh Hashana."

"And how do I fit into all of this?"

"Roy, I know this is a momentous thing to ask of anyone... but back when we were in high school, you told me something. You said you thought all the world's great religions represented different paths up the sides of a steep mountain, all leading to the same summit. You said it didn't really matter to you which path you started climbing, so long as you kept ascending. Back then, I didn't have the courage to take you up on what I sensed was an offer. Do... do you still feel that way?"

Whoa. He hadn't foreseen *this*. But what had he expected from Lily when he'd started calling her again? "So... what you're asking of me is... you want me to become Jewish? Like, uh, Sammy Davis, Jr. did?"

She smiled. "Well, Sammy Davis, Jr. wouldn't have been the example I would've picked... because I can't quite picture you tap dancing... but, *yeah.*"

Roy laughed; he imagined the Black Ministerial Alliance's outraged reaction to his conversion. "Uh, any chance I could defer this decision until after the next election campaign? I don't know if this city is ready for a black Jewish mayor."

Her smile faded. "Oh, I wasn't even thinking of your political career. Maybe... maybe it's too much to ask of you. I'm sorry, I'm so embarrassed—"

"Hey." He took hold of her shoulders. "I didn't say *no*, did I? It's just a heck of a lot to think about. I mean, I just pulled myself from the wreckage of a marriage that came crashing down, in part because of religion. As they say in therapy, I've got *issues.*"

"I understand." She kissed him on the cheek, letting her lips linger against his skin. "Thanks, Roy. For being willing to even think about it. I won't rush you. I promise."

* * * * *

Who in the hell is ringing my doorbell this time of the evening? Cynthia Belvedere Hotchkiss thought. Couldn't she just enjoy a quiet visit with her best friend without all kinds of interruptions? She went to her front door and peered through the keyhole. She didn't like who she saw standing on her front porch. Her n'er do well uncle, Sergeant Quincy Cochrane. But he was a blood relation, so she couldn't just leave him standing there, no matter how much she wanted to.

She opened the door a crack, leaving the chain fastened. "Uncle Quincy, you aren't one to just pop on by for a cup of coffee," she said brusquely. "What's up? I've got company, so make it quick."

"Hi, niece." He grinned mischievously, then held up a briefcase so she could see it. "I got a laptop computer I think you might be interested in."

She could barely conceal her contempt. "You trying to raise money to hit the gambling boats again? This is a new low, even for you. What do I look like — a *pawn shop*? Where'd you get that laptop from? Lift it off some drug dealer you shook down?"

"No, ma'am. This here is a very special laptop. It didn't come from no drug dealer. I think you'll want it, niece."

"I've already *got* a very nice computer, thank you."

She tried closing the door, but he jammed his foot into the opening. "Does the name 'Amitri Zoukeni' mean anything to you?"

"Hell, no. Now *get* your foot *out* of my door, or I'll call the po — I'll report you to the Community Relations Board."

"Would you be more interested if I told you he was MuckGen's main researcher? *Was*, 'cause the dude's stiff and cold now — he was the poor fool that got massacred by a parade float on Saint Paddy's Day."

Her pressure on the door wavered. "What does your silly laptop have to do with MuckGen?"

Quincy showed her the nametag affixed to the briefcase. "This was Zoukeni's laptop. After he got run clean through on Royal Street, he didn't need this no more. He wrote some pretty interesting stuff on this computer, niece. Stuff you'd wanna know about. Stuff them MuckGen folks would likely pay a pretty penny to keep the world from finding out."

"Like what?"

"Like how their big, fancy project that's supposed to earn billions ain't worth a stubbed-out cigar. It don't work. Keeps blowin' itself up."

She stared long and hard at her uncle. "Quincy, is this on the level?"

"Sho' 'nuf. I may not be the straightest arrow in the quiver—"

"*That's* an understatement!"

"But I can't very well lie about all the scientific gobbledygook on this here computer. It's too damn complicated for me to make up. Now, you gonna let me through the door so we can talk proper, or do I take my goods to the Morehouses, see if they're interested?"

She unlatched the door chain. "All right, Quincy. I'll hear you out. Wait just a minute." She turned toward her parlor, at the far end of the foyer and a long, formal dining room. "Lisa, hon? Would you mind taking Nicole upstairs for a while? It's a relation of mine at the door. We need to talk over some... some family business, stuff I don't want to bore you two with."

"No problem, Cynthia," a plump, pretty woman answered. "Nicole and I will take our game upstairs to her room."

Cynthia waited until her daughter and her old college friend had disappeared up the winding staircase. Then she led Quincy toward the parlor. "You say this 'perpetual motion machine' of theirs doesn't work?"

He patted the briefcase. "All the details are in here, niece."

"Let me see some of it."

He sat himself down at a dark oak French Provincial table. "Huh-uh. No sneak previews. You give me a down payment on my finder's fee, and you can have yourself a look."

She smirked. "And what would this 'finder's fee' add up to?"

"Fifty thousand."

"Fifty thousand *dollars?*"

"Cheap at twice the price, niece. We're talkin' 'bout a company that wants to become the next Exxon, right? And in order to do that, they need to buy or lease a buncha land that your church owns. I hear they been balkin' on meetin' your terms. Now, what do you think they'd pay for that land, if they knew you'd throw in this here laptop so's they could keep it out of the hands of the press? I bet they'd like to keep milkin' their investors and the government as long as they can. Maybe long enough for them to hire some more scientists who can make their energy machine work without blowin' itself up."

"But — but *fifty thousand dollars?* Where am I supposed to come up with that kind of money?"

"Hey, you're a New Orleans politician, with a New Orleans politician's war chest. And better than that, you're assistant pastor of the Holy Tabernacle Maximum Gospel Church. Y'all own more real estate 'round here than Carter has liver pills."

"*Get. Out.*" She pointed at the door, her fingertip trembling with barely contained rage. "You — you *skunk*. You *miscreant!* How *dare* you insinuate that I would misuse church funds? You make me *ashamed* that we have any blood in common."

Quincy held his ground. "Who's sayin' anything about misusin' church funds? What I'm suggestin' is that your church make an *investment* in the information economy, one that could pay for itself ten times over practically overnight. And if you don't want to get your church involved, I happen to know you got a nice chunk of surplus change left in that election fund of yours. You haven't made much of a secret that you might just be interested in runnin' for mayor yourself next year. Last I saw, you got about ninety thousand sittin' in the bank, collectin' interest."

"How — how do you know that?"

"That's public record, darlin', available to any interested citizen. And I been keepin' tabs on my favorite niece. Now, under election laws, you can re-donate any sum of that there surplus to a registered charity of your choice. Just so happens I know of a *fine* charity that's always lookin' for donations — BABPO, the Benevolent Association of Black Police Officers. Alcee Hasty, the treasurer, and me are chums from way back. You make a donation to BABPO in the amount of fifty grand, I can assure you it'll be used for a righteous cause. Besides, you *owe* me, niece. Big time. I mean, there I was, the uncle of the bride who married the man who got himself elected mayor. Everybody on the force was placin' bets on how many months it would be before I made captain. But then you go and screw the pooch by divorcing Rio. And me? I'm still stuck on the goddamn Street Crimes Unit after twenty-one years on the force. You know what that done to my rep, niece, after the way you raised my hopes?"

Much as she hated to give her loathsome uncle any credit, Cynthia had to admit Quincy had his facts straight. That briefcase he held pulled at her with the power of an electromagnet. Not only would its contents ensure an enormous profit for her church... but when it became public knowledge, as it most surely would, the momentous technical failure it described would ensure her ex-husband's lofty dreams would collapse into egg all over his face.

She wanted that computer. She wanted it *bad*. But the thought of getting in bed with Quincy Cochrane, letting him put his *stink* on her...

"Look, niece, if you don't wanna do business with me, that's fine. There's the Morehouses; or I can even go directly to the MuckGen folks, see what they'd pay to get their laptop back. But I'd rather give a blood relation first shot at a payday. And like I said, you owe me."

She wiped her forehead, hoping her uncle hadn't noticed the sheen of perspiration which had gathered there. "Uncle Quincy... I apologize for yelling at you before. Just give me some time, okay? It's a lot to think about."

"Sure, Cynthia." He turned to the door. "But don't take too long." He pulled it open. "Twenty-four hours, niece."

As he sauntered down her front walkway to his squad car, parked in *her* driveway (*what if the neighbors saw?*), Cynthia wanted to brain him with a well-aimed potted fern. He was her uncle, for Christ's sake — how could he put her in this kind of position? So far, her maneuvers against Roy had all been above board. But this... this threatened to tempt her down some dark roads.

"Cynthia, it safe to come out now?" Her best friend, Lisa Eymard, stood on the second floor landing. "I'm getting a little tired of playing checkers with Nicole, and I'd love to make a fresh pot of your coffee."

Cynthia watched Quincy drive toward the Eastover neighborhood's front security gate, then sighed and closed the door. "Sure, Lisa. Come on down. I'm sorry Uncle Quincy forced me to be rude."

"Nothing to apologize for, hon. Family can be a cross to bear. This one, though, he sure drives a hard bargain, doesn't he?"

Cynthia felt her face redden. "How much of all that did you overhear?"

The round-faced, round-bodied black woman smiled and raised an eyebrow. "Oh, most of it. Your uncle wasn't trying real hard to keep quiet."

Damn that man! Him and Roy Rio both. "How much did Nicole hear?"

"Don't sweat it, hon." Lisa put her arm around Cynthia's shoulders. Her friend's warm touch was enough to make Cynthia feel instantly reassured. "Nicole wasn't paying no attention. The whole time, she was jabbering away with her girlfriends on her cell phone."

"Well... thank the Lord for that, at least. I wouldn't want her running with any tales to Roy. She's so damned protective of her father."

"Yeah, well, that's little girls and their daddies. Mama busts her ass and gets nothing but grief, but all Daddy has to do is smile and he's a knight on a white stallion." Lisa started to withdraw her friendly embrace, then stopped as her fingers grazed Cynthia's tense neck muscles. "Oohh, girl, you're tighter than a drum! Get yourself over to that sofa, lie down, and let me work on you some."

"I'm all right, really—"

"I'm not taking 'no' for an answer. *Lie down.*"

Cynthia complied. Ever since Lisa had re-entered her life nearly a year ago, her old high school friend had somehow known exactly the right thing to say, the right thing to do. Such a comforting, reassuring presence... Cynthia felt the tensions in her neck, shoulders, and back begin to drain away, like bad, dirty oil from a crankcase.

"Ohh, Lisa..." Her words were muffled by the linen pillow she'd buried her face in. "Where'd you learn to work such magic?"

"Oh... around."

"Roy used to — *ooohh* — used to try to give me little massages. Wasn't never any good at it, though. Nowhere *near* as good as you."

"Why'd you get together with that man, anyway?"

"Oh, I don't know... he seemed like a lost bird when we got introduced, like a little bird that fell out of the nest and broke its wing. I guess I felt sorry for him. Had no *idea* how to be a black man, but he was trying so *hard.* Shaved his head 'cause he thought it made him look like W. E. B. Dubois. Like *that* was supposed to impress anybody, back in the 'eighties! He was comin' off a long-time romance gone bad with some white girl. He was lookin' for her opposite, I guess. And I must've been the *blackest* girl in arm's reach. Uncle Quincy had him pegged right off the bat, though. Called him 'Roy *Oreo*,' said he'd be nothin' but trouble for me. One of the few times I shoulda listened to him."

"How about this time?"

"This time? What should I do about his offer, you mean?" Cynthia clenched her eyes shut. "Tell him to jam that laptop up his ass, right? Then tell the Public Integrity Bureau that Quincy's stolen evidence from a death scene. Be a good, upright church lady. That's what you're gonna tell me, right?" Her voice trailed away to a whisper. "*Shit.*"

"Now why are you puttin' words in my mouth, girl?" Lisa picked up the pace of her massage. "Did I say anything about wanting you to throw that fish back in the lake?"

"But — but I thought..." She felt something granular being sprinkled on her back, followed by something warm, liquid, and turgid. "What's that, Lisa?"

"Just some special massaging sand I keep in my purse. You mix it with a little oil, and it takes a massage to a whole new level. Scours away dry skin, too."

Lisa wasn't kidding. When her friend's fingers resumed their probing and kneading, their touch was like nothing Cynthia had ever experienced. If Roy had been able to make her feel even a *tenth* this good... "Oohh, Lisa, that's *heavenly*. Are you — are you writing things on my back?"

"Just amusing myself."

Cynthia had no idea what those symbols or doodles being traced on her skin looked like, but she felt them speaking to her inner self, the same way songs remembered from her childhood often could. "So... so you don't think it'd be wrong for me to make a deal with Uncle Quincy?"

"*Wrong?* Hon, what's *wrong* with helpin' to take down a company that's tryin' to pull a scam on this city? And if it takes some of the shine off Roy Rio, all the better! You complain to me all the time how he's hoodwinked New Orleans, fillin' the voters' heads with big dreams while he doesn't do *squat* to fix the potholes in their streets. Take the man down a peg. He's got it comin'."

"That bastard... he never supported me during my ministry studies. I was slaving on that degree, trying to raise Nicole practically on my own. But *his* software business always came first, then his *campaign* — *they* were the important things."

"No appreciation from that man. None."

"Could hardly *ever* get him to go to church with me. Not until he started running for mayor — oh, then it was a *fine* thing to be seen in the pews."

Lisa murmured agreement. "Hypocrisy. And what kind of example was he settin' for Nicole?"

"Always disrespectin' me and my ambitions in front of my daughter. The two of them laughin' at his little jokes, her worshipping him like he was some hip-hop star..."

"And all the while Nicole was worshippin' *him*, he was worshippin' somebody *else*, wasn't he? That white girl from his past..."

Despite Lisa's near magical ministrations, Cynthia felt her spine and shoulders stiffen. "Lily Weintraub. That white *bitch*. I saw how he was looking at her all through that FEBO exercise. If I coulda caught her alone that night, I woulda torn her weak blue eyes right outta her head."

"Damn straight, girl. So, you gonna cut a deal with Uncle Quincy?"

"I — I still gotta think about it. Fifty thou is a lot of money. Let me do a little pokin' around first. Get some idea what that laptop is really worth to the MuckGen people. No sense in my stickin' my neck out unless they're crazy-scared of what's on that hard drive going public."

Lisa Eymard said goodnight, then crossed the street to her Buick. *Not that bad a night*, she thought. Cynthia was on the verge of taking the plunge. Quincy Cochrane would prove to be a useful tool, she was sure.

The police sergeant virtually reeked with the taint of Ti Malice. Much as she hated to admit it, she and T.M. were often drawn to the same marks. Natural partners they were, despite the friction between them.

She settled herself behind the wheel. The street lamp overhead was dark. *Good.* She needed the darkness. She removed a jar of special cold cream from the glove compartment, then liberally slathered the cold cream over her face, her neck, her arms and legs, and finally her clothes.

Then Eleggua-Eshu rolled the Lisa guise off himself like a layer of thin, skintight latex. He folded it up neatly and placed it inside a tobacco pouch. Finally, he removed a tiny hat from his vest pocket, exhaled a quick puff of breath on it to expand it, and placed his favorite derby on his bald head.

Of all his trick guises, he'd decided he liked this "Lisa Eymard" the best. Maybe after a few more sessions of special massage, he might tempt Cynthia into a little "girl" on girl action. Wouldn't that be fun?

All in all, a most pleasant night's hexing, he thought as he drove through the Eastover gates. He slowed and looked around him. Grand walls, grand gardens, grand houses... ah, the vanity and presumption of mortals. Mere decades ago, all this luxury had been barren swampland.

And soon, very soon, he told himself, it all would be again.

Chapter 9

"**M**AYOR Rio, do you have any questions? I know these first sessions can be pretty overwhelming, even intimidating."

The rabbi's words barely registered on Roy's consciousness. He was far more aware of the insistent pressure of Lily's hand around his. This was a pretty big step they were making. Sure, all they'd done was visit a rabbi in his office. But given his and Lily's shared history, it was a step as enormous as Neil Armstrong's initial hop to the lunar surface.

"Mayor Rio? Do you have any questions I can answer before we finish up for tonight?"

A sudden squeeze from Lily's hand helped Roy refocus his attention on the short, bearded, friendly-looking man sitting across from them. "I'm sorry, Rabbi. I was in Never-Never Land there for a minute."

"Oh, I'm sure you have a multitude of things on your mind," Rabbi Freidman said, smiling graciously. "Plus, you're contemplating a major life change here. Over the centuries, many observers have ascribed the Jewish people's reluctance to seek or accept converts to clannishness, or a sense of ethnic superiority. But it has actually stemmed from the rabbis' concern for potential converts' well-being. We may be God's Chosen People, but this 'chosenness' doesn't denote any superiority. Rather, it means that God selected the Jews for hundreds of additional responsibilities and obligations — the *mitzvot* of which I spoke of earlier. And, for reasons known only to Him, God also chose the Jews to endure centuries of persecution. Since the time of the Roman Empire, many regimes have enforced edicts which condemned both converts to

Judaism and their adopted religious communities to death. Of course, matters have never been so dire, thank God, here in America—"

"Yeah, maybe not for the Jews," Roy said. He immediately regretted saying it. Rabbi Freidman looked as if he'd just swallowed his tie. Roy sensed Lily sink deeper into the couch.

"Sorry," he said; but then he felt even more foolish for having apologized.

"Oh, please don't be," Rabbi Freidman said, quickly recovering his composure. "I didn't mean to imply that America has had a perfect record of tolerance. I only meant to say that religious tolerance, officially, at least, is the law of the land. And perhaps the time is long overdue for we Jews to set aside old fears and compete with other faith communities for our share of unchurched spiritual seekers. That said, an absence of legal barriers doesn't imply a corresponding lack of *social* barriers. Lily has told me about the resistance the two of you have met from her father. And relations between the Jewish and black communities, so closely allied during the civil rights years, have unfortunately frayed. As the black mayor of a majority black city, I'm sure this must weigh heavily upon you."

Roy felt his impatience intensify. "That's putting it lightly."

"I know I must sound terribly discouraging," the rabbi said. "I don't mean to be. We Jews are a small people, and many of our most illustrious and devoted members have been either converts or the descendants of converts, including even King David. What I'm trying to emphasize is that, with a decision of this magnitude, there are costs which must be factored in, personal sacrifices which each of you will find yourselves making. Mayor Rio, I implore you to be completely honest with yourself about your motivations. Some rabbis will always encourage the spouse or would-be spouse of a Jew to convert. I'm not one of them. I cannot in good conscience recommend that you take this action if you do so only out of a desire to please Lily. You must also want it for yourself, and for any children with which you and Lily may be blessed."

"I'll take that under advisement." Roy stood and shook the rabbi's hand. "Thanks."

"Will I be seeing the two of you again? Same time next week?"

"Schedule permitting." Roy forced a smile and helped Lily up from the couch.

"Thank you so much, Rabbi Freidman," Lily said. "I really appreciate your meeting with us on such short notice."

Rabbi Freidman showed them out of his office. "Of course. We rabbis are like doctors — on call twenty-four seven. It was a pleasure talking with both of you."

They walked through the empty synagogue parking lot to their cars. Roy had driven his personal vehicle, a sleek late model Audi A8. *Ol' Amos would probably hate that German set of wheels*, Roy thought. "That rabbi's a nice guy," he said.

"Yes, he is. A very gracious man."

"He's not your usual rabbi?"

"No. My family attends Beth Judah. Jacob Reiss is our rabbi there."

They stopped next to Lily's car. "So taking me to see Rabbi Jake wouldn't have been discreet, huh?"

Lily stared at the ground while she dug her keys out of her purse. "I'm not the only one who wanted to keep this just to ourselves for now, Roy."

"I know, I know." He opened the door for her. "You want to grab a cup of coffee and some desert? This is one of those rare nights when I can actually squeeze some me-time in."

She reached into the car and placed her purse on the passenger seat. "Sure," she said, her voice tight.

"You mad at me?"

She turned around, looking surprised. "Do I seem mad?"

He couldn't help but laugh. "Actually... yeah, you *do*. Look, I don't know what you were expecting out of me tonight. The rabbi told me to take it slow. That sounded like solid advice to me. Can we leave the big, scary decisions behind for an hour or so, and just try to have some fun?"

Lily hugged him tightly. "That sounds good," she said.

He followed her to a coffeehouse on Clearview Parkway. Roy figured this place was deep enough into the boonies of suburban Metairie that he wouldn't be immediately recognized. With any luck, he and Lily would be able to enjoy their coffee in relative anonymity.

Inside, he quietly shuffled up behind Lily and slipped his arms around her waist. "So what sweet things can I offer my sweet one?"

Not an especially smooth line, he thought, but it seemed to have the intended effect; Lily smiled her biggest smile of the evening. "Oh, I don't know... that Death-by-Chocolate cake looks awfully good..."

"Then Death-by-Chocolate it shall be." He grinned at the young woman behind the counter. "My delightful companion will have a slice of Death-by-Chocolate cake. I, in turn, will have a... oh, you're out of blondies, aren't you?"

"Yeah, just sold the last one ten minutes ago," the server said. She looked at him more closely. "Say, don't I know you from somewhere? Are you on TV?"

"No," he said. "I'll have a macadamia nut cookie and a large *café au lait* — decaf, please." He turned to Lily. "Hon, what would you like to drink?"

"Oh, please give me a big *café au lait*, too, but make mine high-test. I'm on the graveyard shift tonight at the hospital."

He heard the bathroom door behind him swing open. Then he heard himself addressed by a title he never would've expected here — "*Daddy??*"

He immediately let go of Lily's waist and turned around. "*Nicole?* What are you doing here? This is a school night! Does your mother know you're all the way out here in Metairie?"

Nicole ran to him and gave him a vigorous hug. "Oh, don't worry! I'm out here studying with Kaweetha, one of my friends from dance class." She pointed to a tall, slender, dark-complected girl sitting at a corner table. "Mama gave me permission. She kinda likes getting me out of the house. Hey, what are *you* doing all the way out here?"

Shit. "I'm, uh, I had to come out to the Jefferson Municipal Complex for a meeting." He sensed Lily take a deep breath behind him.

"Oh, okay," Nicole said, and then her face perked up with a surge of urgency. "Hey! I wanted to call you later, anyway. I think Mama's up to something wicked—"

"Nicole, don't be telling stories on your mother. Show her some respect."

"No, really! Just listen. Uncle Creepy came over to the house a couple of nights ago—"

"You mean your Uncle Quincy?"

"Yeah, Uncle Creepy. Mama doesn't even *like* him, but lately she's been talking to him pretty nicely on the phone. He's up to something. I don't know what, but I've listened a couple of times with my door open just a crack, and I heard them talking some about MuckGen and about *you*—"

The server set the two pastries and two coffees down on the counter. "Ma'am, that'll be eleven forty-six, please."

Roy turned back to the server. "No, wait, I'll get it."

He didn't have to look at his daughter to know she was staring at Lily now.

"Daddy, who's that?"

Lily stepped away from the counter to where Nicole could see her better. "Roy," she said, "I don't think I've ever met your daughter. Would you introduce us?"

Roy felt his internal temperature plummet twenty degrees. No matter how well he did this, it wasn't going to go down easy. Not with a teenaged girl who, he knew, yearned for her utterly incompatible parents to miraculously reconcile. "Nicole, this is Lily. Lily is... an old friend. We went to high school together."

"Lily..." Nicole whispered the name like it was a curse. *Oh, Jesus,* Roy thought suddenly. *What has Cynthia said to her?* "Then... what I heard Mama telling Miss Lisa... it's all *true—?*"

"Nicole, what have you been hearing from your mother?"

She backed away from Roy, a look of profound disappointment and betrayal darkening her face. Then she turned and ran to the table where her friend sat. Within seconds, they were both gathering their laptops and papers.

"Nicole—!" He took a few tentative steps towards her table. "Honey, this is not what you think..." His daughter refused to look at him. She and Kaweetha headed for the door.

"Roy, what's going on?" Lily sounded confused and distressed, but Roy would have to deal with her later. Already, Nicole and Kaweetha were halfway across the parking lot.

Roy ran after them. "Nicole, wait! Whatever your mother told you about Lily and me, it isn't true! Will you just wait and *listen—?*"

The sound of Nicole slamming the door of her friend's Corolla echoed through the parking lot. Within seconds, his daughter was gone.

Chapter 10

"**M**R. Mayor, I'm sorry I've got bad news to report," Bruno Galliano said.

"Just hit me with it," Mayor Rio replied. His voice lacked any vigor or animation. "Skip the preliminaries. Everybody's got fucking bad news for me lately."

Bruno couldn't recall ever hearing the mayor utter a profanity before, not even in the heat of the campaign. The mayor stared forlornly at a framed photograph of his daughter at the edge of his desk. "Uh, if this is a bad time, Mr. Mayor, I could come back later..."

"*Every* time's a *bad* time. So go ahead and dump your load."

"It's the Secure Emergency Communications System, sir. It's gone down. Again."

Mayor Rio drilled Bruno with an angry, incredulous stare. "SECS is busted? *Again?* The comm system you convinced me and the City Council to invest five point seven *million dollars* in? The system that's supposedly hardened enough to stand up to a Category Five hurricane? *That's* the system that's down again?"

"Uh... yes, sir."

"Well, get the contractors in and have them *fix* that piece of shit. *Again.*"

"There's a, uh, a complication, sir. I can't ask the contractors to perform another fix until... well, until I secure more funding. My office — apart from baseline operating funds, we're out of money."

"Why is this a money issue? Don't we have a maintenance contract in place? Didn't the damn system come with a *warranty* of some kind?"

"The warranty only covers manufacturing and installation defects. The contractor swears up and down the problems we're having aren't due to any inherent defects. It's all external causes, they say. Strange... coincidences, bizarre occurrences the designers couldn't have foreseen. 'Twilight Zone' stuff. And our maintenance contract... you remember your directive on reducing the cost of service contracts? One of your first initiatives after taking office?"

"Yes," the mayor said darkly. "I remember."

"Well, we saved a bundle on the up-front cost of the maintenance contract. But the way we did it was by limiting the number of major repairs included in the base fee to two per calendar quarter. Beyond that, any additional repairs are all, uh, fee for service, time and materials. That's why I burned through my budget so quickly, Mr. Mayor. There's simply no way I could've foreseen the number and complexity of the repairs—"

"That's *your* problem, Bruno. You negotiated the service contract. You procured the system. You got the budget you asked for, unlike a lot of other departments. *You* find a way to make it work."

"But — but—"

"I'm not adding more money to your budget. Don't even ask. There's nothing left in the damn cookie jar—"

His telephone rang. He looked ready to pitch the phone through his window, but he glanced at the extension and reluctantly picked it up. "Alberta, I'm in the middle of a meeting with Bruno. Can this wait? What? She's says it's urgent? All right, all right, put her through."

He covered the phone's mouthpiece. "Sorry, Bruno. It's Annalee Jones from MuckGen. Let me find out what she needs. Should only take a minute."

He uncovered the phone. "Annalee? Alberta tells me you've got some kind of a problem...?" Bruno watched his boss's face grow increasingly troubled. "No... are you *sure*? Are you absolutely certain that's what Cynthia was trying to do? I mean, *extortion*, that's *serious*... So she didn't come out and ask for any *quid pro quo* directly? But you think she's got access to your company's missing laptop? Now let me get this straight — she's hinting there's stuff on there that could hurt you?" He looked up at Bruno. "Annalee, excuse me for just a minute. I'm not — I've got an employee in here with me."

He pressed the phone's mute button. "Bruno, I've got to deal with this. See Alberta on your way out, and let's reschedule."

"But what do I do about SECS in the meantime?"

"I *told* you, SECS is *your* problem. Handle it. Apply for some emergency management grants. Go after some federal money. Maybe Duckie Duckswitt can donate part of his travel meals budget."

He pointed to the door.

Bruno collapsed onto his office couch.

His administrative assistant, Venus Roman, caressed his shoulders. "Why do you look so downhearted, my Bruno?"

"The mayor just told me to give myself an enema with a howitzer shell. He acts as if these SECS problems are all my fault. As if *I'm* responsible for whatever damn gremlins are mucking the system up. He said I can't expect another cent of city money this budget year, told me to go begging for grant money. Swatted me out of his office like a mosquito."

Venus climbed onto his lap, then twirled a finger through his thinning hair. "Oh, come, come, my valiant warrior. It couldn't have been as bad as you say."

Bruno squirmed uncomfortably. She obligingly assumed a slightly different position on his lap, her wide hips crushing him less decisively.

"No," he said. "It was *worse*. He treated me like some know-nothing college intern — every bit as bad as that goddamn Lieutenant Colonel Schwartz used to treat me when I was with the Corps. Maybe I should quit. Maybe I should get the hell out of this damn bowl of a city, head back to East Texas."

Her large, liquid eyes widened with concern. "Oh, you wouldn't leave *me* behind, would you?"

"Of course not, baby. Heck, you're the best thing that's happened to me since my Bunny died. You'd come with me, for sure. I mean, what do you need this penny-ante city job for, anyway? It's beneath you."

"Oh, but I *couldn't* leave New Orleans. Not *ever*." She stroked the sides of his face, then nuzzled his chest. Her lustrous black hair spilled across his lap, soothing him like a cashmere blanket. "Besides, my Bruno would never turn his back on his duty. Not my sergeant, not my glorious soldier. This foolish mayor needs you. For when is the loyal soldier most needed, but when he must shield his Caesar from the poisoned spears of the Caesar's own impetuousness and blindness?"

Bruno chuckled, somewhat embarrassed. "Yes, well, that's very nice of you to say, Venus. You've got quite a way with words, there."

"Your praise honors me," she cooed. "So this unwise notion of quitting — you will put it out of your mind?"

"It's just — I'm not sure I can be *effective* anymore. I don't seem to be able to *persuade* the man to focus on the right issues, not even after that cluster-snafu of a hurricane simulation. Maybe I'd be doing Mayor Rio a worse turn by sticking around than I would by leaving—"

She placed a forefinger on his mouth. Its warmth seemed to fuse his lips together. "Hush, hush. Such lack of confidence... it shrivels my heart to hear it from you. You must be punished." She looked up at him, her eyes dancing with mischievousness.

Bruno's eyes darted to the clock on the wall. His eleven-thirty meeting was barely fifteen minutes away. "Uh, what'd you have in mind, exactly?"

"The usual, my sweet."

"You locked the door on your way in?"

"Of course."

"Is Anita in the next office?"

"No. She went downstairs to smoke. And I asked her to walk over to Walgreens to get some maxi-pads for me."

"Maxi-pads?! Doesn't that mean—"

"Do not concern yourself, my valiant one." Venus unbuttoned her blouse, then began the complicated task of unhooking her massive brassiere. "We have other ways."

Her humongous breasts (size triple D, Bruno estimated) spilled out of the loosened bra. They quivered atop her rib cage like opaque pink jellyfish. As he had often done, Bruno marveled at those breasts' otherworldly smoothness and lack of sag.

She slid off his lap and knelt on the floor, facing him, her breasts enveloping his thighs. Those breasts weren't her sole spectacular feature; from this vantage point, the contrast between her wasp-thin waist and those ultra-maternal hips was, well — *breathtaking. Lord, she's like some fertility goddess from primitive mythology*, he thought. He realized he was already fully aroused, and painfully so. She reached beneath herself and began unzipping his khakis.

"Wait!" he whispered. "Aren't we — aren't we gonna get kinda *loud?*"

"You're right," she said, freeing one hand to grab for the TV remote control on the table behind her. "I'll turn on The Weather Channel."

"Good idea," he gasped.

Turned up loud, the meteorologist narrated a review of America's most destructive past hurricanes, then speculated about the very active storm season ahead. As soon as Venus had freed Bruno from his confining trousers and ensconced him within the embrace of her orbs, she swished loudly, as though she were about to spit out mouthwash. Then she leaned over his cocooned manhood.

She didn't spit — that would've been unladylike. A thick strand of what could only have been saliva poured slowly from her lips and gradually filled the hollow between her breasts. It had to be saliva, but it was golden as virgin olive oil, fresh from the press. It *smelled* like olive oil, too. Venus began manipulating herself around him, and suddenly Bruno wasn't thinking about olive oil anymore.

"Oooh *criminy*, honey, does that ever feel *good...*"

"I am pleased that you are pleased."

He closed his eyes, then opened them again so he wouldn't miss anything. His buddies in the Army, with all their bar bragging about exotic R&R trips to Thailand and old Saigon, none of them could match what he was getting right now, not even with their most outlandish bullshit sex stories.

Yet even with so much to look at, he couldn't keep his eyes away from the damn Weather Channel. Old clips appeared of Dan Rather reporting from Homestead Air Force Base after Hurricane Andrew. Then older news footage, in grainy black and white, of drowned St. Bernard Parish and the Lower Ninth Ward after Betsy, the "hundred year storm" that was followed by another "hundred year storm" a few short years later — Camille, which stripped the Biloxi and Gulfport coastlines bare.

Jesus, he thought. Shame nearly swallowed him whole. June first was, what? Fifty-two days away? Having his dick massaged by a pair of triple-D breasts while he was on the clock wasn't exactly in the public's best interest.

"Ve — Venus?"

"Yes, dear one?"

"How many — *aaahhh* — how many confirmations have you, uh, gotten for my eleven-thirty meeting?"

She kept up her steady rhythm. "Four, I think. Three others said they have conflicts. The remaining invitees have not responded to either your initial letter or to my follow-up phone inquiries."

"Only — * oooohhh!* — only *four?* But we sent out a duh, a *dozen* invitations to emergency managers at all the major health care facilities—"

"Do not let it concern you, monumental one. I am certain that once these four have met with you, news of the worthiness of your presentation will spread like the morning sunshine. Then I shall have plentiful work rearranging your schedule to accommodate all the procrastinators."

He wanted to believe her. He really did. But an awful suspicion had gnawed its way into his mind. "They're — they're blowing me off, aren't they? I've got no authority over them. No *real* authority, no power to order them to do anything—"

"*Bruno!* You must not allow yourself to become soft!" She compressed her orbs more tightly around him and accelerated their up and down motions. "You are a warrior! A *gladiator!* Of *course* you have the power to command!"

Self-pity clung to him like old bubble gum on the sole of his shoe. "No, baby, you don't get it... all I am in this damn job is a *facilitator.* Christ, that sounds like the organizer of some goddamn high school job fair..."

"*Balderdash!* You need no exalted spot on an organization chart — you are an aristocrat, a conqueror of lesser men! No mayor or governor or board of directors need *give* you authority — you were *born* to it!"

Maybe it was the increased friction, but suddenly the flesh surrounding him grew increasingly warm, an almost painfully sublime sensation. He felt himself grow fully erect again. "You — you think so? But what if I can't convince them to do what I need them to do?"

"Overpower their objections with the might of your sword arm!"

"Over — *ohhhh* — power them?"

"*Yes!* Be like Mars, the god of war, my sweet!"

"Ahhh — *aahhh—*"

"Decapitate your enemies! Show the roaring crowd their severed heads! Then make their blackening tongues lick the bitter dust!"

"*AAAAHHHHGG-UH!*"

Right before the commercial break, The Weather Channel's local forecast called for scattered showers, followed by increased humidity.

"Yummy!" Gerard Wolfe exclaimed as he entered Bruno's office. "I just *love* the smell of olive oil! You bring in some Italian take-out?"

Bruno forced a smile. "Yeah, eh, from Cafe Roma. They do great pasta." He checked his watch. Nearly ten minutes to noon, and only two of his four confirmed invitees had shown up, just Dickie Langenstein and now this schlub from Baptist Hospital.

Well, screw the rest of them. If they wouldn't come to him, he'd go after *them*, force them to do their damn jobs, if he had to. Screw the mayor and his tight-fistedness. The hell with those lazy, good-for-nothing pricks in the governor's Office of Homeland Security. He'd do the whole job himself if he had to. He was a *gladiator*.

"Well, gentlemen, let's get this show on the road. Gerard? You got something there in that briefcase for me? Your disaster evac plan? Let's take a look at it."

Gerard, potbellied, prematurely balding, face stamped with a desperately friendly expression, fumbled with the zippers on his briefcase. "Actually, Mr. Galliano, I need to explain something—"

"Just hand it over, son."

Gerard removed a slender manila folder from his case. Bruno estimated it couldn't contain more than four or five pages. "That's *it?*" he said, grabbing the folder from the pudgy man's fingers. "That's all you've got?"

"It — it's a *start*, Mr. Galliano... I've been terribly busy these past couple of months, really swamped..."

He skimmed the few skimpy paragraphs Gerard had provided. It didn't take long. The idiot had printed it out in a fourteen point font, surrounded by inch-and-a-half margins, and even then he'd only managed barely four pages. "This isn't a *plan*," Bruno said, flinging the pages onto the table. "Where're your agreements with emergency transport providers? Where's your list of key staff? There's not even a diagram of your facility's emergency evac routes. This isn't a disaster plan — this is a plan to *formulate* a disaster plan. This is *crap*."

"I'm sorry, Mr. Galliano, I really am. See, Baptist's currently in the middle of a *huge* reconstruction of our labor and delivery, neo-natal, and post-partum care floor. It's a *mess* — there's construction debris all over the place. I'm constantly having to dog the contractors about safety and noise issues—"

"Excuses are *crap*. I already gave you and the others a four week extension, and this is the best you can deliver? Your boss should be embarrassed he hired you. In fact, I think I'll give him a call right now—"

"*No!*" Gerard looked on the verge of tears. "Please — *don't*, Mr. Galliano. Is there any way you can find it in your heart to give me another three weeks? I promise, I swear—"

"Are you *nuts?*" Contempt twisted Bruno's expression into what he hoped was a terrifying sneer. "Three more weeks, mister, and the new hurricane season will be breathing down your neck like the Hound of Hell. Tell you what. I'd never order a man to do something I wouldn't do myself. You stay on after this meeting, and we'll spend a couple hours going over best practices from hospitals around the country. Hell, I'll even go walk your facility with you. But in exchange for my graciousness, you've got till the end of *this week* to write up a complete plan. You got me, son?"

Gerard nodded rapidly. "Yes, sir! Thank you, sir!"

"Good. Okay, let's take a look at what you've got, Dickie. If your plan's especially top notch, I'll wanna share it with Gerard, if that's okay."

Dickie Langenstein's expression remained stony, as it had throughout Bruno's dressing down of Gerard Wolfe. "I don't have anything for you. And don't bother threatening to call my boss. He's fully aware that I've come empty handed, and he supports that decision."

A frontal assault? No weaseling or whining? Bruno braced himself. "What's going on, Dickie?"

"I informed you months ago that our disaster preparation plan is undergoing a thorough vetting process. Multiple committees need to have input. A veto from any committee can start the whole process over again. I informed you in writing that the Louisiana Department of Health and Hospitals has given us until next spring to have our plan finalized. That wasn't good enough for you, apparently. You fired off a series of letters to my superiors which they, to be honest, found insulting and condescending. They sent me here today to tell you personally to cease and desist. You have no direct authority over us."

"I take issue with that. *Serious* issue." Bruno decided to try a bluff. "Regulatory power isn't limited to just accreditation, y'know. The City has multiple permitting authorities that could tie your facility up in knots if you don't play ball. Let's see... conveyances, construction, just to start with the 'C's—"

Dickie's expression didn't change. "I'm sure our legal counsel will be happy to take such threats under advisement and respond appropriately."

"Uh, Mr. Galliano, I've really gotta use the bathroom," Gerard said. "May I be excused?"

"Yeah, yeah, sure," Bruno said. "But don't be too long. You and me've got a long afternoon ahead."

Gerard bolted for the door, taking his briefcase with him. *Probably brought some comic books with him to read on the john*, Bruno thought. He turned back to Dickie Langenstein, deciding to throw him off balance. *Time for a charm offensive*, he thought. "Dickie, I see we've gotten off on the wrong foot. I'm sorry. Doesn't have to be that way. How about you and me go down to the cafeteria and talk things over? Can I buy you some lunch?"

"Save your money." Dickie headed for the door, shaking his head. "Meeting's over, so far as I'm concerned."

"So that's how it is, huh?" Bruno let his feigned cordiality fall by the wayside. "Well, mister, you tell your boss — hell, you tell your *boss's* boss to be expecting a call from me."

"Don't waste your time," Dickie said, halfway through the door.

Bruno managed to keep his anger in check until he heard the elevator ping and its doors open and close. Then he let loose with a savage kick against the office door.

Well, at least he still had Gerard Wolfe in his clutches. He'd get a workable disaster plan out of that ignorant lummox or die trying.

Bruno stuck his head into the men's room. "Gerard? Finish up what you're doing, son. Time and tide wait for no man."

No response.

"Gerard? You hear me?"

He checked the stalls for feet. No feet.

Nearly blind with fury, He stalked to the stair well and descended two steps at a time to the cafeteria. Gerard wasn't in there, either. Nor was he in line at the snack counter at the far end of the hall.

The disgusting fatty had out-foxed him. He'd gotten nothing from nobody, not a single shred of a disaster plan.

Chapter 11

LILY Weintraub watched Roy Rio cut the symbolic ribbon on Baptist Hospital's newly refurbished delivery and neonatal ward. He was surrounded by gorgeous newborn children, and she felt a rapier stab of pain in her heart. She'd spent virtually her entire life caring for other people's children, starting with her own brother. But would she ever have the opportunity to nurture children of her own?

She tried desperately to devise some excuse to pull Roy aside. They'd hardly spoken since that awful night at the coffee house in Metairie. He'd canceled out on their scheduled meetings with Rabbi Freidman three weeks in a row.

She ached for him. The more he'd distanced himself, the more powerfully she yearned for him.

She *hated* that; it wasn't like her at all. What had been happening to her? She felt like she'd become a stranger to herself these past few months... a thoroughly unlikable stranger.

"Lily, I'm sorry to bother you," Dr. Applebaum said. "But Mrs. Hitchens in 641... she's got some nutty notion about you 'laying hands' on her. She insists you're her 'good luck charm.' She's a high risk patient, and, well, anything that might make this delivery go more smoothly..."

Lily watched Roy finish up his brief remarks. "Just — just give me a few minutes, Jon, okay? Then I'll be right over."

"Thanks."

Roy headed for the elevators, surrounded by a phalanx of aides. Lily cut him off just beyond the nursery's windows.

"Roy? Do you have a minute?"

The way he looked at her — the wariness, even aversion — snuffed out the dying embers of her self-esteem. "Sure, Lily," he said after a second's indecision. "Walt, have the guys wait for me downstairs."

Lily led him into an empty lactation consultation room and shut the door. "How have you been?" she asked, doing her best to keep her voice steady. "Are you all right? I've been worried."

"Look, I'm sorry I've been so out of touch." He didn't *sound* sorry. "I apologize for not making a single meeting with Rabbi Freidman since the first one. But things have been absolutely ape house crazy for me—"

"I know. I'm not blaming you."

"I didn't say you were." He rubbed the smooth-shaved top of his head. "Hey. I really *am* sorry about these past three weeks. That scene with Nicole at the coffee house... that was *ugly*. I feel awful you got caught in the middle of it. Cynthia's playing some dangerous games. I wish all this crap hadn't fallen into my lap right after you and I decided to test the waters again."

Lily smiled hopefully. "Thanks. That means a lot. I think Rabbi Freidman had the right idea when he told you not to rush into things. Besides, the best way to learn about Judaism is to experience it, not just attend classes. Did you know Passover's right around the corner? My family and I will be attending second *seder* next Tuesday at the Woldenberg Village retirement center. I — I'd *love* for you to be there, Roy. Just so you could experience it. Besides, it's voter outreach — nearly two hundred senior citizens will be there, and they never miss an election. Everybody would be thrilled to have you as their guest."

Roy looked dubious. "Wait a minute — your *dad'll* be there? Won't I have to wear a flak jacket?"

She shook her head. "That's the serendipitous part. You'll be attending in your capacity as mayor. Dad won't need to know I invited you. Maybe it'll give him an opportunity to see you in a... less threatening light."

"I don't know about this... are you saying we'll have to pretend we don't know each other?"

"Of *course* not. But there'll be hundreds of people there, and it's a much, *much* less stressful way to introduce you to my holidays than, say, inviting you over to first night's *seder* at Dad's house."

"Heck, serving a tour of duty in Afghanistan would be less stressful than *that*." He pulled his Blackberry out of its holster. "Tuesday night, you said? I don't see anything on my schedule that would conflict, but I've really gotta check with Walt and Alberta."

Lily felt her chest tighten. "Roy, I really, *really* want you to come—"

"I'll do the best I can, hon."

"Please, Roy." Lily grabbed his hands, clung to them as though she were drowning. "*Please.* I can't *tell* you how important this is to me..."

He pulled away from her. "I'll do the best I can. Okay?"

She watched him hurry down the hall to the elevator. She couldn't leave the shelter of the lactation room, not quite yet. Not until she'd gotten her trembling under control.

Where had this desperation come from? She squeezed her fingernails into her palms until the pain overpowered her humiliating quivering.

Dear Lord, what have I become?

* * * * *

"You may now eat your Hillel sandwich," the rabbi said to the groups clustered around their tables. "Next comes everybody's favor part of the *seder* — the festive meal! *Gefilte* fish and *matzo*-ball soup will be served in just a few minutes. Many thanks to the wonderful dietary staff here at Woldenberg."

The rabbi switched off the microphone and returned to his seat at the head table, next to honored guest Mayor Rio. Kay stuffed her Hillel sandwich, a combination of *matzo*, *charoset* (a paste-like mix of crushed walnuts, diced apples, and wine), and pungent horseradish, into her mouth. She wished she could enjoy the evening more. But her aura had been buzzing like a pesky mosquito ever since she'd sat down with Daniel and his family.

Already, one elderly lady had choked on a piece of *matzo* and then experienced the indignity of a Heimlich maneuver from a nursing aide. Even that hadn't roused Daniel from his somnolence, though. Her beloved sat through the ceremony like a dormant *golem*, a man of clay.

She reached for Daniel's hand beneath the table. Her warm squeeze elicited zero response.

Last night's *seder* had been an ordeal — Amos had prodded his son unceasingly for the reason behind Daniel's emotional shutdown. Only Kay's and Lily's joint intercession on Daniel's behalf had salvaged even a semblance of a placid family holiday meal. And tonight Lily was seemingly lost in a fog.

Kay waited for the unspoken tensions at the table to boil over. It didn't take long.

"Daniel. Daniel, look at me." Amos Weintraub leaned across the table, still an imposing physical presence, despite his eighty-four years. "I cannot stand this silence anymore. You *must* tell me what has happened to keep you from your work."

Daniel slowly shook his head.

"Daniel, we just read in the *Haggadah* of the Four Sons. Never before have I ever thought of you as my Wicked Son. But if you continue to ignore your father—"

Kay couldn't stand it anymore. "Mr. Weintraub, with all due respect, *please* let your son have his privacy—"

"I saw something really bad at work," Daniel said quietly.

Amos smiled in triumph. "*There!* My mute son has finally spoken. 'Something really bad,' you saw? You cut the grass, Daniel. What could you see that is so terrible it makes you miss work for two weeks? A dead body you found?"

"No..."

"You saw a crime, maybe? If so, you go the police, you report what you know, and all is well! But my son knows what is his civic duty, so it must be something else."

"Dad..." Daniel's voice was tight. "What... what would you do, if... you had to choose between *doing* something, when you knew you'd get hurt real bad... and *not* doing something, when you knew there was a chance lots of other people would get hurt real bad?"

"You are being *mysterious*, Daniel. If you want me to help you, you must give more information. *Specifics*, I need."

"Okay, but..." Daniel looked pleadingly at Kay, as though she could protect him from whatever consequences his mouth might bring down upon his head. "But Dad, you have to, you have to *promise* not to tell anyone what I'm going to tell you. Or I'll get in awful trouble."

"Very well. Now, give to me the details."

In halting, hushed tones, Daniel told the story of what he and his supervisor had seen alongside the Seventeenth Street Canal, and how Tran's vehement concerns about the neighborhood's safety had disappeared upon Na Ong's and Na Ba's arrival.

"Tran... he told me he'd get me fired if I told *anybody* about the water leaking into the yard. He's warned me lots of times to keep quiet. He's even called me at home."

Amos' face took on a hard cast. "Vietnamese mafia," he said. "I have heard of such a thing." He reached across the table and patted Daniel's hand. "You have done the right thing by remaining quiet, Daniel. Good judgement. Much worse than losing your job — you could lose a hand, or your head! This is none of your concern. Be quiet, be safe."

Lily's jaw dropped. "Dad, how can you tell him that? Of *course* it's his concern! It's *yours*, too! That place Daniel described, it's barely a mile away from your house. From the *synagogue*. If that flood wall should ever fail—"

"To make a warning should not be *Daniel's* responsibility! He cuts the grass, that is all! There are other neighbors near that place. Someone else can make a complaint. Someone whose job and safety are not threatened."

"This isn't how you raised us, Dad! Aren't you the man who joined the Polish Army at the age of sixteen, rather than flee to France with your uncle, because it was the *right thing to do?*"

"That was *different*. The German Nazis were monsters. Preparing for war with them was the only possible choice. Here, there are many choices—"

"But only one *good* choice," Lily insisted. "Daniel needs to go the Metropolitan Crime Commission and report official malfeasance. Or he could call a reporter." She turned to her brother. "Daniel, you can do it anonymously. 'Anonymous' means you don't have to give your name. Just tell them what you know. None of your employers ever need know you spoke with anyone."

Daniel stared down at the table. "I'm afraid," he said.

"I *understand* that you're afraid. But being brave doesn't mean that you're unafraid. It means that you confront your fear and deal with it, so you can do the right thing."

Amos held up a warning hand. "Lily, do not push your brother so. He tried for many long, fruitless years to find a job that would give him health insurance, a pension for his old age. I worked hard to help him find this. You have a hundred, a *thousand* times the opportunities he has—"

"That doesn't *matter*, Dad! I want Daniel to be able to live with himself!"

Daniel turned his sad gaze towards Lily. "Couldn't... couldn't *you* report it? Why don't *you* go to that metropolitan whatever?"

"Oh, Daniel..." She shook her head with frustration. "I could, but I won't." Kay detected the shade of a hectoring older sister in Lily's voice. This argument was veering into emotionally dangerous territory — Kay sensed her aura uncoiling within her, writhing with pleasure, fangs dripping venom.

"I won't," Lily continued, "because it's *your* duty as a responsible adult. I've always been proud of you, because I could always count on you to try to do the right thing. Please, don't make me *ashamed...*"

Daniel was silent for a few seconds. Kay watched his face turn a livid shade of red. "If — if you think it's so damn *important* not to keep suh-*secrets—*" he was so angry he could barely spit his words out; "— then, then set a good example! What about *your secret*, Lily? Why don't you tell Dad *that?*"

Lily looked stunned. Amos caught her expression. "What is he talking about, Lily? *What* secret?"

Kay's nipples and groin felt on fire as her aura reached out with its corrupting tendrils. She tried pulling Daniel away from the table. "Daniel! Don't say it! Bite your tongue, honey!"

Caught up in his emotions, Daniel ignored her. He pointed at Mayor Rio at the head table. "*That* secret! Lily's dating that man again! And she's too *afraid* to tell you, Dad!"

Amos looked as though he'd suffered a blow to his solar plexus, expelling all the air from his lungs. "Daughter... is this *true?*"

Lily's porcelain face twisted into a mask of wounded betrayal. "Oh, Daniel, how *could* you?"

"So it *is* true, then?" Amos suddenly looked all of his eighty-four years. "You — you have dishonored your mother's memory the same way a *second* time? And I have to learn of your disloyalty to your people, to your family, on this, of all days?"

"Dad, I'm *not* being *disloyal!* Not to the Jews, not to Mother, and not to *you!* That's an absurd accusation, and totally *unfair!*"

"So then why did you hide this from me?"

"Because I *knew* you'd react exactly like this! Jesus Christ — I'm *forty-three years old*, Dad! I am *not required* to tell you everything that is going on in my personal life! But if you have to know... *yes*, Roy and I have seen each other socially a few times, and, *no*, I have no idea where it's going. But Roy has agreed to at least explore the possibility of becoming Jewish—"

Amos's fist struck the table. "For years, I have tried to introduce you to men who would make observant husbands and fathers, perfectly good men. And yet you insist on choosing one who *may* 'explore' becoming Jewish?" He rose from his seat. "I will go speak with this Mr. Rio. Right now. I will learn his intentions towards you. I do not care if he is mayor or the Emperor of Ethiopia, he will tell me his intentions towards my daughter."

Lily blocked his path. Kay saw people at neighboring tables glance uncomfortably at what had turned into a loud confrontation. "Dad! *No!* Are you out of your *mind?* You will *not* say one *word* to him! Do you want to mortify me forever? *Do you?*"

For a moment, Kay thought Amos would push Lily aside. But then the elderly patriarch stared deeply into his adult daughter's face, and the steel within him melted.

He retrieved his hat and his cane. "There is food for me at home," he said. "I will finish my seder there. Daniel, have your sister drive you home. Or Kay."

"Dad..." Lily took three steps toward her retreating father, then stopped. "You wanted to make me feel guilty?" she said, so softly that only Kay and Daniel could hear. "Well, it *worked*, damn it."

She retrieved her sweater and slung her purse's strap over her shoulder.

"You're leaving?" Daniel asked.

"Yes, Daniel, I'm *leaving*."

"But... but what about dinner? Dad paid for us all—"

"Then Dad flushed a hundred dollars down the toilet, didn't he?"

"Lily, please don't go..."

"You really don't understand, do you?" Her barely restrained voice was sharp enough to make the air bleed. "What you did, Daniel... what you did to me is *unforgivable*. I've practically been a mother to you; I've sacrificed and *sacrificed* for you..."

Kay watched her boyfriend begin to shake. "Lily, forgive him!" she pleaded. "It wasn't his fault—"

"It's *never* his fault, is it? Poor, poor Daniel — a little boy in a grown man's body, never responsible for what he does. You know what? I don't buy it anymore. He knew *damn well* what he was doing. He wanted to hurt me. I saw it in his *face*, Kay." She whirled on her brother. "You got what you wanted. I hope you're pleased. But you know, I think you've actually done me a favor. You've freed me. My whole life, I've wanted *out* of this city. But I stuck around because I was needed. Dad needed me. *You* needed me. But now, like the Israelites set loose by God's wraith on Pharaoh, I'm finally *free*."

"I'm sorry, I'm sorry," Daniel said, repeating the words like a magic incantation. "I'm sorry, I'm sorry, I'm *sorry*..."

Lily shook her head. "'Sorry' isn't good enough. Not this time."

Daniel gulped down a sob as his tears poured out. Kay felt her aura relax inside her, its mission accomplished. The burning which had assaulted her most sensitive parts vanished, leaving her numb and exhausted.

"What did I do? What did I *do*?" Daniel's plaintive cries landed like thunder claps on Kay's eardrums as he ran after his sister. "Lily! I'll make it all better! Just tell me how!"

Kay found herself alone. She watched Roy Rio excuse himself from the head table. A waiter brought four plates of baked chicken, string beans, and sauteed potatoes. She didn't have the strength to tell him to take them away.

Chapter 12

STANDING on the fourth story terrace of Baptist Hospital, Lily faced down her ashen-faced would-be sister-in-law. "Kay, if you've come here to get me to forgive my brother, you're wasting your time."

"But... there's so much you don't know," Kay said. "Things I need to tell you, things that'll sound crazy. But if you'll listen, you'll understand why Daniel was... *forced* to do what he did. And you'll understand so much more. About your family. About your... your childhood." She clung to the railing as though the slightest breeze could topple her to the Napoleon Avenue sidewalk four stories below. She looked sickly and weak, much like she had at the hurricane simulation when she'd suffered that vomiting fit.

Lily checked her watch. She still had thirty-five minutes before her nursing staff conference. She wanted nothing more than to walk away from this awkward meeting, but her stubborn sense of politeness forced her to offer Kay at least a brief audience. "Go on," she said. "But I can't stay out here with you too long."

Kay nodded. "Daniel hurt you terribly. Under... *ordinary* circumstances, there would be no excuse whatsoever for his behavior. But what happened at the *seder* — it simply wasn't his fault. He couldn't control what he said. He was being influenced. All of you were."

"By *what*? The Passover wine?"

"No." Kay stared at the steady lines of traffic passing four stories below. "By *me*."

"*You*? But — what possible *reason* could you have for turning Daniel against me?"

"Lily, do you know what an *ayin hora* is?"

"As in '*kein ayin hora*'? Of course I do. It's an old *bubbe-meise* brought over from Europe. Some spirit or Evil Eye that hangs around Jewish people, waiting for them to make a slip of the tongue so it can make something bad happen. When I was a kid, I remember my mother spitting between her fingers three times and saying '*kein ayin hora*' — 'no Evil Eye.' "

"I wish... I wish your mother would have done that a lot more often. She would have lived a longer, happier life."

"What makes you say that?"

"Lily, *ayin horas* are real. Or at least one is."

"And you know this *how*, exactly?"

"Because I am one."

Lily smiled. "We're talking in a *figurative* sense, right?"

Kay shook her head, more obviously in pain with each passing second. "No. Literal. I'm a bad luck spirit, a *real* one. And I'm part of a conspiracy of bad luck spirits called the Miasma Club. It's been working for decades to destroy New Orleans, to return the city to the swamp it once was. I used to be a... a willing part of that... but not anymore. This hurricane season... the Miasma Club will carry out Operation Big Blow. New Orleans could be wiped out. I need you to, to warn Mayor Rio. *Please*, Lily. I'd do it myself — but I *can't*. There's a thing inside me that stops me. You saw it in action. My vomiting fit at the FEBO meeting? That was my aura silencing me, because I threatened to reveal too much."

She's gone off the edge, Lily thought. *How much of this nonsense has she told Daniel?* "Kay... do you need me to call for a doctor? You don't look well. You don't *sound* well."

"There's nothing any doctor can do for me. Maybe a lobotomy...?" Kay smiled ruefully. "No, with my luck, my frontal lobe would grow right back. You're the only person in this hospital who can help me."

Kay then told her a story whose roots stretched back decades. She told about how the conflict between the Miasma Club and the mortal community had been brought to a head by scientists' efforts to leech away the Mother's miasmatic energy field. She told about the decapitation of FEBO's leadership cadre; how the Miasma Club had sown dissension and distrust among the agencies responsible for protecting New Orleanians' lives and property; how the city's disaster response infrastructure had been systematically degraded; and how Mayor Roy Rio had been purposefully distracted from linking any of the dots.

"What happened to your brother," Kay continued in raspy gasps, "it's part of all this, too. Why *else* would his superiors at the Levee Board be so anxious to cover up the existence of a leaking flood wall? It was Na Ong and Na Ba — they're like me, except they do their work in the Vietnamese community. They couldn't influence Daniel directly, so they acted on him through Tran Ho and Daniel's other Vietnamese supervisors."

Lily's head was spinning. In all her years of nursing, she'd never before encountered an instance of paranoid ideation this intricate and self-reinforcing. She shivered when she contemplated how many years her vulnerable, impressionable brother had spent in a relationship with this madwoman. "Are you saying that what Daniel did to me at the *seder* had something to do with crippling New Orleans' *flood control system?*" Maybe if Lily could poke enough holes in her story, this paranoia would begin to deflate.

Kay miserably shook her head. "No; that was just my aura taking advantage of violent, out-of-control emotions to stir up trouble among Jews. It probes for any weaknesses it can take advantage of — character flaws, flashes of anger or jealousy or hurt. Slips of the tongue are its red meat. It wasn't just Daniel my aura influenced a few nights back. *All* of you said and did things that otherwise would've remained locked inside you. That's why you *must* forgive Daniel."

"So this whole story you've concocted — it's all an effort to convince me to forgive my brother?"

"*No!*" Kay clutched her stomach, obviously in great pain. "I mean, of *course* I want you to forgive him. And to forgive your father, too. But what I really want you to do — what I *need* you to do — is convince Mayor Rio that disaster is on its way. That he needs to focus on hurricane season..."

"Kay, think about what you've been telling me. Look at it logically. There's a big hole in your story. Didn't you tell me that this 'aura' of yours has always acted to prevent you from speaking the truth about the Miasma Club? But you've just told me all their secret plans. You didn't vomit uncontrollably, or even get *hiccups*. How do you explain that?"

"I *knew* you'd be almost impossible to convince." She began visibly trembling. Tears left damp trails down her cheeks. "My aura knew it, too. Both of us knew, in order to get you to believe, it would come down to... *this.*"

"To *what?*"

"The end of any chance... I might have for happiness. To get you to believe, I have to *damn myself.* In your eyes, and in Daniel's eyes, too."

Jesus. She's really getting worked up. Maybe I should *call in some help?* "You needn't worry about any of this getting back to Daniel. My brother and I aren't on speaking terms."

"You won't feel that way in a minute. You'll talk with Daniel tonight, right after I leave. You'll forgive him everything. Maybe... maybe this is all for the best, then. Your family is what matters. This city is what matters. Not me."

Paranoia and *a martyr complex — what a mix.* "Whatever you're going to spring on me, Kay, just *do* it. I'll be happy to hook you up with a therapist. But I don't have much more time right now."

"I've known you your entire life, Lily. I played with you when you were a little girl, when Daniel was a baby. I knew your father as a young immigrant. I knew your mother."

This continuous bringing up of her mother felt cruel; Lily wanted to slap Kay, force her to stop poking that ancient, never-healed injury. *"Really?"*

"Your father had a poker buddy named Yankel who cajoled him into gambling too much. You had a little girlfriend named Hilda. Accident-prone Hilda, do you remember? Whenever you or Daniel played with her, you each ended up with a skinned knee or a broken bone. I was both of them, Lily. I was Yankel *and* I was Hilda."

Lily felt the blood begin to drain from her face. "You — you heard all that from Daniel, didn't you? He told you all those stories. Admit it!"

Kay shook her head. Her jaw trembled now, but she managed to keep speaking. "Do you remember what your father wore on that Sunday afternoon drive to Pontchartrain Beach? I do. He wore brown slacks, a yellow golf shirt, and a blue and white checked sports jacket. Do you remember what Hilda wore? She sat next to you on the back seat wearing a red and white gingham dress. Do you remember what you wore? It was a blue skirt and a white blouse — 'the colors of Israel's flag,' you told your father."

"Nobody — *nobody* remembers details like that after thirty years. You're making it up because you know I can't remember—"

"But there are things you *will* remember, Lily. The two of us were alone in the Buick's big back seat, making enough noise for ten children. Your father pulled the car over to the curb at the corner of Canal Boulevard and Robert E. Lee. He turned back in his seat, glared at you, and said, 'You girls must be *quiet!* You will make me to run off the road if you do not stop with your noise!' He'd been in a bad mood all morning. You started crying. I felt my aura grow excited within me. 'If you make one more word of noise,' he yelled, 'I will turn around and drive *straight* back to the house! And I will send Hilda home, so you have no one to play with!' "

Lily felt her skin turn cold. "My God... I never told anyone about that. No one, not even Daniel..."

"You managed to stay quiet for a few minutes. But then I egged you on to start playing again. My aura must've known what it was about to do — it wanted you to feel *guilty* for what was about to happen. Oh God, Lily, I'm so *sorry*, so sorry I put that horrible guilt on you. But it was *me*, Lily, not you. My aura sensed your father's sadness, the melancholy that had been digging into him all day. I didn't know what it was about to do. I swear to you, I *didn't*. I want to think, if I *had* known, I would've thrown myself out the window.

"But I didn't know what was happening when I felt my face begin to change, when I opened my mouth and began singing in Polish. I got my first inkling of the hell ahead when I saw Amos's shocked face in the rear view mirror — when I heard his nearly choked-off question — '*Rachel? My sister—?*' And then it was too late. The Buick jumped over the bayou's levee. My dear, dear, *sweet* Daniel — just a helpless *baby* — flew out of his mother's arms, through the open window like a plump little white duckling. Then the car hit the water, and your mother's head shattered the windshield..."

Lily steadied herself against the railing. She was eight years old again. She was a screaming child in the back seat of a Buick LeSabre slowly sinking into Bayou St. John. She smelled what she now recognized was her mother's blood, splattered on the dashboard, on the shattered glass. "I thought... I thought it was a false memory. All these years, I've told myself what I saw was a figment of trauma..." She forced herself to stare at Kay. Yes, without much effort, she could strip thirty-plus years from those features, see her as Hilda. Watch her *change*. "I... I used to stare at my father's only photo of my dead Aunt Rachel, dead twenty years before I was born. The torn photo he'd retrieved from the ruins of his family's house. You were *her*, those last few seconds before the crash. *I saw you.* I saw you *change*. And, and it was all *real*..."

"Yes," Kay said. "It was all real. Everything I've told you. I'd change it all, if I had the power."

Lily stared down at the lanes of rush hour traffic creeping through the gathering darkness. Nothing seemed real anymore; everything was just a movie projected onto a screen of smoke, something that could vanish without a trace. "You were my best friend..." she said. "But you killed my *mommy*."

"My aura killed Miriam. My *aura*. It's a part of me, but it's not *all* of me. The decent part of me, the part that loves Daniel, and your father, and *you*, Lily — that part is *begging* you to warn Mayor Rio about the Miasma Club. You want *revenge?* Help smother the evil hopes of the Miasma Club. I know it won't be easy... because I can feel my aura reaching out to you right now. It's excited by your anger, your feelings of hurt and abandonment, your terrible, sad resentment. It wants to use those dark things—"

"*No!*" Lily backed away from Kay, backed away as far as the guard railing would allow. She had felt something. Something seductively invasive that fed, parasitic, on her own emotions. She had felt this very same thing before, when she'd assisted Kay into the bathroom at the FEBO meeting, then returned to the conference room to retrieve her things, only to find Roy waiting...

"You — you *pushed* me into falling for Roy again," she said, her voice a whisper. "That night of the hurricane wrap-up... what I'm feeling now, it's exactly what I felt *then*. I'd been avoiding him for months, but that night — that night, my God, I was a sixteen year-old *schoolgirl* again. None of it real... these past months of feeling out of control, full of desperate yearning, feeling I wanted to *die* if I couldn't get him to marry me... none of it's been *real*. I've been your puppet. I've *always* been your puppet..."

Now Kay backed away, seemingly stunned. "Lily, I *swear* I didn't know. I don't always recognize the more subtle ways my aura works. I have to be looking for it, and I wasn't then. It wanted to distract

Mayor Rio, and it grabbed hold of you, you poor thing, used you as its tool—"

"*Stop* saying '*it*'! It's *you*! *You're* the monster!"

"Yes, I am. But even a, a *monster* can feel love. Even a monster can cry out a warning—"

"And you want me to *believe* you? You actually think, after what you just admitted, I'll run to Roy *now* and tell him all about this supposed plot? You're gaming me. But it won't work, not anymore."

"That's my aura putting words in your mouth—"

"*Stop playing with me, damn you!*" She remembered her mother's nervous, half-comical words and motions, uttered whenever Miriam had just uttered a possibly fateful slip of the tongue. "*Kein ayin hora!* No Evil Eye!" Lily hissed. And she spat between her forefinger and middle finger three times.

The effect was immediate. Kay doubled over, her eyes bulging. She groaned, and the groan became the rising yowl of a cat caught beneath a car's tires. "*Guh*-good," she gasped. "You believe. That... that's the first step."

"*Kein ayin hora!* Shut up, monster!" She spat thrice again, droplets of her saliva hitting the concrete near Kay's feet like tracer bullets. Kay jumped from the path of the flying spittle. Lily's rush of exultation surged when she saw blood trickle from Kay's nose and ears and mouth.

Kay stumbled backward against the guard railing. "Yeh-*yes*, let all that anger out. When you're thinking *cluh*-clearly, you'll pass on my warning..."

"*Never!* I'll *never* be your puppet again! And neither will Daniel! I'll make him understand what an evil, vile piece of *filth* you are! Go near him again — go near *any* of my family — and I'll find a way to hurt you *worse* than you've hurt us."

The demon wept. Whether from pain or sorrow, Lily couldn't tell. Nor did she care. "At least promise me *this*," Kay begged; "whenever you learn a hurricane is heading towards New Orleans, *get Daniel out*. Please, *please* promise you'll do that—"

The demon's feigned concern for Daniel — the man whose life she'd stunted, who could've been an architect or physicist but who'd instead found himself relegated to hauling trash — drove Lily to renewed fury. "*Shut up!* You can't trick me into feeling pity for you!" She advanced to half a stride from the trembling woman-demon. "*Kein ayin hora* — you *bitch!*"

She spat thrice between her fingers — this time, directly into Kay's face.

Kay Rosenblatt screamed. Then, with an implosion of humid air, she disappeared, leaving behind an overwhelming stench of putrefying cabbage.

* * * * *

Kay felt a burning which wasn't burning, a fire which wasn't fire.

She tumbled, blind, through a void of gaseous ice, as though she'd been propelled through Jupiter's core.

And yet she sensed she was returning home.

Not to her house on Elysian Fields Avenue. To a much older home, the womb which had sustained her before her birth into sunlight and the siren call of consciousness.

Water, and soil; sand and clay; roots, tendrils, and vines. All in blind, dreamy competition...

Something hummed and buzzed that was not part of the natural Order of Things Here. Something made of metal, mined from distant places. She felt afraid, because the womb which surrounded her felt afraid. Its water was being sucked away. Its roots and tendrils withered. Its soil, its humus, its muck turned to dust.

Kay felt the womb's anger and hatred. Her whole being seethed with the womb's unbending desire to restore the Proper Order of Things Here...

She awoke on a cold concrete floor. It vibrated. Those vibrations helped shake her numbed flesh back to life.

What the hell had just happened?

She'd made Lily believe her. Lily had responded with the traditional acts of warding off, the three Yiddish words followed by three expectorations. She'd done it three times, the third and final time directly into Kay's face. And then — what? Kay had been swatted across space, for all she knew across time, too, bludgeoned off the Baptist Hospital terrace to... somewhere.

Where was she? What place was this?

She slowly stood. All of her joints ached. She was inside a tremendous brick building, full of machinery and a spider's web of exposed suspended piping, lit only by a few florescent tubes which hung from the ceiling. Giant rotary engines pierced the floor, their bottom halves apparently descending into a basement. Yet even half-submerged, these engine casings towered over Kay, made her feel like a mouse who'd taken shelter beneath the hood of an eighteen-wheeler. Gigantic drive shafts connected the engines to... monster *worms?*

She walked closer to the bizarre manifestations, noting that her aura screamed out its revulsion more vehemently the closer she came. Yes, they certainly looked like worms, titanic metal worms which breached the floor and penetrated the outer brick wall, seemingly frozen in the act of emerging from their underground kingdom.

Not worms — lampreys, with greedy, sucking mouths that never rest.

Kay hadn't thought those words herself. She barely knew what a lamprey was. But her aura, apparently, knew, and it shared with her an image of a blind eel-thing with a round, sucking mouth filled with concentric, circular rows of teeth.

It made her shiver.

She needed to get out of here.

No workmen were present. The windows were dark; it was still night outside. She found a door, unbolted it, and stepped outside.

She found herself on a traffic island, in the middle of a circular road which served as a hub for other roads. She stared back at the brick building's facade and read the large black letters arrayed there:

A. BALDWIN WOOD DRAINAGE PUMPING STATION NO. 1

NEW ORLEANS SEWERAGE AND WATER BOARD

Now she knew where she was — on South Broad Street, in Broadmoor, about a mile from where she'd parked her car. Across the street stood a dilapidated row of stores. Straining her eyes, she read the street sign for one of the spoke roads — Melpomene.

Melpomene. One of the Muses. She realized with sudden, piercing clarity what she needed to do next.

The Muse who lives in the Marigny... I have to go see her. She felt her aura recoil at the thought, and feeling its revulsion redoubled her resolve. *If Lily won't warn Mayor Rio... only the Muses stand a chance of stopping Operation Big Blow.*

Chapter 13

KAY dragged herself to apartment number 301 on the third floor landing of the Royal Roost Apartments. She was bleeding heavily. That Doberman watchdog had really done a number on her down in the courtyard. She'd dispatched it as gently as she could, but not before it had ripped up her arm.

Her left forearm dripped blood onto the damp concrete. She pounded on the door. Already, she felt her wounds begin to heal, although the arm remained a gory spectacle.

Lights flickered in the apartment's back rooms. Kay heard music. She hoped the Muse was alone. She sensed the apartment's occupant peer through the door's security peep hole. "My name is Kay Rosenblatt," she said as quickly as she could. "I know this might sound crazy, but I absolutely *must* talk with you. You and your sisters are the only ones who can help me. I know you know what I am, because I sensed what *you* are when I saw you in the French Quarter. I don't know if you Muses have rules against meeting with bad luck spirits, but this is really, *really* urgent. The Miasma Club has a plan to destroy the city. Only you and your sisters can stop them — the Triumvirate seem really afraid of you guys, so you must be awfully powerful."

She realized with silent amazement that she'd managed to betray the Miasma Club without her aura's interference. If she'd needed more proof of the Muse's beneficent power, all doubts were now banished. *Nothing* had ever silenced Kay's aura so decisively before.

The door opened a few inches, then stopped short at the end of a taut chain. She recognized the beautiful red-haired woman from the

131

French Quarter, who now warily watched her. "What did you say your name was?" the woman asked.

"Kay Rosenblatt."

"You followed me home a few weeks ago, didn't you? You and some guy. You tried being sneaky about it, but you weren't very good."

"That's right. I'm sorry we worried you. It's just — I never saw a member of your Club before, and I had to learn where you lived. I was already thinking about coming over to your side."

"Uh-huh. Right... Hey, is that *blood* all over your skirt?"

"Uh, yes. That dog downstairs—"

"Mrs. Gruenwald's Doberman?"

"I guess so. It jumped me as soon as I came into the courtyard."

"That damned animal. I've been trying to get the SPCA to do something about that dog for months." She unlatched her chain and opened the door. Her eyes grew wide when she saw Kay's arm. "Holy *mackerel* — maybe I should call an ambulance—?"

"It looks a lot worse than it is, really..."

"Well, come on in." She pulled Kay inside and locked the door behind her. "At least let me get some antiseptic for that arm."

Kay followed her through a small living room and a narrow hallway. The apartment was a walk-through collage. Every square inch of wall space and ceiling was covered with photos cut out from magazines — images of musicians and their instruments, running the gamut from jazz giants to eighteenth century opera divas.

They came to the bathroom, whose black-painted walls were caked with scraps of sheet music. The woman turned on the faucet. "Thank you, Polyhymnia," Kay said. "It *is* Polyhymnia, isn't it?"

The woman smiled. "Nope. Weird guess. I'm Felicia. Here, wash off that arm. I'll see if I can dig up a bandage."

Kay scrubbed her left forearm thoroughly. The soap stung, but not nearly as much as she'd thought it might. Only a pair of long, pink scrapes remained on her arm.

Felicia returned holding a shirt. "Couldn't find a bandage, so it looks like I'll have to sacrifice a tee—" She stared, amazed, at Kay's forearm. "Hey! All that blood on my landing came from *those* little scratches? You aren't a hemophiliac, are you?"

"No. Just a really fast healer." Kay dabbed her arm dry with a towel. "I'm surprised you're surprised. Aren't you Muses fast healers, too?"

"Uhh... sure, I guess... whatever." Felicia gave Kay a long, head-to-toe look over, her eyes lingering on Kay's hips and her full thighs. Kay couldn't recall ever having been *examined* by a woman this way; the closest parallel she could come up with was how Daniel stared at her when he thought she wasn't looking. "So," Felicia said, apparently satisfied, "now that you've gotten all close and personal with Mrs. Gruenwald's dog, you want a beer?"

Kay felt herself blushing. "That's very kind of you, but I don't, um, drink. Beer, I mean."

"Hey! This is my own special home-brew we're talking about. Anyway, what've you got against beer?"

"The taste. It's so... *harsh*. It reminds me of... well, a part of myself I'd rather not think about. A nasty part I hope you and your sisters can make disappear."

Felicia smiled. "You don't write song lyrics, do you?"

"I've, uh, never tried..."

"Well, you ought to." She grabbed Kay's hand and pulled her toward the apartment's tiny kitchen. "Anyway, I *insist* that you try some of my beer. Don't worry — it's sweet. Or sweet for *beer*, I guess."

"I, uh, suppose I can't say no. Especially not if this is part of the initiation." Her face brightened. "Is it?"

Felicia opened her fridge and took out a pair of unlabeled, dark brown glass bottles. "*Initiation*'—?" She handed Kay a bottle after unscrewing the top. "Look, before the evening gets any more interesting, I have to ask you something. Are you off your meds, or are you just a little *off*? 'Cause I can deal with the latter, but the former gets kinda hairy, in my experience."

"Oh, I don't take any medications. I hardly ever get sick, except for on Friday the Thirteenth and the Ninth of Av. And when I'm sick on *those* days, there's no medicine in the world that can help me."

Felicia led Kay to the generously broken-in couch in the living room, nudging a pair of cats off the cushions with her bare foot before settling down and pulling Kay onto the sofa with her. "So... how about telling me some about this part of yourself you hope I can make disappear? You got me hooked with that... I'm a sucker for poetic mystery. Oh, and have a sip of that beer. Tell me how you like it."

Kay did as she was told. She preemptively cringed. But the taste was like nothing she'd expected. "*Oh!* It — it *is* sweet. It doesn't taste like beer at *all*."

"I'll take that as a compliment."

"It's, well, it's just *wonderful*." Each swallow radiated a glowing warmth from her stomach to her limbs. She felt marvelously sensitive to everything around her — the embroidered patterns on worn cushions beneath her legs, the columns of dust and cat dander that shimmered around the candles massed in the room's corners. She dared hope this magical beverage might be an antidote for her aura; perhaps if she drank enough of it, the terrible thing inside her would quietly drown?

"It's such an *honor*, being here with you." Kay wasn't sure where those words had come from, but she was content to listen to whatever her own lips, tingling now from the beer, might let loose. "When I saw you at that concert, heard what you inspired from that girl singer, saw the way you haloed around her, so, *so* beautiful... well, actually *meeting* you, it was almost too much to hope for. I was so afraid you'd shun me on sight. But now, tonight — it's a *dream come true.* It's like, I've been living a nightmare, a horrible, *horrible* nightmare, but now, with your help, I'm finally going to wake up.

"You'll save me, won't you?" She grabbed Felicia's hand as though it were a life line. "Maybe I don't *deserve* saving. But you're *good.* I can sense that — you're *good,* and you'll save me whether I deserve it or not. Once I'm one of your sisters, I'll be able to make things *right.* I'll, I'll go back to all the people I've hurt—" her voice cracked; she felt herself about to sob, but she clung to her voice, desperate to get all her words out "— and, and, instead of cuh-*curses,* I'll give them all *blessings*—"

Then she couldn't hold it together anymore. The image of Daniel's face from last week's seder, that beneficent innocence polluted by self-loathing... she collapsed into convulsive sobs, some small part of her recognizing the beer's influence. Without knowing how, she found herself cradled within Felicia's arms, her face cushioned by Felicia's breasts.

"There, there, hon," Felicia said, caressing her hair. "You let it all out." Light pats on her back became a massage, increasingly commanding and soothing. "You tell Felicia whatever it is you've gotta say."

The massage helped Kay quell her sobs. "My whole life... as far back as I can remember, I've been a, a *poison,* a walking, talking *plague*... Oh, Felicia, or Polyhymnia, or whoever you are..." Kay looked up into her companion's gorgeous blue eyes with worship. "What's it like to be *you?* What's it like to help people do more than they ever dreamed they could? To have people *pray* for your touch, instead of dreading it?"

"You really want to know?" Felicia asked.

"More than anything."

"Then come with me to my bedroom, hon, and I'll show you."

ANDREW FOX

Kay shivered, even though the small bedroom wasn't cold. She wasn't used to being naked in front of somebody else, at least not like this. On prior occasions, she'd known the men she'd gotten naked with would become victims of her aura — all the power of the moment had resided with her. But now, naked on this ruffled bed crowded with cats, her hostess disrobing before her, Kay had no power whatsoever. She faced the unknown, like a toddler about to take her first steps.

"Are you cold, hon?" Felicia asked. She peeled off her panties, her last bit of clothing. She was a walking art gallery — her entire body, with the exceptions of her hands, feet, and face, was illustrated with the visages and instruments of famed musicians. She was a woman-shaped microcosm of the fantastic collage that was her apartment. She was *stunning*.

"No, I'm not cold," Kay said. "Just a little... intimidated, maybe."

"Well, don't be." Felicia climbed into the bed and snuggled up against her hip. "I don't bite. Except when I *do*." She began kissing the small of Kay's back, so lightly and softly that Kay quivered. The combination of the beer's after effects and Felicia's kisses was electric; her insides felt like melting caramel, slowly churned.

"Are all the Muses as, um, beautiful as you?" Kay whispered.

"'Muses'? I'm still not sure I know what you're talking about, hon. Is that a new slang term I'm not hip to?"

Kay laughed, more because the kisses had tickled her than because she'd found the remark funny. She leaned back and felt a pair of cats scurry from beneath her back. Felicia adjusted to Kay's more relaxed, prone posture. She shifted her butterfly kisses to the insides of Kay's thighs. Then, with her fore and middle fingers, she gently probed between Kay's legs.

Kay stiffened. "Is — is this part of the initiation?"

"Sure... I guess you could call it that." She began moving her fingers in tiny circles, making them glide and twirl like ice dancers. "Just *relax*, and let Felicia 'initiate' you, okay?"

136

"When will I change?" Kay whispered.

"Oh, according to my fingers, I'd say you're 'changing' already. Enjoy the ride."

Kay closed her eyes. She'd expected the initiation ceremony to be painful; every ceremony she'd ever been obligated to perform with the Miasma Club had involved either humiliation or mutilation, often both. But this ceremony was anything *but* painful. It felt *fabulous*.

She opened her eyes and looked down. Felicia's face had disappeared between Kay's legs. All of a sudden, the pleasurable sensations she had been enjoying intensified a hundred-fold.

She thought she might scream, the sensations were so overpowering. But when she opened her mouth, a far different sound emerged, a wordless prayer of thanksgiving. She was changing. She really was *changing*.

I won't be a plague

I won't be a plague

thank you God for letting me not be a plague...

Her entire body tingled. Her nipples itched, just like they would when her aura would gather its force for some mischief, only this itching sent little bolts of pleasure racing straight to her groin. Her hips began bucking as white light exploded behind her eyelids. And her wordless prayer became a scream, but not one of pain.

Little aftershocks coruscated up and down Kay's body as Felicia caressed her belly. "What... what *was* that?" Kay whispered, exhausted.

"I believe that was called an *orgasm*," Felicia said. "Your first one? If so, I'm honored."

"Am — am I a Muse, now?"

Felicia laughed softly and tweaked her on the nose. "Yeah, honey, if 'muse' is your word for bisexual, then I guess you are. Welcome to the neighborhood, cutie."

Kay, feeling herself falling towards sleep, searched within herself for any signs of her aura. Failing to find any, she smiled the blissful smile of the redeemed.

She snuggled closer to her savior, not minding at all when a cat staked out a position just above her head and tickled her face with swishings of its bushy tail.

Everything would be all right now.

Everything...

Kay was underground. Trapped by the weight of hundreds of pounds of soil, she felt no sense of panic or even discomfort. She recognized this place; she'd been here earlier tonight, just before she'd awakened on the cold floor of the pumping station.

She explored her new self. She was a not-quite-yet flower, a bud whose soon-to-open petals reached for the sunlight waiting above, while her roots expanded fantastically through the black humus.

She sensed something much like herself near the tips of her roots. Although she had no way of seeing it, she could tell this was Felicia. Felicia had also sprouted an undulating network of roots. Her roots and Kay's roots touched, then snaked around each other, as irresistibly attracted to each other as a compass's needle to magnetic North.

Kay felt herself instantly double in size. Her pathways of sensation now no longer limited themselves to her own roots and petals; they extended throughout Felicia's, too. Kay's sap flowed into what had been exclusively Felicia, and she felt Felicia's sap, sweet and pure, flow into what had formerly been exclusively Kay's body.

Peace. Release.

Somewhere beyond the cocooning darkness, an animal yowled, then hissed. Others like it joined it in a swelling chorus.

Be quiet, please. You're disrupting my peace—

More than just discordant sounds impinged on her consciousness. She smelled *muck*. Funky river bottom muck, the kind that appeared along the edges of a bayou at low tide.

Do flowers have a nose?

How am I smelling this if I don't have a nose?

She was waking up, she realized. The cacophonous sounds and pungent odors came from outside her precious darkness, trying to pull her into wakefulness.

No! I won't go! I won't LEAVE!

She clung to the blanketing darkness, grasped desperately for her vanishing sense of well-being. But something vastly powerful added its voice to the forces shoving her towards wakefulness, something buried deep inside her. Something she both feared and hated, and knew as well as she knew herself... because it was a part of herself.

That something *screamed*. Screamed as though it were jumping out of the jaws of death itself—

Kay's eyes popped open. The yowling and hissing came from four cats. The terrified felines had retreated to the tops of the dressers. Backs arched, fur bristling, tails held upright and trembling, they stared at Kay's and Felicia's legs and hissed and spat.

The putrid stench remained. So did the silent screaming inside her abdomen. She tried to sit up. Her legs did not respond.

She pushed herself up on her elbows and looked down.

Her legs weren't there anymore. And neither were Felicia's. What had replaced those four tapered columns of flesh and bone... was *muck*.

She nearly added her own shriek to her aura's internal screaming. But she swallowed her instinctual horror and forced herself to think. *Am I still dreaming? Is this real?*

And if it *was* really happening, was it a necessary part of her transformation into a Muse? Was that why her aura fought it with the ferocity of a cornered wolverine?

She leaned over to nudge Felicia awake. Before she could touch her companion, Felicia's eyes snapped open.

Unlike Kay, she had no compunctions about shrieking.

"What are you *doing to me?!?*" Wild-eyed, she tried pushing Kay away from her, off the bed, but the muck clung to them both, anchoring them inextricably together. "Stop it! *Stop it right now!!*" She slapped Kay repeatedly across the face. Kay whimpered and weakly defended herself. "Sisters!" Felicia shouted. "Save me! For the sake of Creation, *save me!*"

Suddenly, Kay's lower body felt like a sheet of rubber being pulled between two horses stampeding in opposite directions. The pain nearly made her pass out. Then her ears were hammered by a deafening

-SNAP!!!-

and when she was able to open her eyes, she saw she had legs again.

Felicia had rolled off the side of the bed. She cowered in the corner, surrounded now by her cats, and stared at Kay with terrorized eyes. "You... you're exactly what you said... a *plague.* An evil, cursed *thing.*"

Kay felt herself tremble as she realized her dream of redemption had been murdered. "I... I didn't do it," she said. Inside of her, the aura no longer screamed. It laughed. "I thought *you* had done it, that it was part of my transformation—"

"Get out. You're *polluting* my home." Felicia used the edge of the disheveled bedsheets to pick up Kay's clothes and fling them at her. "Get out and never come here again."

Kay sensed the redness of shame spread over her entire body. She struggled into her clothes. "Please," she said. "Even if it's... not possible for me to be one of you, at least *listen* to me. The Miasma Club — the bad luck spirits — they — *we* — are planning to destroy New Orleans. We've been sabotaging the levee system, hurricane preparedness plans, even FEBO." She waited for her aura to choke off her words, but it merely giggling inside her like a demented adolescent. "That's why I came to you. I felt your power shut down my aura earlier tonight. Maybe — maybe you're stronger than we are. If you can shut us *all* down before hurricane season starts—"

Felicia pointed toward the front door. "Get out."

"But — haven't you been *listening?*"

"Get *out*. Before I call the police."

"I'm *not* your *enemy!* I *love* this city! You have to help. You're the only ones who *can—*"

Felicia grabbed an electric guitar and wielded it like a baseball bat. "Do you really expect me to *believe* you? You've got five seconds. Then I start swinging."

Kay was utterly befuddled. "But — but you're a *Muse*. You're all-loving, all-*good—*"

Felicia stormed around the corner of the bed, swinging the guitar menacingly. "GET! OUT!"

Kay retreated. "But—"

"*OUT!!!*"

Kay turned and ran.

Her aura giggled with demented malevolence.

Chapter 14

WHERE *is Owl hiding? And why?*

Kay spent a sleepless night searching fruitlessly for Owl Lookingback. He was the only entity she'd ever witnessed defy the Triumvirate and get away with it. Now that she'd been cut off from the Muses, Owl seemed to be her only hope of discovering even a clue as to how to avert Project Big Blow. But he had gone to ground. His fishing cabin in the Lake Catherine part of New Orleans East was dark, shutters tightly shut. She couldn't find him in any of his usual haunts in the French Quarter or Uptown. He refused to answer his cell phone.

Tormented by her aura's continuous mocking laughter, she returned home an hour before sunrise. She couldn't count on Lily; Kay would have to warn Mayor Rio about Operation Big Blow herself, in person.

Her aura would fight her with every nefarious trick in its arsenal. The thought of the Sisyphean effort it would take to deliver her warning nearly made her despair. She was reasonably sure her Corps credentials would suffice to get her through the door. But what then? Her aura would choke off Kay's voice or twist her words into gibberish.

And even if she managed to get the words out, why should Roy Rio believe her?

She stared at her computer. Trying to mail Mayor Rio a warning was useless; the mischief the Miasma Club could inflict on her package as it traveled through the postal system and City Hall's mail sorting room was virtually infinite. Email was also a hopeless endeavor, thanks to Glenn's talents. But a written warning stood a better chance of avoiding a vicious garbling than a verbal warning — at least she could proof it before the mayor would read it. She would just have to act as her own delivery service, somehow shove her warning into the mayor's hands despite the aura's worst efforts.

Two hours later, she printed out a sixteen-page account of everything which had happened since the most recent Friday the Thirteenth. She read over her hard copy. It seemed all right; not a masterpiece of Western literature, but straightforward and clear.

Of course, she reminded herself, if her aura could force her to vomit, scream nonsense, or come down with laryngitis, it could probably puppeteer her into ripping up this letter before the mayor could read it. Well, she'd make the aura's job as hard as possible. She printed out thirty copies, then gathered a stapler, a box of envelopes, a jar of glue, and her photographer's vest, the one covered with pockets.

By the time the morning sunlight had fully illuminated her den, Kay was ready. Her multiple pockets bulged with copies of her letter, as did her purse and a leather portfolio she'd tied to her wrist. Her final line of defense against her aura's sabotage? She'd glued copies of the letter to her torso and wrapped others around her arms and legs, securing them with rubber bands and spare shoe laces, and she'd stapled copies to her long-sleeve blouse beneath her vest.

Surely at least *one* copy of her letter would survive her encounter with the mayor.

She was as ready as she could make herself. She phoned the mayor's secretary to say she would be delivering an extremely important document. She was mystified that her aura allowed her to speak freely; she wished she knew what devilish ordeals it planned for her.

Feeling as encumbered as a medieval knight, she grabbed her car keys and exited her back door. The morning was gray and oppressively humid, the opening act for a thunderstorm. Ozone filled the air. She prayed her ancient (but well cared-for) AMC Gremlin would start.

Before she could walk across her shadowed driveway to the car, something damp and cold snaked around her ankles. Shackles sprang into existence around her wrists, accompanied by syncopated giggling. Before she could scream, a furry paw clamped her mouth shut.

"A little birdie told us you've been a bad girl," Reynard the Fox said. "A very, very bad girl, indeed."

They took Kay to an abandoned elementary school in Press Park. This was a derelict neighborhood which had lost nearly all its residents once the fact that it had been built atop a toxic landfill became common knowledge; an earlier stratagem of the Miasma Club. Krampus, Glenn, and Reynard locked her inside the dark, dusty gym, its high windows covered by rotting boards. They told her nothing.

She had time to think. Too much time. *My aura set me up again. It let me print out all those copies of my letter and glue them to my body, so I'd be literally covered with incriminating evidence when the Miasma Club abducted me. It distracted me with worries so I wouldn't sense the Club's proximity. Even the weather helped... the ozone odor covered up the cabbage stench.*

They had her. The big question now was: what did they intend to *do* with her?

At last, she heard the lock on the gym's doors click open. A flashlight blinded her. Reynard's musky paws and Glenn's cold steel talons pulled her from the room.

"Where are you taking me?" she said, trying to sound braver than she felt.

"Oh, you'll like it," Reynard cooed in her ear. "Our destination? A delightful shopping mall. Don't you ladies simply *adore* shopping?"

Glenn the Gremlin cackled. "It's shuh-shuh-shuh-*showtime!*"

The Lake Forest Plaza Shopping Mall in New Orleans East had once been the crown jewel of the city's retail sector. Built on thirty acres of drained cypress swamp, in its prime it had boasted four anchor department stores, over sixty specialty shops, and South Louisiana's only indoor ice skating rink.

Trapped in the back seat of the Miasma Club's Chevrolet Suburban limousine, Kay stared at the mostly darkened mall. Reducing Lake Forest Plaza to relative ruin had been one of the Miasma Club's major projects of the late 1980s. A pinch of drug gang activity here, a sprinkling of vandalism there, a leavening of shoplifting, a frosted topping of carjackings and murders, and the poisoned cake had been fully baked.

Now the sole surviving department store, a Dillard's, hung on by a frayed thread. Police had forced the closure of the game room, deeming it a notorious gang hangout and a menace to the public safety. The ice skating rink was a dimly recalled memory.

As Reynard and Glenn pulled her from the limousine, she felt the weight of a terrible emptiness. A handful of lonely cars clung to the uneven pools of light surrounding the mall's main entrance, shunning the darkness beneath scores of broken lamp posts. The acres of decaying asphalt looked even more desolate and lonely than the original cypress swamp had after all of its trees had been cut down, before the water had been drained away, leaving the muck to dry and wither, awaiting the coming of suburbia.

Reynard and Krampus yanked her through the mall like she was a broken chest of drawers being returned for store credit. Struggling was hopeless; they frog-marched her through corridors where no guards or customers ventured, and any stray onlookers would be highly unlikely to involve themselves.

"What do you plan to do with me?"

Reynard laughed and yipped. "Delighted as I would be to tell you, it would be most unfair to spoil the surprise."

Glenn pushed open a door which opened onto a narrower corridor, one which had formerly held rest rooms and utility spaces, now caked with fifteen-year-old dirt. At the end of this corridor lay another door. Kay heard familiar voices beyond it, distorted and echoey.

Once she was shoved inside, she found herself standing at the edge of what she could only surmise had once been the mall's ice skating rink. Smoke and pungent incense made her eyes water. Fires had been lit within thirteen steel drums arranged around the rink's perimeter. The shadows of her fellow Miasma Club members pooled on the curved wall surrounding the rink.

"We have the Jewess," Reynard announced.

"Big fuckin' deal," Fortuna Discordia shouted back. "We should've left that traitorous tramp to rot in that school gym, if you ask me."

"But no one is asking you, Fortuna," Ti Malice's rich baritone shot back. "The Triumvirate required her presence, and so she is here. The only question left is whether we begin the ceremony now, or whether we persist in our efforts to locate the Indian and the Greek."

So Owl and Pandora are still free? Kay thought. Reynard and Glenn shoved her inside the circle of blazing drums. Now she was able to see her fellows more clearly. Na Ba offered a discreet wave of greeting, which made Kay's heart swell with an irrational flutter of hope.

"Now that we have obtained the minimum quorum," Mephistopheles said, "we may begin the ceremony of beseeching and summoning."

Ti Malice stepped forward. "I ask again, would it not be better to make one more effort to ensure the attendance of our full company? If your powers of detection have been somehow foiled by the Indian's machinations, then allow *me* to try my hand. Give me but forty-eight hours. Between us, Eleggua-Eshu and I are tied into the psyches of seventy percent of the mortal inhabitants of this city. There is virtually nowhere the Indian and the Greek can hide—"

"*No*," Mephistopheles said. "There will be no further delay. The ceremony will occur tonight, as planned, when conditions are most auspicious. We of the Triumvirate choose not to include the Indian and the Greek. Their actions will have ramifications for them, ramifications most dire. And now, we begin."

Mephistopheles held his arms out straight from his shoulders. Krampus and Old Scratch, standing on either side of him, did the same. The trio's fingertips touched. Within seconds, in a blaze of arcane flame and light, the members of the Triumvirate merged, assuming their Combined and Terrible Aspect, the devil whose three faces were one.

"Mother of Us All," they/he said, "we come to this place of dire blasphemy to beseech You, to request your Aid, to summon your Cleansing Power. The mortal humans, blind to their connection to You, deaf to their dependence upon You, so prideful and arrogant — they have profaned You upon this very spot. In their ignorance and arrogance, they declared themselves masters of this world, shapers of land and water and air. In this very place, they mocked Your Power and made themselves 'gods' by creating a bubble of northern winter for their petty amusement.

"And yet what have been the fruits of their blasphemy here? Naught but wrack and ruin, decay and despair. Despite the futility of all their works, still they persist — binding Your holy rivers within channels constricting and ruinous, starving Your deltas of replenishing floods, mingling Your salt waters with Your fresh, driving girders of foreign steel deep within Your flesh. And now, their ultimate affront — they seek to purloin your very Power.

"We, the humble children of Your Muck, have fought for three centuries against them. Yet the wounds they continuously inflict upon Your Body continue to fester and bleed. As your humble servitors, we now call upon Your full and unfettered Might to finish the work which we have so lovingly begun. We call upon Your Winds. We call upon Your mighty Waves. We call upon Your cleansing Rains, Your scouring Floods, Your awesome Cyclones.

"Send us Your Storm, we beseech You. Send us Your Hurricane, we pray. As You have suffused us with Your Strength, granting us power to bend mortals' fortunes, we now offer unto You a portion of that Strength You so lovingly bestowed."

The merged Triumvirate cast their terrible gaze upon the gathered company. "Members of the Miasma Club," they/he said, "repeat these words after us. Repeat them in the dozen tongues of your mortal communities; repeat them in the Language which preceded any human utterance. Repeat oh my gathered minions these words:

"Mother of Us All, send us Your smiting Winds, Your awesome Cyclones."

French, Italian, German, Czech, Creole, Yoruban, Dahomean, Gaelic, Vietnamese, Hmong — Kay heard a United Nations chorus answer the Triumvirate's call. She clenched her teeth, yet her lips and tongue still managed to betray her. She shook furiously as she heard her own voice respond, first in Yiddish, then in what she assumed to be Polish, Russian, and Ukrainian. She found herself even more shocked as her mouth and throat formed sounds which she'd never before made — the sounds of winds blasting north from the Gulf, eviscerating barrier islands and wetland groves, sucking roofs off houses, smashing the glass faces of towers which challenged the sky.

"Mother of Us All, may Your Winds drive mighty Waves onto the mortal-infested shores."

She could no more resist the words emerging from her throat than she could a Category Five storm surge.

"Mother of Us All, scour the land with Your purifying Flood."

A flood of shame, fury, and tears scoured her.

"Mother of Us All — we *beseech* Thee — renew Thyself with Thy great and omnipotent Storm — resurrect Thy Pure Body with the power of Thy Hurricane!"

Pagan! Pagan! The Jewish portion of her embryonic soul recoiled from this blasphemous declaration of earth-worshiping fervor. Yet her aura forced her to say the words just the same.

The fire in the pit danced higher. Bolts of emerald plasma licked greedily at the broken ceiling. "And now, my brothers and sisters," the Triumvirate said, "the time has come for us to return to our Mother a portion of what She has so lovingly given us. Take up the Knife of Ill Fortune, whose hilt is carved from the mainmast of a storm-sunk treasure ship, whose blade is forged from the iron armor of the CSS *Louisiana*, the gunboat which failed in its mission to save New Orleans from ignominious defeat. Take up this Knife, and *give*."

Eleggua-Eshu approached the pit first. He lifted the Knife — almost a small sword — held his left hand over the pit, and then sawed off his left thumb.

Kay's soul shriveled deep inside her; her aura exulted when the amputated appendage splashed into the pit's bottom. The flames responded voraciously — the abandoned rink flared brighter than the brightest noonday sun. She was assaulted by an image of miasmatic tendrils reaching southward across the Gulf, jumping from island to invisible island of Gaia energy, stretching at last to the middle of the Atlantic, the womb of tropical cyclones...

Na Ong and Na Ba stepped to the pit's edge next. Na Ba cast a concerned, pitying look in Kay's direction, but only for an instant. Then she turned to the work of hacking off her husband's thumb. After she wrapped his left hand in gauze, he returned the favor, removing his wife's thumb with the efficiency of a *sushi* chef.

Fortuna Discordia went next. She licked the blood from the knife, moaning with pleasure as the droplets sizzled in her mouth. Her gloating eyes never strayed from Kay's as she dismembered her own left hand.

Reynard and Glenn began pulling Kay toward the pit.

"Owl!" she cried. "Owl! *Save me!*"

He'd managed to extricate himself from this blood sacrifice. Could he be watching events unfold in the rink even now?

"OWL—!!"

Glenn held her fast. Reynard stretched her left arm over the pit.

Neither Owl Lookingback nor any other white knight rode to her rescue.

Chapter 15

THE *storm is coming.* Reynard the Fox's fur bristled with delight. The nub of his missing claw throbbed with awareness of a tropical disturbance stirring in the open Atlantic off the western coast of Africa.

He stopped in the Regional Transit Authority's men's room to check his illusory guise in the mirror, then headed off to delete all records of the Authority's emergency transit evacuation plan from the agency's computers, ensuring that thousands of New Orleanians who lacked personal automobiles would remain trapped.

* * * * *

The storm is coming. Even now, it gathers strength near the Cape Verde Islands. Ti Malice, lord of shadows, silently encouraged Quincy Cochrane's efforts to stir up a stink at the Benevolent Association of Black Police Officers' meeting, both about his own upcoming suspension while under investigation for possible malfeasance and about the NOPD's newly unveiled Hurricane Response Plan.

"It's discriminatory!" Quincy thundered to his fellow Association members. "Worse, it's racist on its face! Where do most of us get deployed by this so-called plan? I'll tell you — the Quarter, the Central Business District, Uptown, and the Garden District. The *white* and *green* parts of town. Where do we *not* get deployed? Again, I'll tell you — Central City, Gert Town, the Seventh Ward, the Lower Nine. Not anywhere we'd be in a position to protect *black* lives and property — oh, no, heaven forbid we cops do *that!*"

A fine student, Ti Malice thought. *He's almost as effective at stretching the facts as I am.*

* * * * *

The storm is coming. My circuits buzz endlessly as its outer bands draw near Bermuda. Glenn the Gremlin scurried between banks of servers on the second floor of the Louisiana Office of Public Health's Loyola Avenue headquarters. His cablelike fingers injected viruses into each machine he touched. He corrupted databases of homebound invalids who would need to be evacuated, deleted schematics of emergency shelters, and erased contact information for hundreds of medical personnel who'd be needed to provide care for chronically ill refugees.

What a fine, fine time to be a gremlin!

* * * * *

Three weeks prior to the official start of hurricane season, fifteen hundred members of the National Association of Disaster Preparedness and Emergency Response Organizations packed Hall C of the New Orleans Convention Center for their annual convention. Bruno Galliano felt excited and hopeful to be in this room, surrounded by so many hundreds of his colleagues. He had lobbied hard to get the Association to bring its meeting to the Crescent City this year.

In fifteen minutes, Mayor Rio would officially welcome the attendees, many of whom planned to extend their stays to take part in the excitement of the first-ever third weekend of Jazz Fest at the New Orleans Fairgrounds. Glancing at the breakfast buffet in the back of the hall, Bruno spotted a familiar face — Bob Marino, now two months into his retirement from FEBO.

Bruno joined him. "Hey, Bob, don't you have better ways to spend your retirement than hanging out with us old war horses still on the job?"

Bob shook Bruno's hand. "Good to see you, Bruno. I'm still on the Association's advisory board, and my wife wanted to get me out of the house, so here I am. You know, I can't say I miss being up there on the stage as a head honcho. It's more fun being one of the little people."

"I'm kinda surprised to see you here at all. I would've figured you'd want to wash your hands of the whole emergency management business."

"No. I wanted to wash my hands of *FEBO*. Not the emergency management business." He sighed deeply.

"What's the matter?"

"Bruno, what's the goal of any decent public servant when they enter a big organization? To leave it in better shape than it was when they first walked in the door. And me? I left FEBO in the hands of an incompetent who barely gives a damn. Do you believe in karma?"

"You mean that 'what goes around, comes around' business?"

"Yeah."

"I dunno."

"I wasn't a believer, before. But these last few months have changed my mind. It's been the weirdest thing — ever since I was here back in February, I've been blessed, if you want to call it that, with *negative* karma. Answer me this. In a just world, what should've been the upshot of my winning that jackpot and then retiring, knowing the mess I'd be leaving behind? I'd blow the money on booze and more gambling, throw away my marriage, find out all my so-called friends were shameless leaches—"

"Oh, come *on*, Bob. You're being way too hard on yourself."

"Wait. My outlandish luck didn't stop with Louisiana Lucky Loot. A week after I retired, my wife suggested we make a trip to Atlantic City, just as a lark, to see if lightning would strike twice. Well, it *did*. I cleaned out the place. Three different casinos asked me to leave and never come back. After we got home, I started giving friends and neighbors tips on horses and Powerball lottery numbers. Every damn one paid off. Within days, so many people were lining up to talk with me, I had to start charging fees and percentages just to keep the crowds under control.

"It's fucking *nuts*. Six months ago, my kids were either looking at going to a state college or aiming for a merit scholarship. Now I can send all four of them to Harvard, if that's where they want to go. What the heck am I doing at this meeting? Being here is an *escape*. Here, at least, I can pretend my life hasn't been turned inside-out."

Bruno stared hard at his friend. "This is on the level?"

"As level as Nebraska."

Bruno chuckled with lingering disbelief. "Boy, I sure could do with a little of your problem. If I ever came down with the Midas touch, the first thing I'd do is buy a whole lotta folks around this town a damn *clue...*"

Bob staring past him, a puzzled look on his face. "Who's that woman over there, the one in the red dress?" he asked. "You know her?"

Bruno turned around. "The one with the curves like a roller coaster, sitting in the back row?"

"That's the one."

"Sure, I know her. That's Venus Roman, my administrative assistant."

"Was she at the disaster simulation exercise in February?"

"No, I had her working on other stuff."

"I — I could *swear* I've met her before. I just... I can't place it. Could you introduce us?"

Bruno spotted Mayor Rio enter the hall. "I'd love to, Bob, but I gotta get up there on stage with the mayor. How about we do it at the break?"

"Sure," Bob said, still staring at Venus. "Thanks."

Bruno made his way to the stage. Johnny Redonto, Association President, an emergency planner from Chicago, adjusted the mic at the podium. "Good morning, everyone," he said. "I see you've all straggled in from Bourbon Street. The staff's been kind enough to put out a bowl of BC Powder packets next to the coffee setup." He paused for the perfunctory laughter. "This morning, I'm honored to start our program by welcoming Mayor Roy Rio to the podium for some introductory remarks."

Mayor Rio shook hands with Johnny. "Let me begin by welcoming you all to the great City of New Orleans," he said. "I don't think you could've chosen a more appropriate locale. We are an historic metropolis, essential to the nation's economy because of our energy production, our bountiful seafood harvest, and most especially our port, strategically located at the mouth of the Mississippi. Yet we are a metropolis threatened as few others are by the forces of nature. The embattled nature of our lives here has given us New Orleanians a unique *esprit de corps*, a determination to grab life by the horns and enjoy it to the fullest. This sensibility has produced our wonderful jazz music, our world-famous architecture, our year-round calendar of festivals, and our delightful cuisine. I invite you to enjoy them all—"

A short, square-faced conventioneer approached one of the microphones which had been set up in the aisles. He tapped it to see if it was live. "I am dreadfully sorry to interrupt the mayor, but I have vital news to share," he said. "May I speak?"

Mayor Rio motioned for him to continue. "Of course. I think the Tourism and Visitors Bureau will forgive me if I cut my sales pitch a little short."

The man nodded. "My name is Sonjay Nupta, and I am the Emergency Management Coordinator for the city of Tampa. I have many close friends at the National Oceanic and Atmospheric Administration in Miami. My NOAA colleagues have sent to my Blackberry just now a most disturbing forecast. The first storm of the Atlantic season has formed and has been given the name of Antonia—"

"Hey, I thought hurricane season isn't supposed to start until June first," Mayor Rio said. "It's not even the middle of May yet. The damn thing's getting a jump on us."

"Pre-season storms are unusual, yes, but they are not unknown. The NOAA meteorologists project with seventy percent certainty that Antonia will enter the Gulf within the next two days. Most pre-season storms are weak and poorly organized. However, such will not be the case with Antonia. Prevailing weather conditions, when combined with record-setting water temperatures for this early date, appear to be ideal for a rapid and most severe intensification."

Sonjay paused and looked around the room. "My friends, I have no wish to sound alarmist, but I am afraid we will need to return quickly to our posts, especially those of us who live and work along the Gulf Coast. To have conditions this propitious for a hurricane, this early... were I non-rational person, I would be tempted to think the Gulf of Mexico has prepared a grand welcome for Antonia."

Part II

Ain't Got No Home

"Ain't got no home

An' no place to roam

Ain't got no home

An' no place to roam

I'm a lonely boy

I ain't got no home.

Ooo-ooo ooo-ooo ooo-ooo ooo-ooo

ooooooh..."

Clarence "Frogman" Henry

Ain't Got No Home

Chapter 16

Roy Rio stared across his desk at his Director of Emergency Preparedness and steeled himself. "Okay, Bruno, I know you're itchin' to do it, so hit me with your worst-case scenario."

"We could have a Cat Three or Cat Four storm rolling through our neighborhood as early as this coming weekend," Bruno said.

"Hell *no*." Roy wanted to grab his employee and shake him until he got a different prediction. "That's *not* gonna happen. Not the inaugural third weekend of Jazz Fest—"

"I'm not saying it's a sure thing, but that's what some of the computer models are suggesting. You don't like it? Sue Sun Microsystems."

"Have any storms ever hit Louisiana in May?"

"Nope. But that doesn't mean a thing."

"So when we will know what this storm is really up to?"

"Hard to say until it's past Cuba. Those high surface water temperatures in the Gulf could make it career around like a loose pinball. The NOAA boys say we should have some pretty solid landfall probability maps by sometime Thursday. Even then, though, Antonia could dance a Cajun two-step and mess the computers all up."

"Sometime Thursday... You do realize, don't you, that this whole metro area, from Slidell to LaPlace, is supposed to be crammed full of Jazz Fest tourists from Wednesday night to Monday morning? About two hundred thousand of them, filling up every single hotel and motel room within a hundred miles of the Fair Grounds? Do you know what the Hotel and Motel Association, the French Quarter Business Association, and the restaurant owners would *do* to me if I called for an evacuation, canceled Jazz Fest, and then the storm hits *Pensacola?*"

Bruno squirmed. "I know, I know. That's why you get paid the big bucks."

"Yeah, right. Okay, give it to me straight — worst case scenario, this thing is a Cat Four and projected to ram straight up the Mississippi. How much lead time do I need to evacuate the city?"

"Seventy-two hours. And that's what we've estimated for a normal weekend, with no Jazz Fest in town. A heck of a lot of those tourists aren't going to have cars. They're gonna need buses, taxis, Amtrak, anything with wheels or wings—"

Roy hadn't heard anything Bruno had said beyond 'seventy-two hours.' "*Three DAYS?!?* That's *impossible!* I'd have to declare an evacuation before the NOAA people had even made up their minds what part of the coast the storm is supposed to hit. I'd have to cancel Jazz Fest—" he counted backwards from Saturday "—*Wednesday morning!* You have to do better than that. Give me *options*, man."

"Assuming the State Department of Transportation has finally gotten their contraflow plan straight, we could maybe pull off a fast and dirty evacuation within a thirty-six hour window, get about seventy to seventy-five percent of folks out, and offer vertical evacuation and shelter in the Superdome to everyone else. Or you could order a mandatory evacuation for just the lowest-lying areas, Lake Catherine and the Rigolets and the fishing camps along Haynes Boulevard, tell everybody else evacuation is voluntary but recommended, and pray for the best."

"No mayor in the history of New Orleans has ever ordered a mandatory evacuation," Roy said, rubbing the back of his head. "We haven't even figured out the legal liabilities. I mean, potentially, businesses could sue the city for millions in damages if I make the wrong decision..."

The following evening:

"Mr. Mayor, it's been a day since we learned about Antonia. You have to make up your mind. We need a decision."

Writing adventure simulation software was never like this, Roy thought. As a game coder, you were a god — you decided how many monsters hid in the cave and how many in the abandoned warehouse, which could be vanquished by flame throwers and which by fragmentation bombs. You never had to worry about X factors beyond your control, wind shear from *La Nina* or late spring cold fronts pushing down from Canada...

"Mr. Mayor," Bruno repeated, "we're all waiting, your whole team. The press, they're waiting. The Jazz Fest people are waiting. And more important, half a million citizens are waiting. We need to shit or get off the pot."

Roy stared into the tired, tense faces of Bruno, his chief of staff Walter Johnson, Police Superintendent Pendergrast, his legal counsel, his communications director, and his chief budget analyst. "I say... hell, I say we call it a night and go out for beers."

Bruno stared at him as though Roy had grown a third eyeball. "Uh, Mr. Mayor?"

Roy smiled guiltily. "Dumb joke. Sorry. What's the very latest from NOAA? Is that Canadian front gonna ride down here on a white stallion and save our asses, shove the storm off to the southeast?"

Bruno frowned. "Possibly. Or the front could stall out when it runs smack into a warm front pushing north from the Gulf. That'd leave Antonia free to whack us — or Gulfport, or Biloxi. Heck, there's even a possibility that *El Nina* could drive high altitude, fast moving dry air across the Southwest and Texas and end up decapitating Antonia before it hits land. Then we'd end up with nothing worse than a bunch of scattered rain showers."

"In other words," Roy said, "they don't know."

Bruno nodded glumly.

Roy sighed. He turned to his chief legal counselor. "Patrick, if I declare a mandatory evacuation and Antonia ends up a dud, do we end up getting our asses sued from here to Sunday by every business deprived of one of their biggest money-making weekends of the year?"

Patrick Delachaise shrugged his shoulders. "I hate to sound like the guys at NOAA, but this is *terra incognito* — unexplored territory. A citywide mandatory evacuation wasn't even declared for Betsy. Liability issues? The only way to find out for sure is to have aggrieved parties sue, and then let the cases wind their ways through the courts."

"What's your opinion on our exposure with a voluntary evacuation versus a mandatory one?"

Patrick shrugged. "For what it's worth, I'd guess there'd be fewer and weaker liability issues with the former."

Roy rubbed his forehead. None of this was helping him one bit. "Walt, we haven't heard from you yet. What political implications am I looking at?"

Walter looked up from his laptop. "Based on your possible decisions, you'll land inside one of four consequence quadrants. Luck out with a true positive or true negative, you're golden, a hero, parades in your honor. Stumble into a false positive or a false negative, your ass will be burnt to a cinder."

"Dammit, I'm too tired to remember any of that Statistics 101 crap—"

"Okay. False positive — you assume the storm's going to hit, you call for an evacuation, it goes someplace else, and you've ruined everybody's weekend and profits for nothing. Result? You're cluster bombed. False negative — you assume the storm's going someplace else, you *don't* call for an evacuation, it hits here, and people get hurt or die who otherwise might've gotten the heck out. Result? You're branded an immoral monster. True positive and true negative are the inverse circumstances of what I've just said."

"So you're telling me the worst possible choice I can make is to not call for an evacuation and then have the storm hit?"

"Mr. Mayor," Bruno interjected, "your conscience should tell you that."

"Okay," Roy said, "I realize time is short, so let's deal with what we know for sure. Bruno, what probability is NOAA giving Antonia of growing stronger than a Cat Three?"

"Well, you can never say *never*—"

"Stop. What I need to know is, what are the hurricane experts saying *right now?* Not tomorrow, not in Maybe-Land, but this minute?"

"Right now, they're saying there's about a twenty percent chance it could become a Cat Four."

"A one in five chance. Now we're getting somewhere. Bruno, the Corps of Engineers certifies their levees against a Cat Three storm surge, right?"

"Nobody at the Corps would dare use that term 'certify.' But, yeah, I mean, that was their rough design goal..."

"Good, good. All good." Roy rubbed his hands together. He could feel the pins inside the lock approaching alignment. "Bruno, isn't it true that nearly all deaths from hurricanes result from storm surge?"

"Most of them, yeah. Although the wind'll kill any folks in trailers who decide to ride out the storm."

"Right. Okay." He felt on top of his game again. Maybe being mayor wasn't so different from running a software company, after all. He stood. "Here's what I'm going to do. I'm declaring a mandatory evacuation for all residents living in trailers or mobile homes and all residents living outside the levee system. I'm declaring a voluntary evacuation for everyone else. For those citizens under mandatory evacuation order who don't have transportation, and those citizens who feel unsafe in their own homes but who are unable to evacuate, we're opening up the Superdome as a shelter of last resort.

"Walt, you okay with this?"

Walt nodded. "Yeah, boss, I'm good with that."

"Bruno?"

Bruno nodded, too, though less enthusiastically. "Given all the circumstances, I think that's the best I'm gonna get, so, yeah. But we don't have any plans to provision the Superdome for more than a day or so. You gotta tell people to bring their own food, bedding, medicines, toilet paper—"

"Handle it," Roy said, gathering his papers. "Get the TV and radio stations to run spots. Gentlemen, let's head upstairs. We've got a press conference to give."

* * * * *

A sudden wind gust dislodged one of the boards covering the windows of the Press Park Elementary School gym, where the Miasma Club had been keeping Kay prisoner. A feeble ray of murky light allowed her to examine the makeshift bandage wrapped around her left hand. Her amputated thumb had stopped bleeding. The bandage was encrusted with dried blood, now nearly black. The stump throbbed incessantly with intimations of the coming storm.

She batted aside a fly which had been feasting on the flaky putrescence. Then she unwound the bandage, wincing with anticipated pain whenever it stuck to the skin beneath. She held her hand up to the light. Her severed thumb was already beginning to grow back. Staring at the tiny bulb of new bone, muscle, and skin sprouting in the midst of ravaged scar tissue, some of it still pulpy and damp, she was more appalled than surprised. Of *course* it would grow back. Her body was nothing more than an evil weed, and weeds, no matter how fiercely pruned, always grew back. Unless they were pulled up by the roots.

Reynard and Glenn hadn't taunted her in hours. Whenever she'd been on the verge of escaping into sleep, they'd awakened her from the far side of the door with melodramatic readings from her letter of warning to Mayor Rio, ending their performances in paroxysms of laughter. Were they still out there?

"Reynard? Glenn?"

No sound answered her, save the wind's howlings.

She tried the door. It remained locked. But the light from the uncovered window revealed the door had been gnawed through by termites. She kicked it and was rewarded by the sound of hollowed-out wood splintering. She took a few steps back, then threw her shoulder and full weight against the door. It split in half and fell off its hinges. She was free.

A wind gust from beyond the sagging breezeway nearly pushed her back inside the gym. She saw no sign of Glenn or Reynard. The school's desolate parking lot was empty; only a parade of flattened cardboard cartons and torn roof shingles, which bounced across the cracked asphalt like tumbleweeds, provided some semblance of the life which had once animated this poisoned subdivision.

Leaning forward against the unpredictable wind, Kay stared up at the clouds. They raced from the western to the eastern horizon with the grim implacability of priests walking Death Row, ambassadors of the Angel of Death.

Trembling in the warm, damp wind, she knew why Reynard and Glenn had stopped guarding her. She didn't matter anymore.

Would stubborn old Amos evacuate? If he wouldn't, then neither would Daniel. Although the thought of the evil her aura might do them should she draw close enough terrorized her, she had to find out.

Kay waited until the dozen men in Congregation Beth Judah's small chapel had finished their afternoon prayers. She overheard a few wish others luck with their evacuations. Amos Weintraub remained conspicuously apart from these conversations; this filled Kay with a sense of dread.

He acknowledged her presence with a nod and a slight bow. "Daniel isn't here," he said. "He is out making money, carting away tree branches and such before the wind can blow it into people's houses."

"This is one of his regular work days, isn't it? Why isn't he helping the Levee Board prepare for the storm?"

Amos squinted, as though shielding his eyes from a sudden glare. "Daniel no longer has his job with the Levee Board."

"Oh, no. They fired him?"

"The day after the bad argument with his sister at the *seder*, he went to his boss's bosses to report what he had seen with the levee. Two days later, he is given his walking papers. When I have him apply for unemployment monies, his bosses contest it. I am having to spend for a lawyer to get for Daniel what he is owned."

"That's, that's *terrible*."

"Yes. Well, at least Daniel and Lily are no longer estranged. Whatever you told Lily later that night — I have heard nothing of it, either from her or Daniel — it has allowed a reconciliation, a healing between them. I thank you for this. I would not want to go down to my grave knowing that my two children are embroiled in *tsurris* and hatred, unwilling to speak."

So at least one bit of good came from my confession. No matter what happens to me from here on out, I'll have that to remember.

"Mr. Weintraub, you and Daniel will evacuate, won't you?"

"Evacuate?" Amos chuckled as he put his *tallis* back in its bag. "I did not flee Poland when the Nazis came — I joined the Polish Army. Never in all my years of living in New Orleans have I evacuated for a storm. Not for Betsy, not for Camille, not for any of them."

She sensed her aura begin to tingle. "But Mr. Weintraub, this hurricane season is *different* from any other. I can't tell you why, because you wouldn't believe me, but you and Daniel *must* evacuate—"

"My daughter Lily is required to stay working at her hospital. How could I possibly leave her?" He smiled and shook his head. "No, I have faced down hurricanes ever since 1948, when first I came to this city. Never have I left my home and my synagogue unprotected against looters and robbers. Whatever may blow this way, I leave it in God's hands. I have my Daniel, and he has his little fishing boat, should the water rise too high. Compared to the German army, what is the fury of a storm? *Nothing.*" He smiled more broadly and patted her on the shoulder. "I stay and fight, Kay. I do not run. If my time comes to an end, so be it."

Her shoulder twitched beneath Amos's hand as she sensed that her aura had swallowed juicy bait — bait, she realized, it had specifically sought. "Mr. Weintraub," she gasped, "you've, you've just set yourself up for something *terrible* to happen."

"'Terrible'? What do you mean?"

She had hoped against hope that talking with him here, in synagogue, would grant him some protection. But her aura, her damnable, wily aura, had clouded her judgement. It had maneuvered her into position, then dangled a baited noose over Amos's head. "Mr. Weintraub — the words to drive away an *ayin hora* — *say them*. For the sake of your family, say them and spit between your fingers three times."

The fact that her aura permitted her to make this plea without any attempt to silence her terrified her. "Do it, Mr. Weintraub. Drive me away, like Lily did. *Please*, I beg you, *please...*"

"Drive *you* away...?" He looked around the emptying chapel to see if anyone had overheard her outburst. Then he stared back at her, a sad, concerned look in his eyes. "Perhaps a clean break, it is for the best. I did not understand how Lily was able to pry Daniel away from his devotion to you. Yet now... I think I understand. Goodbye, Kay."

"*Do it*, Mr. Weintraub! Banish me! And please, *please* evacuate!" Her cries echoed through the empty chapel as he passed through the doors, shaking his head. "Take Daniel to a safe place... please..."

Kay watched him put on his coat and hat and quickly exit the synagogue. She knew, with a certainty that tasted of arsenic, that unless she could find a way to destroy herself and the thing inside her, Amos Weintraub's long, eventful life would soon end.

Chapter 17

KAY stood in the middle of her cramped bathroom, her feet surrounded by bags bulging with over-the-counter pharmaceuticals. She'd needed to drive all over town, fighting horrendous evacuation traffic, to find four drug stores which hadn't yet closed their storm shutters. And the shelves at the four stores had been almost bare. She prayed she'd been able to buy enough bottles of pills to do the trick. Suicide, for her, at least, might prove more difficult than it looked in the movies.

She set the first bag of drugs down on top of the toilet seat and began ripping open dozens of little boxes, then cracking apart safety seals and struggling with various types of child-proof packaging. She spread several hundred pills of varying colors and sizes across her vanity's countertop. Antihistamines, acetaminophen, aspirin... that was just the A's.

Suicide not done in the sanctification of God's Name is a grave sin, the Jewish part of her whispered.

But was she *really* about to destroy a body and mind borrowed from God? According to the Triumvirate, she was a child of the Mother, a local swamp goddess or manifestation of the Gaia spirit. But... but... she was also a Jew. And if she really believed what Judaism taught, then *all* things ultimately came from God. Which meant her suicide really *would* be a grave sin.

But isn't a Jew allowed to break almost any commandment in order to preserve a life? And if I'm nothing more than an ambulatory pile of muck and weeds, doesn't Amos Weintraub's life count far more than mine?

Yes, she told herself. *Yes.*

She scooped up a fistful of pills and stuffed them into her mouth. They tasted *awful.* She grabbed a gallon jug of filtered water and took a swallow, barely gagging the pills down, shuddering as the last tablet scraped its way down her gullet. *Crap. Why isn't it possible to kill yourself with an overdose of chocolate pudding?*

Inside of a half hour, she'd managed to force every pill from every bottle down her throat... all except for the contents of one final Rite-Aid bag. Her mouth tasted like a rusty Brillo Pad. *Yick.* Her sinuses felt unusually clear. Was she feeling sleepy? Not any more than she normally did. Her tummy hurt — maybe she was suffering massive internal hemorrhaging? Eh, probably not... a more likely cause of the discomfort was all that water she'd made herself drink, which had stretched her bladder.

Hope wasn't yet lost. There was still that last bag to get through.

When she leaned over to pick it up, a wave of nausea slammed into her.

I'm going to throw up — I'm going to vomit pills like Vesuvius vomited lava...

She stuck her face over the sink. Nasty as the next few seconds would be, it shouldn't be a disaster. She'd been gulping down pills for nearly an hour; most of them would've dissolved by now, escaped through her stomach lining into her blood stream.

Here it COMES—

Her mouth yawed wide as her stomach and throat muscles involuntarily contracted. Yet the sounds that followed weren't at all what she'd expected to hear — where was the SHGLORP! of the vomit splashing into the sink?

Instead, she heard this:

click! click! click! click! click! click! click!

Her eyes widened as she stared down into the sink. It rapidly filled with pills. *Dry* pills. *Whole* pills. Pills that looked fresh from the pill factory. They shot from her mouth like bullets from a Gatling gun, quickly filling her sink to overflowing. Pills bounced off the pill mountain and fell *click-click-clicking* onto the tile floor.

When her purgation finally came to an end, the bathroom resembled a conceptual art installation at the Contemporary Arts Center, some wry commentary on the insidious influence of the American pharmaceutical lobby.

Damn it, she thought, kicking a pile of pills into the hallway. *Damn it, damn it, DAMN IT.*

She'd have to try something else. Something far more violent. And she was running out of time. If only Owl were here... he was the one person who might be able to tell her how a bad luck spirit could die. But he'd somehow made himself so scarce that even the Triumvirate had been unable to find him.

Yet, right after the Friday the Thirteenth conclave, hadn't he prepared her for a crisis of this sort? He'd given her a phone number, told her to use it only in case of a true emergency, if she found herself unable to contact him any other way. She'd laughed off the gesture as an example of his melodramatics, then tossed the card with the phone number in the back of her panties drawer.

She dug through the drawer. She found it — thank God her aura hadn't made her run it through the wash with her dirty underwear.

She dialed the number. A synthesized voice directed her to punch in her code prior to leaving a message. What had she and Owl agreed upon? Oh, yes — "HELP OWL," but in Yiddish. *Helfn Sove.*

She punched in the letter combination, then waited for the beep.

"Owl, it's Kay. Please call me at home. It's a matter of life and death — literally. I need to kill myself, but I don't know how."

She drove to one of the last businesses that still remained open, a pawn shop on Airline Highway, and bought a gun. The thought of using it made her sick to her stomach, and she wasn't sure it would even do the job. But in case Owl failed to get back to her in time, she had to try *something*.

Back in her bathroom, she opened the box that held the used nine millimeter automatic pistol. She made sure the gun's ammunition clip was properly inserted, just like the man at the shop had shown her. Then she placed the barrel in her mouth. Given how nasty her mouth already tasted, the metallic sharpness of tooled steel was actually an improvement.

She didn't let herself think the name of her beloved, the precious name which started with D. She was too afraid she'd fail to pull the trigger.

She took a final glance in the mirror. She looked really dumb with the gun in her mouth; like an overgrown baby sucking on a black steel pacifier. Or an inflatable sex doll for guys with a snuff fetish. Blowing out the back of one's own head wasn't the most glamorous way to die.

Kay pulled the trigger.

She heard the bang. She also saw something that had no business happening outside of a Bugs Bunny cartoon — the back of her throat, propelled by the bullet, stretched above the top of her head like a great wad of Silly Putty. Then the skin and sinews of her neck snapped back, hurling the trapped bullet into the pouch of skin beneath her tongue. The bottom of her throat stretched out like a bullfrog's before propelling the bullet, its momentum nearly spent, out through her startled lips, burying itself within the sink's pile of pills.

Now her mouth tasted *really* bad. She felt like she'd just had her tonsils and adenoids removed, without the benefit of anesthesia.

Fuck. Fuck. *Fuck.*

When her hearing returned, she heard her telephone ringing. She ran to her bedroom. But by the time she lifted the receiver, the ringing had ceased.

Please leave me a message. Please...

She sat on the edge of her bed, checking the phone every few seconds for the series of beeps which would tell her she had a new message. Finally, after four minutes had passed, she heard the tones for which she'd prayed.

"So, Kay," the message began, "I hear you want me to be your Dr. Kevorkian. I've actually got an answer for you, babe. But you ain't gonna like hearin' it. There's only a single way I know of for one of our kind to die. And even that isn't death of the sort you're probably thinking of."

She felt a tiny sprout of hope. At least he hadn't said it was *impossible.*

"I figgur you're familiar with the phrase, 'dust to dust.' Well, for you, or for any of our kind, 'dust to dust' is pretty close to literal. For us, 'death' means losin' our individuality, our separate personality, and getting reabsorbed into what spawned us. And what *did* spawn us? It wasn't only the miasma field.

"You ever give much thought to why all the members of the Miasma Club are so different from each other? Why Balor's like Balor, and Glenn's like Glenn, and you're different from both of them? If you're all pullin' on the same pool of miasmatic energy, why don't you all work the same? Why are some of you tricksters, and others possessors of the Evil Eye? See, each group of human beings that've settled here has brought its own culture, its own beliefs and superstitions. With each new group that moved on in, the Mother pulled certain notions from their subconscious minds, reacted to whatever superstitions and fears they brought with them. Those superstitions and fears provided the new ingredients, the *focus* for what the miasma field gave birth to."

Owl, this is all very interesting, she thought, *but what does it have to do with me* DYING?

"Let's use Balor as an example," the message continued. "He never would've come into being if a critical mass of Irishmen hadn't immigrated here during the early 1800s, and if they hadn't had

172

some common folklore about a big oaf named Balor with a single, giant eye and a nasty little leprechaun named Faebar who lived in the eye's tear ducts. Then, once he was on the scene and doing his bad luck business, he gave validity to those superstitions, kept them alive from generation to generation. And the people's continuing belief, even if only barely acknowledged, helped the portion of miasmatic energy that had become Balor maintain its focus, helped it *stay* Balor. Think of it as a big feedback loop that's managed to keep itself going for a couple hundred years.

"And how do you break a feedback loop? You shut down one of the inputs. The miasmatic energy field's not goin' away. And what's the *other* input? Think about it. Maybe you shouldn't be so quick to wish for your own death, babe. 'Cause the only way it's gonna happen is for your whole belief cohort — the Jews of New Orleans — to either die or get the hell out of town, then stay out. Maybe not *all* of them; maybe just the bulk of them. And what's most likely to make that exodus happen?"

Kay didn't wait for Owl to answer his own question. "A hurricane even worse than Camille," she said, her face sinking into her hands. "You're saying the only way to save Amos... is for New Orleans to die first."

Chapter 18

"**D**AMNIT, people just don't *listen!*"

"Nothing new under the sun, Bruno," Bob Marino said to his friend. They stood on the Superdome's outer observation deck, overlooking Poydras Street and the Dome's giant pedestrian ramp. The density of the crowd below them approached the pandemonium which would follow a victorious Saints playoff game. Traffic lights all along Poydras Street swayed like tipsy Cajun dancers. Sudden wind gusts, mere shadows of those to come, sent empty soda bottles and beer cans and real estate guides (*Free—Take One*) cartwheeling down the six-lane-wide avenue, now eerily empty of traffic.

Bruno stared at the sky. High, broken cloud formations whizzed past with surreal speed. *They look like flights of bombers*, Bruno thought, *over Vietnam*. Feeling his blood pressure beginning to spike again, he looked down once more at the sea of people that stretched five blocks. So far as he could tell, fewer than one person in fifteen pulled a cooler behind them or carried bags loaded with supplies. "I told them, I told them, I *told* them to bring their own food and bedding," he said. "It's been all over the TV and radio — bring enough food for three days. Bring your own toilet paper. Bring blankets and pillows. But then these people walk up to the security checkpoints with nothing more than a bag of Doritos and a beer, goddamn it."

He yanked his cell phone from its holster. "Might as well get some use out of this thing before all the cell towers get blown down." He punched in a number, then angrily punched it a second time. "Crap, this piece of shit is already worthless!"

"Here," Bob said, holding out his hand. "Let me try."

"You a miracle worker?"

"Lately? Yeah, in fact. What number do you need?"

Bruno gave him Venus Roman's number at the city's Emergency Command Center, located in the City Hall basement. Bob keyed in the number and waited for a ring. "Got it. Here."

"Thanks," Bruno said, eyeing his companion with a touch of awe. He placed the phone against his ear. "Venus?"

"Boss?"

"Look, I need you to get a hold of Tom Robbinson at Food for Families. The guy never evacuates. Knowing him, he's over at that big commodities warehouse by the lake, battening down the hatches. Tell him we need every case of ready-to-eat food he's got — breakfast cereal, canned tuna, canned fruits and vegetables, juice, evaporated milk, the works. Oh, and have him bring some baby formula, too. Enough for five hundred babies for three days. If Tom can't round up his own drivers, get Sheriff Hagaman to send three of his deputies out to Tom's warehouse. And make sure he sends deputies who can drive a manual transmission, okay? You got all that, Venus?"

"Sure thing, boss. I'll get right on it."

Bruno re-holstered his phone. "They might not like the menu," he said, looking down at the long line of mostly black faces, "but at least they won't starve while they're here. Thanks for whatever magic you worked with my phone."

"I'm at your disposal. I might not be the Director of FEBO anymore, but I know my way around a disaster."

* * * * *

It's all coming true, Lily Weintraub thought with a shudder. Kay Rosenblatt's nightmare prediction. The storm. The mass confusion. All of it.

As she directed traffic in the middle of the chaotic ICU, she realized that part of her welcomed this chaos — needed it, even. Ever since that life-changing confrontation with Kay, she'd been struggling to lose herself in her work, to distract herself with medication schedules, staff rotations, performance reviews — *anything* that would allow her to escape the realization that her family had been playthings of an *ayin hora* since long before Lily's birth.

"Debbie," she said, "transfer Mrs. Johnson and Ms. Durand to Room 525, away from the exposed windows. Lauren, move Mr. Fourchard next to Mr. Hilliam in Room 529. And see if you can manage to squeeze Mr. Nayland in there with them — Debbie! Be careful with those I.V. lines! Stop acting like a first year nursing student!"

The young blonde nurse halted her patient's wheeled bed and untangled the lines, looking like a scolded puppy. "I — I'm *sorry*, Ms. Weintraub. I'll be more careful."

Lily silently cursed herself. Snapping at a junior staff member like that, especially in front of patients, was *so* unprofessional. This wasn't even Debbie's normal shift — the young nurse had volunteered to pitch in during the emergency. "Very good, Debbie," she said, forcing herself to calm down. "You're doing a fine job. Carry on."

Sheila Zuppardo, her Assistant Director of Nursing, grabbed her arm. "Lily, you got a minute?"

"No, but I'll make one for you."

"I just heard we've got a bad situation in Hematology. Can you come down with me?"

Sheila led her into the blood storage room. Lily's heart sank when she saw a trio of repairmen working on the largest of the hospital's three walk-in blood coolers. The cooler's door stood wide open — and she didn't feel any cold air escaping.

Brian Grambling, Supervisory Blood Technician, emerged from the now room-temperature cooler an enraged bull. "How could you let this happen?" he snapped at Gerard Wolfe, the Assistant Safety Director.

"There was a two-day supply of plasma and blood products sitting in that cooler. Now it's goddamn hazardous *waste*. What happened to the alarm that was supposed to raise holy hell in your office and mine whenever the temperature in any of these coolers deviates by more than five degrees?"

Gerard backed into a table, his fleshy cheeks trembling. "I — I don't know what happened to the alarm. That's a Maintenance problem. Take it up with *them*."

Joe Smitty, the senior man present from Maintenance, stopped disassembling the cooler's temperature gauge. "Oh, *no*. No, *sir*. I am *not* takin' the rap on this one. It's Safety's job to inspect all the alarm systems in this building. When they find problems, *then* they call in Maintenance."

Brian turned back to Gerard. "When was the last time this alarm system was inspected and tested?"

Gerard turned a pastier shade of white. "You expect me to just *know* that? All those records are back in my office. On my computer. And, and the I.T. guy's been trying to restore my hard drive—"

"Hey, fellas," said the technician lying beneath the inoperative cooler as he crawled out. "The folks who need a fire lit under their asses are the dopes in Pest Control. Two wires down here have been gnawed clear through. One's the wire from the motor to the condenser; that's what killed the cooler. The other's the wire that connects this unit's alarm to the juice in the wall. Either we got us a rat with a degree in electrical engineering, or a pretty smart gremlin."

Gremlin... The word made Lily shiver. "Brian," she asked, "what's our remaining blood supply?"

He looked grim. "At normal rates of use, I'd say a day and a half to maybe two days. With the kinds of trauma cases the storm might dump on our door step...?"

"Can we replenish from the Blood Center?"

He shook his head. "They're cleaned out. Every hospital in the area topped off as soon as the mayor issued the evacuation order. And it's a safe bet that nobody's going to be donating blood until Antonia's gone."

Lily turned to Sheila. Hearing the word *gremlin* had plunged her into mental vertigo, but now, of all times, she needed to be thinking straight. "Sheila, make sure the doctors in Surgery have postponed all non-emergency procedures until after the storm passes. We'll need to conserve our blood supply for the burn and dialysis patients and other chronics. I want every nurse who hasn't given blood in the last month to report to Hematology. Set up a mandatory donation schedule. And spread the word to other departments that we need every drop of blood their employees can spare."

"I'll get right on it," Sheila said.

Lily turned to Gerard before he could slink out of the room. She had her own bone to pick with the pudgy Safety Director. "Mr. Wolfe, why are my chief nurses working a disaster protocol that's *nine years old?* This whole hospital's been reconfigured since that plan was written. Weren't we supposed to have a new protocol in place months ago?"

Gerard's lips trembled like slabs of liver being fried in oil. "It — it's in place. You didn't get a copy?"

"No."

"Well, let me get back to my office and I'll email you a copy — oh, *damn*, I forgot. My computer's busted."

He wasn't a very effective liar. Lily felt a swell of anger bordering on fury. "It's not posted on the network?"

"The — the network? Nuh, no, it's not on the network. My boss, he wouldn't let me post it. Confidentiality issues, he said." He squeezed past her. "I'm sorry. I really gotta hit the men's room."

"Put your hands on a hard copy," she called after him, "because I want to see one sitting on my desk by the time I'm done giving blood, a half-hour from now. Do you hear me, Mr. Wolfe?"

He disappeared into the men's room without a word.

Gremlins. Ayin horas. The Evil Eye.

She tried not to think it. But she couldn't block the memory of her little girlfriend Hilda — no, *Kay* — transforming, her face changing to that of Lily's dead Aunt Rachel.

If those things could do *that*... how could she trust that anyone around her was actually who they seemed to be? Was Gerard Wolfe one of them?

She wanted to run. She wanted to keep running until she was out of this city, out of this state.

Instead, she took the only appropriate action she could.

She went to donate a pint of blood.

* * * * *

Roy Rio stared out the windows of his office at the gray clouds sprinting across the gray sky. He knew he needed to get downstairs, to the emergency command and control center in the basement. That's where his core staffers waited for him, in the safest place in City Hall — the building's 1950s-era fallout shelter.

But there weren't any windows in the basement. And the clouds had hypnotized him.

Turn away, he thought. If he stared hard enough, *believed* hard enough, he could nudge the storm aside. He could make it go away, give his city another year to get its house in order.

Turn away. Turn east. East.

Ridiculous. Useless. Childish. And maybe un-Christian, to wish disaster on someone else.

179

Nicole would be safe, at least. She and her mother should be well on their way to Birmingham by now. He'd ordered all non-essential City Hall employees to evacuate or seek shelter in the Superdome. His core staff, the men and women he couldn't spare, had moved to the emergency command and control center.

And Lily...?

He batted aside the temptation to call her at Baptist Hospital. *It must be a madhouse over there*, he thought.

When the hell was the governor going to declare the disaster? The last twelve hours had been an infuriating game of *Which comes first, the chicken or the egg?* He'd called FEBO's Region VI Director in Dallas. He'd asked when he could expect them to get food and water and emergency vehicles pre-positioned ahead of Antonia's landfall...

"With all due respect, Mr. Mayor, FEBO is not a first-response organization. Our acronym stands for Federal Emergency *Backstop* Organization. Your first responders are your own police, fire fighters, and paramedics, plus State law enforcement agencies. Really, legally we're powerless to take any steps to assist you until after your governor officially declares a disaster."

So then Roy had called Governor Bouvine's Chief of Staff...

"Mr. Mayor, I understand where you're coming from, I really do. If I were in your shoes, I'd want FEBO to get their people down there ASAP, too. But you've got to understand, there are serious, *serious* ramifications stemming from the Governor's decision to officially declare a disaster. Legally, it opens the door for the feds to get way deep into our britches. The President can legally request federalization of the Louisiana National Guard. Conceivably, our Louisiana boys in uniform could get sent to *Mississippi*, for God's sake, and the Governor couldn't say *boo* about it.

"Tell you what: when Antonia's peeling away roofs in Plaquemines and St. Bernard Parish, and Grand Isle's getting sucked into the Gulf of

Mexico, *then* Governor Bouvine will declare a disaster. But so long as there's still a chance we're gonna duck this one...? No declaration, no sir."

Then Roy had called FEBO headquarters in Washington and spoken to the Undersecretary for Disaster Response...

"No disaster declaration, Mr. Mayor? Then there's no disaster. And if there's no disaster, then, I'm sorry to say, there's nothing for me to respond to."

Three hours ago, the National Hurricane Center in Miami had upgraded Antonia to a Category Four storm. Even if, by some miracle, Antonia were to make a last-minute hook away from Southeast Louisiana, Category Four storm surge was already muscling its way toward the fragile Louisiana coast. Unstoppable, irreversible, pushing a wall of seawater two stories tall.

And still the Governor held off on declaring.

"So it's just us," Mayor Roy Rio said to himself, staring at the clouds. "Me, my cops, my firemen, a few Levee Board Police..."

It wouldn't be enough. It wasn't enough even during non-disaster times. Bruno had been right in everything he'd said. The storm hadn't even hit land yet, and already Roy had failed.

"Mr. Mayor, it's time to go downstairs."

Roy hadn't heard Walter come in. "Everybody's down in the bunker," Walter continued. "The National Hurricane Center's about to make their final prediction of path and landfall. Then you'll need to deliver a statement to the news people."

"Wait," Roy said. "Let me make one more call."

He'd go straight to the top. William "Duckie" Duckswitt. He stared down at the private number Bob Marino had given him just a few hours ago — Duckie's direct line. Surely the FEBO Director would realize this wasn't the time for picayune bureaucratic nitpicking. His reputation was on the line, too. Even if Duckswitt's people and supplies weren't legally supposed to be in South Louisiana before Governor Bouvine declared a disaster, surely he could at least get them on the road.

He dialed the number, and prayed.

His heart jumped when his call was answered on the third ring.

"Hello—?"

"You've reached the office of William Duckswitt, Director of FEBO. Director Duckswitt is currently on an inspection tour of FEBO facilities in Hawaii. However, your call is important to us. Press 1 to leave a call-back number. Press 2 to leave a message. Press 3 to listen to a brief biographical sketch of Director Duckswitt. Press 4 for a directory of other FEBO Headquarters phone numbers. Press 5 to be redirected to Director Duckswitt's mobile phone..."

Roy pressed 5 and was greeted with five seconds of static. He began breathing again when he heard the mobile phone ringing.

"Hello. You've reached the mobile phone of William Duckswitt, Director of FEBO. Your call is very important to us. —beep— This mailbox is currently full. —beep— Please call back at another time.

"—beep—CLICK"

Chapter 19

MAYBE *I haven't had any luck destroying myself. But Antonia is a billion times stronger than me. Please, God, let the storm accomplish what I couldn't. Let Owl be wrong for once. Let me die. Let Amos live.*

Brackish water from Lake Pontchartrain stung Kay's eyes. Droplets hit her face and torso like bullets, raising instant welts. Her legs from the knees down vanished into swirling, frothing water that had risen to cover the entire length of Lakeshore Drive. The picnic pavilion she had chained herself to now was an island in the midst of an expanded Lake Pontchartrain. Foam-topped breakers, skirting the top of the submerged concrete seawall, smashed into her pelvis.

She welcomed them.

The chain she had wound around herself and the pavilion's support post squeezed her lower ribs. She could sense her aura struggling against her. But it was weak, weaker than she could remember it ever having been. She felt it growing punier with each passing second, thrashing around inside her head, furious at its helplessness. The evacuation must've shrunk the region's population of Jews to a tiny fraction of its former size.

Although the hammering winds made any expression other than a grimace nearly impossible, she managed a smile. For if her aura was dying, could Kay's death be far behind? And if she and her aura died before Amos was killed, her aura's curse would surely be nullified.

She glanced behind her at the tall, grass-covered levee that separated Lakeshore Drive from the more inland parts of the Lakeview and Lake Vista neighborhoods. Already, angry waves lapped against its base. Would her death prove sufficient to break the summoning circle, and would breaking the circle blunt the storm's intensity?

All she could do was pray — and make fleeing impossible for herself once she inevitably panicked, when the water rose up to her mouth. She tossed the chain's padlock's key as hard as she could toward the lake. A gust caught it and spun it high into the distended air. Then the buoying gust abandoned it, and the key plunged into the froth.

A dark finger descended toward the lake from a black cloud about a mile offshore. The finger gyrated and circled, as though uncertain which skimming wave to point at. Then its direction steadied. It pointed straight down, tethered by an invisible anchor. As Kay watched, entranced, a second finger, the first's twin, rose from the surface of Lake Pontchartrain. It stretched upward, elongating in trembling desire to touch its twin.

The two fingertips, thinned to wispiness by mutual attraction, met and melded. The funnel cloud's wasp waist immediately thickened with a massive transfusion of lake water. Dancing now across the foamy waves, it began moving toward shore. Towards Kay.

The funnel cloud blotted out everything else on the horizon. The cacophony deafened her. Her soaked clothes clung to her skin, but the oncoming vacuum sought to peel them off her. She watched layers of sand and gravel and even fish get sucked into the maelstrom. The flotsam ascended into the angry heavens on a turbine-powered spiral staircase. *I'll be flotsam soon; I'll get sucked into a thunderhead and blown to pieces by lightning, God willing.*

As her aura shriveled, the human part of her, that part patterned on lowly animal foundations, asserted its primacy. This part screamed in terror now, screamed as suction distended her lips, pulled on her teeth, and threatened to yank out her tonsils.

The pavilion began shaking. Chunks of the roof burst from the rafters and soared into the black air. She looked up — nothing separated her now from the funnel cloud but hundreds of feet of ravenous vacuum.

I can't breathe

I can't BREATHE—

Her post oscillated with increasing force. She slid up it as it shook itself loose from its slab. Gravity had been thrown violently into reverse. Like a cork popping from the neck of a wine bottle, Kay and the shattered remains of the pavilion achieved dizzying flight.

I'm a dust speck

a dust speck in a whirlwind

An invisible escalator shot her and her associated debris on a corkscrew path hundreds of feet into the air. She found herself blessedly able to breathe again. The prior absence of air had been replaced by a superabundance of air — chunky air, clogged with water vapor, dirt, nails, tree branches, and roof tiles. All these things moved at approximately Kay's velocity, so they floated around her in a semi-solid gel.

She twisted her body so she could look down. Miles to the southeast, the towers of the Central Business District looked like twigs protruding from the ground. The tornado headed due west along the shoreline. It clung to the lakeward base of the levee, seemingly reluctant to jump the fifteen-foot high mound. A few dozen yards from the levee's inland face, a stately row of luxury villas trembled in the suddenly negative air pressure, but escaped devastation.

The twister morphed back into a towering, twitchy water spout when it hit the Orleans Avenue Outfall Canal. Kay choked as she was forced to expel lungfuls of brackish water. The funnel cloud's course immediately shifted to follow the path of the canal. It moved rapidly inland, briefly pausing to suck guard rails and asphalt from the Lakeshore Drive bridge. Then it whizzed southward along the water's surface, bouncing like a billiard ball off the canal's parallel concrete flood walls.

The sturdy Robert E. Lee Avenue bridge gave the twister a foothold back onto land. Freed from constraints, it zig-zagged indiscriminately through Lakeview, a gigantic Weed Wacker which devoured bus shelters, traffic lights, backyard play equipment, and a corner convenience store. It paused for a full three seconds over a large house, methodically picking away the roof before suctioning out the home's contents. Kay watched a bathtub and an intact toilet circle in mid-air fifty feet below her. A little girl's collection of horse figurines and a large pink stuffed bunny floated, tumbling past, close enough for her to grasp.

And then she spotted the blonde brick walls of Congregation Beth Judah, less than two blocks from the cyclone's careening base.

Something kicked her from the inside. Her *aura?* It had been quiescent ever since the funnel cloud had formed out in the lake; she thought it had died. But it had been lying quiet only to gather its strength. It kicked her again, so sharply she gasped. It had never been so *localized* before — it felt like a gut-borne parasite the size of a grapefruit.

The tornado lurched toward the synagogue. Deep within what she realized must be her uterus, she sensed fingers grasping the charged wires of her fear, drawing strength. She felt her aura-thing reach out to the cyclone. It communicated somehow with the twister, modulated its own fury to match the frequency of the tornado's elemental destructiveness.

Through her aura-thing, she felt the cyclone lock onto a path which would slice the synagogue in half.

The mingled contents of the demolished house and convenience store floated all around her. She grabbed a broken broom handle. Holding it like a sword, she jabbed herself between her belly button and pubic bone. The aura-thing recoiled. She thrust the handle into her soft midsection again, harder this time. She sensed it scurry away from the blow, but it was trapped within a narrow bag of flesh.

Now *it* was afraid. She jabbed herself again and again and again, until blood entered her mouth.

The cyclone seemed to hiccup, then stumble. It resumed a random, haphazard path. Its edge scoured the synagogue's small parking lot, sucking up small trees and the synagogue's sign. It tore to pieces a pair of trailers which housed the congregation's preschool. But it left the main sanctuary, with its ark and Torah scrolls and memorial plaques and eternal lamp, nearly untouched. Best as she could tell, only one piece of debris had fallen on the sanctuary's dome.

I can die happy now, she thought.

The tornado's forward momentum weakened considerably when it reached the West End Boulevard neutral ground, a grassy swath more than a city block wide. She remembered when this neutral ground had been the New Basin Canal, a shipping channel from Lake Pontchartrain to the edge of the French Quarter. The bones of the old navigation channel lay between two much younger drainage canals, both fortified against storm surge by the Army Corps of Engineers — the Orleans Avenue Outfall Canal to the east, and the Seventeenth Street Outfall Canal to the west. She could see both of these clearly, two long, skinny fingers of Lake Pontchartrain, engorged now with storm surge. Their concrete flood walls gave her no sense of security; they had been built under Lieutenant Colonel Schwartz's supervision.

Her revolutions slowed. The tornado lurched and stumbled. The thunderhead which had been feeding the whirlwind its kinetic energy broke up, its black boiling mass dissipating into puffs of gray cloud.

Then all at once, she felt herself falling. The ground reached up to bludgeon her.

The sky punished her, too. It rained down wood and it rained down earth. It rained down loaves of bread and it rained down copper wire. It rained down a stuffed bunny and a dozen tiny toy horses.

It rained and it rained and it rained.

* * * * *

"Hurricane Antonia, downgraded to a strong Category Three storm, has just made landfall in Waveland, Mississippi—"

Roy Rio's staff cheered the news from the emergency band radio. Just five hours ago, the storm had hooked sharply to the east, thrown off its original track by a high pressure system which had surprised all the forecasters by muscling its way down from the Midwest. Its final landfall occurred about forty miles to the east of downtown New Orleans.

The cheering made Roy feel both exultant and shamefaced-guilty.

"Glory be to God!" Walter proclaimed.

In all their years of friendship, Roy had never known Walt to be religious. But a salvation of this magnitude could make even a hardened atheist fall to his knees and praise the Lord. *Still*, he thought, *I doubt the folks in Waveland, Pass Christian, and Gulfport are praising God much for His saving mercy right now.*

His male staffers engulfed him in a round of bear hugs and his female staffers showered him with kisses. Survivor's guilt aside, it felt good. It felt damned *good*.

The only staffer who failed to congratulate him was Bruno Galliano. Bruno sat quietly in a corner of the emergency management bunker with his marooned friend, Bob Marino; they both listened intently to the rest of the National Weather Service's update. Roy walked over to them. "So we dodged the bullet," he said.

Bruno looked up, not smiling. "I don't think we dodged it, Mr. Mayor, so much as the shooter got a little wobbly with his aim at the last minute. Probably won't be so lucky, next time."

"Bob," Roy said, "can't you get this guy to lighten up a little?" He clapped Bruno on the shoulder. "How about we save the worries for later. Take some time to be *relieved*, man. Celebrate a little!"

Bruno shook his head. "I'll celebrate when I know in my bones that you've taken all this as a lesson. I'll put on my party hat the day I see you and Walter and your budget team stand up in front of the City Council and *insist* that they reprogram the funds needed for a realistic hurricane response plan. Until then, I'm gonna have to figure it's back to business as usual, focusing on the crisis *du jour*."

Roy felt blood rush to his face. But before he could respond in anger, Bob stepped in. "Bruno, give the man a break," Bob said. "He's not a Ducky Duckswitt; he's doing the best he can in a tough situation. Look, after you're done cleaning up from Antonia, I'm going to devote a few weeks of my retirement to helping you ferret out federal grants. God willing, my weird good luck will rub off on your applications. Then you'll be drowning in money."

"That's extremely public-minded of you," Roy said. "Meanwhile, how about we do a quick damage assessment outside? I need some fresh air. Grab yourselves some rain slickers and come upstairs with me."

A moment later, the three men climbed the steep set of stairs to the City Hall lobby. The lobby's tall glass doors, armored with plywood, admitted only isolated shafts of gray light. Quiet and empty, the foyer felt like a cave. Roy unlocked a service entry door. He had to push with all his weight to get it to swing outward against the pressure of the wind. The resisting gust died suddenly, and he stumbled through the doorway.

Broken fir trees lay like victims of a drive-by shooting across the building's broad front steps. On the far side of Perdido Street, Duncan Plaza's open-air concert pavilion was more open-air than it had been designed to be; its West African-style roof now sat like a thatched sun hat atop one of the plaza's artificial hills.

Roy pulled his slicker's hood over his head. He walked quickly toward the intersection of Loyola Avenue and Poydras Street, where he could see how downtown's high-rise office buildings and hotels had fared. He felt excited — giddy, almost — like a boy heading out on his cub scout troop's inaugural wilderness excursion.

"Don't go too far, Mr. Mayor," Bruno called after him. "Bob and I heard that downtown's crawling with armed looters."

Roy waved him off. "Don't worry, Bruno. I'm a big boy."

A jumble of toppled traffic lights and broken electrical cables obscured the intersection. He stared up at the towering glass walls of the Entergy headquarters and the Hyatt Hotel. The Hyatt had fared the worst; the storm had smashed about a third of its guest room windows. Yet just fifty yards from the hotel's entrance, in the middle of the Poydras neutral ground, the bronze statues of the Cancer Survivors' Sculpture Park, portrayals of New Orleanians young and old, stood undisturbed.

Survivors, Roy thought. *We're all survivors.*

Yes, he was a survivor, too. By the grace of God, he'd been given time — time to recognize his mistakes, time to rectify gaps, time to gather the resources this vulnerable city needed.

There's still time for MuckGen to work their economic magic and fill the city's coffers. Annalee hasn't heard a peep from Cynthia these past few weeks, not since I pressured Chief Pendergrast to investigate Quincy Cochrane; so that's one fire I've managed to stamp out. We'll be much better prepared for the next storm.

Very soon, he knew, reporters from all over the country would descend upon New Orleans, drawn here by the big story: The Disaster That Failed to Happen. No one but Bruno Galliano and Bob Marino need know how close this city had come to the edge.

* * * * *

Kay listened to her bones at work, strained to hear the whispers of mangled cartilage struggling to recapture its original form.

Scritch, scratch. Scritch, scratch. Tap, tap, tap. Pieces of her right cheekbone floated like broken wreckage in the chaotic sea of blood beneath the bruised skin of her face. The subtle vibrations of her cheekbone's reknitting vibrated through the undamaged portions of her skull.

She'd never felt pain like this before. *Never.*

Her healing had never proceeded this slowly before, either. Was this what dying felt like? An accelerating surrender of the body's involuntary functions to entropy and decay?

She tried to move. Excruciating jolts from her left knee and right thigh told her those bones must be broken. Weight bore down on her shoulders and back. She could turn her head just enough to see that a smashed chest of drawers had landed atop her upper torso. She lay face down on a mound of tornado-heaped debris; her shattered cheek rested uncomfortably against the wreckage of a ping-pong table.

Something throbbed against her pelvic bone. Her lower belly felt distended, its sheath of skin stretched almost to the point of splitting. The throbbing — this wasn't the aura kicking her insides. The insistent convulsions she sensed in her lower belly weren't defined or purposeful enough to be kicking; they felt more like tremors, or spasms.

Her eyes flickered in sync with the spasms within her womb. She felt herself drifting down, down, deep into the womb of the waterlogged earth beneath her. She sensed pressure, pressure of water against soil, the probing of surging tide against weakening, slowly yielding canal bottoms. The probing was invasive, insidious, insistent; she sensed the drilling rivulets hit metal sheet piling, then skirt the piling, racing down, down to hidden layers of loosely packed sand and gravel, where they resumed their tunneling.

She had seen the Corps' engineering drawings of the Seventeenth Street Outfall Canal's floodwalls, triumphs of thrift and expediency over safety and redundancy. Her extended consciousness knew precisely when the undermined barrier would suffer catastrophic failure.

She was jolted back into her broken body by a series of what sounded like explosions from the direction of the Seventeenth Street Outfall Canal.

Her eyelids fluttering involuntarily, she watched the clouds flee to the east. She sensed the skin of her belly stretch and press against a jagged mat of splinters.

At some point, she didn't know when, Kay felt water lapping at her bruised and cut feet. Steadily rising water.

Chapter 20

"DAD, Dad! Put that *down!*"

Daniel Weintraub grabbed the recliner out of Amos's arms. His father, his incredible, irascible father, was attempting to drag a sixty-pound recliner up the stairs.

Amos gasped for breath. "It — it was your mother's! Her *favorite* chair! She would never forgive me — *not ever* — if I let her chair drown!"

Daniel realized that nothing he could say would force Amos to relent. "All right," he said, "*I'll* take Mom's chair upstairs. You — you go get those photo albums I left on the kitchen table. Take them up to your bedroom. A *few* at a *time*, okay?"

Amos nodded. He looked stunned at his son's sudden assertiveness. Then he meekly turned and sloshed through the invading water toward the kitchen.

Daniel balanced the chair's weight on his shoulder. What had he just done? He blinked rapidly. He'd just given his father a set of orders. And his father had *followed* them. That had never happened before.

Then again, the Weintraub house had never had a foot of water in it before, either.

He'd just set the recliner down on the second story landing when he heard his father shouting. "Daniel! Daniel, my God! I haven't been *thinking!* We must go to the synagogue, *immediately!*"

He ran down the stairs. "What, Dad? What is it?"

Amos grabbed his arm. "Daniel, we must take your boat and go!"

"But we've still got so much to do here—"

Amos pulled him toward the door. "Forget our things! They do not matter! The scrolls! The *Torah* scrolls — *those* are what matter! If this water rises to the ark — we must rescue them, Daniel!"

He felt a shiver of dread. Each of the scrolls weighed fifty or sixty pounds. And Beth Judah's holy ark held five of them. But preserving them from harm was almost as important as preserving human life.

"I'll go get them, Dad," he said. "You stay upstairs."

"No! I will come with you!"

"But — but you'll take up room in the boat. Then we might have to make two trips—"

"I will brook no argument on this! I *will* come with you!"

Daniel went to retrieve the boat from the shed. When he pulled the back door open, a fresh surge of water pushed into the kitchen. He waded out onto his porch. He couldn't see the grass in his yard. The aluminum utility shed which housed the boat had partially tipped over. He crawled through the narrow space between the sodden ground and the shed's uprooted wall. The doors, badly bent but still chained shut, were useless; the only way to get the boat out would be through the same space he'd just crawled through. He grabbed the wall's lower edge, then lifted. The storm had done the heavy work for him, breaking most of the securing bolts. The shed flopped over like a large, soggy cardboard box. Sliding the boat out was easy — it was already afloat.

He tilted the boat's fifteen horsepower outboard motor out of the water so that its blades wouldn't scrape, then towed the vessel to the back door. His father couldn't swim. He realized he'd feel much more secure having Amos in the boat with him, even if they ended up having to make two trips.

"Dad! Come out this way!"

He helped the old man into the boat, surprised at how tightly Amos clutched his arm. Suddenly, his father, who had always been a titan of unbreakable granite in Daniel's imagination, seemed desperately frail.

At the now invisible border between sidewalk and street, the water climbed to the midpoint of Daniel's thighs. The current pushed him and the boat towards Canal Boulevard and the synagogue. He glanced back at his father. Bad times had always brought out Amos's best side, a stoic, grimly humorous heroism which dated to his days as an artilleryman in the Polish Army. He caught his father's eye, hoping for a quip about Noah and the ark, perhaps a wink to reassure Daniel that all would be well. But Amos, ashen-faced, stared right through him with the stunned incomprehension of a wounded bird.

The water grew deeper. Now it reached his waist. The synagogue was two blocks south. His progress slowed. He thought about climbing into the boat himself and starting up the motor. But he wasn't sure how much fuel it had left; they would need that fuel later, if the water reached their house's second story.

He gasped when he saw Beth Judah. The synagogue had always been a brick and wood extension of his father — inviolable, holy, a fortress-like refuge from the corrupting influences of the outside world. Yet the white dome over the main sanctuary was now marred with cracks. The upper portion of a refrigerator poked out of a jagged hole, as though the dome were a huge egg that had hatched a Frigidaire.

How could God have let this happen? he asked himself. He quickly reminded himself that both the First and Second Temples in Jerusalem had been destroyed, and rabbis still argued over the meaning of those ancient catastrophes. Compared to the rabbis, who was he to dare pose such a question?

He pulled his boat and his father across what had once been a pristine courtyard. Now its white stones, imported from the Holy Land, were obscured by murky, oily water and floating street trash. Water had pushed the synagogue's massive oak front doors open. He waded through one of the doors. The gray outside light penetrated only a few yards into the foyer. He thanked God that he could navigate every room of this building blindfolded, if necessary.

He tried pulling the boat through the doorway. It wouldn't go. Just an inch less beam, and he could've forced it through.

"Dad, I'm gonna have to leave you here. I'll come back with the Torahs one at a time."

Amos climbed unsteadily out of the boat. "I — I will help you."

The force of his father's stubbornness felt like a punch to the gut. "Dad, stay here. Let me do it. *Please.* You could trip—"

Amos twisted out of Daniel's grasp. "Unhand me! I did not come with you merely to sit in the boat and do nothing. I have been lifting these very Torahs since before you or your sister were born. Above my head, I have lifted them! So do not treat me like an invalid! Never forget, for all your life, *I* have taken care of *you!*"

Daniel squeezed his eyes tightly shut. There had been few times in his life when he'd been tempted to scream at his father. He counted backwards from ten to zero, a trick Lily had taught him. "At least... hold my hand. Okay?"

Amos did not protest. Together, they waded into the murky darkness. A clinging blanket of claustrophobia fell upon Daniel. In the short moment they'd wasted arguing, the water had risen several inches. Would it rise to the sanctuary's ceiling, trapping them?

At the far end of the hallway, just below the mounted rows of memorial *Yizkor* plaques, splotches of color swam in the darkness like luminescent jellyfish. Ever since he'd been a boy, Daniel had felt uneasy around those plaques, with their tiny bulbs which were lit on the anniversary of the named person's death; an older boy had told him that ghosts were trapped inside the bulbs, and when the bulbs were lit, they could see you and would try to steal your soul. Amos had told Daniel this was an evil lie. Yet now he couldn't help but wonder if the storm had shattered the bulbs, freeing ghosts which had been trapped for decades.

He approached cautiously, keeping himself between his father and the shifting lights. When he'd waded within ten feet of them, he could see what they were. The water had pushed open the doors to the main sanctuary. Weak sunlight shone through the sanctuary's stained glass windows. The light projected the windows' colors onto the chest-deep water in the hall, and his wading had created waves which caused the reflected splotches of color to shimmer and undulate.

He peered into the sanctuary. The backs of the pews closest to the entrance were still visible above the water, but those closer to the raised *bema* and ark were completely submerged. The sanctuary was built theater-style, with the pews closer to the *bema* lower than those farther back. Judging from where the water lapped against the bases of the *bema*'s twin lecterns, he estimated the water had risen to six inches above the *bema*'s floor. Which meant that at the bottom of the sanctuary's slope, the water already stood almost six feet deep. And it continued to rise.

Why couldn't his boat have been just a smidgeon smaller?

He headed down the slope. His father followed; Daniel sensed the older man's trembling through the tight grip Amos maintained on his wrist. "Dad, stay here. That water down there comes up to your chin, maybe even higher."

"But — but you're not any taller than I am—"

"Yeah, but I can swim."

Amos obeyed him. Daniel wished he felt as brave as he'd just made himself sound. As he dog paddled the last few feet to the *bema*'s steps, he realized he had no idea how to rescue the Torah scrolls. He couldn't swim with them. Even if he could, immersing the scrolls would ruin them.

He crawled up the submerged stairs. Their inundated carpet felt like decomposing algae at the bottom of a pond. At the top of the *bema*, the water reached nearly to his knees. Once it rose another foot, it would be lapping at the bottom of the ark, the gilded enclosure which held the five Torah scrolls.

He stared up at the ark. Its top reached nearly to the ceiling of the sanctuary's dome, culminating in a tree-like spire which symbolized the Tree of Life. He'd been privileged to open the ark's doors on only a few occasions, the first being his *bar mitzvah*. Always before, he'd worn his finest clothes in its presence. He felt ashamed to approach it now in his filthy, disheveled condition.

He reached out to open the doors and determine that the scrolls had remained undamaged. Something wasn't right — his hands met the handles at a strange angle. Either he was tilted, or the ark was. He stared up again at the top of the dome, remembering the hole he'd seen from the outside. The bottom of the falling refrigerator had penetrated all the way through, knocking out a large chunk of wood, plaster, and masonry from the dome's interior. The plunging debris must've smashed into the top of the ark before falling to the floor, tilting it askew.

He took a step closer, then immediately stepped back. The floor boards had sagged beneath his weight. Gingerly, he stepped forward again, probing the invisible floor with his foot. Some of the boards weren't there anymore. Falling debris had punched a hole about four feet square in the *bema*'s raised plywood floor.

He edged around the hole to the ark's doors and opened them. The five Torah scrolls had tumbled into the ark's right corner, worsening the ark's tilt.

What could he do? He grasped the closest scroll and tried pulling it back to its proper resting place. The whole ark moved, groaning with a voice of rending metal and splintering wood. His heart somersaulted in his chest. He backed away.

"Daniel? What is happening up there?"

"I'm — I'm scared the whole ark is going to tip over, Dad."

"Then grab the Torahs as fast as you can! Wait, I will come to help you—"

"Dad, no! You stay there! The water's too deep for you to get through."

"The water is becoming deeper here, too, Daniel! Whatever you intend to do, you must do so *quickly!*"

What *would* he do? Stunned, Daniel realized from his father's words that Amos had no plan at all. It was all up to him.

If he had something waterproof to wrap them in... a big garbage bag might work, but there was a possibility it could leak. Some kind of a little boat would be much better, something he could tow them in. He could probably find garbage bags in the kitchen. What else did the kitchen have that could help him—?

Of *course!* The kitchen also large plastic garbage *cans.* They would float. He could wrap each Torah scroll in a garbage bag for extra safety, then shuttle them in two plastic garbage cans between the *bema* and his boat outside.

"Dad! I've got to go to the kitchen!"

"The *kitchen?* This is no time to *eat,* Daniel—"

"Not for *food* — for garbage cans. We can float the Torahs out to our boat. Isn't that a good idea?"

"Garbage cans for the Torahs? That is very, very disrespectful, Daniel..."

This time, Daniel didn't try to staunch his anger. "*Damn it,* Dad! You put this all on me, and now you want to make it impossible for me to do *anything!* Do you want to drive me *crazy?* We either put those Torahs in garbage cans, or we let them *drown!* Which do you want?"

Disdain vanished from Amos's face, replaced by surprised, bewildered respect. "Go..." His voice had turned thick and raspy. "Go get the garbage cans, my son."

Daniel waded as quickly as he could toward the doors. Amos caught his arm before he could head down the hall. "But do not leave me here!"

"I can't be in two places at once—"

"Do not leave me *here*. The water — it is coming up fast. Too fast. I would be higher up on the *bema*. Take me there, then go. While you are gone, I will place the scrolls on the reading table, which is highest of all."

"But—"

"*Please*, Daniel." Daniel had never seen such fear in his father's eyes.

Hurrying as much as he could, he helped his father wade down the slope. When they reached the place where the water came up to their necks, Daniel sucked in a deep breath and submerged. He grabbed Amos around the waist and lifted him so that his head remained above water, then lunged forward to deposit his father on the *bema*'s steps. He helped him over to the reading table, then leaned him against that relatively high and dry refuge.

"Thuh-thank you, thank you, Daniel."

"The table's good and sturdy. There's a stool right there. You can climb on top if the water gets too high. Don't try moving the Torah scrolls. The ark's too tippy. Are you gonna be okay?"

Amos hugged him tightly and buried his face in his neck. The last time his father had done this had also been in this room, on the day of Daniel's *bar mitzvah*, just after he'd managed to haltingly but successfully chant his assigned portion from the Prophets. "Yes. I — I will be fine. I... I'm so proud of you, my son. I love you, Daniel. I *love* you."

For reasons he failed to understand, Daniel's eyes welled up. "I love you, too, Dad. You're — you're a good daddy. I'll be back as fast as I can."

He swam to the doorway, then waded through the colored reflections on the water's surface in the hallway. He tried running toward the kitchen, but his extreme exertions failed to move him any faster than a determined walk.

After what felt like hours, he reached his destination. Luck shined on him — he saw three large plastic garbage cans bobbing on their sides, partially submerged in a corner. He grabbed the first garbage pail he could reach and emptied it, did the same for a second, then towed the two floating cans to a set of drawers where garbage bags were stored. He tossed a soggy box of plastic liners into one of the pails, then pulled his cargo into the dark hallway.

His father's distant cry reached Daniel's ears when he was alongside the social hall, a three minute slog from the sanctuary.

"Dad! Dad, are you okay?"

No answer.

"*Dad!*"

He hadn't heard a crash. That meant the ark hadn't toppled over. But any relief he might've felt fell victim to his father's ominous silence.

"*DAD!!!*"

He abandoned all logic about the futility of running through chest-deep murk. His mother had died in water. He and Lily had almost died in water. And now...

No. His father had survived the war in Poland, the Holocaust, years as a stateless refugee. Amos Weintraub was a man of stone, a titan who would never — *could* never — die.

By the time he reached the sanctuary, he could hardly breathe. Each heartbeat exploded in his eardrums. "Da... Dad? Are you... are you...?"

Amos wasn't atop the reading table. Neither were any of the Torah scrolls. The ark had tilted even more to the right, but it still stood. Daniel counted only three scrolls on its listing shelf.

He dove into the water. He swam until his forehead smashed into the steps, then dragged himself to the *bema*, lungs aching. His head broke the surface next to the rabbi's lectern.

He couldn't see his father anywhere.

He splashed furiously all across the *bema*'s floor, feeling for an arm or leg. He nearly dove back into the deeper water when he remembered the hole in front of the ark.

The sun had shifted. The colored lights, refracted through the sanctuary's stained glass windows, now swam all around the base of the crippled ark.

He frantically stumbled to the floor's hidden brokenness. *The hole,* he thought. *I warned my father not to go near the ark. But I forgot to tell him about the hole...*

He stared down into the water's depths. Bathed in undulating purple, orange, and yellow light, his father's face stared up at him. One of Amos's arms remained wrapped around a Torah scroll. The other scroll pinned his leg against a slab of broken plywood.

I didn't tell him about the hole...

He followed his father's still-open gaze upward, needing to see the last sight his father had witnessed.

The eternal lamp, hanging from the dome's ceiling in front of the ark. It hung there still. Its light had gone out.

* * * * *

I will greatly multiply thy pain and thy travail; in pain thou shalt bring forth children...

Interior claws had grabbed hold of the two sides of Kay's pelvis. They pulled outward with obscene strength, trying to split her lower body in half. Writhing on her back atop a floating jumble of wooden debris, she stared down at the dome of her distended belly with agonized disbelief.

I'm supposed to be dying — *not giving* BIRTH...

Unless this was *part* of the dying. The pressure between her hips subsided for a few blessed seconds. She couldn't see her legs, but she knew her shattered knee and broken thigh bone had mostly healed. When the rising water had freed her from her cage of broken furniture, blind survival instinct had taken over, and she'd swum to this makeshift raft. But what good were working legs if she were about to expel all of her internal organs through her vagina? What would happen then? Would her empty bag of floating skin be eventually picked apart by the circling gulls? Or would it sink, to be reabsorbed by the sodden and hungry earth?

The pressure began building again. She hitched up the remains of her dress to allow her legs to spread to their widest. She held back a scream, wanting to save that release for when the pain grew even worse. She counted down the twenty seconds she estimated the contraction would take to peak and subside. Yet this one refused to peak — it built and built and *built*. Thirty seconds... *thirty-five*... the pressure ballooned until she thought her beach ball belly would burst.

Push! The word seared her brain like a bolt of lightning. Using muscles she didn't realize she had, Kay obeyed.

PUSH

Now she screamed. Not from pain. From anger — the searing pain fueled an even more intense anger. Anger that she'd been doomed to live her existence as a monster. Fury that she'd been permitted to experience love, then been tricked and maneuvered into poisoning the lives of the very people she'd longed to embrace.

PUSH

She screamed. The scream echoed back from the rows of inundated houses on either side of West End Boulevard. Her water had broken, and it had drowned the whole damned city.

PUSH

She would push it *all* out. All the horror, the self-loathing, the decades of daily defeats inflicted on her by her aura...

My aura — I'm pushing out my aura—

PUSH!

PUUUUUUUUSSH!

The head... it's — it's passing...

The rest slithered out of her in a burning rush. She sucked in lungfuls of air, then struggled to get her elbows beneath her so she could confront whatever it was she'd birthed.

She saw it.

It was a little Kay. A little, dead Kay. Stillborn. Her two foot tall *doppelganger* had the smooth, pink, perfect skin of a newborn. Perfect, angelic, except for its eyes. Its open, dead eyes dominated its face. They were vulture eyes, raptor eyes, with tiny red pupils swimming in irises the hue of corrupted yolk.

Evil eyes.

A wind gust flurried the surface of the water. The floating aura-thing's top layer of skin flaked off. The flakes circled high above Kay like cinders from a dying fire. As she watched, pieces of the thing's face, its nose, its lips, its cheeks, granulated and crumbled, then fluttered free. Only its eyes remained stubbornly intact.

She couldn't bear to see those eyes anymore. She grabbed a floating branch and poked the little body, hoping she could sink it. Instead of sinking, it broke apart. She stabbed it again, more aggressively this time. The limbs and torso crumbled to white ash, like a carbonized log jabbed with a fireplace poker. The ash spread over the water's surface. Yet even as it spread, it retained the shape of a dead Kay. Its red and yellow eyes, still undecayed, stared at her from the middle of an expanding Kay-face.

She beat the spreading face with the branch. She bludgeoned the surface of the water into a foaming froth. She shrieked and flailed until her arms ached, until the horrible eyes had been punctured and drained of vitreous fluid, until they at last vanished into the murk.

All the noise she'd created had blanketed the *putt-putt-putt* of an approaching small boat's motor. Panting and shaking, Kay didn't realize she was no longer alone until she heard a familiar voice call out to her.

"Feeling better now?" Owl Lookingback asked.

Chapter 21

"**W**HERE the *hell* is all this water coming from? The goddamn storm is supposed to be *over!*"

Roy Rio hadn't directed his explicative-laced questions at anybody in particular. He knew that none of his staff, now scurrying to rescue the emergency command bunker's electronic and communications equipment, had any answers. He kicked his way through the half-foot of water that had seeped into the basement bunker, taking out his frustration on this silent, implacable foe.

Did a water main burst? Ninety minutes ago, his entire emergency communications grid had crashed, leaving him effectively deaf and blind. Bruno hadn't managed to get the system properly fixed. Scratch that — *Roy* hadn't given him the funds to get it properly fixed.

He heaved a server onto the top of a wheeled cart, then gestured for an aide to get it upstairs. He didn't want to confront the obvious next question, but he couldn't escape it. *Did a levee break?* Antonia had declined to a Cat Three just before landfall, and it had delivered only a glancing blow to New Orleans. The floodwalls should've held, with capacity to spare.

Yet he couldn't ignore the evidence of his waterlogged shoes and trousers.

Walter, his face ashen, led a police officer to Roy's side. The officer was drenched from the neck down. "Mr. Mayor," Walter said, "this is Officer Barnes. He's got really bad news. *Really* bad news."

"Police Headquarters at Tulane and Broad is surrounded by four feet of water," the dripping officer said, "and it's getting higher by the minute."

"When did you leave headquarters?" Roy asked.

"Over an hour ago... I walked."

"You *walked?*"

The officer grimly smiled. "Our cruisers don't come equipped with snorkels. I'd say we've lost, oh, at least seventy vehicles just in the garages beneath our building."

"Does the Chief know what *happened?*"

"The London Avenue Outfall Canal in Gentilly, that one's busted for sure," the officer said. "The Third District's station isn't too far from there. We had men out checking for anybody who'd rode out the storm, and they heard the flood walls give way. Our two-way radios are still working, at least until their batteries run down. The Chief would've radioed you, but—"

"But down here, we were relying on our high-tech communications grid, not old-fashioned radios. And then the storm turned that grid into four million dollars' worth of scrap. Goddamn... So the Chief had to fall back on the old shoe leather network?"

"Yeah, you right. Though you'd have to call it the shrimping boot network, I guess. That water followed me all the way downtown. I know the land gets higher the closer you get to the river. Still, the Central Business District's basements are gonna be underwater by nightfall."

I'd thought it was over. But it's just beginning. "Has the Chief gotten any reports from Lakeview? New Orleans East? The Ninth Ward?"

"Reports were just starting to trickle in when I left. The Lower Nine... I don't think it's there anymore."

Goddamn.

"All those people in the Dome," Roy said. "I thought... I thought we'd get the streets cleared, and then we'd just send them all home."

"I don't think a lot of those people have homes to go back to anymore, Mr. Mayor."

I'm not ready for this, Roy thought. *I HAVE to be ready. But I'm not...*

The rumble of heavy vehicles outside City Hall rescued him from paralysis. He heard them slosh along Loyola Avenue and turn onto Poydras, heading for the Superdome. "You hear that?"

Officer Barnes nodded. "Big vehicles. Bigger than anything we've got or the Fire Department's got."

"Army?" Roy asked. "National Guard? Let's get up there and see."

The simple act of climbing the stairs began raising his spirits. He took the steps two at a time. If it *was* the Army — they had equipment, they had manpower, they had know-how. Hell, they probably had some giant gizmo developed for the Iraq War that could plug up a broken levee inside of an hour.

He spotted a row of olive-painted trucks paused next to the Civil Court Building. He ran down to Perdido Street, already covered by a foot of water, and sprinted toward the nearest truck. When he got a closer look at his would-be saviors, his brief euphoria deflated. The convoy was disappointingly short — only eight large transport trucks. And the dozens of soldiers who clung to every available handhold looked mud-soaked and bedraggled.

This wasn't the vanguard of a rescue mission. These soldiers were storm refugees themselves.

He banged on the driver's side door of the first truck he reached. "This is Mayor Roy Rio. Who's in charge of this convoy?"

"I'm Private Anne Anderson, Eighty-Sixth Battalion, Louisiana Army National Guard," the driver, a surprisingly petite young blonde woman, yelled. She struggled to make herself heard over the diesel clatter. "We just got our asses chased out of Jackson Barracks by a wall of water. The man you're looking for is Colonel Mike Brunneau, in the lead Humvee."

Roy sprinted toward the Superdome, followed by Officer Barnes. Once they rounded the corner onto Poydras, he saw the convoy's lead vehicles climbing the ramp to the Superdome's upper parking deck. *Are they planning to drive thirty thousand people to high ground? These trucks couldn't carry more than a couple hundred at a time — how are they going to decide who to take first? Won't that set off a stampede?*

They caught up with the lead Humvee on the Superdome's helicopter landing pad. Bruno Galliano and Bob Marino rushed out of one of the Dome's offices and met them at the helipad. A broad-shouldered black man wearing a colonel's bars stepped out of the Humvee. Roy stood a couple inches taller than the colonel, but the Army man outweighed him by a good twenty pounds, all of it muscle. And his dark skin, dark as a that of a native Zimbabwean or Nigerian, made Roy feel almost milky by comparison.

The Army man extended his hand. "Colonel Michael Brunneau, Eighty-Sixth Battalion, Louisiana Army National Guard. And you would be—?"

Roy didn't reply for half a second, stunned the man didn't recognize him. Sure, he wasn't sitting in his office with the Great Seal of the City of New Orleans behind him, but didn't everyone in South Louisiana know his face? "I'm Mayor Roy Rio. What's the situation in the Lower Ninth Ward and New Orleans East?"

"Catastrophic," the colonel replied. "Everything's under twelve feet of water. Best as I can tell, storm surge rammed straight up the Mississippi River Gulf Outlet and demolished any levees in its path. Jackson Barracks is completely inundated. The only vehicles my people were able to save were the trucks equipped with river-fording kits. Everything else got drowned. Didn't lose any personnel, thank God."

"I'm glad to hear these trucks can drive through high water," Roy said. "We're about to get a whole lot of it. At least one flood wall west of the Industrial Canal has broken, along the London Avenue Outfall Canal. I've got thirty thousand people sitting inside this Dome with limited stocks of food. A lot of them are elderly. When will you start pulling them out of the disaster zone?"

Colonel Brunneau shook his head. "We can't. That's not what we came here to do."

"*What?* What *did* you come here to do, then?"

"Set up a base camp for a major search and rescue mission," the colonel said. "You say you've got thirty thousand people sheltering here in the Superdome? What's their status?"

Roy turned to Bruno. "They're, uh, pretty much okay for now, Colonel," Bruno said. "The storm tore a big hole in the roof, and a lot of rain got in, so there are puddles everywhere on the main level. But people avoid that by staying on the upper levels. It's hot in there — the climate control system went down maybe seven hours ago — but there's still running water in the bathrooms. For now."

"What's the food situation?" the colonel asked.

"Only about a third of the folks brought their own food. The deputies and security guards, plus the M.P.s you sent over a couple days ago, have started collecting the food and adding it to the limited stocks of M.R.E.s we've had in place since the start of the storm season. There's been some grumbling and resistance, but the men look to have it under control. The food should last us another two days."

The colonel turned back to Mayor Rio. "There you go. No one inside that Dome is in immediate danger. The accommodations may not be up to Hilton Hotel standards, but they'll live."

"What about the frail elderly I've got in there?" Roy asked. "I've got diabetics, wheelchair-bound, hypertensives... a lot of these folks are gonna start running out of their medicines soon."

"Have them transferred to the New Orleans Arena," the colonel said, pointing to the green tiled basketball stadium which shared its physical plant and parking lots with the Superdome. "My medics will set up a field clinic there to treat the wounded the choppers'll be bringing in."

"Choppers?"

"Our helicopters flew out of harm's way two days ago. Standard operating procedure; after the storm passes, they circle back to where they're needed. That's why I'm securing this landing pad. Within the next two to six hours, dozens of choppers — mine, the Coast Guard's, probably some from the Bellechasse Air Station — are going to start using this as their base for search and rescue. You've got thirty thousand souls here? Well, by rough order of magnitude I'd say we've got five times that number sitting on rooftops or trapped in attics. *Those* are the people we came here to help. We'll get 'em back here, triage them between the Dome and the field clinic in the Arena, then wait for outside forces to come in and pull them out."

"But you'll be coordinating your activities through me, right?" Roy said. "I'm the ranking local political official. I fully support your use of this helipad, of course. I know the head of the Superdome Commission, Joe Tervelon. I'll have Bruno reach him, work out all the details—"

Colonel Brunneau's frown cut Roy off. "You're operating under a misunderstanding. I don't need anyone's permission to use this helipad. I'm commandeering it. I'm under no obligation to 'coordinate' any of my activities with you. My commander-in-chief is the Governor of Louisiana. Until I receive orders from her or from a superior officer, I am to use my best judgement. If you have forces under *your* command which can assist me with search and rescue, I will be happy to coordinate activities with you and with them."

Roy's face filled with hot blood. He hated that — he knew his skin was light enough that his blush of humiliation would be burningly obvious to everyone.

What forces *did* he have? His police department had lost virtually its entire fleet of cruisers. His other agencies had only skeleton crews. The Criminal Sheriff's deputies? The Levee Board's cops? The Harbor Police? None of these answered to him; all belonged to elected or politically appointed minor potentates. Many of these had probably evacuated, cutting themselves out of the command and control loop.

"Well, Mr. Mayor?" Colonel Brunneau asked. "Do you have anything to offer?"

The son of a bitch doesn't have to rub it in. "Not... not right at the moment. I'll get back to you."

"You do that. Until then, you'll have to excuse me. I've got a command post and a field clinic to set up, and choppers due in by nightfall."

* * * * *

"How did you find me, Owl?" Kay demanded.

"Well, ain't that a fine 'howdy-do'?" Owl said. He leaned over the edge of his boat and took a closer look at Kay's precarious raft. "Maybe you'd like it better if I left you to enjoy your private lake on your little yacht here?"

"Why the hell can't you ever give a straight answer?"

He grinned and offered her his hand. "Y'know, you're pretty damn spunky for a gal who's just gone through labor."

She refused his assistance. "And I'm pretty damn 'spunky' for a gal who's supposed to be *dead*, according to you. Or was that just another lie from the trickster?"

He looked affronted. "That wasn't no lie. There were two possible outcomes of havin' your entire belief cohort disappear. *Two.* I explained *one.* That's not a lie, sweetheart. That's an incomplete truth."

"*Damn it*, Owl! Stop jerking me around!"

He rolled his eyes. "Woo hoo! Cut the histrionics, babe. You got no real beef with me. You may not've gotten everything you always wanted, but you got a big chunk of it. You and your aura are *quits*, permanent-like. It's takin' the long wet dirt nap, and you're still breathing. I didn't spill all the beans for ya before 'cause I couldn't be sure how things were gonna go down. Now get in the friggin' boat, will ya?"

This time, Kay accepted Owl's hand. Stepping into the boat, she nearly stumbled over the prone, motionless figure of Pandora, lying beneath a blanket.

"Hey, be *careful!*" he scolded.

"Owl — is, is she—?"

He placed Kay on a seat in the boat's bow, then carefully resumed his station at the tiller. "No, she's not dead. Not yet. Best as I call tell, she's in some kinda coma. She slipped into it right before the winds took the roof off my little cabin near Bayou St. John. Soon as her Ills started popping off, I couldn't rouse her."

Kay's naked shins rubbed against something angular beneath her seat. Looking down, she saw it was Pandora's box. She'd never been this close to it before. She resisted a powerful urge to unlatch it and peer inside.

"Go ahead," Owl said. "Open it. Take a look. Ain't nothin' gonna jump out."

She pulled the box out and opened it. The fragrance of a doused fireplace emerged. Fading sunlight revealed thirteen lumps of colored ash clustered together. The lumps, some purple, some green, others orange or yellow or colors Kay couldn't describe, had begun losing their distinctiveness, blending together into a single motley soot pile.

"She... she really loved those little things," Kay said.

Owl pulled the outboard motor's starter cord. "Yeah, a bit more than you loved your aura."

She pushed the box back underneath her seat. "What about *you*? What happened to your other self?"

"Mine?" Owl headed the boat south. "I haven't had an 'other self' for almost two hundred years, babe. The last of my people got shoved outta New Orleans right around the time Louisiana joined the U.S. of A."

"*What?* But how—?"

"How have I lasted this long?" He smiled, flashing his few remaining rotting teeth. "A steady diet of fire water and tobacco, and bathing only twice a year; I swear by it. Actually, there's a lot to be said for startin' out yer existence as something more akin to a cypress tree or a pool of pond scum than a man. You know how long a cypress tree can last? Half a century or more, if it don't get cut down. Oh, I been gettin' older over the years; don't take more than a quick look in the mirror to tell me that. And now that you're free of your aura, you'll start aging, too. But at a tree's pace, not a woman's.

"Another thing — forget that super-duper healing ability you used to have. Actually, that part's a shame. You're kinda messed up, girl."

Kay's hand rose to the left side of her face. The spastic throbbing of the tissues surrounding her left eye, the burning sting of open wounds across her brow and cheek, all this had been subsumed by the trauma her birth canal had suffered. No longer.

"How bad...?" she asked.

"Pretty bad. You ain't gonna be winning no beauty contests. You woulda done good to have hung onto that aura a couple more minutes, let it work some last-second magic on you."

"No," she said, shaking her head. "It couldn't have left me too soon."

The sun fell behind the office towers on Veterans Memorial Boulevard, on the Metairie side of the broken Seventeenth Street Canal, just a few blocks to the west. Had the canal's western bank been breached, too? Were those office towers now slab-sided, vertical islands in a hugely swollen Lake Pontchartrain?

"Owl," she asked, "how did you manage to keep yourself hidden from the others?"

"Safe houses. I've got — or at least I *had* — a network of hidey-holes built over forgotten Indian burial grounds. They give me a kind of zone of invisibility, make me mystically undetectable to any bad luck spirits less senior than me. Which would be *all* of y'all. And I can extend the zone to others, with some limitations."

"What do you think happened to the rest of the Miasma Club?"

"Oh, I'm sure the big guns are still around. Even with the mandatory evacuation, I'm positive there're still enough blacks, Italians, Irish, French, Anglos, and Germans around, maybe in the surrounding parishes, to keep bad luck spirits like Krampus, Ti Malice, and Mephistopheles juiced. Even if just barely. It was the spirits with the relatively tiny constituencies, you and Pandora and Na Ong and Na Ba, who were the most vulnerable to dissolution... or to what happened to you and, a long time ago, to me."

"So those are the two 'possible outcomes' you mentioned? Either dissolving and getting reabsorbed by the miasmatic field, or... or what? Turning human?"

"Not all the way human," he said. "Like I told you, you're gonna age a whole lot slower than any real human being. And you won't fall prey to most diseases that afflict normal folks; the bacteria and viruses that love human sinus passages don't seem to have an appetite for the stuff we're made of. But you can be hurt. And my best guess is, you can be killed, too."

An entrance ramp to the Pontchartrain Expressway sloped up out of the water like the arched back of a brontosaurus feeding in a prehistoric swamp. As they passed beneath the ramp's shadow, Kay heard shouts from above. Four people, three women and an elderly man, had taken shelter from the rising water. They yelled, begging for rescue.

Kay caught Owl's eye. "Owl...?"

He shook his head. "No room."

She looked back as the boat chugged past the ramp. One of the women, the one with her arm around the elderly man, stared imploringly. "Just him," the woman shouted. "Take just *him*, please..."

Kay desperately wanted to respond, to say something. Anything. Encouragement, apology, sympathy...

The old man reminded her of Amos Weintraub.

She waited until she could no longer hear the woman before speaking again. "Owl, what makes the difference?"

"What difference d'you mean?"

"The difference between those of us who crumble into dust, and the ones who turn part-way human. Is it just chance?"

"It ain't blind chance," he said. "I don't believe in blind chance. Near as I can figure, it has to do with the growth of a 'soul' or some such thing, much as I feel sorta presumptuous usin' that word."

She felt a spark of hope ignite in her breast. "But — but if we come from the miasma, how can any of us have souls? Only God can make a soul, and I wasn't directly created by Him. I'm just one of the Mother's puppets."

"You're bein' narrow-minded, babe. Too blinkered by that monotheism you get fed on Saturday mornings. My people, we believe *everything's* got a soul. People. Animals. Even rocks and clouds and rivers. And if a rock can have a soul, then why not you and me?

"Here's what I figure. Spirits like us, when we get birthed, we come into this world, not with a full-fledged soul, but with something more like the *seed* of a soul. The *potential* for one. A seed needs watering to grow, sunlight to thrive. It don't get those things, it just stays a plain little seed, sittin' there, doin' nothing."

Kay forgot all about the wounds throbbing on the left side of her face. "What would water our soul seeds?"

"Sometimes, we bad luck spirits get inside the lives of those folks we're hexin'. We pretend to be their friends, their relatives, lovers, even.

Our line of work comes with its own occupational risk — that being, if we're good enough at what we do, we can start to fool even ourselves; we can start believin' we really *are* the intimates we pretend to be. Most of us manage to remain tight and hard, and the seed stays dormant. But others of us slip up, let that first tiny shoot emerge. It hungers for the sunlight and water that are all around. And it grows."

"And... and that's what happened to *me?* Being with the Weintraubs for so many years... they helped me grow a *soul?*"

Owl shrugged. "Near as I can figure... yeah. Proof's in the pudding. Your aura turned to ashes. The rest of you didn't. As for Na Ong and Na Ba? I don't sense them no more, but that don't necessarily mean anything. I had me a notion that they'd started really carin' about their Vietnamese folk—"

"I thought so, too."

"But they're young spirits, barely thirty years old. Maybe they ain't been around long enough for their souls to sprout big enough." He shrugged. "They could be two big patches of ash right now, slowly dissolvin' in New Orleans East somewhere."

Kay glanced down at Pandora, who breathed so faintly she might be an olive skinned mannequin. "And what about her?"

Owl looked away. "I don't know," he said.

"Will she come out of this coma?"

"I *said* I don't *know*. Your ears messed up?"

The boat's bow nudged aside the floating corpse of a gray dove, its feathers glistening with gasoline residue. Kay watched the little corpse turn in circles, its wings gradually spreading. "You love her, don't you?"

"Fuck, yeah, I do," he said quietly. "As much as I loved Creek-Flowing-Over-Stones."

"Who...?"

ANDREW FOX

"Long, long story," he said, a bitter tone darkening his voice. "Maybe I'll tell it to you, if we manage to live through the next week."

"You think we won't?" After weeks of trying to nullify herself, she felt a renewed thirst for life — and its corollary terror of death.

"I didn't come lookin' for you just outta the goodness of my heart. Unless I keep you — and Pandora — away from the Miasma Club, I'm a dead man."

"Why?"

"I tried screwin' with their storm summoning ceremony, remember? Me and Pandora went on the lam."

"But it didn't work. Antonia may not've given New Orleans a direct hit, yet it came close enough to crack the levees. Besides, you've been uncooperative and impertinent lots of times before, and you've always gotten away with it."

"That was then." He steered the boat around the branches of a drowned oak, then glanced quickly at the darkening skies to the east. "I used to be unique, babe. The Triumvirate, they never knew what the hell I was, exactly. See, I was already here, waitin' for them when they emerged from the miasma just before the Civil War. I knew what *they* were. They didn't know squat about *me*. And that's been my ace in the hole, why I could always bluff 'em, even though the least of 'em coulda squashed me like a roach.

"But I ain't unique no more, Kay. If Mephistopheles gets within spittin' distance of you, he's gonna realize pretty much instantly what *I* am. And then the gig's up. For me, *and* for you. You tried screwin' with them, too. And now that your aura's gone, you're no use to them anymore. In fact, you're a threat — you can still sense them whenever they're around, and you know how they work.

"We're a package deal, babe. Either we both make it, or neither of us do. They're distracted now by all this chaos. Sated like a python that just swallowed a pig. But they won't stay fat and happy forever. The sooner I can get you and Pandora to one of my safe houses on higher ground, the better."

Too much information, too fast. She couldn't make sense of it all. "You said the Triumvirate didn't appear until just before the Civil War? But the Civil War didn't start until 1861. European settlers had already been living here for a hundred and forty years, building levees and digging canals. Why would the Mother have waited so long before creating the Miasma Club?"

"She didn't," Owl said. "You just assume the Miasma Club you know is the only one that ever existed, right?"

"It's *not?*"

He smiled. "Open your mind, babe. The world didn't start with you, and it won't end with you, neither. Yeah, there was an earlier Miasma Club. I blew it to hell in the Year of Our Lord 1810. But it took strength I don't got anymore, and months of planning and preparation. Months we probably ain't gonna have."

He cleared his throat and spat into the water. "Gettin' dark. Light fades much more, I'm liable to ram us into a tree. We'd better find us someplace to bunk down, a two story house or an apartment building. We need to rustle us up some food. And you need clothes."

In the eastern sky, Kay saw the dusk's first star. No, not a star; a planet, probably Venus, judging from its size and brightness. She shuddered. *Venus... that's one of Fortuna's false names.*

"Owl, will they ever stop? I mean, if the city manages to come back from this, will the Miasma Club just keep on piling disaster on disaster, until the mortals give up and move on?"

"Yeah, that's how it'll be. Unless them scientists stop tryin' to leech off the Mother's energy and she has a change of 'heart.' Or unless you and me have time and luck enough to replicate my trick of 1810. Wouldn't count overmuch on either."

Chapter 22

A baby's wailing awakened Bob Marino. For an instant, he didn't know where he was. Ten stories above his head, the morning's first gray light illuminated a sagging hole the size of a school bus in the Superdome's roof, and he remembered where he'd spent the night.

He sat up and winced, then massaged a protesting muscle in his lower back. It had been a long time since he'd slept this rough; the wild fires in northern New Mexico during the late eighties. Maybe he should've taken Bruno Galliano up on his offer of a bed across the street at the Hyatt? No; the whole reason he'd stayed in New Orleans was so that his crazy good luck could rub off on those around him. And who needed good luck more than these poor souls here in the Dome?

He walked to the railing, where he could look out over the entire Dome. Isolated flashlight beams, probably wielded by Louisiana National Guard soldiers, lanced the darkness in areas unlit by the weak dawn light from the roof hole.

Where were his people? Where was FEBO? *They aren't* my *people anymore*, he reminded himself. Still, it had been more than twenty-four hours since Antonia had made landfall. The Region Six office north of Dallas was only a ten hour drive away.

He heard the *wap-wap-wap* of an approaching chopper. Whose? The Coast Guard's? The Army's? FEBO's? He ran outside to see.

The air on the Dome's upper parking deck smelled and tasted like a blessing after the hot stench of the Superdome. Black water covered Poydras Street. The chopper he'd heard earlier sat on a landing pad two stories above the flood, its rotors still turning. Men in dark blue jumpsuits, Coast Guard men, lifted a medical evac stretcher from its carrying pod, then wheeled an elderly woman towards the improvised triage facility at the New Orleans Arena. There wasn't a single FEBO blue polo shirt in sight.

He pulled his cell phone from his pocket. Until now, apart from one call to his wife, he'd avoided using it, hoping to conserve its power. The phone's battery gauge indicated it still retained nearly a full charge. So far, his luck was holding out. The big test of that luck would be whether he could access any service. He had a big advantage; his phone had an Arlington, Virginia area code.

It was on the same network as Ducky Duckswitt's. Duckswitt's cell number still resided in his phone's directory. He wondered where his ex-subordinate was right now. In Baton Rouge, meeting with the governor? En route to New Orleans? He'd know soon enough, if he could hit a working cell.

After an agonizing second of silence, the phone on the other end rang. He retreated out of the wind so he could hear more clearly. The connection clicked.

"To what do I owe the rare privilege of a call from the ex-Chief Administrator of FEBO?" *That* was no recorded message.

"William? This is Bob. I'm in New Orleans, at the Superdome."

"What the hell are you doing *there?*"

Bob caught himself before he could reply, *What the hell are you* not *doing here?* "I got stuck here when the Disaster Preparedness Convention got cancelled. Where are you?"

The other end remained silent for a second. "I'm in the Los Angeles Airport. I just flew in from Hawaii. Why?"

Bob couldn't believe his ears. Even for Ducky Duckswitt, this was too much. "*Why?* New Orleans is full of *flood water,* that's why! And there's not a FEBO employee in sight."

"Wait a minute... the storm hit Waveland, not New Orleans. Local first responders have been giving my staff and me situation updates since late yesterday afternoon. The last I heard, New Orleans had come through pretty much fine."

"Whatever reports you've gotten are seriously out of date. The Superdome is surrounded by water—"

"Bob, you know as well as I do that all it takes to fill New Orleans with water is a decent thunderstorm. What about the pumps?"

"William, listen to me. This isn't precipitation flooding. After Antonia passed, the pumps were working, and the water in the streets was going down. But that was early yesterday afternoon. Now the water around the Dome's twice as deep as it was yesterday. And I'm in one of the higher parts of town. This isn't rain — this is Lake Pontchartrain. The flood walls have breached. It's a catastrophe—"

"I'll need to get independent confirmation of that, of course."

"*Independent confirmation?* What the fuck do you think *I* am?"

Duckswitt went silent. "Bob, let me remind you of one little thing," he said at last. "You aren't my boss anymore. Let me repeat that. You. *Aren't.* My boss. Anymore. I don't have to put up with either your profanity or your contempt."

"Oh, Jesus..." Bob felt the situation sliding from farce to nightmare. "William, listen, this isn't about me and you. This could be the biggest natural disaster in American history—"

"No. It *is* about you and me, Bob. You think your snide remarks and innuendos didn't get back to me? Remarks about my *amateurism?*"

"Oh, Christ, don't be *petty* at a time like this—"

"You'd just *love* for me to fall on my face, wouldn't you? I'll tell you what. I'll get independent verification of what you've claimed, from the *proper* authorities. And then I'll make my decision on how FEBO will respond. And when we *do* respond, everything's going to be *by the book.* *Real* professional. That means every scrap of paperwork gets filled out, no contract gets signed without three competitive bids, and every doc and nurse we hire gets his or her sexual harassment and diversity training before touching a patient."

The thick damp air seemed to clamp down on Bob's head. "William, *listen* to me, for God's sake! I just spent the night with thirty thousand homeless people in the Superdome. They're going to run out of food and clean water within the next two days. The toilets aren't working — people have started relieving themselves in the stairwells—"

"Sounds like a right fun vacation. Send me a postcard, okay? Or a tee-shirt — they've got great tee-shirts on Bourbon Street, don't they?"

Duckie Duckswitt hung up his phone.

Bob Marino, ex-Chief Administrator of FEBO, now a trapped Hurricane Antonia refugee, stared at the cell phone in his sweating palm. It beeped three times, flashed a Low Battery warning icon, then went dead.

His luck had run out.

* * * * *

"Quincy! Dear, *dear* Uncle Quincy! I can hardly *believe* the luck!"

Cynthia Belvedere Hotchkiss noticed her uncle didn't look pleased as a Lotto winner when he spotted her. Despite the sour look on his face, he steered his boat toward the second-story balcony of the Camelot Quality Inn Hotel. She didn't care whether he was happy to see her or not. All that mattered was that she was about to be rescued from this hell hole where she and Nicole had sought shelter after Cynthia's efforts to maneuver around the endless stalled snake of cars on the I-10 by driving on the shoulder had resulted in a wreck.

Quincy's scowl turned to astonishment when he saw Nicole. "Cynthia *Hotchkiss!*" he yelled across the water. "You mean to tell me you didn't evacuate that *child?*"

Nicole pointed her cell phone camera at the approaching boat and clicked her great uncle's picture. Cynthia nearly slapped her upside her head for *again* wasting the phone's battery power. That unruly, impulsive child had been snapping random photos from the hotel's balconies ever since New Orleans East had turned into a lake.

Cynthia sidestepped her uncle's scornful question by firing off one of her own. "And what about *you*, Uncle?" she shouted across the water. "Aren't you on administrative leave? I would've thought you'd be in Houston by now, watching the disaster on TV with a beer in hand."

"Man's allowed to change his mind," he said. He tossed her a dirty coil of nylon rope so she could pull the boat to the balcony's side. "I been rescuin' folks, takin' them to the water's edge."

"*You?*" She nearly dropped the rope with surprise. "You mean to tell me you've actually been doing your *job*, 'serving and protecting'?"

"So I'm a volunteer, so what?" He grabbed the balcony's railing. "Shit, Cynthia, don't make me sound like no *monster*. I might not always been the greatest cop, but this is still my home. Maybe if you'd bought a certain laptop like you said you would, I woulda taken a nice, long vacation when my suspension came down."

"Maybe if you hadn't kept jacking up the price on me, I would've done the deal."

"Whatever. At least this way, I got to help some old folks off the toppa their houses."

"*Bravo*, good Samaritan," Cynthia said. "Charity begins at home, of course." She steadied herself on Nicole's shoulder and stepped down into the boat. "Now, where do you plan to take us?"

"Downtown to the Superdome."

"Hell, *no*, you won't," she said sharply. "I'm not about to let you deposit me and my child in the midst of twenty or thirty thousand people of that sort."

"What sort, Mother?"

"Quiet, Nicole. What are our other options, Quincy? Surely the Superdome isn't the only high and dry refuge?"

"We could go Uptown," he said. "Strip of land close to the river levee is prob'ly dry. You two could walk down to the Tchoupitoulas Street up-ramp, then walk across the Crescent City Connection to the West Bank."

"Good," Cynthia said, smiling. "You'll escort us over to the West Bank, stay with us until we reach the Red Cross or National Guard?"

"We'll see," he said. "I might wanna keep comin' back for folks, long as my gas holds out. We got room for a couple more passengers if we squeeze tight. There any more folks left here at the hotel?"

"Sure," Nicole said, "there are *lots* up on the fifth and sixth floors—"

"*No*, there are *not*," Cynthia said. "Nicole is mistaken." She pushed the boat away from the balcony. "Take us Uptown. And don't spare the horsepower — this sun is *brutal*."

"Whatever," he muttered. He steered the boat away from the hotel and followed the sunken path of the I-10 expressway west.

A helicopter approached from downtown. It hovered a hundred feet above while the co-pilot signaled to ask if they were in distress. Quincy gave him a thumbs-up sign and waved him on.

"Why did you send them *away?*" Cynthia asked. "They could've gotten us out of here a whole lot faster than you can."

"Niece, there's hundreds of folks somewhere out there that need that chopper a *hellavuh* lot worse than you."

Moments later, a woman cried out to them from the roof of a Wal-Mart garden store annex. Quincy hesitated, then steered them across the drowned parking lot.

"Quincy, what are you doing?" Cynthia asked.

"Goin' to pick her up."

"We don't have *room*. We don't have *time*—"

"Yes, we do," he said, refusing to look at her. "Move your fat ass over on that seat, and there's plenty of room."

"*My* ass isn't fat, Uncle Quincy," Nicole piped up, "I've got room—"

Cynthia reached over and slapped her daughter's mouth. "No more warnings, Nicole! You *sass* me, you get *slapped*. Quincy, you're making an unsound judgement. Wouldn't it be wise to leave her rescue to the professionals?"

"No, niece, it *wouldn't* be 'wise.' I'm the captain of this here ship, and I say—"

"As city councilwoman, I *out-rank* you, Mister NOPD Sergeant."

"Maybe in City Hall you do. But, in case you ain't noticed, we ain't in City Hall."

The stranded young black woman's shouts became more intelligible as they drew closer. "... Lord, *thank* the *Lord!* I been here a day now, thought fo' *sure* I would *die!* Storm tore the roof off my building, walls out my apartment, and then the waters came, and I had nowhere to go... But now you here! Thank the Lord *Jesus!*"

Why couldn't it be one of my church members, at least? Cynthia asked herself, appalled at the thought of sharing her tiny, precarious space with such an uncouth representative of the underclass. *She's* obviously *a crack-head — she'd have to be, to have delusions she could ride out the storm in one of those cheap-ass cardboard-and-glue apartment complexes.* Well, Quincy might have control of the tiller, but he couldn't stop her from making it extremely clear to this young woman that she *was not welcome.*

The boat began striking floating potted plants. They bobbed in the boat's wake, their plastic pots maintaining enough buoyancy to keep the dying mums and azaleas afloat, if not necessarily upright. Then the boat shuddered and lost momentum. Nicole looked down into the water and screamed.

"Mama! *Mama!* It's a *dead* man! A dead man's stuck to our boat!"

Cynthia looked. Like a bloated black tortoise, a corpse had joined their party as a stowaway. It had gotten snared in the boat's prow rope. "*Quincy!*" she screamed. "You see what your foolishness has done! Get that *thing* away from us! It's *diseased!*"

He struggled with the tiller, trying to compensate for the corpse's drag. "Don't go all *mental*, okay? Shit, you act like you never seen a dead body before — how many open casket funerals you done officiated at, anyway?"

"Just get us *out* of here, you *idiot!*"

"Y'all *okay?*" the woman standing atop the garden center called out, obviously unable to see what was causing the commotion. When the boat approached to within a few feet of her roof, however, she saw. Then she started screaming, too. "Oh *God!*" she yelled, covering her face. She ran away from the water's edge, then ran back to look again, her eyes popping wide with horror. "Oh Lord *Jesus!* That could be *me!* Oh *thank* the Lord Jesus y'all come to take me! Praise him! Praise him! Oh *praise him!*"

She tried scrambling into the boat the second its bow scraped the building's rain gutters. But Cynthia was equally quick. "Not so fast, you *fool!* You'll tip us over!" She attempted to block the younger woman. "There's no *room*, we'll send someone back for you, so get *out!*"

The boat rocked under the two struggling women.

"Mama! Stop!"

"Niece, have you gone *crazy?*"

"Mama, you're gonna *tip* us!"

The would-be stowaway began wildly slapping Cynthia's shoulders and the top of her head. Cynthia tried grabbing her wrists, but the other woman was too strong. So Cynthia slapped her back. She pulled Cynthia's hair. Cynthia, more affronted than hurt, shrieked, then grabbed a clump of her opponent's mangy Afro and yanked as hard as she could.

"Mama!"

"Niece, you don't cut this craziness right *now*, I'm gonna toss you overboard—"

Cynthia got one leg onto the roof and grabbed her opponent around the waist, mustering her strength for one last ditch effort to pitch the woman out. But she felt the space between her two legs stretch — the boat was drifting away from the roof!

Just when she thought she'd surely split in half like a turkey's wish bone, she and the woman, still clinging to each other like TV wrestlers, toppled into the water. She didn't have time to take a breath before she went under. Disoriented, blind, panicked, she flailed desperately until she no longer felt the boat's bottom. Then she kicked her legs and reached for the air above.

Something stopped her. Some *one*. The lowlife *bitch!* She punched and shoved until her assailant moved and Cynthia's face broke the surface and she sucked in great mouthfuls of air, blessed, *blessed* air.

She felt a hand slide down the back of her torn blouse. Cynthia steeled herself to slap the *shit* out of the obscenely persistent crackhead. She blinked dirty water out of her eyes. She saw the crackhead clinging to the far side of the boat. Then *whose* arm—?

She turned her head. Eyes the color of a dead fish's belly stared into hers. The *corpse—!*

Cynthia clenched her eyes shut and screamed. She screamed and screamed and screamed.

When she was all screamed out, she opened her eyes again. She didn't feel the dead arm down her blouse anymore. She treaded water, her arms outstretched at her sides. The dead man, floating face up now, sprawled across her lap, mouth open, one eye closed, as though he were winking at her.

She heard an electronic voice say, *"Say cheese."* She realized she'd heard it say the same thing several times now in quick succession.

She looked up at the boat. Quincy stared down at her disdainfully. Nicole also stared down, but at her cell phone, pointed at Cynthia and the corpse. Her daughter's face was expressionless.

"*Say cheese.*" Nicole clicked her camera phone's electronic shutter again, then again.

* * * * *

"So, Mr. Mayor," Bob Marino said regretfully, "don't count on hordes of rescuers from FEBO swarming over the horizon anytime soon. Not while that bastard Duckswitt's in charge."

Roy Rio felt like he was trapped underwater. The hot, humid air sat like week-old soup in the room. Despite the open sliding glass door and the room's lofty position on the eighteenth story of the Hyatt Hotel, no breeze stirred the curtains. Sunken within an armchair by the balcony, he could barely muster the will to look up at Bob Marino, Bruno Galliano, and his chief of staff, Walter Johnson.

"I can't tell you how sorry I am," Bob continued after a long pause. "I had reason to believe my being here would help make things better. But all I've managed to do is make them worse."

"Don't you let yourself believe that, Bob," Bruno said. "Not for one goddamn second."

Roy stared out over the balcony. If he blotted out all context, the view was stunningly beautiful. The noon sun set the watery vista to sparkling. The skyscrapers of Poydras Street looked like blazing obelisks risen from the ocean's floor, the houses of Mid-City and Lakeview a thousand motley islands of terracotta red and slate gray.

New Orleans as Venice. The eighth Wonder of the World.

"The buses... they're all underwater, aren't they?" he asked, speaking more to himself than to any of his companions. "Hundreds of city and public school buses. How did we get so... so *lucky* as to locate every one of our bus depots on lots below sea level? Was that *luck*, or what?"

"Yeah, Mr. Mayor," Bruno said quickly, "we're kinda fucked, so far as buses go. But, look, you can't let yourself dwell on that. Right now, you've got thirty thousand scared-as-shit, dispirited citizens sitting next door in that sweltering Dome. They need to know you're still here with them, Mr. Mayor. They need you to tell them everything's going to be *okay*. Even if that's a goddamn *lie*, they've still got to hear it."

Roy shook his head. "Not... not now. I don't... look, I don't have anything to *say* to those people. What the hell *can* I say? *You* go talk to them."

"Huh-uh," Bruno said, "I'm not letting you duck this. Nobody in that Dome knows me from a pimple on their ass. But everybody knows *you*. Maybe they didn't all vote for you, but you're *still* their mayor. You've *got* to get over there. If you don't, no one will ever forgive you. Including *me*, for the record."

He wished they'd give him time to get his head together. He wanted to look out the window, pretend the view was beautiful, just for a short while longer.

"Walter," Bruno said, "why haven't *you* chimed in? You're his oldest friend. Help us get through to him."

"Leave me alone with him for a while," Walter said.

Roy heard Bruno and Bob leave the room. He waited for Walter to say something. Walter didn't.

"So," Roy said at last, "you're gonna give it the old college try? Hit me with a version of the classic Knute Rockne speech?"

"No," Walter said. "That's too... hackneyed." He swiveled Roy's chair around so that the mayor faced him. "You fucked up, Roy. Big time."

"Huh...?" This wasn't what he'd expected. He waited for some acknowledgement that this was a joke, an attempt to shake him out of his funk. But he could see no trace of compassion in his closest advisor's eyes. "Walt, what...?"

"You heard me right," Walter said. "I've been your yes-man for way too many years. Always pumping you up, inflating that ego, nudging you in the direction of the next big mountain to climb. Hell, I was a better wife than your *wife*. But it turns out, you didn't need pumping up. You needed *deflating*. So consider me a pin. You're a *fraud*, Roy. You sold the voters of New Orleans a false bill of goods."

Roy sat perfectly still, stunned.

"This is your worst nightmare, isn't it?" Walter asked. "The day the whole country suddenly learns the emperor has no clothes. Even worse, the *Morehouses* get to see you buck naked. You thought you'd ride into the mayor's office as the white knight in black skin, right? And the whole town would have to bow down to your glorious resume and good intentions. '*Let's run New Orleans like a Fortune 500 company.*' '*No political machine — just competence.*' It felt damn good, didn't it, to appear on the cover of *Black Enterprise* twice in the same year?

"And really, judged against your predecessors, how good did you have to *be*? You figured, 'Hell, all I need do to beat those guys is be *honest*.' You prided yourself on being a Big Picture Man — all the messy little details of running a city and providing services to half a million people, *those* were for the little folk.

"Well, there's more to running New Orleans than avoiding scandal and praying for a one-punch miracle like MuckGen to fill up the city's coffers. You don't have it, Roy. You never did. You know what those people in the Dome are saying? 'Mayor Morehouse may've been a crook, but he wouldn't have let all them buses drown. He would have got us out of here by now.' You've spent the last three years trying to convince the black poor and working class that you care about them. But you know what? The proof is in the pudding. Because when the levees broke, when the hundred thousand New Orleanians who live below the poverty line really needed their Black Superman, *you weren't there for them*. You'd been whacking off in your Fortress of Solitude, reading *The Wall Street Journal*.

231

"You're an empty suit. 'Mayor Roy Oreo?' Yeah, that's about right. In the end, the fact your skin happens to be black didn't mean a goddamn thing to those poor wretches trapped in the Dome."

Roy felt a sharp pain beneath his breastbone. He wondered, only half caring, whether he was experiencing a heart attack. His vision blurred. Walter's shadow, cast on the bathroom door, grew squat and rotund, as though his spindly advisor had transformed into a ripe pumpkin with legs and fedora.

"You're... you're *fired*," he managed to whisper. "Get the fuck *out*."

Walter smiled tightly. Then he tipped an imaginary hat, an affectation Roy couldn't remember him ever employing before. "Whatever, Roy," he said. "You're the mayor. Be seeing you."

Walter Johnson stepped into a dark men's room off the Hyatt Hotel's deserted lobby. But it was Eleggua-Eshu who peeled off Walter's skin, folded it neatly, and placed it inside his briefcase.

He'd tasted blood, and man, had it ever tasted *good*. Until today, he'd been able to get no nearer to Mayor Roy Rio than the man's ex-wife and ex-uncle. But even the mightiest fortress of virtue had a loose stone *somewhere*.

He'd finally found Roy Rio's loose stone. And he'd yanked it free, letting all the water in the castle's moat pour through.

Chapter 23

I *can't leave New Orleans — I* can't...

Kay stared up at the suspended ramps and giant concrete stanchions leading to the twin spans of the Crescent City Connection, which linked downtown New Orleans with Algiers and West Bank Jefferson Parish. Despite the heat, she shivered. Contemplating crossing that bridge terrified her.

She set Pandora's box down on shadowed, deserted Calliope Street. "Owl. I don't want to go."

Owl Lookingback, burdened by the comatose form of Pandora draped across his shoulder, turned slowly to face her. "Kay," he said, voice raspy with exertion, "we talked about this a good long time, and we both agreed—"

"I *know* what we agreed," she said, her pulse racing, "but I've changed my mind. Can't we go to one of your safe houses along Tchoupitoulas Street instead, hide out there?"

"I'm not so sure they're *safe* anymore. Look, haven't you felt what's been happenin' to the miasmatic energy field over the last three days? All them surges and fizzles? I know you can't draw on the field anymore, but you sure as hell can still *sense* it."

"I *have* felt it. The 'fizzles' I can understand — with all the bad luck the city's been suffering, the miasmatic energy has to run low sometime, doesn't it? But the *surges*—?"

"Came from *you*. And Pandora. When your aura 'died' and all of Pandora's Ills took the dirt nap, the bad luck energy they contained didn't vanish. It got reabsorbed into the miasmatic field."

"Will it get made into another Greek bad luck spirit? Another Jewish one?"

He crouched and set Pandora gently onto the ground. "Not anytime soon. Not till enough Jews and Greeks return to get that process rolling. And who knows if they'll ever return? I'll bet the surviving Miasma Club members are feasting on them morsels of freed-up bad luck energy. It's party time, least for a short while. Then they'll crash. If we can just stay outta their gunsights for three or four more days, we should be golden for five or six months. They'll be hibernatin', hidin' in their hidey-holes, comatose as Pandora, waitin' for the well of bad luck energy to replenish itself."

"So why can't we just hide in one of your safe houses for the next four days?"

"*Tarnation!* Ain't you been *listenin'*? All the rules have changed! For all I know, the Triumvirate's got x-ray super-vision now that can burn right through my little concealment charms. Only way to be reasonably safe is to go someplace they hardly ever go and hunker down. And that 'someplace' is the West Bank, or whatever's left of it."

The very words *West Bank* made her heart thud. There wasn't a single synagogue there, not even a bagel shop. For Kay, it was *Terra Incognito*, the dark, empty place on the map.

"Can — can we stay inside Orleans Parish, at least?" she asked. "Stick to Algiers? I'd be able to see the French Quarter from Algiers Point... *please?*"

"Sure, sure, *whatever*. Just so long as we get the hell out of *here* — I feel like I've got a bull's-eye painted on my ass."

They resumed their slow march down Calliope Street. Close to a hundred people congregated around the entrance to the Magazine Street up-ramp. Kay glanced quickly at Owl. A crowd this size might well serve as an enticing lure to any of the surviving bad luck spirits.

A quartet of armed Crescent City Connection police barred the entrance to the ramp. Two black and two white officers were arguing with a middle-aged black man and a shapely black woman. The woman frequently turned to shoo away a teenaged girl who tried seeing what was going on. Kay thought the black woman looked vaguely familiar, possibly someone she'd seen on the TV news.

And there was something else familiar about her, too.

"Owl," she whispered, "she's been touched by one of us — I mean, one of *them*."

He nodded. "The guy next to her, too. But the scent is less fresh on him. Let's see what goes on here."

"Look," one of the white officers said to the black man, "I don't know a thing about any buses waiting over on the other side. I don't know where you got that story from—"

"From Mayor Roy Rio!" a different black man cried out from the middle of the crowd. "His spokesman said everybody waiting at the Convention Center for a ride out should cross the bridge, 'cause the buses couldn't get over to the Convention Center. You gotta let us cross, man!"

"Yeah, well," the bridge cop said, "I don't know nothing about none of that. If you believe all the rumors you hear, you'd think Moses is gonna part the Mississippi and lead all you folks to Gretna, then feed you gumbo. Me, the last orders *I* got were to maintain order on this bridge."

The man in the middle of the crowd slapped his thigh with outrage. "Man, this is *bullshit!* We got *rights*—"

The woman with the teenaged girl cut him off. "Officer," she said in an imperious tone, "do you know who I *am?*"

The bridge cop gave her a blank look. "I got no idea, lady."

"I'm New Orleans Councilwoman Cynthia Belvedere Hotchkiss. The *Reverend* Cynthia Belvedere Hotchkiss. I must get to Baton Rouge to help coordinate the disaster response as soon as possible."

Kay poked Owl's arm. "I remember now," she whispered. "She's the mayor's ex-wife."

"Some taste he's got in women," Owl whispered back.

"*HA!*" another woman shouted from a few feet away. "She ain't no *reverend!* She's a *devil-woman!* She tried to *drown* me—"

"Shut up!" Cynthia shouted back. "You just *shut up*, you stupid crack whore!"

"Any more of this," the bridge cop warned, "and I'm marchin' *all* y'all back to the Convention Center—"

"Nobody calls me a 'devil-woman'!"

"Nobody calls *me* a 'crack whore'!'

The crack whore lunged at the devil-woman, and the latter cocked her fist, but Cynthia's older male companion came between them. "*Cut it!*" he shouted, pushing them away from each other. "Both you bitches shut your damn pie holes and *simmer down!*"

He turned back to the bridge cops. "Look, officers, I'm really sorry about all this stupidity. I'm a brother officer, Sergeant Quincy Cochrane from the NOPD Sixth District. I'm outta uniform because the flood came too fast and I was off duty. Look, I'll take responsibility for these folks. I'll guarantee their good behavior while they're walkin' over your bridge. Any way y'all can cut a brother cop some slack?"

The four bridge cops glanced at each other. Then the one who'd been doing all the talking motioned for the other three to confer with him. Thirty seconds later, the lead cop walked over to Quincy. He cocked his thumb at the ramp. "Go on up," he said. "But it's no guarantee the situation's any better on the other side."

"Don't need no guarantee," Quincy said. "Just a chance. Thanks." He led the crowd up the ramp.

"Owl," Kay whispered, "do you think it's safe to go with them? Are they too tainted?"

"It's riskier to stay on this side. She's bad news, sure. But the cop's leadin' the parade, not the council lady. The taint's still on him, but either it's worn off with time, or, more to his credit, he's fought it with some tenaciousness. We may not get a better chance to cross."

She swallowed hard, but she couldn't argue with his logic. She picked up Pandora's box and began climbing the spiral ramp to the bridge. Owl kept pace, although, burdened with Pandora, he shuffled like a man shackled to a chain gang. She couldn't help but admire his astounding endurance — it had to be due to more than just his supernatural constitution. He really loved Pandora.

By the time they reached the top, they'd fallen to the back of the crowd. One little gray-haired black man pushed a rusted Sav-A-Center shopping cart loaded solely with a massive gilt-framed oil portrait of a woman dressed in World War Two-era clothes, possibly his mother or his deceased wife. Kay saw smoke ahead of them, on the opposite shore. It billowed from a spot about a mile south of the river, somewhere on the West Bank of Jefferson Parish. She searched for the source of the blaze and was blinded by the sun, its molten orb smudged by plumes of drifting smoke. She jerked her face towards downtown. When her vision cleared, she realized she was now higher than the roofs of the Warehouse District's mid-rise condominium buildings. A wave of vertigo made her stumble.

"You all right?" Owl asked.

"Yes... I'm okay," she insisted, embarrassed that a man twice her age, carrying a ninety-pound woman across his shoulders, should be inquiring about *her* welfare. "Just... a little dizzy."

"Nauseated, too?"

"Some."

"It's our distance from the ground and water," he said. "Your body still thinks it needs direct contact, or at least close proximity with the Mother. It takes your body a while to realize you've cut the umbilical cord."

"Can — can we ever really cut the umbilical cord *all* the way?"

"Sure," he said. "I mean, *I* managed it."

"Have you *really?* If you hate the Miasma Club so much, then why have you never left New Orleans?"

He didn't answer. They approached the steel girder latticework which demarcated the portion of the bridge suspended over the river. Looking up at the looming box of metal beams, Kay saw a placard bolted overhead. It held the symbol of Louisiana, a mother pelican feeding a nest full of her young.

She heard cheering from up ahead. It spread from the front of the crowd progressively back, until people only yards ahead of her were shouting with joy.

"They're coming to rescue us!"

"They'll lead us to the buses! We're saved!"

As the people ahead of her rushed forward, Kay was able to see what had caused all the excitement. A platoon of police officers — regular police, not bridge cops — approached from the span's West Bank approach.

The old man pushing his oil portrait in a shopping cart raced past. "Ain't never been so happy to see Jefferson Parish cops in all my life," he gasped.

The box in her arms suddenly felt twenty pounds lighter. The line of police and the East Bank exodus met at mid-span. Officer Quincy and his companions stopped about ten feet away from the Jefferson Parish contingent. She couldn't hear what the cops said to Quincy and the others. But, as she walked closer, she could see that the cops' faces didn't look friendly, or welcoming.

Not at all.

"That's *nuts!*" Quincy shouted. "You can't seriously tell me we gotta turn around and walk back into the disaster zone!"

"The bridge cops gave us permission to cross!" Cynthia added. "*They're* the controlling authority on this structure!"

The cop in the center of the blockade line crossed his arms. "They're not here. *We* are. And we've got orders not to let you people enter the City of Gretna."

"But we aren't *going* into Gretna," Cynthia replied. "The far side of this bridge is anchored in *Algiers*. Algiers, you must know, is a legal part of *Orleans Parish*. You and your men shouldn't even be *up* here. You've got no right to block our path!"

"Ma'am, this isn't a debating society. There's no way we can track which crossers stay in Orleans Parish and which go into Gretna. And our orders are that *none* of y'all cross over into Gretna."

"But *why*, man?" Quincy asked. "In the name of humanity, *why?*"

The Gretna cop pointed at the plume of smoke behind him. "You see that? That's Oakwood Mall. A gang of thugs from your side decided to loot it. Then they decided that wasn't good enough, so they set it on fire, too. Thirty thousand Gretna citizens have evacuated and left their homes behind, counting on us to keep their stuff safe. So all y'all are gonna turn around right now and walk back to your own side of the river."

Cynthia gestured at the crowd behind her. "Do *these* people look like *thugs* to you? Most of them are women and children, or old people!"

"Look," Quincy said, "like I already told the bridge cops, I'm an NOPD sergeant. I'll personally guarantee none of these folks are gonna make any trouble while I'm with them. All we wanna do is reach the buses on the other side, so we can get to Baton Rouge."

"There are no buses," the Gretna cop said. "Whoever you heard that from is either a liar or doesn't know what the hell he's talking about. Look, I'm not arguing with you people any more. Turn your asses around right *now*."

Kay felt anger and frustration build all around her. As she experienced the same emotions, she sensed something far worse, too. A gathering of malevolence. Hate, triumphant and gleeful, crystallized in the air high above her head...

"*Fuck* this *shit!*" a man a few feet away bellowed. "This is *America!* We can walk anyplace we goddamn *want to!*"

A woman started chanting "*America! America!*" Quickly, the rest of the crowd took up the chant. They began surging forward. As she was pushed forward by the crowd, Kay saw the air above the phalanx of police shimmer and darken, as though a miniature thunderhead were taking shape. The officers unholstered their guns. She smelled the stench of rotting cabbage, and she knew.

"Owl!" she screamed. She couldn't find him. "Owl! Get out of here! *Run!* They're *here!*"

And then she saw it, hovering in the air above the Gretna cops' heads — the Satanic merged form of the Triumvirate, stealing substance from the pulsating thunderhead. Their merged form flickered in and out of clarity like a weak transmission partially captured by a wire antenna. But this insubstantiality did not dampen their triumphant laughter.

"Hail, Kay Rosenblatt!" the Triumvirate boomed with malicious mirth. "Hail to the greatest among us, the one whose efforts bore the most delicious fruit! O Mistress of the Levees, we bow our heads in humble gratitude to thee and thy mighty deeds!"

"I *reject* you!" Kay screamed. "I'm *ashamed* I ever counted myself one of you! I'm with *these* people now, whatever happens to them!"

"Are you so eager to share their fate," the voice which only she and Owl could hear said, "oh little one so greatly changed?"

The Gretna cops assumed a firing stance. The lead members of the crowd, despite Quincy's efforts, had pushed within ten feet of them. The lead officer shouted, "Fire warning shots!"

Kay recoiled as eight service Berettas discharged almost in unison. Not all of the bullets soared free into the smoke stained sky — some hit steel girders fifty feet overhead, then ricocheted back at the roadway. The crowd broke. Kay found herself crushed between those behind her still pushing forward and the panicked people ahead of her who now ran back toward New Orleans. Slammed to the roadway, she struggled to cover her head as shoes and bare feet trampled her. Children screamed. The shopping cart carrying the portrait crashed onto its side, inches from her face.

"Cease firing!" she heard the lead officer shout. "*Cease firing now!*" But the Gretna cops, driven by adrenaline and fury stoked by the presence of the Triumvirate, fired more volleys over the heads of the fleeing New Orleanians.

When the last running feet had stumbled over her, she searched desperately for her companions. Her body throbbed like a giant bruise. Bullets continued ricocheting from the steel overhead, bouncing from concrete into guard rails and back to the roadway. One bullet, its momentum nearly spent, rolled across the concrete and lodged against her bare thigh, burning her skin.

She heard the Triumvirate's laughter, distorted by static, rise and fade and rise again.

"I *hate* you!" she screamed at them. "I'll hate you *forever!*"

"Your method of punishment will be decided later, Kay Rosenblatt. For now, your exemplary service in our cause has earned you a reprieve. But for *you*, Owl Lookingback, our forbearance has come to an end. We know now what you are. *Your* perfidies have not gone unnoted, and they will no longer go unanswered."

She saw Owl lying face down near the far guard railing, shielding Pandora with his body. She sensed a thread of bad luck energy being plucked like a guitar string. The majority of cops had halted their volleys, but a lone holdout fired a last shot. Kay heard the bullet strike steel. She saw Owl's left shoulder spasm and splurt blood as the ricochet struck home.

The towering figure of the Triumvirate, too long and too far separate from its nourishing miasmatic field, lost cohesion. As it shimmered and flickered and fell, Kay's head filled with the untangling voices of Old Scratch, Krampus, and Mephistopheles.

"This is only the beginning, betrayers," the voices said, fading towards the Mississippi below. "Only the *beginning*..."

Chapter 24

H E had to see for himself.

Following the worst night of his life, Roy Rio realized he had just two choices. He could either jump off his eighteenth story balcony, or he could join his citizens inside the Superdome and share whatever horrors and deprivations they were experiencing. He decided on the latter.

Bruno would chew my ass off for leaving the Hyatt without a police guard, he thought. *And Walter... Walt would call me an egotistical fool, playing* The Prince and the Pauper *games while my city drowns.*

Fuck Walter.

He yanked his hood's drawstrings tight and tied them beneath his chin, leaving only his upper lip, nose, and eyes visible; the hooded, sleeveless sweatshirt he'd commandeered should serve as an adequate disguise. The Superdome was so *overwhelming...* a panorama of dehumanizing misery. Or was it? He wondered if a professional anthropologist would look out at this same vista and, instead of seeing chaos, find evidence of communities spontaneously forming, bartering of goods and services, impromptu mutual benefit pacts. The human animal, when challenged by change or hardship, could be a miraculously adaptable creature.

Off to his right, on Concourse D, he saw that Army Guardsmen had organized a food line. He hadn't eaten breakfast yet; actually, he hadn't eaten in over twenty-four hours. Now that he was doing something — *anything*, just moving, being amongst people again — he felt his appetite stir.

He walked towards the end of the long line. As he passed the front of the head serving table, an elderly woman reached out and touched his arm. "Young man," she said, smiling, "sorry to bother you, but I got me three hungry grandchil'rins sittin' on their sleepin' bags, way over *there*, and I just can't carry all this back to them. Is there any way you could help me?"

Roy felt like kissing her feet. She'd given him an opportunity to feel *useful*. "Ma'am, I'd be *delighted* to help," he said. He took paper bowls of Cheerios and canned fruit out of her hands. "You just lead the way."

"You *sure* you don't mind?"

"*Mind?* I couldn't think of a thing I'd rather be doing."

He followed her around the Superdome's terraces, lit only by feeble rays of sunlight which fell like worn crepe streamers through holes in the roof. The woman, tatty wig slightly askew, reminded him of his mother's Great Aunt Dorothy Mae. Despite the severe arthritis which had hobbled her in her final decades, his aunt had always managed to maintain an air of dignity, even when dressed in nightgown and curlers.

They reached the aisle the lady had described. He saw three small sleeping bags, decorated with Ninja Turtles and Disney Princesses, lying disheveled amidst a perimeter of water jugs, old leather suitcases, and toys. But no children in them or near them.

"Now, where did those kids get they selves to?" the woman asked herself. "I thought I told them to stay put with Miss Peggy..."

Roy's stomach lurched. Radio news had reported rumors of awful occurrences in the Superdome, children being dragged into dark, filthy bathrooms—

"*Gram'maw! Gram'maw! Look what we got!*"

He craned his neck in the direction of the child's voice and saw a boy of about six holding above his head — a *balloon animal?*

"What the devil—?" Roy heard his companion mutter to herself. "I can hardly believe what those kids manage to find..." She waved them over. "Daniel! Zenubia! Ar-*thur!* Get back here and come eat your breakfast!"

"No, Gram'maw! You come *here* and meet the clown lady!"

It soon became clear the children wouldn't budge. Roy set his collection of bowls down and followed his companion to the adjoining terrace.

There really *was* a clown.

She sat in the middle of a circle of at least two dozen kids, in full clown regalia — baggy green, purple, and gold costume, giant shoes, red ball nose, and a mask of white greasepaint on her black face. She read to her audience from a stack of children's books, punctuating the dialogue with goofy sound effects. Between stories, she opened a box and pulled out two or three long balloons, which she inflated and twisted into a poodle or a bunny, then handed out as a prize.

Roy watched, half unbelieving. FEBO couldn't deliver basic food and potable water, but some agency had managed to supply a *clown?*

The clown closed the last of her books with a flourish. "Okay, kids," she said, "Harriet needs to take a break, before her voice is all the way gone. I'll do another show in an hour or so. Y'all go back to your mamas and your grandmamas now, and don't forget to *be helpful,* okay?"

"Are you with the Guard?" Roy asked her as she gathered her belongings.

"The Guard?" She looked up at him. "You mean the *Army* Guard? Mister, nobody in their right mind would trust me with a *water pistol.* I'm Hilarious Harriet. Here, here's my card." She handed him a dog-eared business card. "I do birthday parties, Carnival parties, Christmas parties, block parties, graduation parties, retirement parties, weddings, funerals, and *bar* and *bat mitzvahs.* Oh, and I do hurricane parties, too."

"You mean, you aren't with any agency? You're just a — a private citizen?"

"Honey, I don't believe in no agencies or agents. I make my own way. Why am I here? I couldn't afford the gas to Dallas, and my car wouldn't have made it past Westwego, anyway. Hey, you want a Viking helmet to put on top of that hood? I could twist you up one. By the way, the kids get it all for free, but I *do* take donations from adults."

"I, uh, I'm really sorry. I left my wallet back in my hotel room—"

Her greasepaint rimmed eyes went wide. "Shoot — you got you a *hotel room?* Like, with its own *bathroom?* Honey, you can have a Viking helmet, a sword to go with that helmet, and five balloon poodles, all for ten minutes in a working bathroom with toilet paper."

The children's grandmother pulled on Roy's sleeve. "Young man, is that *true?* That you got your own *bathroom?* Look, I'm sorry, I never properly introduced myself. I'm Roberta Jameson. I own my own house in Gentilly, and I'm a good Christian woman. What's your name?"

"Uh, it's, uh, Robert—"

Roberta grabbed his hand and shook it heartily. "Well, Robert, it's a pleasure, a *real* pleasure. Let me tell you, my grandchil'rins — actually, they's my *great*-grandchil'rins — they's mighty *scared* to go potty here in the Dome. See, we can't use the real bathrooms no more, so the Army men got us all doin' our business in two stairwells. One for mens and boys, the other for womens and girls. It's real *dark*, and you gotta feel your way down them stairs until you get to where the water is. Smells *real* bad. The kids, they *hate* goin' down there. You bein' such a nice young man and all, could you see it in your heart to take us back to your hotel room?"

Roy's initial impulse was to say, *Sure, what the heck, follow me over to the Hyatt!* But would that be fair? If he shepherded these five people to the sanctuary of a relatively clean bathroom, wouldn't he be morally obligated to take *everyone?* Or at least all the other children five and under, all the other senior citizens, and all the other volunteer Good Samaritans? "Uh, look, y'all," he said, "I need to think..."

"Look! *There* she is! I *told* you there was a clown in here!"

Roy turned. One of the national cable network news anchors — he couldn't remember which one — led a group of cameramen toward Harriet. Behind them slouched support workers dragging battery carts, a portable generator, and a forest of cables. They began setting up their equipment in a rough crescent around Roy and his companions. The anchor rolled his sleeves up to just above his elbows, then artfully disheveled his tie.

The generator roared into life. The bank of powerful lights burst into luminescence. While Roy waited for spots to stop swirling in front of his corneas, he listened to the anchor's familiar voice.

"This is Ambrose Coppertone, reporting live from inside the Louisiana Superdome, battered refuge for more than thirty thousand victims of Hurricane Antonia. This morning, I'm here to share a story of the miraculous goodness of the human spirit. Strangers share their precious food and water. The elderly find renewed usefulness and dignity in caring for others' children. And, yes, a clown appears, as if from nowhere, to bring precious moments of magic to those children, antidotes to the horror surrounding them."

He thrust a microphone toward Harriet. "Ma'am, kindly introduce yourself to our worldwide audience. Who are you, why did you end up here in the Superdome, and why have you chosen to dress as a clown?"

"Why have *you* chosen to dress as an anchorman?" she shot back. "I'm Hilarious Harriet. I do birthday parties, Carnival parties, Christmas parties, block parties, graduation parties, retirement parties, weddings, funerals, and, uh, what'm I missin', Mr. Robert?"

"*Bar* and *bat mitzvahs*," Roy said. "And hurricane parties."

"Yeah, I do them, too. Rates are real reasonable, I work on a slidin' scale—"

"Whoa, *whoa!*" Coppertone said. "What the people of America want to know is, *why?* Why have you put yourself through the trouble of dressing in greasepaint in such a brutal environment?"

"*Why?* 'Cause that's what I do for a livin'."

"But — but the people here don't have any money."

"Well, maybe they don't have money *now*, but they'll have some *some* day. You ever heard of *free advertising*?"

"Yes, but tell me, what in your own childhood inspired you to bring joy to children? Hilarious Harriet, has there been a special clown in your own life?"

She frowned. "Look," she said, "I gotta ask you something. Is there any way you can, like, flash my cell phone number at the bottom of the screen? I don't have no web address, I'm not that modern. But I got national coverage on my cell phone, so wherever I end up, I can go right to work—"

Coppertone looked at his camera people and made a sudden slashing motion across his throat. The flood lights switched off. Suddenly, their corner of the Dome looked as dark as midnight. "I'm sorry, ma'am," he said, not sounding sorry at all. "That's against corporate policy. Can't accommodate you. Hey, somebody got a waiver form handy? Have her sign a waiver form, then let's wrap up here. I think we can salvage at least a thirty second segment, if we insert some B shots. Maybe some Mardi Gras archival footage, that float with the big clown head — do we have that? Okay, here's the waiver form, ma'am. Just sign at the bottom."

"So you aren't gonna show my cell phone number?"

"No. Just sign the form."

She let the paper drop to the ground. "Y'all don't wanna help a woman earn an honest living? The *hell* wit' you then, I'm outta here." She pushed Coppertone aside, then stepped over the tangle of cables, snagging a couple with her oversized shoes.

Coppertone glanced briefly at the unsigned paper on the ground, then knelt to retrieve it. "Crap," he said. Then he glanced at Roy, Roberta, and the three kids. "Well, we're already set up here. We might as well try to get *something*." He gestured for Roberta. "Ma'am, would you be willing to sign this waiver form? All it says is that we can broadcast an interview with you and your grandchildren, and we own all ancillary rights to your images and words."

Roberta looked afraid. "*Ancillary* — what's *that* mean?"

"It's really simple. It just means you have no right to payment from us for giving this interview, and neither do the kids. Nor can you sue us for any damages or future payments in the case of rebroadcast, or the insertion of your images or words into non-news programs, printed materials, or electronic publication of any kind now known or to be developed in the future. Nothing to it. Now, do you want to have the opportunity to tell your story to America?"

"I — I guess so. Where do I have to sign?"

"Here, here, and here." He looked at Roy next. "How about you?"

Be on national television? *Now?* Disguised as an anonymous nobody? What if he were to be found out? The whole country would think he was a *lunatic*... He backed away from the offered waiver form as if it were a live electrical wire. "No," he said, "I, uh, don't have any good stories to tell, anyway."

"All right," Coppertone said, "just stay out of the frame, then."

Roy backed away. He noticed that a small crowd had begun to gather behind the technicians. A tremendously obese man — Roy, dazzled again by the flood lights, could only see his silhouette — waved his log-like arms and shouted, "Hey, how about me? I wanna tell the whole country what I'd like to do to Hizzoner the Mayor. First off, I'd like to hog-tie him and dangle him by the feet from the top of the Dixie Brewery. Then I wanna dip his damn head a few dozen times in the open sewer Tulane Avenue's turned into. But first, I'd hafta *find* the bum. Where is he? Where's our goddamn *leader?*"

"Yeah, where's the mayor?" a woman shouted.

Other voices quickly joined in. "Where is he?"

"Where's Roy Rio?"

"Where the hell's Roy?"

It became a chant.

"Where's Roy? Where's Roy? *Where's Roy?*"

Part of Roy's mind told him to get the hell out, while his head was still attached to his shoulders. But the greater part of him didn't feel like the mayor anymore. He felt more like what he'd imagined himself as just a minute earlier — an anonymous nobody. An Everyman in a sea of outraged Everymen and Everywomen. Shit, *he* was furious at the mayor, too.

Before he fully realized what he was doing, he added his voice to the crowd's swelling chant. "Where's Roy? *Where's Roy?*"

He saw Coppertone discreetly smile. The reporter motioned for the cameras to begin rolling. "This is Ambrose Coppertone, reporting from inside the Louisiana Superdome, battered refuge to more than thirty thousand hungry, *frustrated* survivors of Hurricane Antonia. Some of those bedraggled refugees have gathered to voice their anger at New Orleans Mayor Roy Rio, who has been conspicuously absent from the scene.

"I have here with me Miss Roberta Jones, grandmother to three young children. Roberta, tell me, how angry are *you* at Mayor Rio?"

"Me? Angry?" she said, looking bewildered. "At the mayor? I, I hadn't thought about it."

"Your grandchildren have been subsisting on corn flakes and powdered milk for days. And soon even that will run out. Isn't it the mayor's fault for not properly provisioning the city's only emergency mass shelter?"

Roberta fanned herself with her hat. "Well, I *suppose* so." She obviously regretted having signed the waiver form, Roy thought. "But he seems like a very *nice* young man. And he did come on the TV before the storm and tell everybody to leave."

"Indeed," Coppertone said gravely. Roy could virtually hear the machinery in the man's head switching gears. Wincing inwardly, he knew what the reporter's next question would be. "So, if you heard the announcement to evacuate, why didn't you? Do you have a car?"

"Oh, yes, I have a car. But those pictures of all those poor people stuck on the highway, they looked so *awful*. I didn't want my grandchil'rins stuck in my little car for a day and a night, with no place to pee."

"And yet, here they are, trapped in the Superdome, in even worse conditions. Wasn't it highly *irresponsible* of you to stay in New Orleans with three young children?"

"Irresponsible?" Now Roberta looked frightened. "Mister Coppertone, please, you gotta understand — I got me a good, strong house in Gentilly. My husband Burt and me, we stayed there through Betsy, and we were *fine* — I mean, the roof didn't come off, or nothin'. And this time, well, I thought we'd just come over here to the Superdome for a day, maybe, just while the storm was on, so the kids could be near lots of other people and not be so scared. And then, when it passed, we'd go... back home."

"But you *can't* go home now, can you?" Coppertone closed on her, pressing the mike nearer. "Your neighborhood's flooded with ten feet of lake water. Shouldn't you have realized that was possible, and gotten your grandchildren *out?*"

She looked on the verge of tears. "But, but — but those levees, they was supposed to be *strong*. I mean, the Army built them, didn't they? How — how was *we* to know they wouldn't hold up?"

Roy couldn't hold it in anymore. Nor did he want to. "Leave her the hell *alone*, man!" he said to Coppertone. "What are you getting all over *her* case for? Didn't you hear her? Her house made it through Betsy. Her neighborhood didn't flood *then*, and that was *before* the Corps of Engineers spent forty years building inland flood walls. You wanna point a finger? Start by pointing it at the damn Corps of Engineers — the *United States Army* Corps of Engineers!"

Coppertone smirked, which stoked Roy's fury even higher. "But surely you believe in *personal responsibility*, don't you? I mean, we can't just abdicate all responsibility for our personal safety and that of our loved ones to *the government*, can we?"

"Wait a minute, wait just a damn minute. How many *bridges* do you drive over each year, Coppertone? Give me a guess."

"Oh, I, uh, I'd have to say several dozen—"

"Make that several *hundred*, 'cause we're including overpasses. Now tell me, do you pull over to the side before driving onto all those bridges? Do you get out and *inspect* the bridges, the support posts, the cables, before you drive onto the span? Or do you just *trust* that the engineers and inspectors have done their jobs *right?*"

Coppertone's eyes narrowed. "Tell me, sir, what's your relationship to Miss Roberta? Are you her son?"

"I'm her goddamn *mayor*, that's who!"

He'd stepped off the ledge. Somehow, as soon as he'd spotted the TV cameras, he had known it would come to this. There was nothing left to do now but back up his preposterous claim with undeniable proof and lay himself open to the fury of the crowd.

He yanked the hood away from his face, his ears burning.

A gasp arose from the crowd, so perfectly enunciated it could serve as the Platonic Ideal of a mass gasp. Even the seemingly unflappable Coppertone let his mouth fall open.

Roberta reached up to touch his face, as if to assure herself through physical contact that it truly was him. The cameramen closed in, jostling each other in their eagerness to capture this moment in a perfect close-up.

"It's the mayor," someone said, repeating the blindingly obvious for an audience of millions.

"It — it really *is* the mayor... holy shit."

Roy knew that astonished *"holy shit"* was echoing across the nation, in the headquarters of FEBO and the Corps of Engineers, maybe even in the White House. Fate had given him his big moment, for ill or for good. Maybe he'd been an impotent figurehead up until now — "an empty suit," as Walt had called him. But now his scream for help would be heard. He might be pilloried as a head-case on every late night talk show, but he would be heard.

Coppertone, eyewitness to wars, earthquakes, and hurricanes, quickly recovered his composure. "Mr. Mayor — why did you feel it necessary to wear a disguise? What did you hope to accomplish—"

"The hell with *that*," Roy said. "Listen — *I am NOT the goddamn story here.*" He swung his arm wide. *"These folks are.* Where's their food? Where's their water? How long are they gonna have to stew in this Dome before they get rescued? I don't *care* whose *fault* it is that they ended up stuck here. You wanna blame someone, Coppertone? Blame *me*. But these people are citizens of the United States of America — and this storm is the biggest goddamn disaster this country's ever seen.

"So where the hell *is* everybody? How come it is that every time there's a tsunami in Bangladesh, we've got the Sixth Fleet there practically overnight, and it's been nearly *three days* since Antonia blew ashore — right here in New Orleans, which is *still* part of the frickin' *United States*, the last time I checked — and our people *still* don't have what we need? Why aren't cargo planes parachuting supplies? Why isn't there a hospital ship docked on the Mississippi? Where the *fuck's* FEBO? Can you tell me that, Coppertone? Can *anybody?*"

No one answered.

Coppertone stood expectantly, microphone extended, waiting for Roy to renew his diatribe. But Roy was all shouted out.

Roberta reached for his face again. With both hands, this time. She pulled his face down to hers and kissed him.

He closed his eyes, enraptured by the sensation of her chapped, weathered lips against his stubbly cheek. He felt the press of other hands, other bodies. People encircled the two of them, reaching out to touch his shoulders, his arms, his face.

Then he heard something he'd never heard before, at least not directed at him. Something other men — athletes, heroes, truly beloved leaders — got. Something he'd yearned for, for oh so many years.

The people were cheering. For him.

Chapter 25

O H *God*, Kay thought. She squeezed Owl's limp hand more tightly. *Don't die on me, old man.* Her surroundings gave her little reason for hope — moaning bodies on rows of blankets on the floor, some lying without any barrier at all between swollen flesh and the polished concrete; the twitchy faces of medical personnel, listening for sounds of approaching helicopters or boats, heralds of a fresh crop of the dehydrated and the nearly drowned...

"Miss Rosenblatt, may I speak with you?"

She followed the Army physician a few yards away. "You're ambulatory," he said, rubbing the salt and pepper stubble on his chin. "Which means that, now that we've patched you up some, I'm supposed to discharge you, send you to the Dome. But I've marked you for air evac. You and your two friends will get a chopper flight to New Orleans International Airport for additional treatment, prior to being flown to a hospital, probably out of state."

The words *out of state* clanged in her head. "But, but *why—?*"

"The old man has a broken shoulder and internal bleeding, in addition to harboring a bullet we haven't been able to dig out. The young lady is in some kind of deep coma which we can't even begin to figure out with what we've got here. As for you... that wound to the left side of your face is pretty bad. You'll require facial reconstruction, probably two or three surgeries, but that's not why I'm having you evaced. There's a chance you could lose that eye."

Kay shook her head. "Oh, I won't lose my eye."

"I wouldn't be so sure. If you aren't kept on a strict regimen of antibiotics, I'm certain infection will spread from surrounding tissues into the eye. Even at this point, we may not have caught it in time."

How can I be so sure? she thought. *Because I started my existence as an Evil Eye spirit. My eye will puff up, grow cloudy and gray like spoiled milk, and every person I encounter will shudder and know deep within their soul the sort of monster I've been.* "Don't be concerned for me, doctor," she said. "My eye will be... *fine.* There are dozens of people here who need and deserve evacuation to a proper hospital far more than I do. I... I *can't* leave." *Not with Daniel still somewhere in the city.*

The doctor frowned. "I can't *force* you to go," he said. "If circumstances were even semi-normal, I'd have to have you sign half a dozen forms notarizing your refusal of treatment. Here, on the other hand..." He let his statement trail off. He stared at a section of floor holding ten pallets with prone patients, and Kay could tell he was already losing interest in her, mentally consigning her to the box marked *Would Not Be Helped.*

"Do you know where my friends will be flown to?" she asked.

He shrugged his shoulders. "I have no idea." He turned away from her, muttering over his shoulder, "You'll have to excuse me — I've got patients to attend to."

She heard a burbling sigh from behind her and turned to find Owl staring at her, his expression fuzzy and blurred. "Kay...?" he said.

She hurriedly knelt by his side.

"Whuh... *where...?*"

"We're in the New Orleans Arena," she said. "In the triage station. After the Triumvirate disappeared, two of the Gretna police officers took pity on us and helped us get here. The doctors... they say you should be fine."

"I sure as shit don't *feel* fine." He winced as he tried moving his left arm. "What'd they stick in my shoulder? A live scorpion?"

"The bullet's still in there. Probably because of the bad luck whammy the Triumvirate put on it. They really hate you. And now, me."

"Yeah? That's not news. Well, shit, they could've done a whole lot *worse*. Those bozos must be losin' their touch." Although it clearly cost him dearly to do so, he turned his head to look at Pandora. "What'd the docs say... about her? Can they do anything for her?"

Kay silently shook her head. "You and Pandora are going to be taken to the airport. There's a better medical field station there. Then you're going to be flown to a real hospital. I don't know where."

"What about you?"

"I'm not going."

"You still afraid?" He looked at her more sharply. "Babe, I got no idea either what's gonna happen to me if I end up in Houston or Little Rock. But I figure this is as good a time as any to find out."

"It's not that," she said. "Well, okay, I'd be lying if I said the thought of leaving didn't terrify me. But the real reason... it's Daniel. He's still in the city. I know he won't leave until he learns what's happened to me."

"You positive?"

She nodded. "His father refused to go. Which meant Daniel couldn't go. His top priority will be to keep his father safe. Beyond that, he'll want to make sure I'm all right. And he won't give up. In some ways, he's as stubborn as his father."

"But what about the Triumvirate? They're gunnin' for you now, too. Don't you want to lie low?"

She shrugged her shoulders. "Whatever will be, will be... If you knew the only way to help Pandora recover would be to keep her here in New Orleans, would you even consider letting yourself be flown out?"

"No," he said. "For her, I'd stay. Just like I'm leavin' for her sake."

Kay smiled a tiny smile. "So wish me luck, then."

* * * * *

"Nurse, how many milliliters of morphine did you just administer?"

The concrete roof of Baptist Hospital seemed to undulate beneath Lily Weintraub's feet, as though she stood on a sheet of rubber laid over an unquiet sea. Heat radiated at her from all sides. It poured from the merciless sun overhead, then reflected off the white roof and railings and the bright aluminum transport beds. She'd spent most of the morning struggling to carry patients up the sweltering stairwells to the roof, those patients most likely to survive a helicopter transfer. Looking at her own arms, now red from the sun, she realized she'd stopped sweating. When was the last time she'd had anything to drink?

They'd been waiting for the promised evac choppers for hours. She'd thought nothing could be more draining than helping to drag those transport beds up three and four flights of stairs. But the waiting, here beneath the sun...

She hadn't slept at all the past two nights. Knowing the monsters were out there, on the streets, inside the hospital, able to touch her any time they wished — she hadn't allowed herself to sleep.

Lily felt a hand on her arm. "Nurse Weintraub, I asked you a question."

She blinked rapidly, trying to force the roof to stop its undulations. "Whu—what?"

"I asked you how many milliliters of morphine you just administered to this patient."

She stared down at the syringe in her hand. It was empty. She had no way of telling how much morphine had been inside it a minute ago.

Someone else stared at her, too. Gerard Wolfe. He'd volunteered to help drag the patients and their transport beds up to the roof, even though the exertion might force him into cardiac arrest. Drunk most of the time (where had he been getting his liquor?), he'd been clinging to her like an errant sheet of plastic wrap, silently begging her absolution. He stared at her now, at the empty syringe in her hand.

"Well?" the doctor said.

"How — how many did you instruct me to give?" she asked. The sick-making undulations shifted from the roof into the spaces within her chest.

"Ten."

"Then — then that's how many I administered."

"Are you *sure?* The patient's color has blanched significantly. Lily, are you all right?"

"Yes, yes, I'm positive. And I'm *fine.*" She forced herself to focus on the old woman lying in the transport bed. "I'll check her pulse and respiration. Right away."

But before she could do anything, she was distracted by the distant whir of rotors. She and her colleagues had suffered through many instances of falsely elevated hope — green Army helicopters or white Coast Guard choppers, specks of potential salvation shimmering against the pale blue sky like flitting hummingbirds, which had seemed to be heading toward their rooftop, only to veer away at the last moment.

She scanned the sky; then she saw it, a white and red helicopter, approaching from the east. No, not one; two. Search and rescue helicopters didn't travel in pairs, did they?

Everyone who wasn't directly tending a patient ran to the railings on the roof's eastern edge. They waved frantically at the approaching helicopters.

She held her breath. She told herself she'd let herself breathe again when the choppers turned away, as they surely must. The lead helicopter signaled. The choppers drew closer, and their signaling repeated. They weren't going to Lakeview. They were coming *here.*

A mass cheer arose from parched throats. Lily released her suspended breath. But then a sharp, very loud crack punctured the cheering. It echoed off the medical office buildings surrounding the hospital. The same sound recurred, then again and again, the repeated retorts bouncing into the echoes of prior discharges, making it seem to Lily that bursts erupted from all around her.

Above her, the tone and pitch of the approaching rotor blades suddenly shifted. The two helicopters, which had been on a steady heading for Baptist Hospital, veered to the left and right.

A few of her colleagues pointed at something down below. She squeezed between two aides and saw the source of the sounds. On the roof of an inundated hardware store at the corner of Napoleon Avenue and South Claiborne, two men raced back and forth like infuriated ants, waving stick-like objects at the helicopters. *Shooting*, she thought. *They're shooting at the helicopters. But why? WHY?*

It was the monsters. It *had* to be. Either they had taken on the forms of the two shooters, or they had corrupted those men, made them think, *"If we can't be rescued, then* no one *gets rescued."*

The two helicopters circled higher, out of range of the bullets, then turned back toward downtown.

"No!" Lily screamed. *"No!* Don't run away! Kill them! You've got guns! You're the *military!* They aren't *human* anymore! *Kill them and rescue US!"*

But the helicopters grew smaller and smaller.

"Come back..." she whispered.

Some of the staff began crying. "Why can't things go *right* for once?" someone shouted. "Why do all these *idiots* just make it worse and *worse?"*

"Why wasn't there a *plan?"* a male nurse hollered. "A plan to get us all out of here?"

Lily watched with righteous satisfaction as multiple faces turned to stare at Gerard Wolfe.

"There — there *was* a plan," he stuttered, his round face blanching beneath its fresh sunburn. "But, but this whole disaster, it's just too *big*, it would overwhelm *any* plan—"

"There *never was* an evacuation plan," she said, her hoarse voice cutting him off with brutal effectiveness. "How many times did you promise to show it to me, Gerard? How many times did I *ask* for it? You never could produce it. Because it doesn't *exist*."

"*No*," he wailed. "That isn't right. I wouldn't — I couldn't — I mean, it wasn't my *fault*."

He stumbled over to her and grabbed her hand, as if only she could grant absolution. His touch disgusted her. She pulled her hand back. Her fury felt liberating, intoxicating. "You're a miserable excuse for a human being. You should've been fired *years* ago. You want to be *useful*? Then help me drag these patients back downstairs. Because those helicopters aren't coming back. Thanks to your lack of planning, we're all going to wait right here until the flood evaporates. If we live that long."

Gerard seemed to melt into the rooftop. She had barely a second to bask in her tirade before she heard a croak, louder than a bullfrog's, from the transport bed behind her. The patient she'd been tending, the elderly woman who'd received an unknown quantity of morphine from her hand, began spasming, pitching her frail limbs against the bed's aluminum rails.

* * * * *

Kay found a battered aluminum canoe, beached on the grassy neutral ground at the intersection of Elysian Fields Avenue and St. Claude Avenue, where the edge of the flood waters lapped against the roadway. She dragged the canoe back into the water. She would use it to travel north, to whatever remained of her home. And, she prayed, to Daniel.

How many times had she traversed Elysian Fields Avenue, either by car or by foot? Thousands? Yet she'd never seen her familiar, care-worn, beloved Avenue like she was seeing it now. The older homes, the raised shotguns and double shotguns and camel-backs, bedecked with Greek columns and linteled posts and filigrees of wooden gingerbread, did not look terribly out of place in their newly aquatic environment. They stood like bald cypress trees, indifferent to seasons wet or dry, accepting both with stoic equanimity. It was the newer homes, the ones built after World War Two, which now looked desperately out of place; those brick bungalows and ranch houses, hunkered down on their concrete slabs, appeared drowned and dead. The water reached almost to the tops of their front doors, whereas their more elderly neighbors, raised four feet above the ground on brick piers, admitted only about a foot of water over their door sills.

She paddled beneath the eerily silent I-10 overpass. Just past the Mardi Gras Truck Stop, now littered with the carcasses of abandoned tractor trailers, the Avenue's six lanes rose out of the waters like a volcanic atoll bursting from the surface of the Pacific. She dragged her canoe up the slope of the overpass and paused at the top to catch her breath. The vastness of the disaster, clearly apparent now, nearly overwhelmed her. During the past hours, she'd been witnessing it one block at a time; her mind had been able to localize the devastation, parse it out, fool herself to believe things were awful only so far as her eyes could see. Yet now she could see horizon to horizon, Downtown to New Orleans East, Mid-City to Lakeview and Lake Pontchartrain — *water, water everywhere, and not a drop to drink.*

What if Daniel weren't waiting for her at her house? What would she do then? Where would she even *begin* looking for him?

She let the canoe slide down the opposite slope, aluminum scraping against concrete, its weight pulling her back to the inundated avenue which would lead her home. Two blocks south of the grand old Zuppardo's Super-Market sign, still partially standing, which provided an unofficial marker for the start of the cemeteries district, she heard a voice hailing her.

"Hey, over there! Do you need any help?"

The steady *putt-putt-putt* of a small motor helped her locate the boat and its pilot. He steered through the parking lot of what had been a small strip shopping center on Old Gentilly Road, a block west. "I'm fine," she called back, waving. Then, not knowing exactly how such a conversation in such circumstances should proceed, she added, "How are *you?*"

"Fine, fine, couldn't be better," the man said. Now that he was a little closer, she recognized his voice. He looked familiar, too; he was round as a barrel, with an oversized Stetson hat.

"Do you need any water?" he called.

"I've got some, thanks."

"You seen anybody who needs rescuing?"

"Not since I left the French Quarter," she said. Finally, she remembered where she knew him from. "Hey, are you Sheriff Herman Chin?"

"Guilty as charged." Even from a block away, she could see his politician's pride at being recognized. "And who do *I* have the pleasure of meeting?"

"Kay Rosenblatt. From the Corps of Engineers. We met at that hurricane simulation last winter."

"Oh, sure, right, I remember! Hey, don't tell anybody else you meet you're from the Corps of Engineers, okay? Lots of folks might not be too forgiving right about now."

"I'll keep that under wraps." Enormous bubbles from a sunken car rose to the surface of the black, oily water and burst in the space between their two boats, releasing a putrid stink. "Hey, what are you doing here? I would've thought you'd be in Metairie or Marrero."

"Hey, you can't keep this fat old Chinaman out of a boat. Actually, things are pretty much under control in Jefferson Parish, and I wanted to get where the action is. So I rounded up a gang of my fishing buddies and a bunch from the State Department of Wildlife and Fisheries, all good ol' boys with boats. We gathered by the Seventeenth Street Canal, pulled out a map, and divided up the neighborhoods. I picked this area 'cause I used to have a grandma lived out here, when we had a laundry in Gentilly. What, you surprised somebody from Jefferson would bother with folks from Orleans?"

"No, uh, not really... Well, actually, yeah."

His round face crinkled, as though the escaped subterranean stench had finally reached his nose. "Pardon my French, but that's the kinda crap we've gotta get past in this state. Black, white, Orleans, Jefferson — we're all *Louisianans*, y'know? That flood water, it didn't stop at the parish line; it flowed straight from Pigeon Town in Orleans right over into Old Metairie. And *all* our problems are like that, y'know?

"I've had a lotta time to think while I've been sittin' in this boat. And I think it's time for somebody who *knows* those problems to step up to the plate. So Sheriff Herman Chin, as of today, is officially running to become the first Cajun-Chinese governor of the great State of Louisiana."

"*Really?*"

"Truly. You're witnessing history in the making, young lady. But there's one thing they're gonna try and tar and feather me with. And that's this damn foolish notion that I'm some kinda 'racist.' Damn it to *hell*, you know how *tired* I get of hearing that? Black people, I love 'em to death. I mean, me and Fats Domino, we go *way* back, he used to eat at my family's restaurant. We go fishing together, four, five times a year. But because I call a spade a spade, because I put my deputies where the crime is and try to protect the blacks from other blacks, I get called *racist*. It *burns* my fat ass, y'know? So, young lady, you tell everybody you see that Sheriff Herman Chin crossed the parish line to personally rescue two dozen black people in New Orleans. I ain't no racist. You tell them that, okay?"

"Uh... okay."

"Hey, here, I got something else for you to do." He edged closer, then pulled a handful of small objects from his rain slicker and tossed them into Kay's canoe. They clattered against the boat's aluminum bottom.

"Anybody you run into, you give them one of those, okay? And say a good word about my campaign."

She glanced down. Sitting in a puddle on the canoe's floor were mementos of every Mardi Gras parade which had rolled through Jefferson Parish in the last twenty years — five refrigerator magnets, each of them a half-dollar-sized likeness of Sheriff Chin's smiling face, wearing a red kerchief and a white cowboy hat.

"Stick one of those on the bow of your canoe," he demanded.

She picked one up and pressed it against her boat's side. Instead of sticking, it fell into the water and sank. "Oh, I'm so sorry..."

"Hell, that's all right," he said. "Forgot the damn things won't stick to aluminum. Been good visiting with you, but I've got neighborhoods to patrol. I hope I can count on your vote. Where're you heading to?"

"Home," she said.

"Well, shit, good luck with that," he said. Then he waved and turned his boat around.

She waved back.

Kay began paddling again and soon entered what had been the cemeteries district. She couldn't see even one of the Jewish cemetery's headstones; just the Star of David weather vane which stood, bent and stripped of its paint, atop the small guard house. Black objects, nearly as long as her canoe, trailed torn shrouds as they bobbed near her path. They looked like logs which had become entangled in sheets, but Kay knew what they were. And who.

She forced herself to look away before she drifted close enough to possibly see any remains of faces. She muffled her reactions with the blackest humor she could muster: *There go your voters, Sheriff Chin. Make sure to get them registered. No sense in letting a perfectly good Louisiana tradition die.*

Three blocks beyond the sunken cemetery, she found herself approaching Mirabeau Avenue. And home.

She was stunned by how much *smaller* her house looked. It was just an optical illusion; her home was a camelback, with a partial second story, and now only that portion of the house stood above the water. She tried remembering how many of her possessions she'd stored within the two tiny bedrooms of her second story. Most of her things — her folk art; her collection of Carnival throws; her dishes and flatware, carefully segregated into meat and dairy, every day and Passover-only — had been in the downstairs rooms. She hadn't moved a single precious object from the first floor to the sanctuary of an upstairs closet; she'd been too busy trying to kill herself.

But she wasn't dead. Only her home was dead. The thought of seeing what had become of her things, collected over a span of a hundred and thirty years, made her want to commit suicide all over again, just a little.

Her bow scraped against the twisted remains of her first story's aluminum rain gutters. She stepped out onto the sloping tiles. Her chimney had toppled over onto the lower portion of the house, smashing a hole through the roof. She stared down into her kitchen. Her refrigerator was just below her. It bobbed up and down ever so slightly; the water had toppled it, but because its door had remained sealed, it had floated upward, almost to the ceiling. One of her kitchen table chairs floated close to the hole, too. Something shiny and rectangular lay across its soaked cushion — a polished stainless steel serving tray which Daniel had given her.

Now it served as a mirror. She saw herself for the first time since she'd ingested hundreds of pills in her bathroom. She was a different person now, and she looked it. Her aura was gone, but it hadn't vanished without a trace; it had left an unavoidable reminder of the century when she and it had been completely aligned. Her guilt, her culpability, formerly hidden, were now written clearly on her face.

She had an Evil Eye.

The events of that Sunday morning when she'd destroyed the Weintraub family flashed through her memory again and again. She watched baby Daniel bounce out the open window as the Buick plunged toward the water. She heard his voice calling her. "Kay! Kay!" But he hadn't learned how to talk that young... how was he calling her?

"Kay! Over here! Kay!"

She heard the approaching motor and shook herself back to the present. She saw him, his face more radiant, more hopeful than she could recall in even her most embellished memories.

Although she knew she didn't deserve the efflorescence of joy she felt, she didn't try to squelch it. She screamed his name and leaped with happiness, then tumbled with a small avalanche of bricks and tiles into the oily water.

Daniel dove after her. Seconds later, she felt his strong arms pull her back onto the roof.

"Kay! Thank God. Thank *God*. Are you okay?"

He squeezed her so tightly that she could barely get an answer out. "I'm — I'm *okay*. What about—"

"I've been looking for you. And looking, and looking! This is the *ninth* time I've come to your house in my boat! Kay, I've had to steal gasoline, because I've been using so much, looking for you. I felt *terrible*, having to steal—"

"It's okay, it's *okay*, darling, everyone's had to steal since the storm." She felt his hair, his face, his shoulders, her fingers alighting on him like nervous butterflies, trying to reassure herself that this was truly him.

"Where have you been?" he asked.

"I've been *everywhere*. I was taken away by a tornado, and then Owl found me, and we ended up at the New Orleans Arena..." She stared at his empty boat. "Daniel, where's your father? Is he safe?"

His lower lip quivered. The joy in her breast froze into brittleness. "He's... he's—" Daniel couldn't get the next words out.

"Oh, no," she said. "No..."

"I tried — tried burying him on the, on the roof of my garage. But there was no dirt to cover him with, and I didn't have a prayer book, and I couldn't remember the right prayers, and I didn't have a *minyan*, and there was no *Chevra Kadisha*. I had to cover my father with *junk*, Kay. Wood, tar paper... But I got him covered before the sun went down."

"How..." Her mouth tasted like ashes. "How did it happen?"

"He wanted to rescue the *torahs* at Beth Judah. The *shul* had all filled with water. I went to get a plastic trash pail to float the *torahs* in — I didn't want to leave him alone, but I *had* to. A flying refrigerator had smashed through the dome and made a hole in front of the ark. I felt the hole with my foot, but Kay, oh, Kay — I *forgot* to tell my father about it! While I was gone... he fell in. He couldn't swim."

So she'd been mistaken when she'd thought the twister had spared Beth Judah's main sanctuary. While she'd been congratulating herself, her dying aura had beaten her one final time.

"Daniel," she said, "I... *I* killed your father." Her voice cracked. "I've destroyed your family. Every *word* that Lily told you about me is *true*. I *am* an *ayin hora*, an Evil Eye, a walking pestilence..."

He took a step toward her. "Kay, I don't—"

"No! Stay *away* from me!" She scurried backward like a terrified rodent. "I know you don't understand. But I'm *death*. I — I *love* you, Daniel — but you have to stay *away*. My aura dissolved, but I don't know if I'm still toxic. I won't hurt you anymore, Daniel, I just *won't*."

He reached beseechingly for her. "I wasn't going to say, 'I don't *understand*.' What I was going to say is, 'I don't *care*.' I don't care *what* you are, Kay, or what you've been. I shouldn't have listened to Lily. All I know is—"

"Look at me!" She pointed at the left side of her face, the throbbing, misshapen side. "Daniel, what I am, it's *written all over my face.* Can't you see? Now it's out in the open, for everyone to look at..."

Faster than she could react, he closed the distance between them and enfolded her in an unbreakable embrace. "Hush," he said. "Just hush *up*. You don't look any different now than you did the first night I saw you. No, that's not right — you look more beautiful now, because you aren't fighting yourself anymore. I *love* you, Kay. I don't want to be without you."

"But, but..." She stopped struggling. Slowly, she accepted the embrace, melted into it. She thought back to his first words upon seeing her a few moments ago. His immediate reactions were always unfiltered, uncensored, like those of a child. Yet he hadn't said a word about her disfigurement.

That meant he didn't see it. Or he *did* see it... but he hadn't felt a need to mention it, because to him, it had *always* been there. He'd always seen through her, seen inside her, as if her skin were made of glass.

He'd been looking at her ugliness for years now. And it hadn't mattered to him.

She pressed the left side of her face against his wet shirt, buried her nose and her mouth in his underlying warmth. Her view of the universe had been all wrong, upside down. She and her fellow creatures of the miasma weren't the supernatural ones, the extraordinary. They were mundane, ordinary as dirt and water. The human beings whose lives they touched were the special ones.

Daniel, simple, extraordinary Daniel — his capacity to forgive and love was a mountain, a levitating, magic mountain. Compared to that, even the Triumvirate's seemingly awesome power was but an insubstantial sand dune, doomed to dissipate before the wind.

No matter how impossible Owl had made it sound, she would find a way to beat the Miasma Club.

Part III

No Joy in Mudville?

Chapter 26

“**A** poet once said, 'No man is an island; entire of itself; every man is a piece of the continent, a part of the main.'"

Had more than four months passed since his now-famous "unmasking speech" in the Superdome? Roy Rio did a quick calculation: four months, a week, and three days. He and his drowned city had finally reached the end of the worst summer in living memory — September twenty-first, the first day of fall, the start of a new season. And here he was, in the just reopened Lower Ninth Ward, giving another speech that, while not closing the circle on his earlier exhortation, at least represented a welcome step in that direction.

He stepped around the portable lectern which his staff had placed, island-like, on what had once been the neat front lawn of John and Tilda Wilson's house on Lizardi Street. The Wilsons, a black couple in their mid-sixties, stood off to the side, arranged there like scenery for the cameras. Roy didn't like that; they weren't scenery. They were fellow citizens who had finally been given the green light to return home. He gestured for them to join him, then put his arms around them, reveling in their closeness. "The poet had it right," he continued. "No man is an island. No neighborhood is an island. No *city* is an island, cut off from its state and nation, free to wither and die with no consequences outside its own narrow borders."

He looked out at the Wilsons' family, who until today had only been allowed to visit their homes during daylight hours. They stood in front of acres of emptied lots and naked slabs, looking like the last few pine trees left behind at the edge of a clear-cut forest. "We're all connected, intertwined, all parts of one greater whole with a common fate. New

Orleans cannot fully prosper while the Lower Ninth Ward remains a shambles, its homeowners in exile, its streets clogged with mud and weeds. America cannot fully prosper while New Orleans — one of its greatest ports, the nexus of a quarter of its oil and gas production, the spawning ground of much of its culture — remains on its knees.

"Today the gates have been reopened to the residents of the Lower Ninth Ward, our neighbors who once built a resilient community of humble but strong houses and streets that echoed with music. They built this place up, and as of today, with our help and blessing, they will take up that yoke one more time. The gates have been reopened. Let them never be shut again!"

Roy stared directly at Bruno Galliano as the Wilson family and friends cheered. Next to him, Mrs. Wilson gulped back a sob, and he hugged her more tightly to him. But Bruno frowned — more of a wince, Roy thought — and shook his head. *"Mr. Mayor, don't make them promises you can't back up,"* Bruno had begged him. *"I understand how important the Lower Ninth Ward is, politically, culturally. But there's no way the Corps is going to make that area safe from even a Cat Two storm surge before 2015, and I doubt they could pull it off given even twenty more years. If you invite people to come back, you're putting them in harm's way. Bite the bullet. Declare the Lower Nine and other untenable parts of the city off limits for building permits. Buy them out. You're the only politician in this town who has a chance in hell of making it stick."*

Every cell in his body had recoiled from Bruno's urgings. Not due to political cowardice; Roy knew himself well enough to rule that out. Of course, there was no denying that, as the black mayor of a majority-black city, he'd pay a steep political price for red-lining out of existence a neighborhood known for its high rate of working class black homeownership.

No... his revulsion sprang from memories of stories his grandmother had told him, tales of her Lower Nine friends' superhuman efforts to rebuild their homes after Hurricane Betsy. As a child, he'd been fascinated to hear how they'd raised their precious little cottages on iron stilts or concrete piers. That land — that parcel of mud and grass — was *their* land, their families' lands, properties which had been paid for by decades of loading and unloading cargoes on the Industrial Canal and the Mississippi, of cleaning white people's homes or hotel rooms, of fixing toilets in public schools. No storm could break that tie.

He cleared his throat and looked away from Bruno. "John Donne concluded his poem by asking his listeners not to respond to the tolling of a church bell by wondering for whom the bell tolls. It tolls for them, too, as well as the deceased, for they are 'involved in mankind,' they are diminished by *every* man's death. If the bell tolls for the Lower Ninth Ward, it tolls, too, for New Orleans. If the bell tolls for New Orleans, it tolls, too, for America. So let us pledge to ensure that from this day forward, the only tolling of bells to be heard on this hallowed ground will be the joyous bells of repaired church steeples and the welcoming bells of rebuilt schools.

"I thank you all for being here. I thank the Wilsons and their neighbors for having the courage to return and rebuild. May God bless them, may God bless New Orleans, and may God bless America."

He felt a shiver of pleasure as applause surrounded him and he replayed his words in his head. Giving a speech had never felt this *good* before. Before Antonia, he'd been an above average businessman, but only a middling, often hesitant politician. Now, however... now the electricity flowed. Antonia had given him his political sea legs. For the first time in his life, he felt he was doing something that *mattered*, that made a difference in people's lives. *Intoxicating.*

He raised his arms, gesturing for all the returnees to join him in front of the moldering shell of a house which would begin its slow crawl back to life this morning. These were his people — *his* people. He was here to help bind up their wounds and make them whole again. He stripped off his jacket and tie and picked up a shovel, intending to shovel away the three-foot-high slope of mud which blocked the home's warped front door.

Cameramen crowded around him, jostling for the best angle. Once they'd all recorded their B-shots, including footage of the flood-imploded homes closer to where the Industrial Canal levee had breached, they retreated with their equipment to their vans. Roy paused to watch the vans' satellite transmission masts fold onto the vehicles' roofs like the forearms of praying mantises preparing to take flight. Then he sank his shovel back into the mud.

"Roy, the cameras are gone," Walter Johnson said in a low voice. "Say goodbye to these folks, and let's get back to the office."

"I'm not done," Roy said. He still hadn't completely forgiven his political advisor that lacerating tirade at the Hyatt. Weirdly enough, Walter had denied ever making those remarks or even being with Roy that afternoon, and other employees had backed up his story.

"From the look of things, you won't be 'done' for another *month*," Walter said. "Come on. The Wilsons have lots of other people to help them—"

"And they've got their *mayor*, too. Do you realize what these people have been through? They need their mayor standing next to them, not just mouthing words, but shouldering part of the load."

"So, does this mean you're going to personally gut every flooded home in the Ninth Ward? How about Gentilly? And Lakeview?"

"Don't be dense, Walt."

"*I'm* not the one being dense. You've got business back at City Hall. FEBO's got us tangled up in red tape. We don't have the staff to handle even a *tenth* of what they're asking for in those project worksheets. We've got to figure out some kind of a compromise—"

"You and Bruno can handle that," Roy said. "Borrow some staff from Public Works."

"We aren't the *mayor*. Only *you've* got the clout to make the feds blink on this."

"Handle it, okay? I'm staying here. I'll head back when the Wilsons break for lunch."

Walter gave up and walked back to his car. Roy couldn't mention it, but he had another reason for lingering. He was supposed to meet with Kay Rosenblatt. And Lily.

Lily... never in a million years could he have imagined her getting tangled up in the legal mess she was in now. Through no fault of her own, so far as he knew, she'd become a symbol of the Antonia disaster. Ugly business, being accused of euthanasia. Even though no grand jury had yet indicted her, she'd already been tried and convicted in the media. With his reelection campaign coming up, he hadn't dared schedule this meeting at City Hall, callous as that sounded; thinking about this necessary caution made him feel dirty.

And then there was Kay Rosenblatt. Driven insane by the catastrophe? That was one explanation for her compulsive yammerings about hoodoo and miasma and a pissed-off Gaia. He would've told his staff to reject her calls and messages if she hadn't said a few things that made a scary kind of sense... particularly about the serial breakdowns of the emergency communications system before and during the storm, which she shouldn't have been aware of, and about that weird business with Walter Johnson at the Hyatt.

Now she insisted the sky was about to begin falling again. Her whole gang of creepy crawlers had been hibernating through the summer, but now the Fall Equinox would wake them up.

The only reason he'd agreed to meet with her out here was that Lily had intervened. He'd been avoiding her since the news of the Baptist Hospital deaths had turned red hot... seeing her and Kay was an attempt to alleviate his guilt.

He saw Lily's car turn off St. Claude Avenue, followed by a pickup truck. Odd that they hadn't driven over in a single vehicle. He made his excuses to the Wilsons and walked a couple of lots closer to St. Claude to meet his visitors.

Kay emerged first. She'd been in some kind of an accident since he'd seen her prior to the storm; he tried not to stare at the livid scars surrounding her left eye. "Thank you so much for agreeing to meet with me, Mr. Mayor," she said. "I've been sensing faint emanations from the Miasma Club all week, but today, the Equinox, those emanations grew much more powerful. They're all waking up, all the ones who weren't disincorporated by the storm. The miasma field has replenished itself, and so the Miasma Club's hibernation is over. You have to be ready for them, whether you decide to accept my help or not."

Roy waited for Lily to exit her car. But she hung back, avoiding looking at him. "Tell me this," he said to Kay. "If you aren't one of them anymore, like you've said, then how do you know what they're up to?"

"I still have a connection to the Otherness," she said. "I can, well, *sense* when a Miasma Club member is nearby, or when they're wielding the miasmatic energy they pull from the Mother."

He sighed and shook his head. "I'm still having a hard time believing all this."

"Believe it, Roy," Lily said, shutting her car door. "I didn't want to believe it, either. But I've been forced to."

He stared at Lily a little too long. She'd gained weight these last few months; her once classically proportioned face had grown puffy. And she'd taken up cigarettes, too. She stood as far from Kay and from him as she could and still remain within speaking distance.

"You don't have to believe just *me*, Mr. Mayor," Kay said. "Your own chief of staff swears he didn't browbeat you right after the storm, and he's got an alibi that's been confirmed by five other people. Assuming different identities is a Miasma Club specialty; I used to do it myself. He's not the only member of your staff who was affected by the Miasma Club. Bruno Galliano has Fortuna's sickly-sweet stench all over him; I could smell it as soon as I walked into City Hall."

Bruno under an evil influence? That would explain a lot of what went wrong. "All right," he said, "assuming I decide to accept your help, how is this supposed to work? You'll be on loan to my office from the Corps of Engineers as my official liaison, right? But in actuality, you'll be serving as a... a goblin detector?"

"That's right. Now that they're awake, the Miasma Club will be hungry to finish what they started. The city's flat on its back now, and they'll try their best to stomp on its windpipe. There's a terribly ominous juxtaposition coming up in three months. This year, the Winter Solstice, the darkest day of the year, falls only eight days after a Friday the Thirteenth."

"Friday the Thirteenth... uh, yeah. And, uh, *how*, exactly, are you going to help me stop all this evilness? Sorry if that's a dumb question — I'm just trying to wrap my head around all of this."

"You're a key part of New Orleans' recovery — I hardly need to tell you that. Every day, all over the country, refugees are making decisions on how quickly to return, or whether to return at all. Congressmen are trying to decide whether rebuilding New Orleans and strengthening our storm defenses are worth the hundreds of billions it'll cost. And they're all looking at *you*, waiting to hear your plans, so they can plan accordingly.

"Before the storm, the Miasma Club never succeeded at influencing you directly. Instead, they preyed on people connected to you, like your ex-wife and her uncle. But during the disaster, one of them, probably Eleggua-Eshu, must've sensed some new vulnerability in you, some weakness or fallibility you hadn't previously shown. He went after you more directly than ever before. That's what they do, Mr. Mayor — they hunt for weaknesses, then exploit any they find.

"The Miasma Club doesn't have to accomplish much to derail the rebuilding. All they have to do is make you look indecisive or weak, or influence you to make hasty, radical decisions. There's an election coming up. You're going to be attacked. Even without the Miasma Club's meddling, that's a precarious situation for a leader with your responsibilities to be in. How can I help? I can warn you whenever a bad luck spirit is present, so you can use that knowledge to keep yourself from making bad decisions. Are they pushing your buttons? Are they making you jump at a wrong choice? Should you trust your immediate impulses or take a step back?"

Roy rubbed his forehead. "So you're asking me to doubt myself, to continuously second-guess my decisions — and this is supposed to *help* me?"

"*No*, that's not what I'm saying at all. I want to be your sentry so you *don't* have to continuously second-guess yourself. You'd only need to look for false motivations when I warn you a Miasma Club member is near. Without me alerting you, you'll be forced to doubt yourself all the time. Because in every important meeting you'll have, you'll never know whether that judge or bureaucrat or campaign contributor sitting across from you is truly who they appear to be."

"I've got the same problem with *you*, y'know," he said. "Tell me why I shouldn't suspect you're still one of *them*, playing a double game? Wouldn't it screw me up just as much, to falsely warn me that a visitor is one of *them*, so that I'd automatically reject whatever it is they're advising?"

"Are you asking me to prove that my aura is truly gone?" Her fingers traced the scar tissue which surrounded her left eye. "There's this. When I was a full-fledged bad luck spirit, any injuries I suffered would heal up in a matter of minutes. This scar has been with me since Antonia, since my aura died. Lily's brother Daniel can verify that."

"Yeah? But you've already admitted Miasma Club spirits can change their appearance. So that scar doesn't prove anything."

"Okay. I know Lily's told you how she was able to ward me off at Baptist Hospital before the storm. Lily, I want you to repeat what you did that night. Say the Yiddish phrase for 'no Evil Eye,' then spit between your index and middle fingers at me three times."

"*Kein ayin hora*," Lily said hoarsely. Roy saw Kay flinch with anticipated pain. Then Lily spat three times between her fingers, directly into Kay's face.

Nothing happened.

"There," Kay said. "Are you satisfied?"

"Look," he said, "how do I know she said the right thing just now? You could be clouding her mind, or something."

Kay's cheeks turned red. "You — you're making it *impossible* for me to help you! I can't prove a *negative*, damn it!"

"I've done my 'civic duty'," Lily said to Kay. "I'm leaving now."

"Lily," Kay said, "*please* don't go! Help me think of some way to convince him! You aren't doing this for *me!* Think about Daniel! Think about his future!"

Lily's face turned livid. "If *you'd* bother thinking about his future, you wouldn't be planning a *wedding* with him, would you?"

"Wait," Roy said to Kay. "You're getting *married?* To Daniel Weintraub?"

"Of *course* to Daniel," she said. "We can't have any celebrations until the end of his eleven months of mourning, so we're planning it for next April."

"I only pray I'm rotting in prison by then," Lily said, "so Daniel can't force me to attend."

Roy tried sorting through the potential implications of this news. "Wait a minute... why now? Lily's told me you've had Daniel wrapped around your little finger for years. You could've gotten him to marry you any time you'd wanted. And even old Amos couldn't have stopped it."

"Oh, it shouldn't be too hard to figure out," Kay said bitterly. "I'm marrying him now so I can get my hands on Amos's money, of course. Here's the truth, not that either of you will believe it. I wouldn't allow myself to marry Daniel while my aura still existed. It was capable of manipulating or pushing me into doing almost anything, but never *that*. Now that it's gone, I don't see any reason to avoid happiness any longer. Just like I can't see any reason to argue with you any longer, Mr. Mayor. Good luck and good bye."

"Hang on a minute," he said. Kay paused, her expression a mix of exasperation and hope. "I can't say I'm a hundred percent on board with this, but let's give it a trial run. When is the Corps making you available?"

"As early as tomorrow."

"Let's start tomorrow morning, then. I'll be back out this way, at the Jazzland amusement park, meeting with some MuckGen people and the City Council about MuckGen's proposal to lease the land the ruined park sits on. Your hobgoblin buddies might be tempted to put in an appearance. You game?"

She hesitantly smiled. "I'm game."

"Good. Meet my people in the reserved section of the City Hall parking garage, first level, at eight-thirty sharp. Oh, one more thing — pass along my congratulations to Daniel on your engagement, okay?"

Lily glared at both of them with barely contained loathing. "I hope the two of you enjoy a *beautiful* friendship," she said before getting into her car.

"Lily, wait," he said. "I'm sorry I missed the memorial service for your father. Is there anything I can do...?"

"Just *save* it, Roy. You want to do something for me? Stay away, just like you've been doing. I needed you during the storm. We all did. I *don't* need you *now*."

She slammed her transmission into Drive and made a sloppy U-turn through hillocks of dried mud, raising a plume of dust that drifted above the hastily patched levees.

Chapter 27

ROY Rio stared up at the rusting skeleton of the Mega Zeph roller coaster, once the signature attraction of the Six Flags New Orleans Jazzland amusement park. Just a few years ago, this attraction had been a linchpin of Roy's economic renewal plan for New Orleans East; now it served as a microcosm of the city's physical and financial ruin. The city treasury was on the hook for nearly twenty million dollars in loan guarantees, thanks to his ramming the deal through the City Council at the beginning of his term. He and his advisors had assumed a family attraction like this was an investment impossible to lose money on. But now Six Flags, embroiled in disputes with their insurers, had announced their intention to break their lease and walk away from this mud-caked collection of ruins, leaving the city holding the bag.

However, a white knight had appeared on the horizon — MuckGen. Their post-storm surveys revealed this land was ideal for their needs. They were interested in assuming Six Flags' lease. For Roy, this potentially solved two problems at once — the city could continue meeting its debt service obligations and even turn a bit of a surplus on the deal; and MuckGen could perform an end-run around Cynthia's obstructionary schemes. Assuming, of course, that Roy could convince the City Council to approve the lease transfer. That's what today's field trip was all about.

The group paused next to a bumper car ride whose dozens of electric cars were caked with thick coats of dried mud. "What we've documented in the months following the storm and the subsequent drainage of this quadrant of the city has been simply astounding," Annalee Jones of

MuckGen said. "Our earliest post-Antonia readings out here in New Orleans East showed an eighty percent decline in bio-energy levels from pre-storm readings. Since then, however, energy levels have been rebounding virtually exponentially. Already, in just the past seven weeks, they've attained ninety-two percent of the pre-storm levels, on average. The trend line shows no sign of abating. To use a crude analogy, Antonia seems to have powered a gigantic flywheel in this area, which may potentially store far greater quantities of bio-energy than any ever measured previously. One of the epicenters of this dramatic surge in energy storage is right here, buried beneath Jazzland. We estimate that, within a year, these seventy acres may contain more recoverable and exploitable bio-energy than the fifteen hundred acre tract we sought to lease or purchase prior to the storm."

Cynthia stared dourly at the mud soiling her leather boots. "Mayor Rio," she said, addressing her fellow Council members as much as him, "have you fully considered all the alternatives to this proposal? Six Flags has stated they intend to walk away from all this ruined equipment, and MuckGen has said nothing about removing it, either—"

"Actually," Annalee said, "we would prefer that the rides and facilities remain in place. Some of our data suggest that the presence of this decaying equipment may in some way be abetting the bio-energy surge, perhaps by placing additional stresses on the soils."

"Precisely," Cynthia said, obviously pleased. "So if we accept MuckGen's proposal, my district gets saddled with a permanent eyesore, visible from every major highway that crosses through New Orleans East. Besides, as I've said for months now, their technology and business plan are *highly* speculative. Who's to say they'll be financially capable of maintaining their lease payments five years from now? We could be kicking loan default just a few years down the road, at little or no benefit to the city. Mayor Rio, you *say* you've canvassed all the other national and regional amusement park operators, and none have expressed any interest in reviving Jazzland. But have you considered having the city run the park itself? We own the land. Once Six Flags abandons this equipment, we'll own that, too. Why let a middleman make all the profits, when they could flow into our general fund, instead?"

You and the Morehouses would like that, wouldn't you? Roy thought. *Hundreds of cronies who could be put on the payroll; endless opportunities for graft...* "Councilwoman, our municipal workforce can barely keep a playground in decent operating condition. How do you expect them to run an operation like this? And where are we going to get the money to refurbish all this equipment, thirty-five mechanically complex rides? We're already leveraged up to our eyeballs, and tax receipts are projected to be down sixty-five percent this year."

She smiled her most devilish grin. "May I quote you, Mr. Mayor? About our municipal workforce, I mean. I'm sure our city employees will find your comments about their work aptitudes most enlightening, come election time."

Roy didn't let himself rise to the bait. Instead, he glanced at Kay Rosenblatt. She signaled with a shy wave that things remained "all clear," that no unseen demon or gremlin had taken command of his ex-wife's mouth; Cynthia's provocation was entirely her own.

"Mr. Mayor," Councilman Sappare said, "I don't think you should reject my colleague's suggestion out of hand. I think her proposal merits some study."

Sappare was Cynthia's closest ally on the Council. Cynthia could try to assemble a coalition to defeat the lease swap motion, but Roy knew her influence on her fellow council members was more limited than the sway she held over her church's elders. Not only that, her obstructionary tactics would be much more visible to the public, who might wonder why a mayoral candidate would oppose an arrangement so obviously in the city's best interests.

"The Council has the authority to study and debate any proposal it likes," Roy said. "As for my administration's view on the matter, I think I've made that clear. Unless any of the other Council members have questions for Ms. Jones or other MuckGen staff, I suggest we adjourn and head back to City Hall."

This was one proposal which met with unanimous agreement. Kay motioned for Roy to remain behind. "Mr. Mayor," she said, "I have to warn you — the Miasma Club are dead set against the MuckGen project. Your announcement earlier this year of the city's support for the consortium was a big impetus for all the Club's members to focus on Project Big Blow."

"But if the goblins are against MuckGen, isn't that all the more reason I should be *for* them?"

"It's not that simple. I'm no technical expert, but the 'bio-energy' MuckGen seeks to tap into, all the power that's been surging back in the soil here since the flood — that's the Mother's energy. MuckGen intends to exploit the miasmatic field, the same pool of energy which used to power my aura's bad luck potencies. No good can come of it. Even if MuckGen's initial projects seem to work perfectly, ultimately, they can only lead to disaster."

He still wasn't sure how far he should trust her. She could be combining a truth — the Miasma Club's aversion to MuckGen — with a false warning, in order to weaken his support for the company. "I don't know about that," he said. "If what you say is true, wouldn't MuckGen's pilot studies have run into some reversals already? I mean, they've been experimenting with harnessing this bio-energy for several years now..."

His Blackberry buzzed. He checked the number before answering. It was Nicole, calling from Houston. "Excuse me for a minute," he told Kay. "I need to take this."

He walked to the shelter of a concession stand to get out of the wind. "Hi, precious," he said. "What are you doing, calling me in the middle of a school day?"

"Hi, Daddy." Hearing her voice, so full of longing, made Roy long for her, too. Thank God her distress over Lily had been short lived. "It's my phys-ed period. Coach wouldn't let us suit up, because it's raining, so all the kids are just wandering around the gym."

"Sounds like fun."

"It's *not*. I don't like the kids here. All the Houston kids think the New Orleans kids are trash. You know what they call us? 'Antonia bums'."

Roy winced. "Have you told your teachers about that?"

"There's nothing they can do — I mean, we've had assemblies and everything, with the principal telling everybody to be considerate. But afterward the local kids go right back to their bad-mouthing."

"Just hang in there, baby. I know it's tough."

"Daddy, I want to come home."

"Baby, you're coming home for a long weekend in just four days—"

"I don't *mean* for a long weekend. I want to come back to New Orleans for good."

"But hon, your mother's house won't be in livable shape for months. She's made it very clear she's staying in Houston for now, where most of her congregants ended up, and only making occasional trips back here. She's your custodial parent, so you've got to stick where she is."

"Why can't *you* be my custodial parent?"

He sighed. "Nicole, we've been through this before. Your mother would never agree to that. And the only way a judge would switch custody against her wishes would be if I could prove she's an unfit parent, which I can't." *And I certainly wouldn't try it in the middle of this campaign — I'd lose every divorced mother's vote out there.* He stared out at the silent expanse of ruined Ferris wheels, roller coasters, and game booths. "Besides... I think your mother's right. New Orleans... it's not a place for a young girl to be, not now."

"But I looked up my old school Xavier Prep on Google Earth, Daddy. They didn't flood. Their website says they'll be reopening for the spring semester. You could go over there and enroll me *today*. Then I could be back with my friends—"

"Nicole, I already said no. But you'll get your chances to see your friends. With your mother planning to run for mayor, she'll have to at least rent an apartment here. Maybe you can negotiate something with her, like staying with her in her place while she's here, then staying with me when she returns to Houston."

"Oh, Daddy, that would be *wonderful!*" She paused. When she spoke again, her voice was noticeably subdued. "Daddy... are things, you know... *okay* there? The stuff I read on the internet... it makes New Orleans sound so *awful*. But things are getting better every day, aren't they?"

He stared at Kay Rosenblatt. She watched him with the wary eyes of a sentry, certain the monsters would try again. Was his city strong enough to withstand them? Was *he?*

"Daddy? Are you still there?"

"Yes, I'm here..." He forced himself to look away from the ruined midway, away from Kay Rosenblatt. He concentrated on his memory of the Wilsons and the volunteers helping them to rebuild their home. "Honey, you're right. Things *are* getting better every day. And as mayor of this city, as your father... I'll make everything right again, I promise. I promise you that, Nicole."

"I believe you, Daddy. If anyone can make things better, it's you."

* * * * *

How easily mesmerized these humans are, thought Glenn the Gremlin.

The woman from Mexico — hardly more than a girl — pulled the gray motel sheets more closely around her swollen belly. Marianna Cortez stared, glassy eyed, at Glenn's face. According to her limited comprehension, what she stared at was a twenty-two-inch television screen which miraculously played a continuous stream of Mexican soap operas and Spanish-language celebrity interviews. The owners of this shabby motel on Airline Drive, close to the dividing line between Orleans and Jefferson Parishes, were far too cheap to pony up for a satellite dish capable of capturing such distant transmissions; this despite having a clientele made up entirely of Mexican workers and their families, drawn to Southeast Louisiana by a bottomless demand for cheap construction labor. But rectifying that situation had been child's play for Glenn. He'd easily extended his form from a cathode ray tube and converter box on one end, through hundreds of yards of cable, to a satellite dish which appeared, unnoticed, on the rear roof of the motel's laundry room.

Glenn's mission was to keep her close at hand, under continuous observation. This modest gambit had proven the easiest way to accomplish that. The shows captured her like fly paper would a fly.

None of the other women who spent their days in this motel, waiting out the long hours until their husbands or boyfriends returned from gutting houses in the city, had such programming in their rooms. Usually they crowded in here to watch, taking up every inch of bed and floor. This, however, was one of the exceedingly rare times when the girl with the swelling belly had been left alone. He found it far easier to tolerate his boring, monotonous mission when it was just him and her alone. Otherwise, the press of so much disorderly, dirty flesh, coated with disgusting mammalian excretions, made him itch to retreat to more sterile surroundings.

Why would the Mother want to grow one of her Mobile Service Units inside one of Her enemies — and such a filthy, stupid *creature, at that?* Despite his nigh-infinite processing power, he could not understand the reasons for this bizarre choice. Having been the last of the current cohort of Miasma Club members to appear, Glenn had not personally witnessed the arrival of any members more junior than himself. But he had questioned a few of his fellows regarding their origins. None reported that they had experienced a "birth" or a "childhood," not even the ones who outwardly appeared to be human. They had simply burst into existence, fully formed, already "adult" and aware of who and what they were.

He stared disdainfully at Marianna Cortez's swollen belly. *What will this newest Service Unit, now growing in the girl-creature's womb, be able to accomplish upon being expelled from its cage of blood and filthy flesh? Won't it be a helpless lump of meat and bone, utterly dependent upon its gestation unit's flabby udders for sustenance?*

Why didn't the Mother simply create more Mobile Service Units like himself? Hadn't he been the most proficient Unit to date, the model most deserving of replication? Indeed, he'd recently proven this by being the first of the Miasma Club to fully recover from his post-Antonia hibernation. True, the members of the Triumvirate had woken first, but their full functionality had been slower to return than his had been. Their sleepy commands had slithered into his auditory receptors: *Seek out the newest of our number. We are depleted. The Mother yearns for new Servants. She has already set the process in motion, in ways unlike ever before... now She commandeers the wombs of our enemies. New communities of human beings are flowing into New Orleans, replacing part of that multitude which we have driven out. These new infestations are potent clay, for they are rich in faith and superstition. Bring us the fresh Servants once they have emerged from their gestational sheaths of human flesh...*

Even in a massively depopulated New Orleans, finding such precious blobs of replicating cells, sheltered within womb bags common to the entire female populace, was no trifling task. The destruction of the great majority of the region's hospitals had both complicated and focused his search. Prior to Antonia, he could have infiltrated the medical records computers at those hospitals and clinics with prenatal services or maternity wards, quickly compiling a list of pregnant humans, their anticipated delivery dates, and their addresses.

In the disaster's aftermath, however, most of the restored clinics had been forced to retreat to pre-computer age methods of record keeping. He had expended several precious nights visually scanning the contents of hundreds of scattered filing cabinets, stuttering bitter curses at the inefficiency of it all. Still, he'd been able to compile a list, one which he'd shared with his fellows as they had emerged from hibernation.

The list, he'd quickly learned, was woefully incomplete. Many of the human newcomers, especially those whose origins lay in countries to the south, had come to New Orleans without the benefit of legal status. Such persons avoided the health care system until absolutely necessary. He assumed that most of these non-legal newcomers would go to a hospital when the time came for their offspring to emerge. But his orders had not given him the luxury of waiting until after birth events to locate his future comrades.

So he'd searched out those places where the non-legal newcomers were known to congregate — the downtown street corners where crowds of them would wait to be collected by contractors' trucks; the tents where free food and clothes were distributed; the decayed motor lodges along Airline Drive where the illegals were allowed to take shelter, in exchange for unpaid work repairing those flooded buildings. He'd patrolled these places, extending his sensors to their utmost limits in an effort to detect a glimmer of the Mother's touch.

Five nights ago, disguised as a portable generator in a Salvation Army tent, Glenn had sensed her. Marianna Cortez. Pushing her rusty shopping cart loaded with donated canned foods, the petite, dark haired girl had passed close enough for him to register the Mother's influence — her womb held a network of cells rapidly assuming human form, but growing in a way alien to their basic nature, possessed of luck-shaping potentialities which would soon reinforce the Miasma Club's depleted ranks.

He'd followed her home, sticking to the shadows as she'd pushed her shopping cart along the muddy sidewalk next to Airline Drive. Then it had been a simple matter for him to devise a plan to ensure she would remain within this tiny motel room, spending the remaining months of her pregnancy under his watchful gaze.

And yet... was this not a waste of his matchless talents? Wouldn't the Miasma Club benefit enormously by redeploying him to seek out the *other* gestating Mobile Service Units?

How advanced was Marianna Cortez's pregnancy? He reviewed the medical texts he'd recently assimilated. From external evidence, she appeared to be near the end of her second trimester, although she would have been made pregnant shortly after the storm. The growing Mobile Service Unit should, by now, have all of its organs and subcomponents in place.

Three more months remained until the Winter Solstice. His cathode ray tube flickered as he contemplated that infuriating fact and the monotony it portended for him.

Marianna Cortez shifted on the bed and rubbed her taut stomach, fingers tracing circles around her distended belly button. He focused his sensors on his hidden comrade-to-come. *I can replicate every function of the human creature's gestational sheath,* he told himself. *I could build an incubator device. I could download the specifications, abscond with the materials. I could install this incubator within the Miasma Club's den.*

Thus, Marianna Cortez is unnecessary.

He indulged himself, expending a few microseconds of processing time diagramming the schematics of a surgical extraction device. His circuit boards nearly overheated with visions of slicing scalpels and multiple clamps to pry the womb open. After freeing his new brother from its cage of Marianna Cortez's flesh, Glenn would become a self-transporting temporary incubator and carry the immature Mobile Service Unit to the Miasma Club's den, where he would build a more permanent incubator device. Then he could return to the search. The hunt.

He prepared to drop his guise of an obsolete Zenith console TV. He accessed medical texts, determined where and how deeply to slice...

Then the door to the room burst open. Five women crowded inside, chattering in Spanish, carrying bags of prepared foods from a taqueria truck. Marianna Cortez greeted them warmly and made room for them on her bed.

Glenn the Gremlin canceled his transformation, grumbling to himself. His logic circuits reminded him that patience was a virtue — impulsive acts on his part would likely earn him severe reprimands from the Triumvirate.

But he would not remain patient forever.

Chapter 28

KAY rested her cheek on Daniel's chest, enjoying the feeling of his arms around her. "How was your day?"

"Tiring," he said. "But that's good, 'cause that means I did a lot. A customer told me I probably have enough work yanking out ruined sheet rock to last me a hundred years."

"Cleaning this city up might take a hundred years," she said quietly, staring out the open flap of their tent toward the dark, silent Lakeview street. She and Daniel had been the first to return to this block. Two months after starting the long process of rebuilding the house which had once belonged to Amos Weintraub, they remained the street's only inhabitants.

"I can't wait for our trailer to get here," Daniel said.

"I guess if it doesn't get delivered tonight, I'll just have to host Owl and Pandora in our tent."

"What about washing up?"

"We'll do what we've been doing," she said, "go use the Red Cross showers on Pontchartrain Boulevard."

He leaned over and sniffed her arm pit, then playfully crinkled his nose. "*Phee-eew!* You never used to smell bad, ever. Except for those couple of days each year when you'd smell like vegetable stew. But now you smell just like a woman."

"Like a woman who didn't get a chance to shower yesterday. Is it really bad?"

"Not bad. Just different from before."

"Yeah. I've become a 'real girl,' like Pinocchio at the end of the movie."

"I'm glad you didn't become a 'real *boy*' like Pinocchio. I couldn't have proposed to you, then."

A sense of insecurity washed over her. "Daniel, do you... still *like* me?" Her eyes misted over, a phenomenon which had imposed itself on her with increasing frequency these past few months.

"Kay—"

"What you felt for me — it wasn't just my *aura*'s doing, was it?"

He placed her hands on his cheeks. "I love you, Kay," he said, carefully enunciating each word. There was no pretense in it, no calculation or falseness.

Her momentary panic subsided. "I love you, too, hon," she said, feeling grateful and relieved and amazed, all at once. This rainbow palette of emotions awed her, this work of hormones coursing through her blood, neurotransmitters firing their subterranean fireworks within her increasingly human brain.

Becoming a "real girl" was hard work.

She heard the approach of a heavy diesel engine. They hopped off their cot and raced to the end of the driveway.

"It's our trailer," he said. "I *know* it is! Ohboy ohboy ohboy! Hey, I've got an idea. After you see Owl and Pandora, let's both take a shower in our new trailer, and then we'll do it? On a *bunk bed!*"

She smiled. They'd just done "it" that morning. Twice. "Daniel, you're like a teenager..."

"I'm making up for lost time." The far end of their street suddenly blazed with headlights. "I *told* you!" he said. "Ooooh, check it out — they're driving a Ford F-350 Super Duty, quad rear end, with a Power Stroke diesel V-8. Man, I'd sure love to have one of *those*."

"You can tell all that just from the headlights?"

"Sure!"

The truck, pulling a twenty-two foot long travel trailer, braked beside them. A workman rolled down his window. "Where y'all gonna want this?" he asked, quickly scanning the property. "I wouldn't recommend that driveway — I mean, we could do it, but with that slope, it'd take a whole lot of blocking and shoring to level it out. Couldn't do it tonight."

"How about the back yard?" Daniel said. "That's flat."

The man frowned. "Unless you want me to knock down a corner of that garage, there's no way I see to squeeze it through there."

"Well, I guess that leaves the front lawn," Kay said. "The grass is all dead, anyway."

Working with a speed that told Kay this was their last assignment of the day, the men secured the trailer on the brown, brittle lawn. "Paperwork says you've already got water and electric restored," the supervisor said to Daniel. "But we can't mess with that stuff until daylight. Have to come back in the morning to install the extension lines."

"Can we stay in it tonight anyway?" he asked eagerly.

The man shrugged his shoulders and handed Daniel a set of keys. "Suit yourself."

The two men stomped their boots on the sidewalk to dislodge trapped sod, then got back in their truck. Daniel raced up the set of wooden steps to the trailer's door.

"Hey!" he yelled at the departing truck. "None of these keys fit!"

The truck slowed but didn't stop. "That's FEBO's problem," the driver yelled back. "We're just subcontractors. That shit with the wrong keys's been happening to us all week."

"Can you bring the right keys in the morning?" Kay called after him.

"We don't do locks and keys. That's a different subcontractor. It's FEBO's problem. Sorry!"

The truck drove off.

She stared at the long aluminum box they'd both been dreaming of. "Aww, hell," she said. Daniel retrieved a hammer and crowbar from his pickup. "Uh, hon, I don't know if busting the lock's a good idea. We'd be destroying government property."

He immediately set to work on the door. "The government destroyed *my* property by putting up crappy levees," he said. "I'm returning the favor."

Kay had anticipated her reunion with Owl and Pandora for months. But she never would've expected *this*. Neither of them had provided a hint of the changes they'd endured.

"Ain't she a *beaut?*" Owl asked, pointing at his car, a weathered BMW parked in front of Kay's and Daniel's trailer. "I tell you, Kay, San Antonio is the *mecca* of used cars. Eighteen years old and barely has two hundred thousand miles on her. Best car I ever owned, and boy, is she *fast!*"

"That's — *wonderful*, Owl," Kay said.

Desperate for even a momentary distraction from the shock of seeing her appallingly transformed friends, she humored Owl by making the appropriate *oohs* and *aahs* over his new car. The BMW didn't look too bad for an eighteen year old sedan; the cream-color paint on the doors and side panels still had a sheen, making it easier to overlook the streaks of gray primer on the hood. Inside, apart from the driver's seat being patched with duct tape, most of the leather was intact.

The car looked factory fresh compared to Pandora and Owl. Prior to the storm, Pandora had appeared half a decade younger than Kay. Now, she could pass for Kay's mother. Her once lustrous midnight-black hair was streaked with silver and gray. Before, she'd had the poise and posture of a dancer; now, her shoulders slumped, and her back had curved from what seemed to be advanced osteoporosis. A mosaic of blue varicose veins marred her cheeks and nose.

And Owl... Owl looked like a perambulating cadaver.

"Can I, uh, invite you two in?" Kay asked. "I sent Daniel over for coffee with his buddies at Russell's Marina Grill. I figured the three of us need to do some talking in private." She opened the door to the trailer. Pandora followed her up the steps.

"Hey, gals," Owl said. "Aren't you forgettin' about somebody? This here setup ain't exactly senior-friendly. I'm liable to bust a hip or something."

They helped him climb the three wooden steps. Kay couldn't help but stare at his forearm; its paper-thin flesh sagged between his bones like a broken window shade.

She helped him sit in the least cramped chair at the tiny dining table. "I'm sorry I can't offer you much. All we have is some canned goods."

"You got some apple sauce, maybe?" he asked. "Damn dentures don't fit me no more, and I got this latest set just two weeks ago."

Kay looked through the contents of her minuscule pantry, just transferred from the tent. "Would canned peaches do?"

"Fine. If I cut 'em up small enough, they slide right down my throat, no chewing required."

She pulled her can opener from a drawer, then glanced at Pandora. "How about you?"

Pandora shook her head.

"You *sure?* I mean, you came all the way back from San Antonio, and I can't get you a *thing?*"

Pandora stared sadly at her. "You're angry," she said.

Kay stopped opening the can of peaches. "*Angry?* About *what?*"

"I didn't give you any warning over the phone. I didn't tell you... what to expect."

"Well..." Kay tossed the peaches into a bowl, splashing syrup across the narrow countertop. "Well, I would've *appreciated* a little heads-up."

Pandora rubbed the liver spots on her left hand. "I didn't want to worry you unnecessarily. I thought... maybe coming back to the miasma fields would reverse what had happened to us in Texas."

"No such luck," Owl said.

"At least... at least our rapid aging has stopped since our return," Pandora said, a tremor of spousal reproach in her voice. "In San Antonio, I was so afraid... so horribly *afraid* I would lose you at any moment. That I'd look away from you for just a second, and when I'd look back, you'd be gone." She held her withered hands in the air. "Kay, I don't care about *this*. It wasn't fear of dying which made me convince Owl to bring us back. It was fear of having to live six months, or even only a week, without him. After losing all my Ills... I couldn't *bear* losing him, too."

Owl frowned. "There's a world of sweetness in what you just said, babe. But an even bigger load of *pigheadedness*. Do you realize what we've probably come back to? You coulda died peaceably in a nice hotel bed back in Texas. Not that I'd want you to die, of course, but if you have to, that's how I'd want it. Now...? Now we'll be hunted down, trapped like muskrats for our pelts." He turned to Kay. "Are they awake yet?"

She nodded. "I can sense them, distantly. They've been awake since the Equinox."

"They haven't come after you yet?"

"Not yet."

He looked both thoughtful and worried. "Maybe they've had more important stuff on their agenda then getting revenge on you. Like replenishing their ranks."

"But *baklava*," Pandora said, "haven't you said that would take many, many years?"

"In typical times, yeah. Freed up miasmatic energy that returns to its source remains defuse, unfocused; it gets scattered through the miasma fields like little deposits of oil trapped in shale rock. But these aren't normal circumstances, babe." He turned to Kay. "You told me on the phone you've been working in the mayor's office. What're his demographers sayin' about who's been coming into town?"

"You mean returnees?"

"I mean newcomers. CNN says New Orleans is fillin' up with Mexicans."

"Not just Mexicans," Kay said. "Laborers have been coming here from all over Latin America and the Caribbean. Dominicans, Colombians, Ecuadorians... Daniel sees them every day on work sites next to his. He's even starting to learn a little Spanish."

"They're catnip for the miasma, and you better believe it," he said. "Third Worlders pouring into a region that's grown steadily more secular, less inclined to superstition. These newcomers bring more than strong backs. They bring *belief. Faith.* And not faith in some sanitized, bloodless Christianity. Those people are bringin' with them a syncretic Catholicism, one that's mixed with a thousand years' worth of aboriginal pantheism.

"Old gods found new niches as saints or angels. They aren't dusty old relics, scraping around for a few crumbs of vestigial remembrance and dread. They're alive and vital in the minds of the faithful — constant presences, powerful, worshipped. If I were part of the Triumvirate, I'd be expectin' taps on the shoulder from some Aztec and Mayan deities sometime soon, a winged serpent or a god-king with a head of polished gold."

"What will this mean?" Kay asked. Her throat had gone dry. "For the city? For us?"

"Expect a renewed Miasma Club that's stronger than it's been in two centuries. Tryin' to kill a city that's *weaker* than it's been for two centuries. One more Antonia, or something like it, and that's all she wrote. The feds won't pay tens of billions a second time to bail us out. Everything south of the I-10 highway will be left to the mercies of the Gulf of Mexico."

"What... what can we do?" she asked.

Pandora slammed her palm on the table. "Why do *we* have to do *anything*? Haven't we already suffered *enough*?" She grabbed Owl's arm. "Why can't we just enjoy whatever time we have left? Why do we have to get involved? Why can't we just have some *peace?*"

Owl patted her trembling hand. "We're already involved, just by bein' who we are. Babe, I warned you it would be like this if we came back. It's us or them now. We know too much, and they know we do. After the Winter Solstice, maybe, we won't pose much of a threat to them, 'cause they'll be a dozen times stronger than they are now. But until then, they're vulnerable, down on numbers. So we've got a little more than two months to make our move. Either we take 'em down before then, or we crawl under the blankets and wait for the hatchet to fall."

"But your safe houses—?"

"Might protect us for a while. Not for long, though. Those Aztec spirits that'll be joinin' the Club? Me and them share some lineage, same as Ti Malice and Eleggua-Eshu do. Give 'em time, they'd be able to sniff me out."

Pandora clenched her eyes shut. But her tears escaped, descending pathways of wrinkles only weeks old.

"You want to go back to San Antonio?" he asked, gently. "Just say the word."

She shook her head. The motion was barely noticeable at first, but quickly grew more and more insistent. "Any chance to keep you, *any* chance... is better than no chance. I won't go back to Texas. *No.*"

He squeezed her hand. "Well, all *right*, then. I'll get you set up in one of the Uptown safe houses, and me and Kay'll go about our business—"

"*No*. I won't let you put me up on a shelf. I'm not made of glass, Owl. If you're going to be risking your life, I want to be right by your side. For every moment we have left."

He remained quiet. "Your call, babe," he said at last.

"The Winter Solstice," Kay said. "This year, it falls just eight days after a Friday the Thirteenth. Is that why it's our deadline?"

He nodded. "Two days of superstition and dread, coming barely a week apart, culminating in the darkest day of the year. Every time a newcomer showed up to join the Club — and I remember this with all y'all, from Mephistopheles to Glenn the Gremlin — it was always on a Winter Solstice that followed a Friday the Thirteenth."

"I remember, too. I was around when Glenn and Na Ong and Na Ba joined us. So... what do we do first?"

"We look for allies," Owl said. "We're gonna need 'em."

"Father Luc," Kay said, "I'm so sorry to disturb you. But everyone I've talked to said you're the best person to ask—"

The priest, standing in the courtyard of what had once been Mary Queen of Vietnam Church, pointed to a box containing hard hats. "Safety first. Put on a construction hat."

Kay obliged him. A bulldozer idled nearby, waiting to smooth over the site in preparation for rebuilding. "Now," Father Luc said, "what can I do for you?"

"I need to know if a married couple named Na Ong and Na Ba returned to Village de l'Est after Antonia. It's very important that I find them."

"Is this a joke?"

Kay was taken aback. "No, no, of course not. They're friends of mine. They used to live here, not far from your church."

"Na Ong and Na Ba, you say? Truly?"

"Yes."

He scowled, then gestured with a flip of his hand for her to leave. "I am sorry, but I have no time for little jokes. I do not wish to be rude to a visitor, but I must ask you to return at another time."

Mystified and hurt, Kay withdrew. A young Vietnamese couple had been waiting quietly behind her. The young woman held a basket filled with containers of food and a Thermos, which she handed to the priest. She appeared to be five or six months pregnant, her lithe figure incongruously round in the belly.

Not knowing who she could try to question next, Kay headed back to Owl's and Pandora's car, parked several blocks away near Chef Menteur Highway. The young couple finished exchanging pleasantries with Father Luc. Then they joined Kay as she walked down the gravel driveway.

"Excuse me," the man said when they were out of earshot of the priest. "*Were* you joking just now?"

Kay stopped and turned toward him. "No! Why does everyone here *insist* that I'm joking?"

"You, uh, you probably don't know much about Vietnamese culture, do you?"

She shook her head.

"Well, it's as though you asked the Father if he'd seen, oh, Mickey and Minnie Mouse."

"Or Dracula and Batgirl," his wife added. "Father doesn't have much of a sense of humor."

Kay shrugged her shoulders. "I wasn't trying to be funny. Those are their names."

"Maybe if you describe them," the young woman said, "we could help you. My name is Anh. This is my husband, Paul. We have lived in this neighborhood our whole lives. We know everyone."

Kay did her best to describe Na Ba and Na Ong, trying to remember clothing they frequently wore. Anh's eyes brightened with recognition. "Did they go to church?" she asked.

"I — I think so."

"Paul, do you remember that strange older couple who would stand in the back of the church at Sunday morning Mass?"

"The ones who hardly ever talked to anyone? And weird accidents would happen whenever they were around?"

"Right, like the baptismal fount overflowing — you remember that? And they never took Holy Communion." She turned back to Kay. "These people wore old-fashioned clothes like those you described."

Kay grew excited. "Have you seen them recently?"

The young woman shook her head. "No, I'm sorry. But we have a friend who owns the most popular restaurant around here. We were heading over to his place next, to help him paint his dining room. You are welcome to come with us. He's been cooking from a trailer since two months after the storm, feeding everyone who has come back. If anyone would have seen them, it would be him."

Kay thanked them profusely. She found herself instantly comfortable with these two. Something about them felt reassuringly familiar, as though she'd known them and liked them for years. "When are you due?" she asked Anh.

"In mid-February," Anh said. "Yes, I *know* I look like I'm nine months pregnant already," she added, laughing. "It's because I'm carrying twins, a boy and a girl."

"How *wonderful!* Congratulations! They'll be so lucky to have each other as playmates. Have you picked out names yet?"

Now it was Paul's turn to laugh. "No," he said, "but maybe we should call them Na Ong and Na Ba? What do you think, Anh?"

Anh blushed. "Don't tease, Paul," she said. "Kay, do you have children?"

It was Kay's turn to blush. "My fiancé and I... we'd love to start a family. But... I don't think I'm able to have any children of my own."

"Oh," Anh said. "I'm very sorry."

"It's okay. Ever since the storm, I've developed a new appreciation for other people's children. Kids are so scarce here now, with the schools still closed. Even the birds have only recently started to return. Maybe... if it would be all right... maybe I could come and baby-sit for you sometime? My fiancé Daniel is marvelous with kids. I mean, I know we just met, and I don't mean to impose—"

"Oh, it's no imposition! That's so *generous* of you to offer, really! But people have been marvelous to us ever since they learned we're expecting, especially when I tell them it's twins. My little babies have a whole *army* of 'aunts' and 'uncles' waiting for their big arrival. We'll even have an *au pair* if we need one. There's a church volunteer here from California, a Vietnamese girl named Ling. She plays her guitar for the workers while they rebuild their stores. She even sings for my babies; she insists they can hear the music. She's often at the restaurant where we're going. Maybe you'll get to meet her, too."

They turned east when they came to Chef Menteur Highway. Kay soon heard the sounds of rebuilding — power saws cutting boards to size, dozens of hammers striking nail after nail. They approached a modest strip mall, its innermost timbers and pipes laid open to the bright fall sun. The commercial signs and billboards along the highway had been twisted by storm winds into rusting origami. But one billboard had been recently restored. A political sign, emblazoned in fresh swaths of red, white and blue:

VAN GOODFELLER

MAYOR

WE DESERVE A FRESH START

Van Goodfeller? Kay wondered. *The fried catfish king?* She hadn't heard that he'd decided to run against Mayor Rio and Cynthia Belvedere Hotchkiss. How formidable an opponent would he make for

Roy Rio? With all his fast food restaurants, he'd benefit from almost universal name recognition. The primary election was just three and a half months away, with a run-off, if necessary, scheduled for six weeks after.

"Here we are," Anh said.

"Kay!" Owl called out from three storefronts away. "Any success?"

Pandora wheeled Owl in a rented wheelchair toward Kay and her companions. "Not yet," Kay said. "But my new friends remember Na Ong and Na Ba. They've got a friend at this restaurant who may have seen them recently."

"Good," Owl said, "because Pandora and me, we're scorin' zip so far."

Kay made introductions, and then the five of them entered the restaurant. The pungent scents of fresh plywood and dry wall couldn't overpower the much more pleasant aromas coming from the kitchen, those of curry and sweet cabbage and peppers sauteed with strips of pork.

Kay heard a guitar being strummed, a soft, wordless melody being sung. "There's Ling," Anh said, "the girl who's volunteered to be our *au pair*."

Kay saw a pretty, young Vietnamese woman sitting on a plastic lawn chair, playing a guitar; she started to say hello, but the word caught in her throat. She *knew* this woman. She didn't recognize her face; but the sense of familiarity, of intimacy sharp and overwhelming, nearly bowled her over. She'd been *inside* this person, and this woman had been inside her, too. They had become, for a few ecstatic and terrifying moments, a single, unified being.

A choked whisper escaped Kay's lips. "*Felicia...?*"

The young woman shared Kay's look of shocked recognition. "You've changed..." she said.

"You — you have, too," Kay said.

"You two *know* each other?" Anh asked.

Ling/Felicia rose from her chair, clutching her guitar like a shield. Her eyes darted from Kay to Owl to Pandora. "I'm sorry," she said to Anh and Paul. "I — I must go."

She darted for the door, her graceful movements marred by a lameness in her left leg. Owl maneuvered his wheelchair to block her way. "Am I meeting Terpsichore?" he asked. "Or is it Euterpe?"

She pushed past him with a wordless cry of dismay.

"Felicia, wait!" Kay called after her. But the young woman limped into the parking lot. Kay followed. "Felicia! Don't run off! I want to talk with you!" But the cacophony of construction noise suffocated her entreaties.

She felt a hand on her shoulder. Owl had risen from his wheelchair. "Get after her, girl," he ordered. "We need her!"

Felicia had already limped into a field of tall switchgrass which lay between the shopping strip and a network of canals and lagoons.

"Go!" Owl shouted.

Kay pursued Felicia, without an inkling of what she'd do once she caught her.

Chapter 29

KAY plunged into the neck-high switchgrass, batting the sharp tips away from her face. She heard the *swish! swish!* of Felicia's flight through the grass, about fifty feet ahead of her. "Felicia!" she yelled. "Stop running! I only want to talk with you!"

The fleeing Muse didn't reply. But her limp slowed her — Kay didn't remember Felicia suffering a lame leg in May. Maybe the devastation and depopulation of New Orleans had turned Felicia lame?

She heard a clattering thump ahead of her. Felicia cried out. She saw the Muse tumble into the grass. She caught up to her less than ten yards from the road. Felicia frantically tried to free her lame leg from a twisted jumble of aluminum siding, a trap hidden in the tall grass.

"Are you hurt?" Kay asked, gasping.

Felicia stared up at her with terrified eyes. "Don't touch me!" she hissed. "Don't come *near* me!"

"Why are you so afraid—"

"*No!* Don't *touch* me! I couldn't bear it! I'd rather *die* than be absorbed by you, you, you *filth!*"

Kay remembered the shock of waking next to Felicia, unable to tell where her body ended and Felicia's began. "I — I can't do that to you anymore. The storm changed me. I'm not an *ayin hora* now."

"You're *lying!* Every word that comes out of the mouths of your kind is a lie! Damn me for my curiosity! I never should've toyed with you months ago!"

Kay heard a car screech to a halt on the nearby road. "You got her?" Owl shouted.

"She's hurt, Owl! I think she twisted her bad ankle!"

"Good deal; that'll make her easier to handle. Get her over to the car. Pandora, get the special chains out of the trunk, babe."

Felicia had listened to every word, clearly terrified. She yanked at her bad leg with strength forged by desperation, fruitlessly trying to dislodge the bent aluminum panel which had wound itself around her calf and ankle.

"Kay!" Owl shouted. "Did you hear me?"

"I — I don't want to touch her, Owl! It'll make her frantic—"

"Just do what I say! Get her in the car!"

"But—"

"Do you want to save your city?"

"Of *course* I do!"

"Then get the damn Muse in the car!"

Kay bit her lip. She'd go along, for now. But this time, *this time*, that man was going to explain himself.

She placed one foot on the aluminum panel and twisted it away from Felicia's leg. "Where — where are you taking me?" the Muse demanded.

"I don't know. I'll find out when you do..."

Felicia began screaming again when she saw Pandora waiting with manacles and chains. "Slap 'em on her, Pandora," Owl commanded from the car.

"Is this really necessary?" Kay asked.

Owl shot her a sour look. "Hell, yes."

Kay stuffed Felicia into the back seat, between herself and Pandora. The Muse began weeping. Kay noticed Felicia wasn't confined by ordinary chains. Hooks had been welded to the links, and dangling from

the hooks were sheet music, old-style single-song records, and books —
The Awakening by Kate Chopin; a text on New Orleans's indigenous
architectural styles; *When Gravity Fails* by George Alec Effinger.

"It'll be all right," Kay said softly.

Owl turned onto Chef Menteur Highway and headed toward the
Bayou Sauvage wilderness preserve and the storm-shattered fishing
camps of Lake Catherine. They soon left the flood-damaged shopping
strips and shoddy, Oil Boom-era apartment buildings of Little Vietnam
behind. The old two lane highway, built atop a much older Indian path
connecting the New Orleans area to the Mississippi coast, took them
through dense thickets of scrub oaks and cypress. The road curved onto
a narrow neck of land surrounded on two sides by grassy swamps and,
glittering in the distance, the open waters of Lake Pontchartrain and
Lake St. Catherine.

It was hard to tell where the land ended and the water began.
Staring out the windows, Kay felt her blood respond to the pull of an
omnipresent restlessness. A hungry itchiness crept over her entire body.
She glanced at Pandora. Her friend stared out the opposite windows at
an identical vista, shivering and rubbing her arms.

"Pandora, do you feel it, too?"

"Yes! *Yes!* What *is* it?"

"Maybe what a diabetic feels when her toe goes black with
gangrene," Owl said, "and then her foot, and then her whole leg. It's the
soundless scream of the miasma, of our Mother, of this whole, entire
place."

We don't have time for more mystical mumbo-jumbo, Kay thought.
"Tell us what you know, Owl."

"It's not what I *know*. It's what I've come to believe. A theory I've
had some opportunities to test over the past two centuries. And maybe
I'll test it again come this next Solstice. Anyway, it'll have to wait. We're
here."

He parked a dozen yards away from the entrance to a pivoting steel suspension bridge. Its entrance was blocked by four flashing barricades. Designed to swivel on a central pivot to allow boats to navigate the pass, it sat in a partially open position, just a corner of its western end touching the road; storm surge from Lake St. Catherine had stripped its gears and forced it out of alignment.

Owl climbed out of the car with his cane. "This is the Chef Menteur Pass Bridge. We're gonna have to cross it on foot. Everybody out."

Kay coaxed Felicia out of the back seat, then helped her take the long step from the highway's edge to the askew corner of the drawbridge. The Muse had changed her appearance — while Kay had been distracted by the omnipresent unease, Felicia had lost her Vietnamese features and reacquired the Franco-Celtic appearance she'd sported when Kay had first met her. Whatever power the shackles contained had made her more docile, too; she allowed herself to be led onto the bridge without protest, as though she were sleepwalking.

"That's where we're headed," Owl said. He pointed to a large structure of crumbling red bricks which sat near the bridge's far end. "Fort Macomb. One of my safe houses." Surrounded by a moat, the red-brick octagon, supported by earthen berms, sat on its tiny island with the wizened exhaustion of an ancient tortoise. "It's almost as old as I am. Built on Houma Indian land after the War of 1812."

He led the group towards the wreckage of what had once been a marina, adjacent to the fortress and its moat. Pleasure craft lay scattered like smashed toys around the toppled ruins of the marina's boat sheds, restaurant, and marine supplies buildings. Owl pointed his cane at the filthy water. "You see those four, five acres of water?" he said. "Forty years ago, all that was land. Storms, erosion, and canal-digging by the oil companies let the fort's moat grow and grow like an untreated tumor. You're looking at South Louisiana in miniature, right here. I'll bet Antonia ate away at least a hundred square miles of land and wetlands between here, Terrebonne Bay and the mouth of the river, lettin' the open sea come that much closer."

Kay shivered and rubbed her painfully itching arms. "Is that why we're feeling these *awful* sensations?"

"Yup. We're standin' near the bleedin' edge of South Louisiana. You may not realize it, but you're watchin' a war between the land and the water. And the land's losin', badly. It's been losin' ever since James Eads and his engineers figgur'd out how to channel the Mississippi so it would dump the tons of soil it collects between Minnesota and here off the edge of the continental shelf, rather than depositin' it 'round the bottom of Plaquemines Parish. Before Eads, all that dirt had been cloggin' up the shippin' channels at the mouths of the river. Eads's channels shot it all out into deep water, so the channels wouldn't have to be dredged every year. They had no idea what the unintended consequences would be."

He struck the soggy ground with his cane. "Why do you think the miasma field is *here*, beneath New Orleans and parts south, instead of someplace else? This land we're standin' on — *all* of New Orleans — it's less than eight hundred years old. You know what eight hundred years is in geological time? Not even an eyeblink.

"Before Eads built his channels, before the Corps of Engineers built their levees, sea and land maintained a rough balance. The ocean ate the land down here. But the Mississippi, thanks to her annual floods, sucked off the top soil of tens of thousands of acres and built *more* land, wherever she had a mind to. And that's how it was, for thousands, maybe millions of years... erosion battling sedimentation, destruction battling creation, water at war with the land... but the two forces remained in rough equilibrium."

Kay began to understand. "All that turmoil, constant, *violent* change... occurring incredibly fast in geological time... that would produce *energy*, wouldn't it? Great, seething cauldrons of energy?"

"Damn straight, it would," he said. "Energy of a rarified type, way I figgur it. Try to imagine yourself as our Mother. Imagine the *pain* of constantly gettin' fingers and limbs chopped off, while at the same time, *new* fingers, new limbs was sproutin' from bizarre places, the small of your back, the middle of your forehead. Imagine the roilin' you'd be feelin' in your guts, the constant pain. What kinda energy would build and build and *build* inside you?"

"Bad luck energy..." She felt as if a curtain had been lifted. "But... but it would only *seem* like bad luck to those who had a concept of bad luck, to those who had built a system of beliefs around supernatural powers which could grant either fortune or misfortune..."

"People, in other words," he said. "Those big-brained primates who seem hard-wired to interpret any facts they can't understand as religion. Is a lightning storm which sets a forest on fire the result of bad luck, the enmity of the gods? The trees don't think so. Heck, the fire burns away the underbrush and lets in sunlight to let new trees sprout and flourish. But if people had built a village in that same forest? Well, y'know, it had to be that Zeus was mad at 'em, or somebody had offered a second-rate sacrifice to Yahweh."

"Or someone had walked under a ladder," Pandora said. "Or broken a mirror. Or let a black cat cross their path."

"You're both gettin' the idea." He removed a ring of keys from his pocket and unlocked the padlock which secured the entrance to the foot bridge leading to Fort Macomb. "'Kay, you know your history of New Orleans pretty well. What's the first thing the settlers did after building themselves a church, a government building, and some houses?"

"They built a levee to protect themselves from Mississippi River floods," she said. "And a little later, they dug a navigation canal that connected Lake Pontchartrain to the back of their town."

"That's right. They changed their new environment to better suit themselves. Oh, human beings aren't the only animals who do that. Beavers and ants do it, too. Human beings just happen to be the best at it. Now, the people who were here the earliest, the Bayougoula and Choctaw tribes, and my own people, the Houma, they were sensitive enough to the 'mood' of this place to know better than to screw with it.

But the French and the Spanish, they had prideful notions. So they set about messin' up the eons-old balance between land and water."

He led them into a dank tunnel through the fort's outermost rampart. They emerged onto what had once been Fort Macomb's inner parade ground. This protected redoubt, surrounded by masonry casemates, was clogged with tall weeds and scattered construction materials left over from an abandoned renovation project.

Owl sat on a worn set of brick steps to rest. "Imagine you're the Mother, your whole body a mass of open sores... and then a bunch of little critters come along and drool *acid* into your wounds. 'Cause that's what the French and Spanish and later on the Americans did. They stopped the river's floods from depositin' new soil wherever it willed. Their canals invited water into places it had never gone before, speedin' up erosion and subsidence. In a matter of decades — no time at all to Her, remember — the Mother found the growth of Her limbs slowed, their destruction speeded up. When a human being's body gets invaded by germs, what does that body do to defend itself?"

"It makes antibodies," Kay said. "So we... *we're* the antibodies?"

"Not just us," he said. He looked at Felicia, still lost in her trance. "Her and her sisters, too."

"The *Muses?* That doesn't make sense — they *oppose* the Miasma Club."

He slowly rose to his feet. "No, they don't. They *complement* the Miasma Club. They're the other side of the same coin."

"I — I can't believe that. Owl, I never told you this, but I've experienced her *essence*. She's the *opposite* of all we used to be—"

"Right, the opposite face of the *same* coin," he insisted. "Let's take her inside and wake her up. Then you'll hear the truth from her own mouth."

He led them into a dim casemate whose gun portals faced the Chef Menteur Pass. The old smoothbore cannons had been removed more than a century ago. They rounded a corner. The land which had once supported this section of the casemate's outer edge had worn away, and a portion of the floor and lower casemate wall had toppled into the water below. Sunlight reflected off the waves busily eroding more of the fortress's base.

"Damn," Owl muttered. "This hole wasn't here before Antonia. Another twenty years, this whole place'll be nothin' more than a pile of bricks on the bottom of a much bigger Lake Borgne."

He looked around the muddy floor. Kay noticed scattered pots, pans, a tin cup, a pair of camping chairs, plus the rusty, dirt-spattered remains of what had once been a small kerosine camp stove. "Eh, most of my stuff's still here," he said. "What's left of it." He took the chain which shackled Felicia and secured it to an iron clasp protruding from the wall. "Pandora," he said, "sorry to ask this, but I need you to lean through that hole in the floor and fill up that big pot with lake water. Kay, give her hand."

Kay had a bad feeling about all this, but she did as she was told. Owl directed them to bring the full pot next to where Felicia had slumped.

"Now get me one of those chairs," he told Kay. He sat facing the insensate Muse, then grabbed a handful of her red ringlets and plunged her head into the brimming pot.

"Owl!" Kay shouted. "Stop it!"

He batted away Kay's arms with his free hand. "Leave me be!" he said. "She don't have to breathe, anyhow. She just thinks she does. This'll wake her up enough to get some answers out of her."

Felicia's body did not remain slack for long. Owl had to apply all the leverage he could muster to keep her face inside the pot. Finally, he released Felicia's head.

"Ahh-ahh-AAAAHHH!" The Muse gulped in air as water cascaded down her face. She glanced wildly around her. "Where — where am I? What are you doing to me?" She beat at her arms and legs, inadvertently flailing herself with the chains. "This horrible *itching* — what are you *doing*, you monsters?"

"We ain't doin' a thing," Owl said, "aside from constrainin' you. What you're feelin' right now, that's the Mother's doing. Right beneath your feet, your Mother's flesh is being eroded away, a few clods every hour." He looked at Kay and Pandora. "She's feelin' it even worse than us three, 'cause unlike us, she's not even partly human. If we could get Fortuna or Reynard chained up here, they'd be reactin' exactly the same."

"*No!*" Felicia screamed. "I'm nothing like you monsters!"

"Awww, bullshit," he said. "I'm so sick and tired of you Muses actin' like you're some angels of Goodness and Light, while us bad luck spirits are pond scum. I've got news for you, *sister*. We're *all* pond scum."

"You're — you're *insane*," she said. "My sisters and I, we inspire great works of art, while you *creatures* — all you inspire is *hate*, misfortune, and *destruction!*"

"Yeah, yeah, yeah," he said, "I've heard this song before. It's a bunch of *hooey*. You and your oh-so-pure sisters are just as effective as the Miasma Club at deflectin' human activity away from things the Mother hates. You just do it a different way, usin' carrots insteada sticks. You want an example? Lemme tell you about a buddy of mine, a guy named Everette Maddox. He's dead now. Drank himself to death at the Maple Leaf Bar on Oak Street. Probably one of the best poets this town's ever seen. Brilliant guy — if he'd applied himself to it, he coulda been a successful engineer or architect, he had that kind of a mind. But livin' here in New Orleans, he got a double whammy — Reynard the Fox seduced him into drownin' himself with drink, and Calliope the Muse nailed his heart to the cause of poetry. I used to go hear him read every Sunday at the Maple Leaf, the one day a week he roused himself from his drunken stupor. I knew what was happenin' to him. Heck, I even told him what Reynard and Calliope were doin'. I pleaded with the guy to get the hell out of New Orleans while he still could. But he didn't want to go. Oh, he believed me. But he still wouldn't leave."

He leaned closer to Felicia. "The drink killed him, yeah. But so did the *poetry*, sister. He threw his life away to follow Calliope's siren song. You wanna know what his final collection of poems was called? *American Waste*. Think about that."

"You've cherry-picked one example to fit your ridiculous contention—"

"Oh, I got dozens more. When I see a wrecked life in this town, I know I'm just as likely to smell the lingerin' perfume of a Muse as I am the stink of the Miasma Club. What's New Orleans famous for nowadays? Our decadent 'culture.' You go back as little as eighty years, and New Orleans was still the Queen City of the South. We made Houston and Atlanta look like pikers, and Birmingham and Memphis weren't even close to our league. But now? Even before Antonia, all them places had left us in the dust. Why? 'Cause they was takin' care of business while we were busy makin' floats for next Carnival season."

He snapped his fingers beneath her nose. "*There! Carnival's* the proof of the malign influence you Muses've had on this town. What other place in America dumps millions of dollars annually into a six-week-long drunken party? Meanwhile, we've got the most *abysmal* public schools in the whole country; three quarters of our 'graduates' can't read anything harder than Dr. Seuss. We Miasma Club members can take the lion's share of credit for that. But not *all* the credit. Whadda you have to say to *that*, sister?"

Felicia's eyes flashed with disdain and defiance. Kay couldn't help but envy the Muse's pride, her lack of shame.

"Eh, I'd do better talkin' to one of these crumblin' brick walls," Owl said, shaking his head. "So let's try another tack. What were you doin', Muse, hangin' around Little Vietnam?"

Felicia spat near his feet. "I'd sooner explain that to a cockroach on the wall than I would to you, *vermin*."

He smiled grimly. "Thanks, sister." He pulled a lighter out of his pocket. "Thanks for givin' me an excuse to do *this*."

He grabbed a book of sheet music attached to her chain, a collection of Antoine "Fats" Domino's greatest hits, opened it to "Blueberry Hills" and dangled the page over his lighter. He spun his thumb, sparking a flame.

Slowly, the page's lower edge began turning brown. Kay watched Felicia's chin tremble. The spreading crescent turned a darker shade of brown. Tears tumbled down the Muse's face. When the page began to smoke, Felicia screamed.

Kay grabbed the lighter away from Owl. "Stop it! Don't *hurt* her!"

"Of all the cotton-pickin' *idiocy*—"

She tossed the lighter through the hole in the casemate wall, into the water.

"I don't *need* that lighter," he said bitterly. "I may be an old husk, but I'm still strong enough to rip up some sheet music, or to smash one of them old vinyl records."

"I won't let you *torture* her!"

"Gimme a break, woman! She's no better than *Fortuna*! Would you be so damn stubborn about lettin' me interrogate Fortuna Discordia — hell, let's use your word, *torture* her — if gettin' cooperation outta her was the only way to save your city?"

"It'd still be wrong," Kay said, quietly but firmly.

"Yeah, well, that's easy enough for you to say, 'cause you don't know what *I* know. You got any idea why I'm so certain there's not a nickel's worth of difference between a Muse and a bad luck spirit? I *know* it, 'cause I seen it proved before my own eyes."

"Tell us, Owl," she said. "Convince me."

He tossed the book of sheet music and its length of chain onto the floor. "This goes back a ways. A long ways, to before any of you existed. To 1810."

"The year you blew the original Miasma Club to hell?"

"Yeah, figuratively speakin'. It was a weird, hard time. The Americans had just taken over the Louisiana Territory. None of the old-timers around here were too happy about that. The Americans poured in like the tide, fresh boatloads of 'em every week. They built themselves a whole new section of the city, Faubourg St. Mary, upriver of Canal Street, so as they didn't have to mix with the 'foreigners.'

"They weren't near as congenial with my people, the Houma tribe, as the French had been. The French treated us like we was a fellow nation. The Americans treated us like we was lice. Three years earlier, in 1807, the members of my tribe made the decision to get the hell out. They disappeared from this area practically overnight."

"Just like my people did, right before Antonia," Kay said. "And Pandora's people, too."

"Yeah. That's when I became like I am now, like you and Pandora are. Oh, a lot *younger*," he chuckled. "Still had all my teeth. But I hid what had happened to me from the other bad luck spirits; the *Club de les Miasmatiques*, we called it then. I was afraid; I had no idea what they'd do to me if they found out. Turns out, based on what they did later to Creek-Flowing-Over-Stones, I was right to be afraid."

"She was your lover?" Kay asked softly. She glanced surreptitiously at Pandora.

Owl nodded. "My first wife," he said. "Her people was the Choctaw tribe. The Choctaw and the Houma never got along too well, but that never came between me and Creek. We'd been the first two of the bad luck spirits to rise. Like Adam and Eve, kinda. Our Eden didn't last long, though. Before we knew it, there was snakes in our garden — first French, then Spanish bad luck spirits.

"Me and Creek's seniority didn't matter *none* to 'em. See, the whole time she and I were gettin' gradually weaker, what with our peoples' numbers dwindlin' due to diseases the newcomers brought from Europe, the younger spirits, they was gettin' stronger. And then came this flood of Americans. That hoard of fresh human minds, of new fears and superstitions, set the miasma field to churning. All the members of the Club knew it was just a matter of time before we'd be meetin' new comrades. But we also sensed the miasmatic energy that fed us wasn't infinite. Creek and me had felt our own power diminish when the French and Spanish spirits had risen, and when the Muses had, too. If there was to be newcomers, at least some of us was gonna get the short end of the stick."

His face hardened. "And that's when the Club decided to do what would make me hate them forever."

"They... they *killed* her?" Kay said.

"Worse than that. They cut her off. Banished her. Creek had been growin' steadily weaker. Unlike the Houma, the Choctaw didn't move away all at once. They dribbled away, a few at a time. It was like watchin' her die of tuberculosis. After my overnight transformation, I prayed she'd transform the same way, before she could suffer too much more. I kept prayin', but on the Fall Equinox of 1810, the Club forced matters to a head.

"By then, Creek was the weakest of the bad luck spirits, and the only woman among us, besides. An earlier version of Reynard the Fox had made himself our leader. He decreed that Creek would be cast out. The Club would perform a ceremony which would cut her off from the Mother, confiscating the energy that had sustained her for the new American bad luck spirits to come.

"I — I couldn't stop them. I was too weak. Too powerless. I had to stand by and watch my own wife condemned to gradual dissolution, like she was a pillar of salt. Do you know what I *owed* that woman?" The pain in his voice made Kay shiver. "*Everything!* Everything, damn it, right down to my own sorry-ass existence. If she hadn't loved me... if she hadn't taught *me* to love, to be more than just a thing of spite and malice... then I wouldn't have had even a shred of a soul when my people up and left. And all of me, not just some, would've gotten reabsorbed into the miasma."

"I owe you the same thing," Pandora said softly.

"Eh, I wouldn't give me that much credit." He took her hand and kissed it. Then he turned to Felicia, his expression softer now. "Y'know, sister, I *did* meet a decent Muse, once. Melpomene, the Muse of Tragedy. She came to Creek and me when Creek was fadin' fast and in the most horrible pain you could imagine. Said she'd been irresistibly drawn to us, despite the revulsion bad luck spirits caused her.

"And the three of us, we figgur'd a whole lot out over the next two months. We figgur'd out that our two opposing teams were actually Eros and Thanatos, two sides of the same coin, servin' the same goal. We figgur'd out how to take 'em all down, the whole lousy, stinkin' bunch, the *Club de les Miasmatiques* and the Muses alike. 'Cause one team couldn't be destroyed without destroyin' the other.

"We pulled it off on the Winter Solstice of 1810, in the swamp north of town, at the lowest spot of the sack of soggy land New Orleans would later occupy. The place where the floods from the river and the lake settled the hardest, where the muddy membrane between the surface world and the miasmatic field beneath was at its most thin. I tricked the bad luck spirits into coming there the night of the Solstice. Melpomene did the same with the Muses. The two groups — siblings, though none of them knew it — fought like bears and she-wolves stuffed into the same cage. And while they were fightin', my wife sacrificed what remained of her person, her own separate existence. And Melpomene, bless her memory, made the correspondin' sacrifice. Bein' made of the same stuff, though havin' opposite 'charges,' they let themselves be pulled together like magnets. They willed themselves to merge."

Kay's face blanched. She saw Felicia's face go white, too. "My God, Owl, what you're describing — Felicia and I — that nearly happened to *us!*"

She quickly described what had occurred in Felicia's apartment mere weeks before Antonia had struck.

Owl nodded with recognition. "Yeah, well, maybe you two will believe me now, huh? Since your almost-merging took place while you slept, soon after, *ahem*, your visit to the Isle of Lesbos, it's pretty clear your subconscious desires are what got that ball rollin'. What do two lovers want more than ultimate Oneness, after all? But unlike you two, Creek and Melpomene went all the way. Their willed merger set off a chain reaction. All the Muses and bad luck spirits started gettin' absorbed into each other, amalgamatin' like rain drops flowin' down a pane of glass. And once they'd all lost their separateness, they got sucked back into the miasmatic field that had birthed them.

"So I got my revenge on the whole rotten bunch, even though I had to lose Creek to do it. I was gonna lose her anyway. Turns out I got a lot more than I'd bargained for, too. The good year 1811 marked the beginning of New Orleans's golden age, a half-century of prosperity unlike anything the town had ever seen, or would ever see again. See, plungin' the Muses and the *Club de les Miasmatiques* back into the miasma gave a monumental shock to the Mother's system. She didn't start poppin' out fresh servitors again until fifty years had gone by.

"Meanwhile, by 1820 New Orleans became the second wealthiest city in the whole country. Those are the years when all them mansions in the Garden District got built, and Andy Jackson whupped the British army on the fields of Chalmette. You think that woulda happened if it hadn'ta been for me? Shit, the city shoulda put a statue of *me* ridin' a horse in front of St. Louis Cathedral, insteada ol' Andy. Indian fightin' bastard...

"Well, if you know anything about history, you know the good times stopped rollin' for New Orleans right about 1861, the year Louisiana threw its lot in with the Confederacy. That's also the year after the first members of the current Miasma Club and Muses made their appearances, and no coincidence, that. I was there, waitin' for 'em. I'd known they'd be back, sooner or later.

"It wasn't long before the city fell to the Union. None of Louisiana's ironclads got finished in the city's shipyards in time. The fire rafts that were supposed to burn up Farragut's invasion fleet drifted off course. All the submerged torpedoes that were supposed to blow up Farragut's ships got corrosion in their fuses or water in their gunpowder. It was a symphony of bad luck. New Orleans fell without the city's militia firin' a shot. After the war, the zip and zing of the antebellum decades never returned. You three were there to see the rest. From Reconstruction to Antonia, it's all been downhill."

"Fifty years without a Miasma Club..." Kay said, awed by the notion. "Owl... can you do it again?"

"I don't know," he said. "I wouldn't be sittin' here if I didn't think there's at least *some* chance. But back in 1810, the big banishment required a willin' Muse and a willin' bad luck spirit to spark it off. And right now, we got neither of those."

"What about *me?*" Kay asked.

"Or... or *me?*" Pandora said.

He shook his head. "Neither of you is a full-bore bad luck spirit anymore. Pandora and me, we've both got just a few dribbles of Otherness left. Kay, you're in better shape; best case scenario, you've still got a few hundred years of existence ahead of you. The ceremony would force you to give up all your remaining Otherness, all those years. But it won't be enough. We'd have to involve others. Mortals who'd been touched by either bad luck spirits or Muses, preferably by both. Mortals who'd be willing to surrender whatever gifts they'd been granted, or maladies they'd been cursed with. Ideally, our co-conspirator would be a big shot, somebody who'd risen high on the wings of borrowed Otherness, somebody who'd willingly fall a long, long way."

Kay stared at the captive Muse. "What about Felicia?"

The Muse maintained a facade of defiance. "What about me?" she asked. "Can I be *forced* to sacrifice my sisters and myself? Doesn't it have to be done *willingly?*"

Owl slowly stood. "Yup. It won't work any other way. That's why you're gonna stay put between now and the Solstice." He gestured for Kay and Pandora to head toward the exit. "Come on, ladies."

He leaned on his cane and looked back at the Muse. She had begun trembling again and scratched furiously at her sides and arms. "Let's see whether six weeks of close proximity to the Mother's pain makes you a little more *willing*, sister," he said.

Chapter 30

ROY Rio didn't like being cornered, especially not in his own home.

Home was supposed to be his sanctuary. But he couldn't have met with these three men at City Hall. The news media would've been all over the story. Not to mention his campaign opponents.

But first things first. Before he sat down with these men — the Reverend Samuel Flint, founder of Detroit's Operation: LEAP (Leadership Engaged for African Progress), the Reverend Jayberry Jeremiah, director of Chicago's By Our Own Bootstraps organization, and Merle Morehouse, Roy's cousin, ex-mayor of New Orleans, and now president of the Urban Progressive Congress — he had to know if any of them was a ringer.

Kay Rosenblatt had greeted the visitors with Roy before withdrawing with him into his study. "What kind of read do you get on these guys?" he asked.

"They are who they say they are," she said quietly.

"Are you *certain?* Men like them don't come all the way to New Orleans just to wish a brother good luck on his campaign. They want something from me, something *big.* I can't afford to mess this up. If I do, I could either sink my reelection or get mired neck-deep in mud."

Kay stared out the window at the nighttime gloom of Audubon Park, seemingly lost in her own thoughts.

"Kay? Did you hear anything I just said?"

"I — I'm sorry, Mr. Mayor. It's just... I've got a lot on my mind right now."

"Anything wrong?"

"Yes... no." She looked searchingly into his eyes. "Mr. Mayor, do you think the ends ever justify the means, when those means are *terrible?* If there was a chance, a *slim* chance, but a *chance,* that you could save the lives of thousands of people, would you be willing to torture someone to get that person's cooperation?"

"That's... an *interesting* question. But now isn't the time to debate it. You're *sure* my visitors are clean?"

"There's no taint of the Miasma Club on the two reverends. The other one, Mr. Morehouse... he's been touched by a bad luck spirit, but it was a long time ago. The residue is old."

"Merle's been away from New Orleans for more than three years. So he's clean?"

"They haven't influenced him recently enough to affect how he'll behave toward you tonight."

"Okay," he said. "I need to meet with them alone." He headed for the door. "Kay?"

"Yes?"

"Thanks."

He entered the living room. Reverend Jeremiah scanned the contents of Roy's floor-to-ceiling bookshelves with the laser-like focus of a censor searching for evidence of blasphemy. Reverend Flint, a shorter man of softer build, who sported a massive pompadour reminiscent of Little Richard's, watched Jeremiah's obsessive search from the comfort of the leather upholstered couch and chuckled.

Ex-mayor Morehouse, the most conventionally handsome of the three, appeared the most ill at ease. He wouldn't sit, refusing to accept even a modicum of Roy's hospitality.

We've never been kissing cousins, Roy thought. *And things between us have only gotten worse since my campaign. Given the way I criticized him and his political cronies, I shouldn't be surprised.*

"Can I get any of you some coffee?" he asked.

"I'm good," Flint said. "We just ate at a nice little joint in the Quarter."

"None for me," Morehouse said coldly.

"No," said Jeremiah, not looking away from Roy's books.

Roy regretted that Kay had given the three visitors a clean bill of health; had she said that any were tainted, his job would be straightforward — usher them out as fast as he could manage. But now... now he had an obligation to hear them out.

"You have a very extensive library, Mayor Rio," Jeremiah said. "I see hundreds of books. Science fiction. Computer science. Architecture." He examined a framed black-and-white photo. "Who are these two white men, standing next to an antique computer? I can't read their signatures."

"Those are Ralph Baer, the inventor of the Odyssey home video game machine, and Nolan Bushnell, the founder of Atari," Roy said. "I met them at a gaming convention a year or two after I started my own software company."

Jeremiah frowned. "Do you know what I *don't* see, Mayor Rio? I don't see any volumes by W. E. B. du Bois or Richard Wright. Or a single book of Langston Hughes' poetry. This attractive parlor contains a portrait of two white video engineers, but none of Martin or Malcolm. Why is that?"

Roy felt his ears burning. "Cynthia took the W. E. B. du Bois with her when we split up our belongings."

"Surely you could have picked up your own copy," Jeremiah said. "If you'd wanted to."

Quicker than he'd imagined, they'd put him on the spot, embarrassed him as searingly as the school kids who'd once taunted him with the nickname Roy Oreo. "I'm sure you didn't come all this way to chide me on my apparent lack of race consciousness. Let's get down to brass tacks."

"I'm not scolding you," Jeremiah said. "I merely point out an issue which should be painfully obvious. You have a problem."

"And it's a problem we think we can help you with," Samuel Flint said. "What percentage of the Black vote did you get in your first election? A quarter?"

"Thirty-two percent," Roy said.

"Less than a third. What put you over the top was near-unanimous support from White voters. But you can't count on pulling off that trick again. Four years ago, there weren't any White candidates. Roy Rio, the non-politician, the software entrepreneur, was the closest thing to a White that Whites could pull the lever for. But this go around, there's a *real* White businessman in the race. That catfish guy, Van Goodfeller. So if I'm a White voter standin' in the booth, I'll be thinkin', *why vote for a Black man in whiteface when I can vote for the real thing?*"

"Am I gonna be charged for all this high-level political analysis," Roy said, "or are you giving away samples for free?"

"Don't play dumb, Roy," Merle Morehouse said, his voice as flat and featureless as the denuded Lower Ninth Ward. "I'm sure your people have run the numbers for you. Even with half the pre-storm Black population scattered around the country, you'll still have to raise your Black voter percentages by a good ten points just to get into the runoff. If you hemorrhage support from both sides, it's possible you could find yourself watching a Goodfeller-*Hotchkiss* contest from the sidelines. Catfish King versus Ex-Wife." He allowed himself a brief, tight smile.

"I like my chances just fine," Roy said.

"Brave talk," Morehouse said. "But I think you're whistling past the graveyard. People will remember the strong words you spoke in the

Superdome when it was surrounded by water. But voters will also remember the things you *didn't* do. Like making sure evacuation buses stayed high and dry. Maybe that's not fair. But politics isn't fair."

"Face facts," Flint said. "You simply *can't win* without capturin' a whole lot more Black hearts and minds. And we don't think you know how to do it."

"But with our help," Jeremiah said, "you can learn how. All three of us lead organizations of national scope. We can help you connect with those Black voters scattered in Houston, Dallas, Atlanta, Memphis, and Birmingham, persuade them you're the leader to bring them home. What happened in New Orleans last summer can be made to become the seed of a glorious new flowering of the Civil Rights movement. Black folks got denied their civil right, their *human* right to seek safety — they were denied passage across the Crescent City Connection bridge. A federal government and a state government dominated by White interests left a hundred thousand poor Black souls to drown, starve, and suffer in a cesspool created by the criminal incompetence and indifference of the Army Corps of Engineers. The three of us can bring enough marchers here to make Selma look like a small town Easter parade."

"There's truth in some of what you're saying," Roy said, "but you weren't here. *I was.* Mistakes were made, sure, *terrible* mistakes, but to claim the driving force behind what happened was racial animus — that's just *bogus.* Other forces were at work, stuff you guys have absolutely no knowledge of—"

"Stop thinking like a software engineer," Morehouse said, "and start thinking like a politician. A good politician knows that when perceptions clash with facts, it's *perceptions* that come out on top. Surely you're aware that a good percentage of Black New Orleanians believe that wealthy White Uptowners blew up levees in the Ninth Ward in an effort to keep the flood waters away from their own neighborhoods."

"That's an urban legend," Roy said, "complete bullshit. Mostly White neighborhoods in Lakeview and Mid-City got flooded out as bad as Gentilly or the Upper Ninth. If 'Evil White Masterminds' were trying to protect themselves, they sure did a lousy job of it. That rumor's one of the most destructive things that's come out of this storm."

"Of course it's destructive," Morehouse said. "But it's out there, and it's spreading. *Perception* trumps facts. If you don't bow to that law of political reality, you're going to get steamrolled."

"The anger is out there," Jeremiah said, "growing stronger. We can help you *ride* that anger. Act in concert with us, and you, Mayor Roy Rio, can become the figurehead of a renewed Civil Rights movement."

And all we want is your eternal Soul. Roy almost smiled. If he were living a cheap horror movie, that would be the next line of dialogue. *Act in concert with us...* They hadn't gotten around yet to spelling out what *that* meant, although he had his suspicions. "Why come to *me?* You've said it yourselves that I'm not the only major Black candidate in this race. Cynthia would leap at your offer without a second's worth of thought."

"Consider our approaching you first a courtesy," Jeremiah said.

"She already talks the language of Black voters," Flint added. "And she's developed a strong base of evacuee support in Houston. Honestly, you need us more than she does."

"Besides," Morehouse said, "you're the incumbent. If we got Cynthia Hotchkiss elected, it would take her months, maybe years, to build the same relationships with the city's business community that you've got right now. You want to get down to brass tacks? That's the real crux of the matter. Your relationships."

"Money is going to start pouring into this town," Flint said, his eyes dancing. "Billions of dollars in reconstruction funds. And since most of that money is federal, it comes with federal socioeconomic constraints attached. Small, disadvantaged business set-asides. Minority-owned business set-asides. HUB Zones, SBA goals, the works. Our people want a piece of that."

"*Your 'people'...?*" Roy said. "Do I take that to mean Blacks in general? Or are we talking members of that exclusive club, the Friends of Jayberry, Samuel, and Merle?"

Morehouse frowned. "I *told* you he'd be like this," he said to his two companions. "I grew up with Percy Pureheart here. Can't you see the golden halo floating over that bald head? We're wasting our time."

"Let's not be hasty," Jeremiah said. He turned to Roy. "Do not jump to reflexive disdain of our 'friends,' Mister Mayor. We perform the sanctified work of redeeming this sinful Nation. Of lifting a repressed, long-suffering people from the darkness of economic and cultural bondage. Such an awesome task cannot be accomplished through spirit alone, nor through words—"

"It takes *bucks*, man," Flint said. "A whole *lot* of 'em. You ever heard of the Stafford Act?"

"Of course," Roy said. "After the past five months, I can recite it in my sleep." He knew exactly where the discussion was headed now. "One hundred and eighty days after the disaster, all contracts for recovery work must be given to local businesses, to aid in the affected region's economic recovery."

"That's right," Flint said. "The first six months, the big boys, the national conglomerates, they sweep in and soak up all the work. But after that, it's the little guys' turn. But those little guys need to be local. Or at least they need to *look* local, legally. And business partnerships are perfectly legal."

"Front companies," Roy said. "That's what you need my help with, right? You want me to hook up your buddies from Chicago, Detroit, and New York with small Black-owned or women-owned businesses here in Southeast Louisiana. You're asking me to help you siphon off recovery dollars from my community, a community that'll *die* without those dollars recirculating through our economy."

Jeremiah sighed. "Your scope of thinking is far too narrow, Mister Mayor. As a Black leader, a privileged member of the Talented Tenth, you cannot allow yourself to be merely concerned about the welfare of the residents of a single city. Your community, you must not forget, is a nationwide one. The business people we seek to aid are allies in our struggle. By helping us to help them, you do not hurt the Black citizens of New Orleans — far from it! Rather, by building a stronger, more self-sufficient national movement of Black uplift, you raise your local constituents up. You give them pride and hope, assets even more precious than recovery dollars."

Christ, this man sure can talk, Roy thought.

He stared at the three men who awaited his answer. *I could go to the FBI. I could offer to wear a wire, get all these shenanigans down on tape. The feds could nail them under the RICO Act.*

But it would still mean getting down into the mud with them. And there'd be the grand jury, and all that press, and thousands of people wondering whether I'd originally been in bed with these three, then cut a deal with the feds to get my neck out of the noose...

No. Let Merle, Jeremiah, and Samuel be somebody else's problem.

"Well, Mayor Rio?" Flint said. "Are we gonna be able to do some business?"

"Get out of my house," Roy said.

The men remained silent for a moment. "You're certain you know what you are doing?" Jeremiah asked.

"As certain as I'll ever be."

For the first time since he'd arrived, Merle Morehouse smiled. "Thanks, Roy," he said. "Oh, I mean that sincerely. I had my worries you might act against type. But you followed the script I'd predicted, word for word." He chuckled. "It's *all* about Roy, isn't it? All about how Roy feels about Roy Rio. It doesn't matter what you actually get done, so long as at the end of the day you can tell yourself, 'My hands are clean.'" He glanced at Jeremiah. "Moral vanity, isn't that what it's called, Reverend?"

He turned back to Roy. "Despite what you think of me, I really do love this city and its people. This town desperately needs a mayor who is willing to crawl down in the mud and do what needs doing to get the job of recovery done. So, cousin, I'm going to *enjoy* helping Cynthia Belvedere Hotchkiss whip your ass."

"Get out of my house," Roy said. For good measure, he added: "And get out of my city."

* * * * *

The worst thing about politics, Cynthia Belvedere Hotchkiss told herself, *is having to deal with slugs like Gerard Wolfe.*

She turned away from the window of her fifteenth floor suite in the French Quarter's Monteleone Hotel. It pained her to waste time and attention on this fat, sweating, trembling white man; but it was necessary. He could yet prove to be a useful tool. "I don't appreciate people who renege on their commitments, Mr. Wolfe," she said. "Do you want a job in my future administration, or don't you?"

"Of *course* I do," he said quickly. "I've been living off FEBO checks and Red Cross assistance ever since Baptist Hospital was evacuated. But... but I've been thinking. About this whole grand jury thing. I — I don't want to go to jail for perjury, Councilwoman Hotchkiss."

"People who tell the truth as they remember it aren't committing perjury. It was *your* complaints to the District Attorney and the State Attorney General's Office that got grand jury proceedings started against Lily Weintraub. Without your testimony, the grand jury will be unwilling to indict, unless other witnesses can be found to corroborate your original complaint. Why are you contemplating withdrawing your offer of testimony? Have your memories of Antonia *changed* in the past three months? Memories grow *less* reliable with the passage of time, not more."

"But — but back in July, I was still terribly *angry*. Nurse Weintraub humiliated me in front of the entire senior staff. Made it sound like the whole crisis had been all *my fault*. Then I got fired. I mean, the hospital laid off hundreds of people, but they made it clear I was being fired because of *performance*. Do you have any idea how small the community of hospital safety managers is? How much people *talk?*

"So I thought, hell, if she's made it so *I* can't get a job, I'm sure as hell gonna make it so *she* can't get a job. I watched her on the roof of the hospital, when the rescue helicopters turned away. I saw her give too much medicine to the old lady who then went into cardiac arrest. And sometime over the prior two days, I'd heard people, nurses and maybe a doctor, talking about what they might have to do with the really sick patients if rescue didn't come."

"So you accused her of carrying out a mercy killing. If you repeat that story for the grand jury, I'd place good odds on Weintraub's indictment." *The bitch would certainly be convicted in the court of public opinion,* Cynthia thought, *which would serve my purposes just as well.* "Why are you wavering?"

Wolfe's small eyes seemed to withdraw deeper into the puffy flesh of his face. "I — I was *drunk*, Councilwoman Hotchkiss. After the flood waters surrounded the hospital... I found some liquor. Those people I heard talking about euthanizing patients — Lily might've been one of them, or she might not have been. *I can't remember.* And even up on the roof... it, it could've been that she made a *mistake* with that medicine. We were all ready to pass out from the heat. I — I *just don't know.*"

If she were a man, now would be the appropriate time to grab his shoulders and shake him like the jellyfish he was. Cynthia would enjoy that. But she was a lady. And ladies had their own ways of making a point.

"Mr. Wolfe, I understand that you're having qualms. Sending someone away for premeditated murder is a serious act. But now that you've begun the process, you can't simply run away. You *must* testify before the grand jury. To refuse to do so would pervert justice itself."

"But — but I—"

"And consider *this*. Your own hands are less than clean in the matter of the debacle at Baptist Hospital. A grand jury might find that you share in the liability for the deaths. Your refusal to testify in the matter of Lily Weintraub could shine a spotlight on your *own* culpability."

She watched his lower lip begin to tremble. She'd threatened him with the stick. Now to dangle the carrot once more.

"Later today, I'm going to meet with three very influential friends who are going to help make me the next mayor of New Orleans. *You*, Mr. Wolfe, are going to help make me the next mayor. After you testify according to your written statements, you will be welcome to your choice of hazard mitigation jobs in my administration; even Bruno Galliano's job, if you wish it. Or, if you would prefer employment outside New Orleans, my friends could offer you any number of select positions in Chicago, Detroit, or New York. The choice is yours — professional oblivion, or a secure future with unlimited growth potential."

She watched sweat roll down his forehead. "I'll... I'll stick by my original story, Councilwoman."

Cynthia smiled. "Good choice."

I'll tie that white bitch around Roy Rio's throat like a noose.

* * * * *

Kay had dreaded returning to Fort Macomb. She shivered as she sensed the full extent of the Mother's pain once more. Was she about to make a terrible mistake?

At moments like this, the most helpful guide she could rely upon was to ask herself, "What would Daniel do?" And once she'd answered that question — the answer came swiftly and surely — she recognized what she had to do. Consequences and friendships be damned.

Making sure her flashlight and pair of bolt cutters were tied securely to her belt, she climbed the gate guarding the bridge which led to Fort Macomb's ramparts. She found Felicia huddled against the wall, shivering. Felicia's eyes sprang open when Kay shined the flashlight's beam on her face. The Muse's slender arms looked as though someone had gouged them with a garden rake, turning her skin into a papyrus of bloody hieroglyphics.

"What — what are you going to do?" Felicia said.

Kay removed the bolt cutters from her belt. "I'm going to set you free."

"Is this some kind of trick?"

"I'm not that clever," Kay said. "Owl would probably call me 'a bear of little brain.' Or something much worse, if he knew what I was doing. If I remove these charms, will you be strong enough to help me cut through the chain? I don't have the hand strength I used to have."

"So... this *isn't* a trick?"

Kay severed a hook that attached a Neville Brothers CD to the chain. She slid the CD across the slick stone floor, freeing Felicia from its power.

"Be *careful* with that!" Felicia said. "Don't throw those things away like, like *garbage*. Do you know how many hundreds of thousands of recordings, instruments, and books were ruined in the flood?"

"I'll be more careful, okay?" She snipped another wire, this one holding a George Alec Effinger paperback novel.

"Just don't leave these things here. Take them home with you. Treasure them, like they're meant to be treasured."

Kay continued removing the charms, stacking them carefully on a dry spot on the floor. "Are you feeling any stronger? More in control of your own will?"

Felicia nodded. "Yes. But, like you, I'm not as strong as I was before the storm. My sisters are mostly in fine shape. One thing a disaster of this magnitude does is draw in artists in its wake. Painters, sculptors, architects, and writers who come to be a part of history. But music... at least the music of *this* place... it's *communal*, not individual. It needs families, communities, *neighborhoods*, to thrive — or it wilts and disappears."

She leaned closer to Kay. "Do you understand what I've *lost?* Gentilly, the Ninth Ward, the Seventh Ward, Broadmoor... those places were as vital to my musicians as spawning grounds to salmon. I don't know if my full strength will ever come back. But I think I'll be strong enough to break this chain, once you remove that last charm. Are you sure that's what you want to do?"

"That's why I'm here."

"You've abandoned your goal of destroying the Muses and bad luck spirits?"

She paused before removing the last of the charms. "I didn't say that. I just don't think keeping you here against your will is the way to do it. Owl said your participation has to be willing. I don't believe being coerced constitutes 'willing'."

"I agree." Felicia set her hand atop Kay's, the first time the Muse had willingly touched her since their near merging. The touch was not without kindness. "So, little goblin, how will you convince me? You're asking me to commit suicide, and to collaborate in the deaths of all my sisters. What can you *possibly* tempt me with that would make me even consider this?"

"Just keep your eyes open. That's all I ask. I'm counting on your love for your musicians to bend your heart. You're able to sense the presence of the Miasma Club. Track them, follow them, see how they crush aspirations and cripple lives. Your lameness — that's the mark of the Miasma Club, a reflection of the destroyed neighborhoods and music clubs, dead bodies floating face down. And they want to do it again. And *again.* Until there are no people left, no *musicians or music* left, in all of Southeast Louisiana. How can you *accept* that? Don't you want to stop it?"

"Do you agree with your friend," Felicia asked, "that the Muses are just as corrosive to human progress as the Miasma Club?"

"I... I don't know. I don't want to think so. But I've learned Owl is rarely wrong."

"You're acting against his instructions right now, aren't you?"

"Yes." She looked back into Felicia's face. "You can prove he's wrong by helping us. I'm going to cut away the last charm right now. I'd like your word that you'll observe the Miasma Club over the next two weeks. Then I want you to meet with me and let me know what you've decided."

She cut the wire holding the final charm, a vintage boxed set of Ernie K-Doe's hit singles. "Do I have your word?"

The Muse wrapped the denuded chains around her fists and pulled. On her fifth yank, the padlock's clasp snapped open. "You have my word, little goblin," she said. "I will watch, and I will ponder."

Kay placed the charms in her knapsack and assisted Felicia off the floor. "Thank you. Can I give you a lift back into town?"

"No. I have people I must see. I'll make my own way."

Kay led her across the weed-strewn parade yard and onto the bridge. "Can I ask you one more thing? Why were you so interested in Anh and Paul, the young couple in Village de L'Est who are expecting twins?"

"I, oh... I can't tell you. Not yet, at least. All I can say is... they're something *new*. Something none of us Muses have ever known before."

"I hope you'll trust me enough, sometime, to tell me the rest."

"I — I hope so, too."

They climbed the fence together, Kay assisting Felicia due to the latter's lame leg. "Good bye, Kay," Felicia said. "You'll be seeing me again. I promise."

"Good bye, Felicia. And thanks." She started walking across the drawbridge.

"Kay?"

She turned around. Felicia still stood on the eastern bank of the Chef Menteur Pass.

"My real name..." the Muse called after her, "the name you need speak aloud to have me come at any time... is Euterpe the Giver of Pleasure, the Mother of the Double Flute."

Chapter 31

"**K**AY Rosenblatt, you're a damned *fool*."

Owl's furious phone call had summoned her back to Fort Macomb. She'd been expecting the call for days, so she'd had time to prepare herself for this face-to-face tongue lashing.

Owl lifted a broken segment of chain from the casemate's damp stone floor. "If I was a younger man, I'd wrap this around your neck, young lady, and pull the ends until that peanut-size brain popped outta your ears. When did you set her loose?"

"Four nights ago."

He threw the chain against the wall. "You *do* realize that the Winter Solstice is barely five weeks away? By all that's holy, woman, what the hell were you *thinking?*"

"Torturing Euterpe wasn't going to work." Her voice remained quiver-free; she was proud of herself. "It was wrong. Not only wrong, it was counter-productive. She has an incredibly strong will. All you were doing was giving her more reason to distrust and defy you — she would've let the Mother's reflected agony drive her insane before she'd have helped us. But now I've given her a reason to trust me. She promised she'll observe the Miasma Club over the next two weeks, then decide whether ending their evil is worth the sacrifice of herself and her sisters."

His eyes rolled toward the dripping ceiling. "What a rube. Don't you think she would've promised you *anything* to get you to cut her loose? Our stumbling across her was a *miracle*. None of us have near the sensitivity for Otherness that we used to. She, on the other hand, can sense us a mile away. So what do you think the chances are that you'll ever have that next conversation with her?"

"You're *wrong*. She told me her true name. Her *full* true name. Just by saying it, I can compel her to come to me."

"Uh-huh," Owl said. "Have you tested it?"

"Tested it?"

"Yeah — tried it out to make sure it works, that it wasn't some bullshit."

"I'm asking her to trust me. How can I ask that if I don't trust her in return?"

He snorted, then scratched the back of his neck. "Aww, hell... Gotta work with the cards I get dealt, like always. So, assumin' your new best buddy sticks to her word and gives us a Muse to work with, you got any brilliant ideas on who we're gonna get to fill out the rest of our dance card?"

"I've had some thoughts. My best starting place, of course, is people I've affected myself. There's Lily. The poor dear would probably jump at the chance to cleanse herself of all the taint I've smeared her with. Maybe, by making her a part of protecting the city's future, I can undo some of the terrible harm I've done to her."

"Fine. But don't forget, without a full-blooded Miasma Club member workin' on our side, we'll need at least one mortal who's been touched by both bad luck spirits *and* Muses; even better, two mortals so double-touched. My buddy Everette Maddox woulda been perfect, but he's dead."

"Double-touched...? I can't be certain — I'd need Euterpe to confirm it — but I think Lily might've been double-touched."

"She write poetry, like Everette?" Owl chuckled. "*I once had an overbearing father / Whose meddlings were a terrible bother / My future sister-in-law / Stuck bad luck in my craw / And I can't catch a man with a hawser!"*

"Oh, stop it. Listen. Her whole professional life, she's demonstrated an aptitude for healing way beyond the norm. That's the main reason she was appointed Director of Nursing at such a young age. I remember, when I saw her for the first time in a quarter century, sensing something *new* about her — a residue of Otherness, but not one I'd ever placed there. More recently, I... I've sensed the same residue on one other person. The mayor."

"Rio?"

"Wouldn't it make sense? Look at all the things he achieved so young. He founded his own software company straight out of college. Then a couple of political talent scouts asked him if he wanted to be New Orleans's next mayor. A complete political novice, he got himself elected over a veteran candidate who'd been hand-picked by Merle Morehouse."

"So? I don't know of any Muse of Software Design. Or a Muse of Politics, neither."

"Polyhymnia, apart from being Muse of divine hymns, mimetism, and sacred poetry, is also the Muse of geometry. And the same kind of mental talents that solve geometrical problems can be put to work solving software problems."

"That's a stretch."

"And think about this," she said. "What's mimetism? Isn't it a talent for physical mimicry? If you combine that with a special ear and voice for sacred poetry, don't you get a man who could quickly master the skills of political self-presentation, just by studying successful politicians?"

"Yeah, yeah, whatever," he said. "I'll give you an 'A' for creative thinking. But what good does it do us? Let's take your notion as a given — Roy Rio was touched by Polyhymnia at some point. And you've told me Eleggua-Eshu managed to get to him during the Antonia disaster. So he's double-touched. Not only that, he's a mortal of great prominence, with lots to lose. Theoretically, he could choose to sacrifice a second term, and that could be the capstone sacrifice we need for the ceremony to work.

"*But* — and this is a *big* BUT — would you *want* him to make that sacrifice? I can't say I've got much of a sense of what Van Goodfeller would be like as mayor, but I've got a pretty good picture of what that Hotchkiss woman would do. And it ain't nothin' pretty. She'd be virtually a one-woman Miasma Club."

"Mayor Rio wasn't my first choice," Kay said. "Would the District Commander of the Army Corps of Engineers be prominent enough to serve as a capstone mortal?"

Owl's face sharpened with sudden interest. "You talkin' about your boss? That Schwartz guy?"

She nodded. "He's fighting for the survival of his career now. Four different independent oversight and review committees have begun investigations. Congress needs a scapegoat. But the Corps tends to protect its own. There's an even chance he'll escape all this with nothing worse than a reassignment."

"Why would he help us? You think he'll spring back to being a model officer and gentleman now that your aura's gone?"

"I seriously doubt it. I never could've exerted influence on him to the extent I did, for the length of time I did, if he hadn't been open to being influenced. But he's not a monster. I'm *positive* that buried somewhere in that self-righteous chest, there's a part of him that's *horrified* by the consequences of his choices. If I can manage to convince him of what's at stake, and how a selfless act on his part can help set things right... Owl, if he's willing to come completely clean in front of the cameras, commit *hari-kari* on his Army career — will that be enough to make the banishment ceremony work?"

Owl thought for a moment. "Possibly," he said. "So let's take stock. What've we got so far? We've got a Muse on the loose. We've got Lily, who despises you, so there's a good chance she'll tell you to screw off when you ask for her help. We've got Schwartz, who you insist you can browbeat into behaving one-eighty degrees opposite of the self-serving careerist you've known for twenty years. Even assuming we can manage to get those three wobbly dominoes to stand up in a line, it still might not be enough."

His eyes lit with a sudden notion. "What about Lily's brother? He's had a worse run of bad luck than she's ever had. Probably wouldn't take too much talkin' to get him on board, no? He already trusts you."

Kay felt as though the ground had disappeared from beneath her feet. "No. Not Daniel. Absolutely *not*."

"Why not? By stripping away his bad luck residue, you might even reverse his brain damage. He could get a chance to be a normal man."

"He *is* a normal man. He's, he's *better* than normal. Leave him *out* of this! I don't hear you volunteering *Pandora!*"

"'Cause takin' part in the ceremony would kill her. There's no comparison."

"I said *no!* You're always, *always* forcing me to bear the brunt of your schemes!" She waved her stunted left thumb in his face. "You didn't get *your* thumb cut off! You didn't let Pandora get *her* thumb cut off! But it was perfectly okay with you that they came and grabbed *me*. You could've stopped this whole disaster before it even happened. If you'd confided in me a year ago, you would've had your willing bad luck spirit — *me* — to use in the banishment ceremony. Then I could've been on the look-out for any of the Muses, and when I chanced into that encounter with Euterpe, I would've been *ready*. We wouldn't have had to pull anybody else into this. We could've done it all *ourselves!*"

"Yeah, and if the queen had balls, she'd be king," he said. "I'm not all-knowing or omnipotent. I'm just a worn out ex-bad luck spirit, a trickster shaman whose wick's nearly burned down to the nub. So sue me. Look, I hate to keep pokin' at what's obviously a sore point, but I'm tellin' you this as a friend. You love Daniel, right? So how can you deny him a chance to be cured? I mean, at least give him the opportunity to decide for himself. Maybe cuttin' grass and haulin' away debris isn't all he'd like to do with his life."

"What's so *wrong* about cutting grass and hauling debris? He comes home every night tired and filthy, but *proud*. And I love that about him."

"Fine, dandy," Owl said. "But he's a grown man. You're not his mommy. *He* needs to be the one to make that choice. Why do you want to deny him that? Take a look inside yourself, girl!"

"Don't you go near him. He's *fine! We're* fine! If I find out you've tried manipulating him in any way... I'm *out*. Are we clear on that?"

"Clear as fresh snow melt."

"Good."

She stalked out of the casemate. Owl was wrong, for once. She didn't need to take a long, deep look inside herself. She already knew her feelings and the terror at their root.

Losing her thumb, her face, centuries from her life span? Even her very existence? All these were sacrifices of small significance, compared with the risk of forever losing Daniel's love.

* * * * *

Roy Rio scheduled his first rally of the campaign season for Central City, a seemingly impregnable bastion of support for Cynthia Belvedere Hotchkiss. He'd decided to meet the threat the three civil rights leaders posed to his reelection head on. He would show her, as well as the Reverends Jeremiah and Flint and, most especially, Merle Morehouse, that he didn't have any intention of surrendering the working class Black vote.

Yet now he stared across cordoned-off Martin Luther King, Jr. Boulevard with disbelief and dismay. From atop a two-story commercial building facing his podium, the giant likeness of his ex-wife stared down at him from a massive billboard. When the news cameras scanned his audience, there would be Cynthia Belvedere Hotchkiss, giant-sized. Already, two camera crews had begun taking footage of the billboard.

Cynthia had managed to outfox him. In front of the entire local media, she'd turned him into a patsy.

He smacked his fist into his palm. "Walt, how could you and your people have let this *happen?*"

"We didn't let anything 'happen,' Roy," Walter said. "We assumed we had that billboard locked down ourselves. That ad must've gone up last night. Mighty quick work; I'm sure it cost Cynthia a bundle."

"I don't care if it cost her an arm and two legs. If we had a contract for that billboard spot, what happened?"

"Obviously, we got out-bid. Must've been an escape clause that allowed Outdoor Display Systems to accept a higher offer. Maybe if you'd *consulted* with me before pissing off Jeremiah, Flint, and Morehouse, we could've avoided this. Anyway, what do you want to do? Should we cancel and reschedule at another location? I could come up with a plausible excuse, some emergency back at City Hall—"

"No." Roy shook his head vigorously. "Any reporter worth a dime would figure out I was running scared. Besides, we've hired brass bands, flown in dozens of Mardi Gras Indians from refuges all over the country — they brought their costumes, they want to march. I can't disappoint all those people."

"So are you just going to pretend Cynthia's face isn't there? That's impossible. I mean, *look* at her — she's got her arms outstretched like she's a black female Jesus treading water with a drowned Antonia victim floating in her lap. I hate to admit it, but that ad is a *classic.* That billboard is going to be the story of the day; heck, the story of the *week.* Nobody's going to remember a word of your speech."

"So I'll improvise. I'll find a way to respond to the billboard in my remarks."

"No, no, *no*," Walt said quickly. "I don't want you going off message. That's just asking for trouble. Stick to the script, and let's just get this one over with."

"But if I play it safe, I'll watch Cynthia and Goodfeller waltz right past me into the run-off. You think I'm incapable of thinking on my feet? How about that impromptu teleconference I gave in the Superdome?"

"The circumstances were completely different. No matter what you say, that billboard is going to trump you. Any chance you watched CNN or MSNBC this morning?"

"No."

"That billboard there? That's just one of hundreds. They popped up overnight, not only in New Orleans, but in refugee-heavy neighborhoods in Dallas, Houston, and Atlanta. Her new sugar daddies just pumped an oil field's worth of cash into her campaign."

Roy turned away. "I'll figure something out."

"You'll stick to the script?"

He didn't answer. He stepped up to the podium and stared at the roughly three hundred faces waiting for him to begin. It was an entirely black crowd, with the exceptions of a few white reporters and some church volunteers from out of state. And Kay Rosenblatt, his watchdog, or watch-spirit.

"Thank you all for being here today," he said, glancing quickly down at his notes. "I know it's a cliché for a politician to begin a speech that way. But today, six months after Antonia, I must truly and humbly *thank* you for being here, for having made the Herculean effort to return and begin the rebuilding process. I know that many of you have been stymied by recalcitrant insurance companies, those companies which promised you 'good hands' but instead have given you the back of their hand. Others have found themselves tangled in the webs of governmental bureaucracy. If any of my offices have proven themselves hindrances, I most sincerely apologize. I pledge myself and all the resources of my administration to widening the road home to a superhighway, whose only speed limit will be the boundless limits of your courage, persistence, and resilience."

It was a good start, a strong start. If the audience and the cameras weren't here, he'd shoot the bird at his ex-wife's overblown portrait. "No city is merely the sum of its streets, buildings, bridges, and parks. A city lives or dies, thrives or withers, by the character of its people. Why are we world renowned? The reason people travel from around the world to visit New Orleans is *you* — the music you make, the food you cook, the myriad, wonderful ways you have chosen to celebrate life—"

A breeze ruffled the papers atop the lectern. One page blew onto the grass. Roy silently cursed. He'd just started finding his cadence, and now his concentration and rhythm were broken.

Without wanting to, he glanced up at the billboard. CYNTHIA BELVEDERE HOTCHKISS FOR MAYOR, it read. SHE SUFFERED WITH US.

She suffered with us.

Those words, and all they implied about him, made him tremble with rage. How *dare* she insinuate that he had sat comfortably on the sidelines? Especially after she'd lied to him about having evacuated Nicole. If she hadn't driven like a maniac, she and Nicole wouldn't have gotten stuck in New Orleans East, and the photograph that billboard was based upon would never have been snapped...

Off to his left, Kay Rosenblatt waved wildly. She signaled him with a slashing finger across her throat to stop the speech. She pointed at someone in the crowd. Roy tried looking where she pointed, but no faces stood out.

The crowd grew restless. He glanced down at the disheveled clump of his speech. It was fucked. *He* was fucked, unless he could spin gold from this mound of shit.

He'd have to go off script, rely on his instincts — despite what Walt said, despite what that Rosenblatt woman wanted. They both assumed they knew better than he did; but had either of *them* gotten themselves elected mayor?

He stuffed his speech into his pocket.

"Ladies and gentlemen, I apologize for letting myself get distracted. I was, uh, *admiring* that billboard over there, across the street." Many in the audience laughed; he'd finally mentioned the elephant in the middle of the room. "I'm sure my ex-wife did suffer during the storm. We *all* suffered. But for Cynthia to imply that her suffering was special, that her having floated in the flood waters is a reason to vote her in as mayor — that's just *wrong*."

A murmur of agreement rippled through the audience. "She didn't get my daughter to safety. Do you know she actually *lied* to me about that? She wasn't like so many of you, stuck where you were because of lack of a car, lack of a bus, lack of any money to get out. No — she wrecked her Cadillac SUV driving like a crazy woman in evacuation traffic, trying to jump the line. And now she thinks the consequences of her recklessness, her endangerment of my own daughter, make her 'special' somehow. To be perfectly honest, that makes me *sick*."

Some in the crowd applauded. All men, Roy noticed. *They must be sick of their bitches, too.* "Y'know, chalk one up for Cynthia. Her people out-hustled my people with that billboard there. Some days, you just don't get what you were expecting. Perfect example — this *Renew New Orleans Now!* comprehensive plan that I commissioned."

Boos erupted. He nodded. "Yeah, I hear you. Supposed to be *my* plan, right? I mean, I appointed all the committee members, picked them from Xavier and Dillard, Tulane and Loyola, got *all* the experts together. A real blue ribbon panel, y'know? And now, before I had an opportunity to officially review it, their plan's been leaked to the media. And a whole lot of people are upset, really bent out of shape by what's in that plan.

"And you know what? *I* don't like it, *neither*."

Cheers, scattered but loud — "You tell 'em, mayor!"

—"Don't let them men take my house away!"

—"Nobody turns *my* family's property into no park without *my* say-so!"

He held his arms out to the protesters among the crowd. "'Shrink the footprint' — it sounds almost *sensible*, doesn't it?"

"*No! No!*"

"Now, listen, now, just listen. These men on this committee, these are smart people. I mean, if we can't expect certain parts of the city to be properly defended against storm surge for years to come, maybe *never*, then it just doesn't make sense to rebuild those neighborhoods. Common sense, right? But consider what those three words, 'shrink the footprint,' *really* mean. Look at the map in the plan. *Whose* neighborhoods are getting 'shrunken'?"

"*Ours! Ours!*"

"Right. The Ninth Ward. Gentilly. Broadmoor. The Seventh Ward. New Orleans East. The only black neighborhoods that aren't on their hit list are Treme and Central City. *Two* neighborhoods. Just *two* that won't get turned into 'green space' or 'storm water collection basins.' They want to take away your land and squeeze you into a pair of neighborhoods where it's 'safe' for black people to live. They want to put you on *reservations*, folks.

"*Reservations*. How ironic is that? Who's gonna march after I finish? The Mardi Gras Indians. Black men who dress up as Native Americans, who honor those allies from long ago who helped some of our people escape from slavery. Those first Americans got *screwed*, didn't they? They were lied to and cheated by the government. Their women and children got massacred in places like Wounded Knee.

"But they didn't take it lying down. Before Wounded Knee, there was a dust-up called Little Big Horn. General Custer got his ass handed to him. And, you know what? *We* don't have to take it lying down, either."

"No, we *don't!*"

"No takin' it lying down!"

"No reservations! No way, no *how!*"

Roy beamed. Damn, this felt good. Maybe even better than his surprise press event in the Dome had. He felt like a god, a light-bringer, a conduit for forces which could not be withstood.

"So what's it gonna *be*, people? Wounded Knee, or Little Big Horn? Are we gonna let Custer push us off our land?"

"*No!* NO!"

"Are we gonna let a bunch of professors and planners erase communities it took us generations to build?"

"*No!* NO!"

"Are we gonna take it *lyin' down?*"

"*No!* NO!*"

"Then come *on*, Indians!" He summoned dozens of waiting men dressed in feathered, beaded costumes, heads crowned with war bonnets towering ten feet high. "Come on, Indians, and show 'em what you *got!*"

Kay tried reaching the mayor's side. Ignoring her had been a bad mistake — she'd sensed Eleggua-Eshu in the crowd. The mayor's words, liable to set the city's residents at each others' throats, were proof of Eleggua's power.

Worse, Eleggua had friends with him. She nearly gagged from the stench of fermenting cabbage; her skin prickled with emanations of Otherness.

She tried squeezing through the phalanx of sheriff's deputies, staffers, and reporters who'd surrounded the mayor. A sudden eruption of horn music and a crash of drums deafened her. The Fresh Birth Brass Band led the Indians down Martin Luther King, Jr. Boulevard toward the waiting crowd.

A deputy pushed her back. "Mr. Mayor!" she shouted. "You've got to get *out* of here! It's not *safe!* Get *out*, Mr. Mayor!"

Someone yanked her away from the circle surrounding Roy Rio. "Don't *you* tell him to go away!" A stocky black woman had grabbed her arm, eyes glimmering with rage. "He *belongs* here! He's *our* mayor! *You* the one needs to go away, *bitch!*"

Kay pulled away. The woman's plastic cup burst against her shoulder, spraying her face with cola and crushed ice. Trying to put as much distance between her and her attacker as she could, she stumbled against the backs of a group watching the Indians.

"*Hey!*"

"What the *fuck?*"

"I'm sorry, I'm *sorry*," she said. One of the men she'd stumbled into shoved her, hard, propelling her deeper within the crowd. She bounced off affronted bodies like a billiard ball, each collision provoking more outrage and curses. A fist struck her left cheekbone, just below her scar. An elbow bruised her ribs. She realized that if she fell, a legion of stomping, kicking feet would ensure she'd never get up again.

A leg smashed into her knees. She felt herself going down. She covered her head with her arms and tried rolling toward the curb, away from the kicking feet.

She tumbled onto the street. Feathered war bonnets blocked her view of the sky. She sensed Otherness nearby, very close. Its presence flitted about her like a cloud of gnats attracted by the blood on her busted lower lip.

Felicia...

Kay saw the Muse dancing not ten yards away, second-lining behind the Fresh Birth Brass Band's tuba player. Despite the Muse's ebony skin and West African features, Kay was certain it was Euterpe. If she could reach her, maybe the Muse would protect her from the violence being channeled by Eleggua-Eshu—

A chunk of curb exploded next to her. Fragments of concrete peppered her thigh and side. A crack like abbreviated thunder which echoed off the brick buildings lining the avenue. She heard a second gunshot. Then a third. People began screaming. A separate volley, from the far side of Simon Bolivar Avenue, answered the first. Someone bellowed with pain. One of the green-shirted church volunteers crumpled onto the street.

Police and sheriff's deputies forced their way into the crowd. The compact mass of people scattered, fleeing toward half a dozen shabby side streets named for the Muses. Kay had to shield her head yet again to avoid being trampled.

More shots. The brass band's music, already faltering, crashed to a halt. Through a jumble of legs, she saw the Fresh Birth's tuba player clutch his chest, then topple forward. The Indians, weighed down by their bulky costumes, swayed amidst the chaos like royal palms buffeted by hurricane winds.

She pulled herself to her feet. A tall, unnaturally thin black man stared at her from across the street. His black shirt displayed the motto *By Any Means Necessary.* He didn't wield a gun of his own. He didn't have to. He seduced other people into using *their* guns.

Ti Malice smiled, folded his hand into a pistol shape, and pointed his forefinger at Kay's forehead.

She turned and ran.

A bullet ricocheted off steel shutters covering the door of a closed dollar store, inches away from severing Kay's windpipe. She stumbled over an upended shopping cart, then glanced behind her. Ti Malice pursued her leisurely, confidently, leading a small mob of men wielding bottles and knives.

She struggled to remember Central City's street layout. Were they chasing her into a trap, a cul-de-sac? Were Eleggua and another mesmerized mini-mob lying in wait for her just around the next corner?

Stay calm. Concentrate on mundane things — the street sign...

YES! The street sign!

Her flight had led her onto Euterpe Street.

She needed somewhere to hide, if only for a minute. She ran down an alleyway between two abandoned houses. If her notion didn't work, they'd catch her very soon.

She ducked inside a shed nestled in a tiny back yard, then hid behind a rusty washing machine. "Euterpe, the Giver of Pleasure, the Mother of the Double Flute, come to me," she whispered. "I *need* you. Euterpe, *come*."

She heard running footfalls drawing closer.

"*Euterpe...*" she whispered fiercely, teetering on the edge of despair.

"I'm here, little goblin," a voice said behind her. "You've chosen an interesting circumstance for our reunion."

"Euterpe! Thank God you came! Ti Malice has gathered a mob—"

"I know," the Muse said. "Rise, and leave this foul hiding place."

"But—"

"Come."

She followed Euterpe out of the shed. Ti Malice led a group of six armed men into the small yard. Hope swelled in Kay's breast when she saw the malicious grin on his face disintegrate into shocked dismay.

"Be gone, abominable creature," Euterpe commanded. "And release your hold on those men's emotions."

"How — *how*—?" Ti Malice sputtered. But he quickly recovered his composure. Like a basilisk confronted by a mortal enemy, he magnified his bulk, quickly expanding to three times his typical height. "You are still overmatched, Kay Rosenblatt, despite your repulsive ally. Even if this Muse proves able to counterbalance my power, these men behind me outnumber you six to one. I need not feed their anger anymore — it is already stoked to a white heat. The only way you will leave this place is as a battered, violated corpse."

"Overmatched?" Euterpe said. "I think not, demon."

She thrust her long brown arms toward the sky. Then she pursed her lips and emitted a trilling whistle unlike any Kay had ever heard. Combining the sonic intensity of a hawk's hunting cry with the melodiousness of a double flute, the whistle echoed off surrounding rooftops, each echo bursting afresh with renewed vitality.

Two women emerged from behind the shed. One, wearing a crown of red roses, dark ringlets cascading down her back and caressing her hips, looked like a black Aphrodite who had just stepped out of a lost Botticelli painting. The other was an ebony whirlwind, a dancer formed of quicksilver and zephyrs, who whirled in a protective circle around Euterpe and Kay.

"Meet my sisters," Euterpe said defiantly to Ti Malice. "Erato, she who inspires the poetry of love, passion, and remembrance, and Terpsichore, Muse of the Dance. They accompanied me to the parade, where they witnessed your evil. You have lost the initiative, monster."

Erato glided amongst the six angry men, her feet barely disturbing the jumble of dead leaves on dusty bricks. She lightly touched each of them, caressing the curve of one's cheekbone, tousling another's hair. Kay watched the fury melt from the men's faces. Viciousness and murderous intent were displaced by the innocence of small boys waking from a nightmare, their release heralded by confused, wistful smiles.

"Are you so sure of your dark powers," Euterpe said to Ti Malice, "that you are willing to challenge all three of us?"

Ti Malice deflated to his normal height. Although he managed to maintain his steely arrogance, Kay could see he'd been humiliated most searingly. "There will be another time, Kay Rosenblatt," he said, spitting the words at her like bits of rancid meat. "Another time, when you are without your watchdogs. We whom you betrayed grow stronger with each passing week. The wombs of the very fleshlings you seek to protect will provide the means of your annihilation."

His form shimmered, then dripped away into shadows cast by tall houses which surrounded the yard. The half dozen men, each rapturously lost in yearnings for some beloved, also drifted away.

"Thank you," Kay told Euterpe. "Does this mean you've decided to help me with the banishment ceremony?"

"That is a discussion for another time," she said. "Our people are wounded and dying. We must attend."

Terpsichore, whose gyrations had never completely stopped, accelerated her dance. Dead leaves swirled around Kay, faster and faster, until she found herself encased in a kaleidoscopic cocoon.

When the wind ceased and the leaves fell upon her feet, she found herself very much alone.

Chapter 32

"**R**OY, either you're an evil genius, or you're the luckiest son of a bitch who's ever entered politics."

Lucky? Roy Rio had felt evil's touch insinuate itself into the strands of his spine like a cancer. His incendiary speech yesterday — it hadn't all come from *him*, had it? He'd gone over this again and again in his mind, talked it out with Kay Rosenblatt like a penitent in the confession booth. An outside influence had tasted his anger and frustration, then twisted it into something hideous.

So why the hell did Walter Johnson look so *happy?*

"You aren't threatening to resign," Roy said. "And you haven't slapped those survey results down on my desk like some angry thunderbolt from Zeus. Care to tell me what it is you've got to smile about? My first official campaign event turned into a riot. Eight people shot. The editorial page of *The Times-Picayune* is practically demanding I be strung up from a tree—"

Walter's smile grew bigger. "Believe it or not, we're back in this thing. We're back in the race." He spread a set of printouts in front of the mayor. "These just came back a half hour ago. Look. As you can see, you've totally tanked with white voters, up and down the economic strata."

"That's *good* news?"

"No, but it's nothing we weren't expecting. Your white support was melting away to Van Goodfeller anyway; all this latest incident has done is accelerate a trend. But just *look* at your numbers with black likely voters. Since last week's poll, you've gone from twenty-seven points behind Cynthia Hotchkiss to virtually neck and neck. She's only four points ahead, inside the margin of error, even with all those billboards of hers."

Roy slowly shook his head. "I don't get it. I've been getting slammed, and not just by New Orleans media, but all over the country. Even *The New York Post*. What did they call me? A 'racial arsonist.' Four years ago, I was the 'post racial' candidate, the 'competency counts' candidate. And now I'm the second coming of Huey Newton."

"Yeah, but look who's been slamming you the *hardest*. It's Fox News, Sean Hannity, Glen Beck. It's Rush Limbaugh foaming at the mouth. The entire right-wing freak show is howling for your head. It's *gold*, man. If I had a hundred million dollars to spend, I couldn't buy us this kind of coverage."

"So what are you saying? Black voters have started circling the wagons?"

"Circling the wagons? Roy, they're *armor plating* them and mounting fifty caliber machine guns on top."

Roy rubbed his forehead. "But this, this is just an emotional reaction, right? How long can it last? The primary election isn't until January."

"You think *I* don't realize that? But you've found your groove, man. You've got to stay on the attack. Not just against Cynthia — against that Renew New Orleans Now! Committee, those legions of egghead planners who want to tell us our business, and the state and federal agencies that've let us down. Stoke the resentment, but do it in a systematic way. I say we start a Bum of the Week club. Every week, we hold a press conference to denounce somebody. Show the people you're a fighter who won't rest until this town gets fixed."

"That sounds like a great way to make a whole bunch of new enemies."

"Well, sure, but if you can't get yourself reelected, what will it matter? Save the nice-nice for *after* the election."

"Who do you think we should start with?"

"Might as well begin with the low-hanging fruit. The Corps of Engineers. Everybody and their mothers hate those sons of bitches."

"Kay Rosenblatt and I have a meeting set with Colonel Schwartz next week."

"He's in some hot water, isn't he?"

"There've been a lot of rumblings that he'll get transferred. That would pretty much scotch his career. So far, he's been digging in his heels, denying he ever did anything but follow the book. Kay and I... we've got some ideas on how to convince him to come clean. Get him to open up the Corps' closet at a press conference and let all the nasty old skeletons tumble out."

Walter raised his eyebrows. "The Rosenblatt girl has that much dirt on him?"

"She knows where all the bodies are buried. And a whole lot more stuff, besides."

"Man, if you can pull that off, *and* take credit for it, then I can practically *guarantee* you a spot in the runoff. *Fantastic.* Meanwhile, there's some internal housecleaning you need to do. Baggage you need to toss overboard. It won't be pretty, but it'll pay off down the road. And if we time the announcement for the day after Schwartz's press conference, the news of our guy's 'resignation' will probably get blown out by the aftershocks of the Schwartz thing—"

A series of angry knocks on Roy's door cut their conversation short.

Shit, Roy thought, *Bruno asked for an emergency meeting.* Their meeting had been scheduled for two. It was 2:12.

Approaching the door, he intended to tell Bruno to come back in ten minutes. But his livid homeland security manager pushed his way into the office, glaring at Walter like he meant to break the slighter man in half. "Was that *me* you were just talking about? Am *I* the 'baggage' that gets tossed overboard as soon as Colonel Schwartz cuts his own throat?"

"Hey, hey, I didn't even mention your name," Walter said. "And what were you doing listening in on our conversation, anyway?"

Roy stepped between the two men. "Bruno, you are *way* out of line." *Have the hobgoblins gotten to him again? Kay told me he was a risk.* "Look, I'm sorry I kept you waiting. But that's no excuse for acting like a maniac, pulling accusations out of thin air—"

"*Thin air?*" Bruno whirled on the mayor. "You think I'm *deaf?* You think I haven't heard all the malicious gossip around here since the storm? I've been referred to as *deadweight*, *political poison*, the *bus drowner*, and now, by your Chief of Staff, as *baggage* that needs to be *tossed*. I know damn well who he was talking about."

He stalked toward Walter. "You want to get rid of me, Johnson? Well, I'm gonna make your day, son. This was gonna be a private meeting between me and the mayor, but since you're his personal Machiavelli, you might as well hear this, too. Mr. Mayor, with all due respect, yesterday's performance — not a speech, but a *performance*, because I simply can't believe those words came from your heart — left me *disgusted* and *appalled*. If you insist on following the script laid out by this, this *propagandist*—" he pointed a trembling finger at Walter — "I *resign*."

"Bruno, just wait a minute," Roy said. "Walt didn't have anything to do with my off-the-cuff remarks yesterday—"

Bruno didn't seem to hear. "Oh, Mr. Mayor, how *could* you? How could you *sanely* imply that the members of the Renew New Orleans Now! Committee — I'm talking men like Henry Lance Campbell and Lionel Partridge, presidents of two of the biggest black colleges in the South — are plotting to commit ethnic cleansing in New Orleans? Have you lost your *mind?*"

"Look, maybe some of my remarks yesterday were intemperate. I was, uh, swept up in the heat of the moment. But the position I staked out — that people should have control over their own lives and property, their own levels of risk — it's legitimate. If you can't get on board with that, I need to know, and I need to know right now."

"But do you *realize* what you'll be doing? Every time you let your Department of Safety and Permits sign off on a rebuilding permit for a house in the Lower Ninth Ward, you're giving your seal of approval for that family to invest their savings there, to *risk their lives there*. Because you know as well as I do, the Corps of Engineers won't have those levees up to spec inside of five years. That area may *never* be safe from catastrophic flooding. So how can you *invite people* — and I'm talking *poor* people, without the resources to rebuild and rebuild and rebuild yet again — to put their lives at risk?"

Roy heard the righteous indignation in Bruno's voice. And, although he was loath to admit it, that passion to protect people shamed him.

But Walter was right, too. For whatever reasons — instinct, corrupting influences, *whatever* — Roy had cast his lot with a policy of *laissez faire*. In front of the whole country, he'd staked the rationale for his reelection on the notion of letting individuals decide for themselves what was proper and safe. To go back on that decision now would torpedo his candidacy faster than any possible blunder or misstep. He *had* to stay the course.

"Bruno, there are two philosophies of governing," he said. "One philosophy assumes that citizens need to be protected by the state from the consequences of their own bad decisions. The other assumes that citizens are rational decision makers who, if they're given adequate information, will choose to act in their own best interests. Strip away the emotions from my remarks yesterday, and what I said was: hey, people, I trust you to make the decisions that are best for you and your families."

Bruno nodded reluctantly. "Mr. Mayor, you're preaching to the choir here. I'm a Libertarian. I know your talking points backwards and forwards. But there are a ton of complicating factors. You say you trust people to make rational decisions once they've been given adequate information. But the information people are getting is anything *but* adequate! The Corps says everything is hunky-dory with the levees now, and it's getting better every day. Independent reviewers say that's bullshit. Who is the common joe supposed to believe? Then there's coastal restoration. Who knows if those plans'll get funded? And if they *do* get funded, who knows if they'll *work?* In the meantime, we're expecting thousands of people to make life-defining decisions on whether to rebuild or to start over someplace else.

"And for a lot of folks, it's not gonna be a rational decision. It's gonna be an *emotional* decision. It's gonna be, 'My granddaddy bought this land, and my daddy built this house, and me and my wife rebuilt the place after Betsy with our own hands, and we're never gonna leave it.' The American people are the most generous people in the world, and most of them are more than happy to help us. But what are the American people gonna say to Congress if they give us billions to rebuild, and we don't rebuild *smart*, and then another storm comes along and drowns us all over again? Won't they say: *Fool me once, shame on you; fool me twice, shame on* us?"

Roy rubbed his forehead. Nothing Bruno had said was wrong. *But you can't make that case to the voters of New Orleans. They won't swallow it. You can't get reelected on a platform of Eat Your Damn Spinach.*

"Bruno, I'm not saying your points don't have merit. But they aren't gonna help me get reelected. Look. Election season is not the right time for this debate. Passions run too high. How about we revisit this a year down the road? We'll have better information then."

"Roy," Walter said, "why are you trying to talk him into sticking around? He's made up his mind. We don't need any loose cannons. Let him go."

Roy motioned for Walter to be quiet. "Bruno, I'm asking you. Will that work for you?"

Bruno shook his head. "I can't condone a bait-and-switch, Mr. Mayor. You don't suddenly switch signals on people after they've sunk tens of thousands of dollars into restoring a house. No. Either you repudiate your remarks from yesterday, or I can't in good conscience stay on as a part of your administration."

Bruno, Bruno, Bruno... I've met you half-way, offered you a ladder. But I can't force you to climb down. "Then I accept your resignation."

Bruno blanched. "You — you do?"

Aww, shit... he doesn't want *to go. He really thought he could get me to change my mind.* "Are you willing to stay on long enough to ensure a smooth transition?"

He watched all the starch leak out of Bruno's stance. "Sure, of, of course. I'll, uh, I'll do whatever's necessary. May I... may I be excused?"

Roy walked him to the door. Events were piling up so quickly. Was he doing the right thing? *Is this what the monsters want? For me to second guess every decision I make?*

An even worse thought pressed itself into his mind as he watched Bruno retreat down the hall. *Do they want me to fail? Or do they want me to* succeed?

What if the monsters trying to wipe out this city want me to win?

* * * * *

"I didn't think you'd come," Lily Weintraub told Kay. "Not when I said I'd only give you my answer standing in front of my parents' graves."

A cool, early December breeze tousled Kay's hair. She quickly glanced around Beth Judah cemetery. The graves of Miriam and Amos Weintraub lay in a corner near the Mid-City terminus of Canal Street. Streetcar tracks, damaged by the eight-week-long flood, sat rusting in the middle of the neutral ground. Amos's headstone wouldn't be installed and unveiled until eleven months after his death. For now, the only marker of his presence was a raised rectangle of earth, covered by newly grown grass.

"I've always found cemeteries to be peaceful, welcoming places," Kay said. "They don't repulse me, or frighten me."

"This one should," Lily said. "It's not that often a murderess is compelled to stand before the graves of two of her victims."

The venom in Lily's voice burned Kay's ears, but she accepted it. "This isn't the first time I've come here. I've visited your father's resting place half a dozen times, and your mother's many, many times before that. I... I love them, too, Lily."

"How can you *say* that? After what you *did* to them? Do you even know what love *is?*" She fumbled with a cigarette; the breeze made lighting it a struggle. "Can a — a creature like you have any *understanding* of love?"

"I love your brother," Kay said quietly, trying her hardest not to respond in kind to Lily's wrath. "You know that, don't you?"

"*Do I?* He *seems* happy. But he's like a six-year-old boy... trusting, eager to please, excited by any scraps of affection. What *you* get out of the relationship... *that's* what gives me pause. Daniel worships you. Do you need the worship of a human being, even one as mentally feeble as Daniel, in order to exist?"

Whatever optimism Kay had felt regarding this meeting melted away. Had they progressed at *all* since Kay's confession of her sins weeks before the storm? "Oh, Lily... sister of my heart ̶ "

"Don't *call* me that! Don't you *dare!*"

"I thought we'd gotten past this. Didn't you intercede for me with Mayor Rio?"

"Oh, and look how *that* turned out. Some job you've done of 'protecting' him. He's changed into a man I hardly recognize, ranting and raving on the TV news." Her cigarette, reduced to a nub, went out. She tossed it aside and quickly lit another one. "I was at a low point. I'd just been arrested, publicly humiliated, then informed that a grand jury would possibly indict me on a murder charge. I wasn't thinking straight. You manipulated me. And now you're trying to do it *again*. Tempt me with promises you can make the monsters disappear, along with this black cloud of bad luck that floats over my head. Why the hell should I trust you?"

"Lily, if I could peel my skin back, so that you could see what's truly inside me, I would."

"I'd *love* to peel your skin back, then pin it up on a corkboard like a bug's carcass."

"I know you hate me."

"Then *why don't you just leave me the hell ALONE?*"

"I... I can't," Kay said. "I won't. Because I love you."

Lily shook her head. "That's... that's ridiculous. And obscene."

"But it's also true."

The two women both stared at the graves. The wind died down.

"So how is this supposed to work?" Lily asked. "If I go through this mystical car wash of yours, I get scrubbed of all my stored-up bad luck, right? What happens then? Do I quit smoking? Does the grand jury say 'the hell with it?' Do I get my job back? My reputation? Do I suddenly loose these twenty-five pounds I've put on since Antonia? Do my mother and father rise from their graves? Do I get my *childhood back?*"

"I... I don't know. I can't predict all the results. But I do know one thing for certain. The Miasma Club will be dissolved. They'll be forced to merge with the Muses, and the whole lot of them will get sucked back into the miasmatic energy field beneath the city."

"Muses..." Lily laughed. "Your story just gets more and more convoluted, doesn't it? Why not pull Santa Claus and the Tooth Fairy into it, too?"

Kay took a cautious step closer to her. "There's something else you have to understand. In addition to cleansing you of your residual taint of bad luck, the ceremony will strip you of your gift from the Muses... the special empathy you've always had for the suffering, what's allowed you to become such a successful nurse."

Lily shrugged. "It's not like that 'gift' does me a whole lot of good now. I'm blackballed, and the terms of my bail don't let me leave the city to find work somewhere else. I'm *trapped* in this damned place. If there are no Jewish bad luck spirits left, how come my life has continued to *suck?*"

"It's the others. They've hated me ever since I betrayed them, and they know you're important to me, so that has made you a target, too. They can't affect your luck directly. But they can influence other people within their own ethnic communities to do unfortunate things which hurt you. The only way I know to stop it is to destroy them. And the only way I can destroy them is with your help."

Lily took a quick drag off her latest cigarette. "That's not true. I'm not the only person in this town who's been touched by both the bad luck goblins and the Muses. You've admitted that yourself."

"Yes, but the Winter Solstice is only weeks away. I can't find other potential participants before then—"

"What about Daniel?"

The question froze Kay's heart.

"If participating in this ceremony is supposedly so good for *me*, why wouldn't it be equally as good for my brother? I mean, you *love* him, right? Why wouldn't you want to scrub *him* of his bad luck taint, too? Unless you've been lying to me?"

"No, *no*, that's not it at *all*." Kay knew that Lily had her. "The truth is... *yes*, I *am* afraid of what the ceremony might do to Daniel. But I'm not afraid it'll harm him. I'm afraid... I'm afraid it will *help* him. That it'll change him, and he won't be the same anymore."

A knowing, sly look appeared on Lily's face. "So you're afraid if he changes... if his brain manages to heal... maybe he won't love you anymore? He could find someone *else* to love?"

Kay trembled, but she nodded yes.

"You know what? That's the first thing you've ever said to me that I believe without hesitation. I'll make a deal with you, 'sister of my heart.' You want me to be a part of this?"

"My fondest wish is to undo the harm I've done to you."

"Well, I'm in — but *only* if you make Daniel a part, too. He'll agree in a heartbeat. And you know why? Because he'll think getting smarter will make him a better husband for you. He won't have the slightest notion that with an unfettered mind, he'll see you in an entirely different light." She pointed to her parents' graves, her hand shaking with barely contained emotion. "And he'll come to recognize the implications of... this."

Kay stared at the graves, too, but didn't see them. Her vision had grown waterlogged, as occluded as it had been when she'd stood bound before a thrashing Lake Pontchartrain.

"You've taken from me almost everything I've ever loved," Lily said. "And now you claim you want to make amends. *Prove it.*"

Kay's tears moistened the young grass which had grown over Amos Weintraub's resting place. She remembered a story from the *Yom Kippur* prayer book — how God had instructed an angel to find the most precious thing in the world and bring it to Him. The angel, after searching many days and nights, came upon a thief who plotted to kill a man and his family so he could steal their belongings. But the thief, observing the family's evening prayers through their window, changed his mind. Reflecting upon what he had been about to do, he shed a tear. The angel caught this tear, the Tear of Repentance, and brought it, the world's most precious treasure, to the Lord.

Kay stared at her tears glistening on the grass. She nodded yes.

* * * * *

Bruno Galliano switched off his TV, feeling disgusted with himself. He realized he'd been sitting on his couch for two hours, aimlessly clicking through channels.

Shit-canned. Two days later, he still could hardly believe it. He'd never been fired from a job before. Sure, he'd offered to resign, but that had just been a threat, an attempt to pull the mayor back from the edge. Yet there was no escaping the hard fact that Mayor Rio had fired him.

And he was letting himself wallow in it, like a teenager whose first love had just dumped him.

He yanked himself off the couch. *Shitfire and hell.* Bunny never would've let him wallow like this. Bunny would've made him get off his sorry ass yesterday morning. That woman had been made of oak.

Christ, he missed her.

Someone knocked on his door.

If it was the mayor, come to say he'd changed his mind, what would Bruno do? Tell him to go to hell? No. He was a good soldier. If Mayor Rio wanted him back, if he'd seen reason, Bruno would return to his post with nary a sour word.

He pulled the curtain away from the window. It wasn't the mayor.

It was Venus.

He opened the door. "Vee — *Venus?* Where're you been? I haven't heard a thing from you in six months. I'd been afraid something had happened to you in the storm—"

"Hello, my Bruno. I've missed you, too."

She was exactly as he remembered her. Green eyes he could swim in. Hips... he could swim in those, too. A breeze carried her scent to him, cloves and olive oil. He sensed his benumbed body returning to life.

"May I come in?" she asked.

"Of — of *course*, sure, come right in." He blushed when he realized he wore nothing but a two day old undershirt and a pair of jockey shorts. He hadn't shaved in three days. "Look, pardon my appearance, okay? If I'd known you were coming—"

"You'd have baked a cake?" She strode past him into his apartment, her voluptuous thigh brushing against his leg. "Don't apologize."

"Can I get you something to drink?" He blurted this out before he remembered he had nothing drinkable in the house, save tap water. "Oh, hell, scotch that. I really need to get to the grocery store."

She sat on the couch and patted the cushion next to her. "I don't require anything to drink. Only your company."

He sat. She erased the space between them. "How long have you been back in town?" he asked. "Where did you end up evacuating to?"

"Somewhere safe. It doesn't matter. All that matters is that I'm back here now, with you."

"I never back-filled your old job. I'm sure you could go back to work, if you want to. But Venus, there's something I need to tell you. I'm, uh, I'm moving on to another job—"

"So I've heard."

"Shit. Word sure gets around *fast*, doesn't it? I'll bet that skinny bastard Walter Johnson has already held a press conference, blaming me for everything short of sinking the *U.S.S. Maine*."

She began massaging his shoulders. Man-oh-man, what a *touch* that woman had! "They don't deserve you. They never did, none of them. Soon they will crawl back to you like the worms they are."

"Ohh, *oohhhh*, that feels *good*, honey. Look, Venus, I don't know what your situation is, but if you need your old job back fast, I'm sure I could work something out."

"I thank you from the bottom of my heart, but without you there in the office next to mine, the job would seem unbearable. And there is a woman working in the mayor's office now, a newcomer, a dreadful, *terrible* woman. She makes me afraid. She should make you afraid, too."

"You aren't talking about Kay Rosenblatt, are you?"

Venus's fingers stopped their kneading. "Yes. *Her*."

"Rosenblatt? I've known that woman since my days in the Corps. She's mild as milk. You've got more *oomph* in your pinky than she's got in her whole body."

She slid onto his lap, facing him, her lips barely an inch from his. Her breath smelled like after dinner mints — the fancy restaurant kind, served in silver bowls by the cash register. "Never judge a person's potential for evil by her meek looks. This Kay Rosenblatt has insinuated herself into your mayor's trust. She pulls him onto a dark path. All those things Mayor Rio has said on the television news which have shocked you?"

"Yeah?"

"They were the poisoned fruits of Kay Rosenblatt's black heart."

She kissed him. Suddenly the room wasn't there anymore. Only her: her mouth, her lips, her tongue. He had no idea what she was doing with her tongue, or how any human appendage could possibly do what that tongue was doing.

She broke contact, leaving him exhausted but hardly satiated. Caressing his chin, she captured his dazzled gaze with eyes as deep as the Mediterranean and said, "Now, my shining centurion, I want you to tell me all you know about Kay Rosenblatt's plans for Mayor Rio."

Chapter 33

Now *I know how a punching bag feels*, Roy Rio grumbled to himself. Van Goodfeller and Cynthia had tag-teamed him through this entire televised debate, a pair of rival wrestlers who'd formed a treacherous, temporary alliance to beat him down. Roy had just finished his summation. Now Goodfeller was delivering his, with Cynthia's turn coming last.

"... And so my claim on your vote is a simple one," Goodfeller stated to the cameras. "At this time of unprecedented crisis for our city, we cannot afford to be divided. Not by appeals to racial or ethnic solidarity, not by setting neighborhood against neighborhood, and not by scurrilous calls for class warfare. The job of our chief executive is to unite this battered city in a common purpose. As a proud, lifelong resident of New Orleans, I was shamed to the core of my being when our current mayor implied to the whole country that the disaster we have suffered has so degraded us that our only path forward is that of resentment and revenge. Should you choose to elect me as your next mayor, you have my solemn promise that I will never, *never* make you ashamed."

Ouch.

And now it was Cynthia's turn.

"I'd like to begin my closing remarks with a warm welcome," she said, slathering Roy with an unctuous, Cheshire Cat-like smile. "I'd like to welcome Roy Rio to the Black race. Oh, it may have taken him a while to decide he's a Black man, but better late than never. I have here a gift for our new Black man, a little guidebook put together by members of my congregation, exiled in Houston. This here book's got a handy list of local soul food restaurants, Black-owned barber shops, and churches which welcome people of color; ones that survived Antonia, of course. Use it in good health, and welcome to the family." She tried handing him the book. He refused to touch it.

"It's always a cause for celebration when a new Black man joins us," she continued, "but — not to look a gift horse in the mouth — I must say I do question the timing. Not to be impertinent, but this sudden conversion of yours, it wouldn't have anything to do with Van Goodfeller's getting into the race, would it? A sudden loss of your support from White voters... that *couldn't* have any bearing on this momentous life change, could it?"

Roy, painfully aware the rules disallowed him to say a word in response, remained silent. Cynthia smiled. "No, I didn't think so. That would be *too* crass. Besides, the way to judge a man's sympathies is through his actions, not his words. You had a fine evacuation plan put together for the big public housing projects, didn't you? Made fast use of all those R.T.A. buses to get the poor folks to safe havens. And for those left behind, who could complain about the way you provisioned the Superdome? I mean, people have told me it was like dining at Commander's Palace! And then, after the storm, it was a fine, *fine* thing, the way you comforted the families of those little old Black ladies who got put down like mangy *dogs* at Baptist Hospital." She reached into her purse. "In fact, I've got pictures here I'd like to show the folks at home, pictures of Brother Roy doing his sanctified work..."

She looked at them, did a theatrical double take, and then slapped her cheek with feigned shock. "Good heavens! Brother Roy, say it ain't so! You aren't with the victims! You're with the killer — Lily Weintraub, Baptist Hospital's angel of *death!*"

She held the two photos up for the cameras. Roy saw they'd been taken in the Ninth Ward the day he'd met with Lily and Kay. Nightmare — this was a *nightmare*.

"Brother Roy, *why* would you choose to associate with a nurse who betrayed her sacred trust? It couldn't be that you were seeking to reignite an old high school romance, could it? I mean, what kind of a leader seeks out company like *that* at a time like *this?* What kind of a *man?*"

Whatever composure Roy had managed to maintain boiled away. "How did you get those?" he shouted, grabbing at the photos, heedless of the fact that cameras recorded everything. "Did you hire some private detective to follow me? Pay off a member of my security detail? Lily's an old friend, damn it! And she's *innocent* until proven guilty in a court of law!"

The college auditorium erupted into chaos. Roy's police detail kept a swarm of reporters at arm's length while Walter pulled the mayor toward the back exit.

Roy stumbled down the steps which led to the parking lot. "Let *go* of me, Walt! Let me go back and talk with them!"

"Not when you're like this," Walter said. "One more performance like tonight's, and you might as well cede the election."

Roy stared out at the dark waves of Lake Pontchartrain, whipped to a froth by a rapidly approaching cold front. He hadn't let Walter shove him into a police car; he wouldn't give Cynthia the satisfaction of watching footage of him fleeing the scene on the ten o'clock news. He'd recover his composure, and *then* he'd depart.

He cursed the day he'd married her. How could he ever have deluded himself that he loved her? Why hadn't he seen then, thirteen years ago, the deviousness, the selfishness, the *cruelty* that were so glaringly obvious now? He'd let a serpent into his bed. He'd wanted to give Nicole a real family, of course; he'd really wanted the marriage to work. But in the end, all he'd succeeded in doing was providing Cynthia with a reference manual on how to wound him.

A lone man approached. He was dressed in an NOPD uniform, but he wasn't part of Roy's security detail. Officer Thomas, the head of the detail, waved that he'd let the man through. The weak light of a street lamp illuminated the visitor's face. Roy recognized him. Quincy Cochrane. Cynthia's uncle.

"You come to gloat?" Roy asked.

"No, Roy, I haven't come to gloat," Quincy said. "I've come to help."

The word set off alarm bells for Roy — he'd been "helped" by hidden spirits a little too much these past months. He searched for Kay, then saw her standing near his security detail. She held a yellow card the size of a playing card above her head, a signal they'd arranged. Green meant a person was clean. Red warned that an individual was under the influence of the Miasma Club, or was an actual member in disguise. Yellow meant somebody who'd been tainted by their touch in the past, but who wasn't now under their direct influence.

He turned back to his visitor. "We aren't relations anymore, Quincy. And we've never been friends. So what possible reason could you have to want to help me?"

Quincy spat into the grass. "Disgust. With my niece. I was in the audience just now. Those billboards she's put up, and the things she claimed tonight, her 'heroism' and 'sacrifice'... she turned my stomach. I'm no prince. But even a dirty cop's got his limits."

"Go on," Roy said.

Quincy told him what had really happened in New Orleans East after the storm to Cynthia, Nicole, himself, the stranded woman, and the dead man whose iconic image now emblazoned hundreds of billboards around the nation.

"Nicole was the one who snapped those photos," Quincy said. "She did it to shame her mother. But Cynthia's *unshameable*. She confiscated Nicole's camera phone. Instead of erasing the photos, she decided one of them was dynamite, *good* dynamite. A few weeks ago, right after Morehouse and those preachers endorsed her, she came into a whole bunch of new money. So a photo of her being a selfish *brat* got turned into the cornerstone of her campaign. And the refugees stuck in Houston and Dallas wanna canonize her now... Saint Cynthia of New Orleans East."

Roy felt the black cloud which had descended upon his head disperse. This could be a turning point, the game changer. "Are you willing to repeat what you just told me to reporters?"

Quincy laughed. "Are you kiddin' me? Hell, *no*. I got just five more years before I can claim my full pension, and Cynthia might get herself elected as my next boss. Too risky. *Way* too risky."

"What about that woman she tried tossing off the boat? I'll bet she'd talk."

"I never learned her full name. I'd recognize her if I saw her again, but she could be anywhere in the country now."

Roy's heart sank. He saw where this was heading. "So that just leaves..."

"Yup. Nicole."

"No, no, absolutely *not*. I won't put my daughter through that. I won't ask her to make a choice between me and her mother."

"She's practically a grown woman. She don't want to do it? She can say no."

How could Quincy be so *blind?* "Do you have any idea of the position you're asking me to put her in? I can't drop that question in her lap and expect her to be able to decide rationally. If she says 'no' to me, she'll feel like she's rejecting me, no matter how much I try to reassure her. But if she goes ahead and tells her story to the media, Cynthia will never speak to her again — you know how vindictive she can be."

Quincy rubbed the back of his neck. "Try lookin' at it this way. Don't you think Nicole is starin' out the windows of her school bus in Houston every day, starin' at those billboards of her mother in the water with that dead man on her lap, thinkin' to herself, *I know what really happened?* How do you think she's gonna feel if her mom wins this election based on a lie, a lie Nicole helped her tell? I'll bet she's just *itchin'* to tell the truth. Right now, it's too scary. But if she knew that you know what happened... that might be just the little shove she needs."

"No," Roy said. "I won't do that to my daughter."

Quincy shrugged his shoulders. "Then you're gonna *lose*, man. I'm throwin' you a life line here."

Roy remained silent, staring out at the unsettled waters.

"Okay," Quincy said. He set a computer briefcase at Roy's feet. "You got a strong moral backbone, even if you don't have the stones to knock off my niece. Makes me feel more certain you're the one who should get this."

"What is it?"

"Somethin' I kept safe through the storm. Somethin' I thought I'd make a killin' off of, but now I think different. Now I think you're the man who needs to take care of this. Have your tech advisors take a good, long look. I'm trustin' you to do the right thing with it, Roy. 'Cause honestly, I got no damn idea what the right thing is."

* * * * *

Daniel embraced Kay so hard her joints cracked. "It's really *true?*" he said. "You and Mr. Owl, you've figured it all out? All the bad things are gonna go away? Lily gets to be happy? And — and I get to be a *normal* guy?"

This was almost too painful for her to bear. Lily had pegged Daniel's response nearly word for word. "Darling," she said, "please, *please* don't get your hopes too high. There's a *chance* things could get much better. But even if the ceremony works exactly as planned, the end result could be only that things don't get *worse*. And it'll be dangerous, incredibly dangerous. Owl's only done it once, and that was two hundred years ago—"

"I don't care about all that," he said. "Lily's already said she's gonna be a part of it, right?"

"Yes, but—"

"Then everything's gonna be *all right*. Lily's *smart*. She's the smartest person I know. Except for Dad, and the rabbi, I guess."

Kay buried her cheek in his chest. "Darling, the last thing in the world I want is for you to get hurt. Promise me, *promise me* you won't let your hopes get too high. Even if everything happens flawlessly, the end result could be so subtle it's almost invisible. Or it might happen so gradually that it'll take years for us to notice you've changed at all. Do you understand?"

She looked up into his eyes and could see he hadn't listened to a word. His face was full of dreams. "You know the best part of all of this?" he asked. "I'm gonna be a *normal guy* on the day we get married! I can give a speech to all our guests, a speech I wrote myself. A *good* speech. And — and maybe I can even go to *college*, just like Dad always wanted. I can be a doctor, or a scientist, or — or maybe even a *rabbi*. Honey, I'll make you so *proud!*"

"I'm *already* proud of you. I couldn't be *more* proud—"

"We need to celebrate!" He pulled her toward the door of their trailer. "Let's go to Russell's. I can buy everybody dessert—"

"No, Daniel, *no*." She stood her ground. "There's nothing to celebrate. Not yet. The day after the Solstice... we'll see."

"Why do you have to be such a *downer?* All I want is to be *happy!* Why can't I go out and celebrate that I'm about to be happy?"

"We're happy now, Daniel," she said softly. "Aren't we?"

"I'm going to Russell's," he said. He walked to the door, then paused, waiting for her to smile and run to be with him.

She didn't move.

He opened the door and went out.

It's good this is happening now, she told herself. *An advance taste of how things will be. The little spats. The shows of independence. The resentment which will inevitably grow, the more he comes to understand what I was, and what I did to him.*

This is how it will have to be.

She waited until the burbling grumble of his truck's engine faded, then went outside. The night had gotten colder. The cogs of Owl's mystical wrecking machine were beginning to fall into place. Lily was on board, now that Kay had fulfilled her end of their bargain. Lieutenant Colonel Schwartz? She and Mayor Rio had met with him twice over the past week. One more meeting should suffice to get him on the team.

One more key participant remained unaccounted for.

"Euterpe, the Giver of Pleasure, the Mother of the Double Flute, come to me." She waited for the Muse's gentle touch upon her shoulder.

Moments passed. She again called out the name of the musical spirit who had promised to heed her summonings.

Yet Kay remained alone.

* * * * *

All I ever tried to do, Lieutenant Colonel Branson Schwartz told himself, *was carry out my assigned missions and stay within the funding limits laid down by Congress. What was so evil about that?*

He stared forlornly out the lobby windows of the Army Corps' headquarters building. Protesters waited at the edges of the parking lot. They waited with their hand-painted signs and their silly baby pools filled with doll houses and toy cars and brown water, meant to represent their drowned neighborhoods.

Well, he wasn't going to run that gauntlet and absorb their abuse. Not tonight. He'd found an isolated spot to hide his car, a couple blocks toward downtown, on the far side of River Road. He could get there through the back exit.

He began navigating the maze of corridors which led to the rear doors. He wondered whether the protesters had recognized Mayor Rio a few minutes ago, when he'd left the building with Rosenblatt. Shouldn't they scream *"baby killer"* at the mayor, too? Hadn't he had a hand in the disaster? It just didn't seem *fair*. If what Rosenblatt had told him was true — and more and more, he found himself unable to deny the truth of her claims — then he'd been played for a patsy virtually his entire career. Those creatures had used him; he'd been a *tool*. A hapless tool for things that shouldn't even exist.

He stepped outside. A wet warm front had pushed its way north from the Gulf, bringing fog. Schwartz couldn't see the Gretna shipyards on the far side of the Mississippi. The river itself, Schwartz's main foe all these years, lay partially hidden beneath a blanket of mist, like a python slithering through tall grass.

It simply wasn't fair. His trusted assistant had manipulated him, pushed him into cutting corners and overlooking substandard work. And now she expected him to fall on his sword in public, take the full measure of blame, disgrace himself?

"Fucking insanity," he said.

Whatever he did, he knew he was doomed to be made the scapegoat; he'd been in the Army long enough to know how the politics at the top worked. They'd tie the red thread around his neck, then force him into the wilderness before shoving him off the edge of a cliff, all the while deluding themselves that they'd solved the problem of faulty levees.

He crossed River Road. Sheets of fog separated him from the protesters up the street. He was nearly positive none of them had seen him.

If he was doomed to be the scapegoat anyway, shouldn't his last act as an Army officer be taking down the Miasma Club? Sure, he'd be leaping on a live grenade to do it. And nobody would line up afterward to present him a medal. But at least he'd be able to live with himself after leaving the service. He'd find someplace quiet to retire, far away from levees and rivers and storm surge. The desert. That would do.

He'd call the mayor first thing in the morning. He'd tell him he was on board, that he'd do it.

The fog obscured the curb where he'd parked, but he saw the swingless swing set at the edge of a playground, so he knew his Dodge wasn't far. Walking closer, he saw the roof of a basketball court shelter, rusty and sagging, hover in the fog like a battered flying saucer from a fifties B movie. He heard voices from beneath the shelter. Were some neighborhood kids trying to put together a game? *Weird time to play basketball*, he thought. *Can't see the hoops.*

"Lieutenant Colonel Schwartz, I presume?"

The sudden question startled him. A female voice, off to his right — he hadn't heard her come up beside him. "Bruno Galliano sends his regards," she said.

He looked at her. Long, black hair, olive skin, wearing a short dress which barely contained her breasts and hips. "Do I — do I know you?"

"We've met once or twice," she said. "At meetings at City Hall. Where you defended the sturdiness of your precious levees."

Oh, hell, he thought. *She's a protester. She must've seen me leaving, even with all this fog.* "Ma'am, I'm terribly sorry for what happened to your home," he said, turning toward where his car waited. "But this isn't the time or place for a debate about causes. Contact me through the Corps of Engineers website, and I'll be happy to have someone answer your questions."

"That's not good enough, Colonel Schwartz."

"It'll have to be." *The impertinence of these people...* He picked up his pace. Something jutted against his chest, stopping him. *A paw—?* No, it couldn't be. A hand. But the arm it connected to bristled with brown fur.

"Don't be in such a hurry to leave, Mr. Lieutenant Colonel," the imposer, still indistinct in the mist, said with a vaguely French accent.

"You look like a man in need of relaxation. A nice swim, perhaps." A hood hid his head and face, but the nose which protruded from the hood... it wasn't human.

This guy's wearing a wolf costume, that's all. Some kind of nutty environmentalist. He cocked his fist. If he had to fight his way through these assholes, then so be it. "I'd strongly suggest you don't mess with me. I'm fully trained in hand-to-hand combat. Back off." He pulled his car keys from his pocket and inserted them in his fist. The ignition key protruded from between his knuckles, a potential eye gouger.

"Oh, don't bother with your car keys," the woman said. "A friend of ours disabled your vehicle."

"You freaks have messed with my *car?*" He took a swing at the clown in the wolf costume. The man backed away from Schwartz's punch with the lithe swiftness of an actual canine. No matter — he was out of the way. Schwartz took off across the fog-draped playing field. He kept a gun in the Charger's glove compartment. That would keep these idiots at bay until a tow truck could come.

He glanced over his shoulder to see if they followed.

Bad move.

He crashed into something rock hard. The impact sent him sprawling. What the hell was a *wall* doing in the middle of a soccer field—?

But it wasn't a wall. He'd crashed into a man. A man so wide and tall, Schwartz couldn't see above his chest — the fog hid the rest of him.

Something in the fog gibbered and cackled. It sounded like a monkey coked up on amphetamines.

"I'll — I'll take as many of you bastards down with me as I can," he said, struggling to regain his wind.

"Oh, we don't intend to lay a glove on you, Mr. Lieutenant Colonel," the man in the wolf costume said. "It's not our way. We'll leave that to our followers, the good people of New Orleans, who have a perfect right to express their grievances. And here they are now."

Multiple hands thrust through the fog and grabbed Schwartz.

"It's *him!*"

"The son of a bitch, I've *dreamed* of getting my hands on him—"

"—levees made outta *cardboard*—"

"Ruined my home—"

"*Baby killer!*"

They had him by the arms and legs. They dragged him across the grass. Toward the basketball court shelter.

"What — what are you people going to *do?*" He twisted in the mob's grasp so he could see what lay ahead of him. He saw it, then wished he hadn't.

In the middle of the basketball court sat an inflatable baby pool. A foot of water engulfed plastic houses and stores and school buildings and toy cars and trucks.

"*A nice swim, perhaps.*" That's what the wolf had said.

He tried whipping his arms and legs free, but the mob held him fast.

"Balor, umm, Balor doesn't like this," the giant said. Irish accent — an Irish giant? Schwartz still couldn't see his face, lost in the darkness of the rafters. "Can't they just beat man some? Teach him a lesson?"

"Shut up, you big, wussy lummox." Thick Irish brogue, also from high up in the darkness. A coked-up monkey's brogue. "This is America. Here, the *people* decide, you witless cyclops. I'm getting down for a better peek."

The mob dragged Schwartz to the edge of the baby pool. They shoved his face into the water.

He forced his head up with the brute strength of panic. What he saw then snuffed out his last shred of resistance.

Inches from his face, on the edge of the pool, sat a cackling leprechaun, four inches tall, with the face of a goat, wearing only a green top hat and a matching set of green swim trunks.

Chapter 34

"**M**A'AM, I'm sorry we had to call you over here, especially at this hour. We think we know who we've got here. But we have to be sure."

"I understand." Kay swallowed hard, then followed the police officer up wooden steps to the large, FEBO-issued trailer which housed the city's temporary morgue. She'd been half-expecting this summons for days now, ever since Lieutenant Colonel Schwartz had failed to report to his office Monday morning. And then she'd seen that news report earlier tonight, officers wading into the river at the edge of the French Quarter, tourists gaping at a waterlogged corpse...

The officer opened the door. The stench of formaldehyde nearly knocked Kay back outside. The floor and walls of the trailer vibrated with the constant hum of powerful generators. Ten cadaver coolers and two autopsy tables left hardly any space in which to move.

Another man entered, dressed in a white lab coat. He squeezed past them and stood next to one of the coolers.

"We fished this man off the rocks by the Moonwalk promenade late this afternoon," the officer said. "Bunch of tourists who'd just gotten coffee and *beignets* from Café du Monde spotted the body. Best as we could tell, it'd been in the river a few days. No identification, but it was dressed in a uniform with Army insignia. The victim was somewhere in his late fifties. Dark brown hair with lots of gray. Five feet, ten inches tall. You reported Lieutenant Colonel Branson Schwartz missing a couple of days ago. He doesn't have any family. That's why we called you."

He gave Kay a sympathetic frown. "You ready to take a look?"

She nodded. The officer gestured to the attendant. "Go ahead, Pete. Open 'er up."

She'd tried to prepare herself. She'd visualized terrible wounds, mutilations. But what confronted her now was more bizarre and grotesque than stomach-turning. It was Lieutenant Colonel Schwartz, all right — but a Branson Schwartz whose portrait had been painted by a child using drippy water colors. He'd always prided himself on his cut physique. Now he'd lost all angularity. Puffy, bloated, and gray, he looked like a gingerbread man which had been left out in a rain storm.

"Is that Branson Schwartz?" the officer asked.

She nodded. The attendant closed the drawer.

"How did he die?" she asked.

"Best as we can tell at this point, he drowned," the officer said. "They'll open him up and find out for sure. But there's no sign of major blunt trauma or a puncture wound. The only bruising we found was on his lower back, but it wasn't nearly enough to have killed him. I need to ask you some questions, okay?"

Kay nodded.

"Had he been depressed? Was he acting any differently than normal?"

"He was under a lot of stress. There's been a lot of pressure, from his superiors and from the public. But he hadn't been acting out of character, not at all."

"I know it's hard for you to judge this, but did he blame himself for what happened? For the levees breaking?"

"He didn't blame himself, Officer. That wasn't in his makeup."

"This doesn't appear to be foul play. And it wasn't an accident — otherwise, his pockets wouldn't have been empty. In your opinion, could he have committed suicide?"

Even days spent marinating in the Mississippi River hadn't completely expunged the distinctive scents of Fortuna Discordia, Reynard the Fox, and Balor the Fomorian from Branson Schwartz's corpse.

"This wasn't suicide," she said.

No sleep for the weary... nor for those who'd watched their carefully formulated plans drown.

Kay felt limp as an old scrub rag. Following her visit to the morgue, emergency consultations with Owl had crowded out any time for sleep. And now, she'd spent the first part of the morning in the mayor's office, bringing Roy Rio up to speed on this latest setback.

"Are we checkmated?" Mayor Rio asked.

"Owl doesn't think so," Kay said. "Lieutenant Colonel Schwartz was... a very important piece on our side of the board. His profile fit the needs of the banishment ceremony almost to a tee, and we invested a lot of precious time trying to get him on board. But that doesn't mean he was the only person who could fill that slot."

"Who else is there? Aside from me?"

"Bruno's friend Bob Marino could possibly fit our needs. Before the storm, I heard reports at a Miasma Club meeting that a special action squad had tampered with Bob's luck field while he was in town last February."

"He and his coworkers won millions playing Louisiana Lucky Loot," Roy said, nodding. "They all took early retirement, leaving FEBO to Ducky Duckswitt."

"Right; the Miasma Club managed to decapitate FEBO. But Bob didn't stay free of bad luck for long. It came crashing back on him when he returned to New Orleans in time for Antonia."

"Uh huh. Bruno's told me that Bob's life has been a bucket of crap ever since the storm. One of his sons was badly injured in a car accident; Bob was the driver. A month later, part of his house got obliterated in the explosion of an underground gas main. Then he and his wife separated."

Kay rubbed the scar above her left eye. "I'm no expert like Owl, but it sounds like what Fortuna did to Bob Marino turned him into a bad luck vortex."

"You mean, like a magnet for bad luck?"

"More like a — a vacuum cleaner. She created a vacuum in his luck field. It stayed empty for a while, but it couldn't remain empty forever."

"When he was winning all that money, wasn't his 'luck field' filled up with *good* luck?"

"I don't know that there *is* such a thing as *good* luck," she said. "At least, not as a distinct phenomenon that can be separated out from the energy of life itself. The mere existence of life implies good luck. Life, living — *that's* what good luck is. The 'good luck' of winning the lottery or finding a soul mate, I think that's really just the absence of bad luck energy..." She thought about the circumstances which had led to her upcoming marriage. "Or maybe a triumph over it. Even the gifts of the Muses — for all their power, all they can do, I think, is nurture bits of potential which already exist within someone."

Mayor Rio leaned back in his chair. "Metaphysics," he said, then shook his head. "Never thought I'd have to deal with *that* as mayor of New Orleans. Garbage collection? Fixing pot holes? Sure. But *metaphysics*...?" He laughed. "Let's get back to Bob Marino. Why didn't his 'luck field' just fill back up with the same amount of bad luck it had held before the Miasma Club messed with him?"

Kay struggled to come up with an appropriate analogy. "Think of it in terms of... oh, of a river that gets dammed. Before the dam is built, the river and its banks stay roughly in equilibrium; there might be some erosion when snow melts increase the river's flow, yet a rough balance remains. When the dam gets built, the river shrinks to a trickle on the downstream side. But the force of the river keeps building and building on the dam's upstream face. If the dam breaks, the river rushes through in a destructive torrent. The old banks aren't nearly wide enough to contain the flood, and they get washed away, quite violently."

"Jesus... so Bob's like a stretched out balloon, getting pumped full of bad luck until he threatens to pop? I don't think it'll be hard to convince him to get out from under *that*. Question is, how much good can he do *us?* You've said we need somebody prominent, somebody who's got social and civic status to sacrifice. Bob's retired. He wasn't the head of FEBO when Antonia struck."

"I know, I know. I'm not saying he's the perfect candidate; but he may be the best we've got. Thanks to his timely retirement, he's still got a sterling reputation as a public servant. So he's got that to sacrifice. And the fact that he's likely to soak up a huge amount of miasmatic energy in the time he's here could work to our advantage, too — it might weaken the Miasma Club.

"But there's something else we need to resolve before we can risk contacting him, certainly before we dare fly him down here. We don't know how the Miasma Club discovered our plans."

"You're *certain* they killed Schwartz?"

"I'm certain."

"They could've been tracking you. They could've followed us to any of our three meetings with him."

"But that doesn't explain their decision to eliminate him," she said. "They weren't close enough to eavesdrop on our conversations; I would've sensed them. Unless they'd learned of our plans for Lieutenant Colonel Schwartz, they would've wanted to keep him around. He was so hated and distrusted by the storm victims, his staying on as the local head of the Corps would've given thousands of potential returnees another reason to stay away—"

Her nostrils twitched with a familiar and detested scent. Her adrenaline spiked the same instant a desperate knock sounded on the door. "Mr. Mayor!" she cried, grabbing a heavy paperweight from a table. "It's Fortuna! She's *here!*"

"Kay Rosenblatt? Is that you?" The voice on the far side of the door wasn't Fortuna's — it was Bruno Galliano's. "I've *got* to talk to you! It's an emergency!"

"That's Bruno," Mayor Rio said, rising from behind his desk. "I haven't seen him since I accepted his resignation."

Before Kay could protest, he opened the door. Bruno rushed in, not even acknowledging the mayor's presence. He grabbed Kay's wrists. Fortuna's scent wafted from his skin like a rancid aftershave. Kay managed to free her hand holding the paperweight. She pulled back to swing it at his head. But she stopped her attack cold when she saw his face. Devoid of the murderousness she'd expected, his features displayed only pain and self-loathing.

"They told me at the front you'd be here," he said. "You've got to help me. When I saw the news about Branson Schwartz — I knew he'd died because of *me*. It's on my head. It's on my head."

"*You* killed him?" she said. "Did Fortuna—"

He shook his head furiously. "No, no, I didn't kill him, not the way you think. Not with my hands... with my *mouth*. Venus Roman, my ex-secretary..."

"You mean Fortuna Discordia. She's been playing the part of Venus."

"Whatever. She's... she's not *human*. She did things to me — I, I *let* her do things to me, unholy things, things Bunny would've been ashamed of, may God save my soul. And she got me to talk."

"What did you tell her?" Mayor Rio said.

Bruno crumpled onto the couch. "What I overheard when I stood outside your door, the morning I resigned. How you and Kay planned to convince Schwartz to come clean to the press. How you'd use his *mea culpa* to help you win a spot in the run-off election. Venus wants your ex-wife to get elected. She bragged to me about what she'd done to Bob Marino. She said she'd do worse to Schwartz, to make sure he couldn't help you. And to keep me quiet, she kept giving me what I... what I wanted."

Kay shot Mayor Rio a look of relief. He signaled his understanding with a tiny nod. At least Schwartz's murder hadn't been precipitated by the Miasma Club's learning their plans for the dissolution ceremony. Apparently, that remained their secret. For now.

"What do you want from me, Mr. Galliano?" she asked, feeling an instinctive sympathy for the broken man.

"Protect me from her. Even though I know what she is now... I... I don't *trust* myself. Ever since Bunny died, I've been out of my head with loneliness. And Venus... she made herself into just what I wanted. What I wanted so bad." He turned to Roy. "Mr. Mayor, I've always been a good soldier. Under normal circumstances, I *never* would've betrayed your trust. But, you've gotta believe me, *no* man could resist what she hands out. And... and I was pissed as hell at you, too. So that made her job even easier."

He turned back to Kay. "She said you used to be just like her, but you've changed somehow. She hates you — she wants nothing better than to stymie you. So I figure you're the only one I can turn to. You've gotta find a way to keep her away from me. Even now, knowing what I know... those lips, God in heaven, those *lips!* I can't get her out of my head! You've gotta put me somewhere where she can't get at me. Can you keep her *away?*"

Kay placed her hands on Bruno's shoulders. "I — I think I can, if you'll help us. And in doing so, help yourself, too."

"Yes, *yes*, I'll do *anything*. Just so long as she can't use me again."

"I need to talk to the mayor alone."

Roy gently pulled Bruno away from Kay. "Bruno, there's an empty office three doors down, on the other side of the hall. Wait for us there."

His eyes constricted with panic. "But — but—"

"Lock the door if you have to."

"It won't *matter*. If she finds me, she'll make me unlock the door. How can I make you *understand?*"

"Jesus, man, pull yourself together." Roy pushed him to the door, all gentleness gone, and shoved him into the empty hall. "That one," he said, pointing to the open office. "Get your ass in there and lock the door behind you."

Kay and Roy watched until Bruno closed the door behind him. Then they returned to the mayor's office.

"Fuck," Mayor Rio said under his breath. "Never thought I'd see the day..."

"Are you all right?"

"I guess. It just shook me up. To see him reduced to... that. We've had our differences, but I've always respected the hell out of him. Now..." He didn't finish the thought. "What can you do for him?"

"I'll call Owl. I'm sure he'll be willing to hide Bruno in one of his safe houses until the Solstice. Can you have one of your deputies drive him there?"

"Sure."

"I'll ride with him, to make sure we aren't being followed."

Mayor Rio stared at the place on the couch where Bruno had collapsed. "Can you use him in the ceremony? You said Bob Marino's participation might not be enough by itself. Maybe if he and Bruno held a joint press conference...?"

"I was thinking the same thing."

"Ten days..."

"Ten days," Kay echoed.

Ten days to go, she thought. *And I'm still without my Muse.*

Chapter 35

"**I**'VE recovered Professor Zoukeni's laptop for you," Roy Rio said.

Annalee Jones's eyes widened with surprise. "Amitri's computer! How did you find it?"

"The police picked it up."

"But I thought — from what she implied on the phone, I thought Councilwoman Belvedere Hotchkiss had somehow gained possession of it."

"I don't think she ever had it, no. But she might've been expecting to obtain it. Thus her call, to get a sense of what it might be worth to you and MuckGen." He stared out the windows of the office suite MuckGen had recently leased on the thirty-first floor of One Shell Square, the city's most prestigious office tower. Vast tracts of New Orleans still remained dark, nearly seven months after Antonia. "How familiar are you with the contents of this laptop's hard drive, Annalee?"

"Not very; only in the most basic way. Amitri was the discoverer of the Orleans bio-energy field, and he was one of our most important researchers. I'm sure his computer contains several years' worth of data on the practical exploitation of the bio-energy's unique properties. Amitri suffered several serious equipment malfunctions. In our last conversation, he mentioned that only one laptop containing his backup files had survived. But after his accident, when we were unable to find it among his possessions, we assumed it had been lost or stolen. The rest of the team has been trying to replicate his experiments ever since."

"They're doing this now?"

"Of course. We've got parallel teams working around the clock. We've been able to triple our research staff in just the past month. You'd be amazed at how the grants have been rolling in ever since Antonia. The Department of Energy, the National Science Institute, NASA, even the Defense Department — they all see enormous potential, and they all want to help fund Louisiana's recovery. The NSI chief said he thinks New Orleans could become the Houston of renewable energy."

Roy's fingers tightened around the laptop briefcase's handle. "Tell your people to be especially careful tomorrow. Tell them to expect things to go wrong. Dangerously wrong."

"Why tomorrow?"

"Tomorrow is Friday the Thirteenth."

She laughed, clearly grateful that Roy had broken the bubble of weird, new tension between them. "Oh, oh, Mr. Mayor — I didn't think you were such a *kidder!* Thank you so much for returning that computer. It should speed up our work considerably—"

"Annalee, I'm not joking around. If your people don't take special precautions tomorrow, they could end up hurt. Or dead."

"You're *serious?*"

"Take a look at Professor Zoukeni's summary notes. Every single one of those catastrophic 'accidents' took place on a Friday the Thirteenth. That's no coincidence. It's central to the very nature of this bio-energy he discovered — what a layman might call 'bad luck energy'."

"So... you've examined the contents of the hard drive, then?"

"I have, yeah, and so have some of my advisors."

"That's proprietary information."

"The laptop was recovered in conjunction with a police investigation of a violent death. That made it official evidence."

"So why are you giving it back to me? Is the investigation concluded?"

"I'm giving you back your company's laptop for the same reason my interlocutor gave it to me. To ask you to do the right thing with it. As much as it kills me to say it, this technology is nowhere near ready for practical applications. It may never be — according to Professor Zoukeni's own findings, it's incredibly volatile and dangerous. Worse, I have... reason to believe that any attempt to utilize the bio-energy outside South Louisiana will propagate certain destructive phenomena normally unique to this region, spread them throughout the country like poisonous spores. MuckGen needs to pull the throttle back, *way* back. Go over Zoukeni's findings. Replicate them, and bring in some outside firms to validate them, too. Study the energy, sure — but stop trying to harness it. It *won't* be harnessed, Annalee. Not without spreading disaster everywhere you try to exploit it."

Annalee remained silent for a moment. "This... this is simply *crazy*," she said. "Do you have any idea what it is you're asking us to *do?* The federal government has invested millions of dollars; soon they'll invest *billions!* We're on the cusp of our initial public offering, which could bring in *tens* of billions! Can't you understand what this will mean for New Orleans?"

"I understand. Believe me, I understand. Asking this of you, it's tearing my heart out. But I need your answer soon, Annalee. You've got nine days to absorb the implications of what's on this laptop. By the Winter Solstice, December twenty-first, I need to hear that MuckGen will shift its efforts from applied research to more basic, theoretical research."

"Or else what?"

"Or I will unilaterally terminate your lease on the Six Flags tract in New Orleans East, citing a threat to public safety."

She shook her head with amazement. "What's *wrong* with you? What's wrong with this *city?* People warned us — 'Don't bother investing in New Orleans; the powers-that-be hate change.' I thought they were talking nonsense. But now..." She whirled on him. "Have you thrown in with the Morehouses? I thought you were one of the *good* ones, Roy. One of the *sensible* ones. But you're just as determined to commit economic suicide as the rest of the troglodytes around here. What do you want? A *pay-off?*"

He didn't respond to the barb, although it wounded him more deeply than he would ever admit. He placed the laptop on the conference table. "I need my answer by the Solstice," he said.

He had one more errand to attend to before he could go home, crawl into bed, and pray for dreamless sleep. He'd assigned an NOPD detail to stand round-the-clock guard at Lily's Riverbend cottage. Knowing her state of mind, he expected she would take it the wrong way. He wanted to set her straight.

And he didn't want to be alone, not right now.

Their meeting began much as his meeting with Annalee had ended — with hostile incredulity. Lily stared at the NOPD cruiser parked outside her front windows. "So now I'm under house arrest?"

"Of course not," Roy said. "He's there for your protection. You heard what happened to Branson Schwartz. But with the grand jury proceedings still pending, I can't 'disappear' you into one of Owl Lookingback's safe houses like I did Bruno. The attorney general would assume you'd broken your parole."

"I watched the TV debate between you and Van Goodfeller and Cynthia," she said, her voice as flat as a soda which had been left open for weeks. "She did everything she could to pin me to you, and you scrambled away as though I were a piece of spoiled fish. You even fell back on the old 'innocent until proven guilty' dodge — you couldn't find it in your heart to tell the public you don't think I'm a murderer."

He glanced around the living room. Whenever he'd visited here prior to the storm, her small house had been immaculately maintained, practically a museum. Now it looked more like a freshman dorm room during final exams. The floor was obscured with piles of old newspapers and emptied cartons of take-out food. Overflowing ashtrays lined the once spotless coffee table. The room looked like the inside of his head.

"It's... just politics, Lily," he said, knowing even before he said the words how weak they would sound. "Politics... it's..."

"A dirty business. Yes, I know."

"Dirty. And brutal, sometimes."

Lily, her face a puffy version of the chiseled visage he remembered from high school, looked directly into his eyes. "Let me ask you a question. And I'd appreciate an honest answer."

"Go ahead."

"Did you assign that policeman to guard me because I'm an important component in Kay's plan? Or did you do it because you... care for me?"

"Both," he said.

"That's taking the easy way out." She turned to him and, surprisingly, smiled. Roy thought he detected a bit of mischievousness, as well as cautious hopefulness. "Care to assign percentages?"

"Math wasn't my best subject."

"Bullshit." She walked to the couch, pushed a pizza box onto the floor, and sat down. "All right, I'll let you off the hook. I can't be a hundred percent certain of my feelings, either. Not after learning that an *ayin hora* has been messing with my head and my heart for, what, thirty-five years?"

Her smile vanished. "Kay admitted to me that she caused my old feelings for you to flare back to life last February. But what I've never had the guts to ask her is this: what about our original romance? Did she cause that to happen, too? Oh, she's claimed she ran away from me after killing my mother, that she didn't come back into my life until Daniel was a grown man. But she was able to take on any face she chose. She could've been any one of three hundred girls at our high school. Did she try to cause more *tsurris*, more heartache for my father, by making me fall in love with you?"

"And what if she did?" He sat down next to her. "Would that make what we had together any less real? According to Kay, those bad luck spirits can't make you do anything that some part of you isn't already inclined to do. People fall in love for all kinds of tangential reasons. Maybe they'd just suffered a loss and were at a low point, and they meet someone who's especially kind. Maybe something about the other person subliminally reminds them of a parent — the new girlfriend wears the same perfume as dear old Mom did, say. All those tangential things do is get the ball rolling, that's all. Once it's rolling... well, then those two people find out whether they can stand each other, after the first wave of infatuation subsides."

"Can we... stand each other?"

"Yeah... yeah, I think we can." He picked up one of the ashtrays. "So long as you cut *way* back on the cancer sticks. I thought you'd given up cigarettes back in nursing school."

Her face colored a deep red. She grabbed a bag from off the floor and began emptying the ashtrays into it. "This isn't *me*, Roy. At least, not the me I *can* be. Nine days from now, on the Solstice, I'm going to go through something maybe no other human being has ever been through. I'm afraid. And I'm anxious as hell. Anxious for it to *happen* — for me to be freed of this curse I've lived with since I was five years old. One way or another, I'll be free. Either I'll be dead, or I'll be a different and better person — maybe the person I was supposed to grow up to be, before I ever met Kay Rosenblatt."

She sat back down, closer to him this time. "Maybe a person worthier of... well, of sharing your life. Do you think I don't *know* what I've been like to you this past year? When I haven't been a clinging vine, I've been a demanding, selfish teenager, or a shrew."

"Come on, you weren't *that* bad—"

"Yes, I *was*. If *I'd* been in a relationship with me this past year, I'd *detest* Lily Weintraub. Either Cynthia was so earth-shakingly awful that I've only seemed half bad, or you've got the patience of a saint."

"Or..." He didn't want to confront this next thought, but it couldn't be avoided. "Or maybe Eleggua-Eshu was playing me the whole time, the same way Kay played you." He shivered inwardly as he remembered the crushed look in Bruno Galliano's eyes. "Yesterday morning, I saw something that repulsed me so badly I acted like a complete asshole, just to get it away from me. I saw a brave man, a career soldier, a man I respected as much as anybody... reduced to a human jellyfish. I saw what a person looks like when he's lost all trust in himself. I... I don't want to end up like that, Lily."

"You won't, Roy. You won't. There's no way you could."

"But I *could*. You weren't inside my head when I gave that 'cowboys and Indians' speech in Central City. Eleggua-Eshu *had* me. For those fifteen minutes, he *owned* me. Remember what I said before, about the bad luck spirits being unable to force you to do something you aren't already inclined to do? That speech wasn't an aberration. Eleggua reached inside me and pulled out something already there, a part of *me*, then pumped its volume to the maximum."

"The riot wasn't your fault—"

"It doesn't *matter* whether it was my fault or not. They've got me questioning myself, and in the ugliest way possible. I just visited the MuckGen people and laid down an ultimatum. Did I do it to stop more disasters from happening? Or did I do it because that's what the Miasma Club wants? Hell, for that matter, why did I want to be mayor in the first place? Sure, I wanted to show Merle Morehouse and his whole family I could do it better than they could, without the cronyism and the kickbacks. And there was the sheer challenge. I told myself I was smart enough, savvy enough to beat the city's problems — the piss-poor public schools, the crumbling streets, the out-of-control crime — not just pay them lip service, like the past eight or ten mayors had.

"But what lay underneath all that? What was I *really* after? What I'm so damn afraid of is that Eleggua-Eshu showed me the true answer: I want to be validated, Lily. I want to be accepted by my own. I ran for mayor because I didn't want to just be some software engineer who makes urban adventure games for African-American teens — I wanted to be the elected leader of a majority-Black city. I wanted to spit in the eye of every goddamned son of a bitch who ever called me 'Roy Oreo'."

She grasped his hand. "Even if that's true, that doesn't mean all your other reasons for running weren't *also* valid. We're *all* mixtures of venality and selflessness. Didn't you just tell me it doesn't matter how love *begins*, only where it takes you? How is this any different? Your reasons for running hardly matter anymore. What *matters* is how hard you've worked these past four years, what you've been able to accomplish—"

"And what *have* I accomplished? New Orleans is on life support. Half the population may never come back. And this election has probably set back race relations in this town by forty years."

"You're exaggerating—"

"*Am* I? Do you know how I felt while I was giving that speech in Central City? I felt *good. Damn* good. I had that crowd eating from my hand. Do you know what a glorious — and *scary* — feeling that is? What if this ceremony a week from now doesn't work? What if the Miasma Club hangs around, and I get reelected? Eleggua tried awfully hard to get me votes by appealing to voters' fears and resentments, using my voice. *My voice.* What does that *mean?* Does it mean I'm the kind of mayor they want, one who'll help turn New Orleans back into a swamp? Am I going to end up like Bruno, despising myself for letting them use me, but unable to say *no* to that drug they keep feeding me?"

"Roy, I won't let that happen. I *won't.*" She pulled him close and rested his head in the hollow of her neck. "Maybe I haven't been able to be strong for myself... but I *will* be strong for you. Nine days from now, for the first time in my whole life, I get to hit back. I get to *fight*. Given the chance, I'll drag the whole Miasma Club back down to hell."

This is a side of Lily I've never seen, he thought with equal measures of gratitude and wonderment. *Maybe she's got more of Old Amos in her than she or I figured.* "I never knew you had this much she-devil in you," he said. "Not that I object..."

"There's a lot about me you never took the time to find out." She pulled his mouth to hers, at the same time pushing him backward onto the couch and straddling his hips with her knees. Her hands unbuttoned his shirt. She caressed his chest, blindly seeking access to his shoulders and upper arms.

He'd never imagined Lily this way. Even in his most explicit fantasies, her demeanor had reflected her name — delicate, reserved, receptive. A flower who awaited the bee's approach, not a Venus Flytrap which sought to swallow the bee whole.

Maybe that had been a failure of his imagination.

Even so, he discovered to his dismay that this cognitive dissonance had canceled out his arousal. If he wanted to avoid being a total cad, he'd have to work hard to give her the response she seemed to demand.

She pulled back from their kiss. "Do you want to go all the way, Roy?" she asked, her face fully alive for the first time in recent memory — as alive and vital as it had been during their first furtive high school dates. He could see her fear of rejection, but her hope and desire burned stronger. "Grant the last wish of a woman who might not be around after the Solstice?"

"You're sure you want to?"

"As sure as I am about anything."

"Uh, are you, y'know, on the Pill, or something?"

Her smile puckered. "Are bears Catholic? Does the Pope shit in the woods? These last ten years, I've needed to be on the Pill like a fish needs a bicycle. Do you have any condoms on you?"

"Actually, I think I just might..." He pulled his wallet out of his pocket. "Yeah. I do. I visited one of the Health Department's STD clinics last week. The staff kidded around some and made me stick a couple of 'souvenirs' in my wallet." He held up a square foil packet like it was a winning lottery ticket. The bright orange packet read: *Play It Safe! Compliments of the City of New Orleans Health Department.*

Lily gave it a closer look. "Ummm... City STD clinic. How romantic..."

"There's a Walgreen's on Carrollton. I think they're open twenty-four hours..."

"Let's not break the mood. Any port in a storm. I'm sure the City Health Department's procurement standards are plenty strict, right?"

"Uh, sure, sure..."

"You want me to put it on you?"

He thought about the mental prep work he needed to do before the condom could be worn. "Uh, that's really sweet, but I, y'know, that's one thing I like to do myself. If that's all right."

Actually, he *hated* condoms.

"Suit yourself, sweetheart," she said, rising from the couch. "I've gotta go pee, and I'll get these clothes off. I think I can find some KY Jelly, too."

As soon as she disappeared down the hallway, Roy stripped off his clothes, laid back on the couch, and forced himself to relax. He closed his eyes and tried imagining Lily as she had been in high school. Perfect, porcelain skin. Pert breasts, perfectly shaped...

He heard her brushing her teeth furiously in the bathroom.

He ripped open the foil packet. The condom went on easily enough. He noticed it had a reservoir tip. A thoughtful touch; he'd have to compliment the folks at the Health Department about that.

"Roy, come on back to the bedroom, okay? It's a little less cluttered."

He rose from the couch. He felt vaguely stupid, walking with the condom on, feeling it smack against his legs.

The bedroom was dark. Lily's indistinct form could've been a pile of pillows. "I'm sorry," she said. "I'd rather keep the lights out, if that's okay. It wasn't a good idea, undressing in front of a full-length mirror just now. I've turned into Queen of the Cellulite Planet."

"Only partly true," he said, groping for the side of the bed. "Keep the 'queen' part. Drop the rest."

She pulled the covers aside so he could get in. "You okay?"

"I'm fine."

"Is there... anything special I can do for you?"

Now *that* sounded more like the Lily he'd expected — a little shy, a little demure. Reassured, aroused by the sudden sense of familiarity, he felt his blood swell in all the right places. "Just let me hold you, hon."

She felt warm, as though she were running a slight fever. Now it was his turn to let his fingers do the walking. Her legs were just as long as he remembered. A little fuller, but that was all right. He'd changed some, too. Everybody did, with time.

He kissed her neck. The fusion of well-worn fantasy with present sensation helped him to stop over-thinking every movement. He sensed his body respond and was grateful.

"Uh, Roy, wait just a minute, sweetheart... let me get a little KY down there. I'm sorry. I'm a little nervous..."

"That's okay. Take your time."

He heard the click of a squeeze tube being opened, followed by a flatulent squirt.

"There. Okay. That should be better," she said.

It was.

Oh, there was still the frustrating nuisance of the damned condom, though. Roy could tell the Health Department's buyer had aimed more for maximum durability than maximum sensitivity. Still, wasn't this the experience he'd anticipated and dreamed about for decades? He wished his teenaged self could be standing invisibly by the side of the bed.

He shifted positions, bringing his body into fuller contact with hers. She shivered slightly and wrapped her arms around his back. Roy felt the loose flesh hanging from the undersides of her upper arms quiver against his shoulder blades. The sensation stirred memories. Bad ones. They thrust him back into his marriage bed... and the final time he and Cynthia did anything together in that bed.

Uh, oh.

He felt himself losing the firmness he'd worked so diligently to acquire. *Aww, shit... how could I let myself go there?* The only solution available to him was to recapture firmness through brute sensation. He picked up his pace. If the sounds Lily made were any indication, she hadn't yet noticed his difficulties. If it weren't for the damned condom...

The digital clock on her nightstand registered midnight.

Suddenly, she felt *great* to him. Maybe it had taken her this long to break through her nervousness; he felt her onrushing tide of lubrication all the way through that thick set of fishing waders the Health Department had foisted on him.

"Roy, you feel really, *really* good..."

"You... you, too, hon..."

"Why'd we wait so long... to do this?"

"Damned... if I know..."

He felt his heartbeat accelerate. Then a sling catapulted him through the roof for a brief visit to the moon.

He crumpled on top of her, all strength gone. He couldn't let himself rest for long, though; he had to make sure his set of waders didn't slide off into the sea. He reached down to hold the bottom rim of the condom while he disengaged.

The thing didn't feel quite right. The rim was way thicker than it should've been, as though the latex had bunched up. "Uh, Lily... would you mind clicking on the light?" He felt her fumble for the switch of a lamp.

The light revealed what he'd suspected. The base of his member was constricted by a ring of silly pink jewelry.

"Uh oh... looks like the levees broke," he said.

She glanced at the clock. "Well, it *is* Friday the Thirteenth." She gently patted his testicles and smiled. "Probably nothing to worry about, though. I'm pretty sure my eggs have all passed their expiration date."

"Not that it would be such a terrible thing..."

"Yeah, well... I might not be around in another eight days, remember?"

He hugged her. "Don't say that, okay? Don't think it."

"I guess you need to be going, huh?"

"Yeah. But the cop cruiser will stay here, around the clock. Until the Solstice."

She pulled a robe from her closet, and they walked out to the living room. "Hey, you mind if I tell you something?" she asked while he dressed.

"Depends what it is."

"I don't want you to feel obligated to say it back to me. It's just... I'm really clear about this now, and I want to say it while I've still got time. My feelings for you have been tested in about every way possible. And now, all the doubt and the hurt... they just don't matter anymore.

"I love you, Roy Rio. And I'm going to save that silly broken pink condom as a good luck charm."

Roy squeezed her hand. Then he finished buttoning his shirt.

"I love you, too, Lily Weintraub."

As he shut her front door behind him, he was ninety-eight percent sure he'd really meant it.

* * * * *

Kay held Harold "Tuba Slim" Zeno's newspaper obituary to her breast, protecting it from the driving rain while she climbed the stairs to Euterpe's last known residence.

She'd tried a dozen times to summon the Muse since the riot, but Euterpe had ignored her summonings. Now, Friday the Thirteenth had arrived, and the Solstice was nearly here.

From the shelter of the balcony, she stared down at the dark, rain-slick streets of the Bywater neighborhood. *"Our people are wounded and dying... we must attend."* Those had been Euterpe's final words to her. Yet now Harold "Tuba Slim" Zeno, founder of the Fresh Birth Brass Band, shot through the lung the day of Mayor Rio's speech, was dead. If Euterpe had been clinging to his bedside in a protective vigil, she did so no longer. Kay held the obituary between her palms like a paper rosary and recited, "Euterpe, the Giver of Pleasure, the Mother of the Double Flute, come—"

The apartment door opened. Euterpe wore the same visage she'd worn the day Harold Zeno had been shot. The same features, perhaps, but not the same aspect. Her glorious halo of wiry, black hair now was shot through with bolts of gray. The shining dark brown skin of her face had been eroded to murky muddiness by a steady flow of tears.

"He's gone and buried," she said. "I am willing to hear you now, little goblin. To listen."

Rainwater coursed off the centuries-old roof and gushed through broken gutters, splattering onto the courtyard flagstones below. "The Solstice is only a week away," Kay said. "Will you help us?"

"Death... it defeats us all, doesn't it?" The Muse's gaze drifted past Kay to the curtain of rain. "What good are skill and dexterity, acquired through years of mortal labor, if breath has fled? I *hate* the Miasma Club. Even Antonia's devastation didn't make me hate them this much."

"I'm sorry," Kay said. "I'm so sorry for your loss. But it's within your power to prevent other Harold Zenos from dying. Will you help us?"

Euterpe's eyes took on a steeliness frightening in its intensity. "Yes."

"Will any of your sisters stand with you?"

"Of all my sisters, Erato is closest to me. She knows my sorrow, and she shares it in the marrow of her bones. She will sacrifice herself and more, even if this means tricking and betraying her other sisters."

"What about Melpomene? Her ancestress helped Owl with the first banishment ceremony two centuries ago."

"The Muse of Tragedy is not without sympathy for your plight and your aims. Within her great and knowing heart lies some faint, passed on memory of her predecessor's sacrifice. She can be counted upon."

"Good." That short, simple word did little justice to the upsurge of hope Kay felt. "I've arranged for a cover story for you to use, a reason for your sisters to gather against the Miasma Club at the Broad Street Pumping Station the night of the Solstice. The mayor will be holding a campaign rally nearby, at the site of the old Falstaff Brewery. Two citizen parades are scheduled to converge at the rally. One will come from Broadmoor and Central City, a group of women who call themselves the Krewe of Broadmoor Muses. Their route will take them directly by the pumping station. Tell your sisters that the Miasma Club plans to cause an explosion at the pumping station, timed for when the Krewe of Broadmoor Muses will be marching by."

Euterpe's face grew thoughtful. "There's enough of the truth in that to make it a good lie. After our confrontation with your ex-ally and his desecration of the Indian march, my sisters are spoiling for a fight. They will quickly rally to defend a group of women who honor us by taking on our name."

"I thought they would." Kay's pride at her newfound skills at strategizing faded, though, as she thought of what would happen to the Muses. Abetting their extermination felt like having to put down the world's last herd of unicorns. "Euterpe, are you... at peace with what's going to happen?"

"Our disappearance?"

"Yes. I'm already mourning for you."

"Don't." For the first time that evening, Euterpe smiled. "Even now, something new comes to replace us. Without this knowledge, there is no way I would even consider betraying my sisters. From our oblivion, a new birth will arise, one which can fully flourish, untainted by the evil machinations of a Miasma Club. Our successors have the potential to be better than us, far better, but only with the proper nurturing and guidance... otherwise, the city will eventually face renewed catastrophes. And in my absence and that of my sisters, that care and guidance, dear little goblin, will be entirely up to you."

* * * * *

In the final hour of Friday the Thirteenth, Pandora found her one-time allies gathered around a mold-stained conference table in the shuttered downtown Charity Hospital. Even if her remaining affinity for Otherness had not led her to this barely lit room, her nose would have — the Miasma Club's stench of fermenting cabbage overpowered even the sickening odors of mildew, putrefying medicines, and the omnipresent dust of rotting dry wall.

She lingered in the partially closed doorway of the conference room, unseen for the moment, as Mephistopheles finished addressing his remaining eight compatriots. "And this first wave of strange, new births? Are we prepared to accommodate them a week hence?"

Glenn the Gremlin bounced up and down in his chair. "Yes-yes-*yes!* My mission will be accomplished flawlessly, with an error rate of zero-point-zero. You can cuh-cuh-*count* on me!"

"And you, Fortuna Discordia?" Mephistopheles asked. "What is the status of the coming birth-spawn within your purview?"

"The little yellow mommy-to-be is scheduled for a C-section at Touro Infirmary on the Solstice—"

"Hold!" Old Scratch said suddenly. He turned to stare at the doorway. Pandora felt his gaze scorch the air. "We have an interloper in our midst. An apostate."

With no more reason to cling to the shadows, she stepped hesitantly into the conference room, taking quick, tiny breaths, like a bird's.

"Woman," Ti Malice said incredulously, "have you come to *die?*"

"No," she said. "I've come... to live. I want to live."

Fortuna stared at Pandora as though she were the bottled remains of a two-headed piglet. "By the Mother's damp soil, what's *happened* to you?"

Pandora stared down at her hands, once delicate as fine china. "Owl Lookingback did this to me. While I was helpless, he took me hundreds of miles away from the Mother. I was trapped in San Antonio for months, forced to watch my body wither, my youthfulness trickle away. I prayed that, with my return home, vitality would return. But the Mother has refused to take me back into Her embrace."

"Why have you returned to us, cousin?" Old Scratch asked.

"Intercede for me, O Thee of the Triumvirate. Plead the case of a shamed and humbled relation, a cousin who has gone astray but who seeks to repent. Agree to call upon the Mother to restore me, and I will grant you a boon."

Mephistopheles appeared unmoved. "And what sort of 'boon' can we expect from such a desiccated specimen?"

"Owl Lookingback still considers me his precious love. I am privy to his plans, and those of his fellow conspirator, Kay Rosenblatt."

"You will tell us where he resides?" Mephistopheles asked.

"And the Rosenblatt woman's foul allies?" Ti Malice added. "Do you know how to neutralize whatever hold she has upon the Muses?"

"I can do that," she said. "And much, much more. On the night of the Solstice, I can deliver both of them into your hands, along with the nine Muses and the mayor of New Orleans. Are not the terrible pumps at Broad Street the gravest mechanical sin ever committed by mortal kind against the Mother? I will show you how to explosively erase that sin, at the same time dooming the whole nest of your enemies to death by fire."

Chapter 36

B RUNO Galliano stood at the entrance to the Louis Armstrong International Airport's Concourse C, nursing a cup of coffee. He hadn't stood out in the open like this in over a week; he felt as exposed as an infantryman on Normandy Beach on D-Day morning. Owl Lookingback had promised that the object hidden inside his little black bag would suffice to hide them from detection by the Miasma Club, at least during the short time required to pick up Bob Marino and drop off Bob and Bruno with the mayor at the old Falstaff Brewery site. But the small black velvet bag which hung from a handle of Owl's walker didn't appear very formidable.

He checked his watch again. Bob's plane had been scheduled to land ten minutes ago. What if something had happened? Bob was a bad luck magnet, wasn't he?

"Relax, Bruno," Owl said. "His flight's here. I'll get you and Bob into the safe embrace of the New Orleans Police Department in a jiffy."

Bruno scanned the distant faces of all men in suits walking toward the terminal's exit. "There he is."

Bob looked a lot thinner than the last time Bruno had seen him. His suit jacket flapped against his ribs with every step.

Four more hours, Bruno thought, *and our shared nightmare will be over.*

Bob saw Bruno, waved, and picked up his pace. When the ex-FEBO director passed a security checkpoint, his shoe snagged on the edge of a rubber mat. Bruno saw Bob's ankle bend at an unnatural angle. Bob's face tightened with pain; he grabbed a nearby chair to keep himself from falling.

"You okay?" Bruno asked, feeling nausea grow in the pit of his stomach.

Bob's face turned white. "I think — I twisted it pretty badly. Good thing I don't need my ankle to give a press conference."

Bruno had Bob lean on his shoulder. "Do you need us to get you some help?"

"I'll be all right. I'll take a fistful of Advils. We can grab that on the way out. Maybe a bag of ice, too."

"It'll all be over before the nine o'clock TV news," Owl said, pushing his walker toward the garage. "Afterwards, we'll head over to the Carousel Bar and toast better days to come."

Solstice Saturday, 1:58 P.M.

In the parking garage, a cloud of mosquitos gathered from seemingly nowhere and descended upon Bob Marino, swarming over his face and crawling inside his suit, biting him savagely.

Solstice Saturday, 2:10 P.M.

Owl cursed under his breath when he spotted the sea of blazing red brake lights ahead of him on the I-10. *Half the city's population is stuck out of town, and we've still got traffic jams?* He peered into his rear view mirror. "You doin' okay, Bob?"

Bob's face had swelled ominously. "Hang... hanging in there," he said.

"Maybe you should exit, use a surface road?" Bruno asked anxiously.

"We'll be through this in a few minutes—" Owl heard something burst under the BMW's hood. The needle on the dashboard's temperature gauge climbed into the red zone. Clouds of steam obscured the view out the windshield.

"The Miasma Club — have they *found* us?" Bruno said.

"It's not an attack—"

"How can you be *sure?*"

"'Cause I *am*, damnit! What I got in that little black bag's like an extension of one of my safe houses. We're cloaked as good as a Romulan Bird of Prey in *Star Trek*, okay? Your pal Bob is suckin' up bad luck energy faster than he can breathe. This shit's not being aimed at us — it's just *happening*."

He nursed the BMW down the Bonnabel Boulevard off ramp. It managed to limp as far as the corner of Bonnabel and Veterans Memorial Boulevard. Then its engine shuddered and died.

Owl pulled his walker and an oil-stained rag from his trunk. He opened the hood. *Water pump's given up the ghost.* "Everybody out," he shouted. "We're gonna hafta catch a cab."

Solstice Saturday, 2:33 P.M.

Kay gathered her hair from the floor of Euterpe's bedroom and placed it in one of two wooden boxes. Lily had shorn her with scissors and electric clippers, and Kay had finished defoliating the less accessible parts of her body with a razor. No spot had been spared.

Hair represented growth, fecundity, vitality. Even if she survived the day's events, none of it would ever grow back. Her hair would be a thing of the past, along with her extended lifespan.

She watched Lily assist Euterpe. Even her future sister-in-law, who had been silently smug throughout Kay's denuding, appeared sad as the Muse's gorgeous locks fell to the floor. *It's like taking a hammer to one of*

Michelangelo's sculptures, she thought. Yet even shorn of her hair, Euterpe still possessed radiance which made Kay tremble inside.

Daniel was waiting when Kay left the bedroom. "Gee," he said, "you look just like that bald Vulcan lady in the first *Star Trek* movie."

He didn't seem displeased. "Is that a good thing?" she asked.

"Yup. Vulcans are really, really *smart,* aren't they? And I'm going to be getting smarter, too. So we'll still be a good match."

Will we? she asked herself as she stared into his innocent, boyish eyes. *Or will Lily get her wish, and like Adam after biting the apple, you'll learn embarrassment, revulsion, and shame?*

Solstice Saturday, 3:07 P.M.

The cab drove Owl, Bob, and Bruno east on Tulane Avenue, traversing a decayed commercial corridor which Antonia had drowned and left for dead.

"You doing all right?" Bruno asked his friend.

Bob's eyes briefly fluttered open. "Sorry," he said. His voice sounded distant and weak. "Christ, I almost feel like I'm coming down with the flu..."

"He'll be all right," Owl insisted. Bruno saw the old Indian's fingers tighten around the cords of his little black bag. "We're almost there. You won't have to say much at the press conference, Bob. Just tell the folks you fucked up at FEBO, big time, then get out of the way and let Bruno spill his guts. Hey, you ever been inside that Broad Street pumping station where Kay's gonna stick the shiv in the Miasma Club?"

Bob didn't answer.

"It's a real marvel, that pumping station. Do y'know it's built on exactly the same spot where I performed the first banishment ceremony? One of the lowest spots in the whole area, eight or ten feet below sea level—"

Bruno touched Bob's forehead. "Aww, *shit*," he said. "He's burning up!"

Bruno saw their driver glance nervously at them in the rear-view mirror.

"We just have to get him through the next two hours," Owl said.

"He won't make it!" Bruno recognized Bob's symptoms. "Those mosquito bites all over him — he's got West Nile virus!"

"He *sick?*" the driver asked. "He got a *disease?*"

"He's okay," Owl insisted. "Just get us to the Falstaff Brewery building."

Bob convulsed. Then he leaned over and vomited onto the floor.

"Oh, no, oh no *no!*" the driver said. "He infect my cab. He spread his sickness! You must get out, right now!"

"Listen, bud," Owl said, "we're almost there. You just do your goddamn job, okay?"

Bruno saw the driver's eyes grow more terrified in the mirror. "No! I pull over! I pull over now, and you get *out—*"

A pickup truck darted from an intersection into the middle of Tulane Avenue.

"*Look out!*" Bruno yelled.

The cab smashed into the truck, then spun and careened backward into an abandoned motel. Its rear end plowed through the windows and walls of the motel's office, creating a mass of rubble which lifted the Crown Victoria's spinning rear tires high into a cloud of plaster dust.

Bruno took a few seconds to collect his senses. He heard the sounds of cracked window glass falling onto the sidewalk and the driver groaning. He undid his seatbelt — he'd been the only belted passenger, he realized — then looked to his companions.

Owl was conscious. "Think I might've busted my shoulder," he said. "You okay?"

"I'm fine," Bruno said. "But Bob...?"

His friend had suffered facial contusions, but his eyes were open, blinking rapidly.

"I seem to be in the best shape," Bruno said. "Let me get the two of you out of here."

His door refused to budge. He crawled to the opposite side, but his best efforts couldn't open that pulverized door even an inch. "I'm gonna have to drag you two into the front seat and out through the driver's door," he said. "It'll be murder on any broken bones..."

"Just do it," Owl said.

Bob was so disoriented and feverish that he hardly reacted to Bruno's manhandling. Owl was much lighter. Bruno grabbed his belt and pulled him across the seat back, doing his best not to jostle the wounded shoulder. To his credit, Owl barely groaned. But then his deeply set eyes widened with alarm. "My *bag!* I don't have it anymore!"

"Let me look for it," Bruno said.

He didn't find it in the car. The rear windows had been partially open at the time of the crash. Could the bag have flown into the street?

He rushed outside. He spotted the bag lying in the middle of Tulane Avenue.

A car heading east swerved to avoid the wrecked pickup. Its front right tire flattened the bag.

Bruno darted into the road. "Don't bother," Owl called out. "It's useless now."

Bruno looked helplessly at the mangled bag. "What was in it?"

"A Houma fertility fetish, made of clay from beneath one of my safe houses."

"I'm calling 911," Bruno said. He pulled his cell phone from his jacket pocket. The phone failed to respond. Its tiny screen was cracked.

"We can't afford to all wait here for cops, anyway," Owl said. "Too much chance the Miasma Club will find us before the police do. You take Bob and go. The brewery's only five or six blocks away."

"What about you?"

"I'd only slow you down. Sitting here, maybe I'll attract the Club to me, give you enough time to get to the mayor's security detail."

"You'd sacrifice yourself?"

Owl grunted. "Heck, this here old lemon's almost squeezed dry anyhow. Go."

Bruno collected Bob. His friend was barely conscious now; Bruno dragged him as much as supported him. Bob's infirmity left them no choice but to cut through the back streets, shortening the distance to the Falstaff Brewery building. Their path took them through the evacuated remains of the city's criminal justice complex.

He heard the rumbling of a large motor creep up behind him. Could Owl have sent a cop cruiser looking for them?

What pulled alongside wasn't one of the NOPD's new Crown Victorias — it was a stretched Chevy Suburban, black with blacked out chrome. The tinted passenger window descended. A roly-poly black face peered out. "Mr. Galliano and Mr. Marino, I presume?"

Bruno's throat went dry. He heard multiple locks click unlocked, doors swinging open.

"You're a very, very selfish man, Mr. Marino," the black man said. "This whole afternoon, you been stealin' what is rightfully ours, gulping it down like a starvin' croc. This has hurt us plenty bad, y'know."

Although the black man's eyes crinkled with pain, he managed to eke out a smile. "My selfish friend, the time has come for the Miasma Club to return the favor."

Solstice Saturday, 3:46 P.M.

Roy Rio checked his watch again. The old Falstaff Brewery building loomed at his back like an eroded mountain, its western face shimmering with the glare of the descending sun. The only communication he'd received from Annalee Jones of MuckGen in the past week was a preemptive "cease and desist" order regarding his termination of their lease, which he supposed was answer enough. And Bruno Galliano and Bob Marino had been AWOL for hours.

"Walt," he said, "give me status on both parades. Where are they now?"

Walter Johnson shot him an exasperated look. "I just checked ten minutes ago. The marchers from Gentilly and the Ninth Ward were at North Carrollton and Canal. The Krewe of Broadmoor Muses hadn't rolled yet, but they were about to get started. So now they're both four or five blocks farther along."

"Radio the captains again. We're starting the speeches at five sharp, whether they're here or not. Have them pick up the pace. Especially the Broadmoor Muses — they've *got* to stick to schedule."

Walter tried using his two-way radio. "I can't raise anyone. All I'm getting is dead air."

"Borrow one of the cops' radios."

Walter did as he was instructed. "Same thing. The radio's got juice, but there's just static."

"Didn't FEBO just spend one point five million dollars to upgrade our supposedly hardened comm system? Jesus — it's not even raining."

"Gremlins, I guess," Walter said.

The word made Roy's skin crawl.

Solstice Saturday, 4:05 P.M.

Kay led Daniel, Lily, and Euterpe to the main entrance of Drainage Pumping Station Number 1, the long, red brick building which sat above

South Broad Street's subterranean canals. She'd been a century younger when this station had been built; back then, the city had covered less than a third of its present expanse. The gigantic screw pumps invented by Albert Baldwin Wood had allowed miles and miles of new suburban neighborhoods to spread into what had been the Mother's swampy redoubts. Nine months ago, those neighborhoods had borne the brunt of Antonia's wrath.

She turned to Lily. "Do you remember the night you banished me? When you made me disappear?"

"Of course I remember," Lily said. "That was when it all became inescapably real for me."

"This is where I landed. I awoke on the floor of this pumping station."

"What's so special about this place?" Daniel asked.

"It's a nexus," Euterpe said. She failed to elaborate.

"It's a place of connections, a place of power," Kay said. "Like Stonehenge in England is supposed to be. Owl says the ground is thin here, so the wholeness of the Mother's spirit is closer to the surface." *Owl*, she thought. *Why isn't he here, waiting for us?* "It's a battleground, too. For a century, man's engines have warred here against nature's floods."

"Kay," Euterpe said, "I can't *feel* you. If you weren't in eyesight, I wouldn't know you're only a few feet away."

Kay closed her eyes and concentrated on that special sensitivity to Otherness which, although diminished, had never completely left her. "I can't feel you, either. It's this place. It's got to be. Let's get inside and find a hidden place to wait. Owl will have to catch up."

She pressed the buzzer next to the door. The station's caretaker failed to come. She tried the intercom button. "Mr. Price? This is Kay Rosenblatt, from the Corps of Engineers. I'm here with my colleagues."

Minutes passed, and still no answer. She began to feel afraid. The station was never left without a caretaker. And where was Owl?

She took the pass key the mayor's people had gotten her and opened the door. The building's stale air throbbed with the electric hum of the station's three constant duty pumps. High dormer windows, coated with decades of grime, allowed dying sunlight to leak into the cavernous space. A dozen hanging florescent lamps floated beneath the three-story tall ceiling like rusted metal jellyfish, sputtering on and off.

"Let's see if we can find Owl and Mr. Price," she said.

The station's ten pumps, only their outer steel housings visible, transformed the station's otherwise utilitarian interior into a Daliesque landscape. Giant rotary motors extended their long drive shafts into even more gigantic metal "worms" — the Wood screw pumps, twelve or fourteen feet in diameter, whose "heads" plunged through floor and basement into the intake basin along the station's eastern wall, and whose "tails" likewise plunged into the discharge basin on the building's opposite side.

"Could they be up there?" Euterpe asked, pointing up at a utility shed and office, mounted on stilts, which towered fifteen feet above one bank of pumps. The shed was surrounded by a porch-like walkway, accessed by a flight of metal stairs.

"That's Mr. Price's duty station," Kay said. "That's the first place we should check." She planned to have Euterpe put the caretaker into a deep sleep. The office might serve as a good spot for the ceremony; it was high above the floor, which soon would be awhirl with battling Muses and bad luck spirits.

Leading her companions toward the stairs, she stumbled over something and nearly fell. A shoe and ankle protruded from behind one of the towering rotary motors.

She felt as though a void had opened beneath her feet. "Oh my God..."

Bob Marino lay upon the hardwood floor, his neck bent at an unnatural angle. Thin metal pipes had been thrust into his ears and nostrils and punctured his torso, making him look like a grotesque human porcupine.

Lily shrieked. "What — what did they *do* to him?"

"Those skinny pipes," Daniel said, "they almost look like, like *straws...*"

"They sucked him dry," Kay said. "Sucked all the miasmatic energy he'd accumulated back into themselves. Euterpe, you'd better get your sisters here."

"They aren't due to arrive for another twenty minutes," she said.

"Summon them *now*. How quickly can you do it?"

"I'll need to put distance between me and this place. Otherwise, my call won't be heard."

"Then go, with all the speed you can muster."

Euterpe vanished in a cloud of shimmering mist, redolent of cinnamon and cloves.

Lily looked stricken. "They're here *now?* But — but Pandora wasn't supposed to lead them here until just before five—"

Her words were cut short by a loud moaning from the upstairs office.

Owl's moaning.

"Oh, God, it's Owl," Kay said. "I'm getting him out of there."

Lily grabbed her wrist. "Are you *insane?* That's just what they'd want. Wait for the Muses!"

"No. He's in agony. If he's alone, I'll tend to him. They may not know I'm here — they can't sense me, and the noise of the pumps may've muffled our voices."

"But what if they're waiting for you up there?"

"They'll crow and brag before physically attacking me, probably long enough for our allies to arrive."

"And what if you're *wrong?* We can't work any mumbo-jumbo without you. You're more important than Owl."

The moaning grew louder.

"I'll go get him," Daniel said.

"*No!*" Kay and Lily whispered in unison.

"Kay, you aren't going up there without me," Daniel said.

"And *you* aren't going up there without your sister," Lily said.

"Fine," Kay said. "We'll all go, then." Fear made her lightheaded, but she wanted to laugh at their ridiculous argument. She loved them both, so very much.

When they were half-way up the stairs, Kay heard Pandora weeping. She bounded up the steps and flung open the door to the office.

The caretaker, Mr. Price, had been thrown into a corner like a discarded rag doll. Owl lay on the floor; unlike Mr. Price, he was still breathing. He looked like a pile of broken sticks held together by a few scraps of clothing. Amazingly, he was still conscious. Pandora crouched next to him, her face nuzzled against his caved-in chest. "Kay," she said, "Kay, you've *got* to help him! It's all gone wrong, terribly *wrong...*"

"Not... your fault," Owl managed to say. "*My* fault. For once... didn't think everything through... enough." His eyes met Kay's. "They're... in basement. Messing with engines. Sorry, babe... I fucked things up for you..."

Kay put the two boxes containing her and Euterpe's hair on a desk, then knelt by his side and used her skirt to wipe sweat from his forehead. "Don't try to talk. The Muses will be here soon. While they're battling the Miasma Club, Pandora can bring you to Touro Infirmary—"

He shook his head, then coughed up blood. "No," he gasped. "I'm... done. All... all up to you, now. You're—" He coughed again, and the convulsion sent a tremor through his whole body; but she thought she heard an echo of his old, sardonic laugh. "You're... the *shaman* now, babe..."

421

He convulsed once more, then remained still.

Pandora wailed. "Oh, Mother, *why?*"

"Kay," Lily asked from the doorway, "what do we do now?"

"You all die a terrifying and awful death," called a deep voice from below. "Is that simple enough?"

Ti Malice's voice. Kay rushed out onto the platform. The remnants of the Miasma Club stood on the station's floor — Ti Malice and Reynard the Fox, each gripping one of Bruno Galliano's arms; rotund Eleggua-Eshu; Balor the Fomorian; Glenn the Gremlin (*with a newborn baby stuffed into a pack on his chest?*); and the Triumvirate: Old Scratch, Krampus, and the dread Mephistopheles.

They're not all here, damn it! Kay counted again. *Only eight — where's Fortuna?*

"Old Scratch," she shouted, "is Fortuna afraid to face me?"

"Don't dignify the traitor with a response," Ti Malice snarled.

"I'll overrule that," Old Scratch said. "Kay Rosenblatt was a valuable member of our company for nearly a hundred and fifty years. Now that her extinction is at hand, I would offer her this one last favor: an answer, paltry as that boon may be." Kay thought she detected a smidgeon of sadness in his red eyes. "Fortuna Discordia is completing a recruitment. She harvests twins for us, human-seeming babes which the Mother has sent us to replace our departed Na Ong and Na Ba. So in your last moments, please be aware that whatever misbegotten plan you and Owl Lookingback formulated was doomed to failure even before its conception. The Mother has always replenished our ranks, and She ever shall."

Kay bowed to him, as much from abiding habit as her surprising sense of gratitude. "I thank thee for thy small kindness, Old Scratch of the Triumvirate."

"To hell with this pseudo-courtliness," Ti Malice spat. "Foul traitor, have your human pets come out of their hiding place. There is something I wish to show them."

Daniel joined her at the railing. "I'd like to show you a stick in the eye, you skinny geek!" he shouted.

"Your pets need to watch their tongues," Ti Malice said. He and Reynard dragged Bruno, white with fear but otherwise unharmed, before Krampus. The green lizard demon rubbed his talons together with glee as his strawberry red tongue slid out of his mouth. Then its forked tip, dripping with green saliva, lightly brushed the captive's cheeks and lips. Bruno screamed as drops fell on his face and burned his skin.

"Krampus, don't hurt him!" Kay shouted. "It's *me* you all hate, not him!"

The lizard demon's flat nose quivered with irritation. "But Krampussss... *hungry*," he said. "Fortuna... sssea-sssoned thisss one... ssso *nissse-ly*..." He forced Bruno's mouth open, thrust his talons inside and, before the helpless man could scream again, yanked out his tongue.

Krampus flung the fat morsel of flesh high into the air, then snatched it at its apex with his own whiplike tongue. "Mmmmm," he said, "tassstes... like *chicken*..."

Bruno's eyes rolled into their sockets. He collapsed onto the wooden floor.

"*No!*" Kay screamed. The losses of friends pummeled her like a fusillade of bullets, each new impact striking before the pain of the prior outrage had time to register. Owl couldn't help her. She was the shaman now. She held her fists above her shaved head and shouted, "Euterpe, the Giver of Pleasure, the Mother of the Double Flute, come to me *now!*"

The Muse immediately materialized on the platform, her arrival heralded by a sonic boom which shook the brick walls. "No — not yet!" she pleaded. "The children are endangered! I sensed their mother's terror. You must give me a chance to save them!"

"Where are your sisters?" Kay said.

"They come momentarily. Please, you *must* let me go, before any harm comes to the twins—"

"Where are they?"

"Still within their mother's womb, at the Touro Infirmary birthing center. I don't know which of the demons threatens them."

Fortuna, Kay thought. "You need to save the babies, and I need to retrieve Fortuna. Can you carry me when you leap across the emptiness between places?"

"I don't know, I've never *tried* such a thing..."

Wisps of mist began seeping through the loose caulking surrounding the station's ancient windows. Kay saw the air surrounding the Miasma Club shimmer and sparkle. Scents of almonds, cloves, and spices overpowered the haze of rotting cabbage. The Miasma Club glanced about with confusion and alarm.

By twos and threes the Muses materialized. They wielded their avatar symbols as weapons, grimly determined to protect their namesakes who now marched toward the pumping station.

Urania the Heavenly, Muse of astronomy, dazzled Balor's sole eye with a burst of radiance from her celestial staff. Veiled Polyhymnia, Muse of sacred hymns and geometry, thrust her golden protractor deep inside Glenn the Gremlin's chest cavity and overwhelmed his logic circuits with a jumble of formulae.

Beguiler confronted dark charmer when Erato the Lovely, Muse of love poetry, tried softening Reynard the Fox's cruel heart with targeted caresses. Thalia and Melpomene, twinned Muses of comedy and tragedy, flung their respective masks at Eleggua-Eshu's and Ti Malice's heads with the skill of Olympian discus hurlers.

Clio, Muse of history, cracked open her leatherbound chest of books beneath Old Scratch's long nose, seeking to ensorcel him with her library's hypnotizing glamour. Terpsichore the Whirler, Muse of the dance, lassoed Krampus with his own flailing tongue.

In the center of them all, Calliope, eldest of the Muses, tallest and most grave, faced down dread Mephistopheles. Their contest of wills provided a gravitational well around which all the other combats orbited.

"Will you try transporting us *now?*" Kay asked Euterpe.

"If doing so is the only way you will release me, *yes*, I will try. But there is no chance I can carry the demon Fortuna back here with me."

"You let me worry about Fortuna. Daniel, keep your sister and Pandora safe, as best you can."

"Wait!" Lily said. "How can you still carry out the ceremony? Bob's dead, and Bruno can't talk!"

"Call Mayor Rio. Tell him to execute our final fallback plan. Tell him I'm sorry." Kay flung her arms around Euterpe's slender waist. "*Go!*"

To Kay, the pumping station and its denizens crumbled around her like statues made of drying salt crystals. She knew this was a relativistic effect which meant *she* was crumbling, decomposing into particles tiny enough to breach the barrier between *place* and *no-place*.

She recoiled from the burning touch of vacuum colder than Saturn's frozen rings. Only those parts of her pressed against Euterpe were spared. *I don't have the body for this anymore...* She felt her lips split and her tears freeze against her sightless eyes—

And then she found herself sprawled on the floor of Touro Infirmary's maternity ward. As she struggled to focus her nearly frozen eyes, she heard Anh, the mother-to-be she'd met almost two months ago, shrieking: "Help me, someone *help me!* That man — he's not my doctor, and he wants to cut me open! I haven't had my anesthesia! He'll *kill* me!"

Kay's vision cleared. She saw an intern, wavering in a trance, standing over Anh's distended belly, scalpel in hand, having strapped her legs and arms to the birthing table. Euterpe grappled with Fortuna in the far corner.

Kay slapped the scalpel from the intern's hand. When he bent to retrieve it, she slammed her knee into his chin, smashing his skull against the birthing table's steel pedestal.

"Who *are* you people?" Anh wailed. "Why do you want to steal my *babies?*"

Kay tried to talk, but her lips were glued together by frozen blood. She stumbled to the door and unlocked it, allowing orderlies to restrain the ensorcelled intern.

Euterpe and Fortuna rolled and wrestled on the floor, evenly matched in strength. They raked each other's skin and clawed at the other's eyes, with first Euterpe gaining the advantage, then Fortuna.

I can't be sure this'll work, Kay thought. *But my culture and Fortuna's share a dread of the Evil Eye. Those few minutes I spent digging through an Italian-English dictionary may prove to be my best time investment ever...*

She rubbed the frozen blood from her lips. Then she pulled Fortuna away from Euterpe. "Be careful!" the Muse shouted. "You are no match for this beast!"

"You bald *whore*," Fortuna snarled at Kay. "With one fingernail, I'll cleave your carcass from cunt to cranium—"

But before Fortuna could make good on her threat, Kay spat thrice between the index and middle fingers of her free hand. She grabbed Fortuna around the waist and shouted, not *Kein ayin hora*, but its Italian translation:

"Non Malocchio!"

Then her skin burned with subzero cold again — she and Fortuna tumbled head over heels through *no-place*. Kay buried her face against the bad luck spirit's warm back, protecting her eyes and mouth. In the deathly vacuum, she couldn't hear Fortuna's scream, but she felt her hated rival's chest spasm with exhalations of shock and fury.

Sensing the coming return of gravity, Kay rolled on top of Fortuna just before they tore through the dimensional barrier. They plunged several feet to land hard on the floor of Pumping Station Number 1.

Kay recovered first. They had materialized at the edge of the wild war between the Muses and Miasma Club. Fortuna groggily shook her head. Still kneeling on her chest, Kay grabbed her by the hair and yanked her head from the floor.

"This is for what you did to Colonel Schwartz!" She smashed the Italian spirit's head against the hardwood floor, twice. Then, ducking as Terpsichore and Krampus bounded close overhead, she dragged Fortuna alongside a massive rotary motor. "And *this* is for what you did to Bruno!" She flung her, head first, into the motor's circular steel sheath.

Euterpe materialized ten feet away. She glanced at Fortuna's crumpled body, then eyed Kay with fresh respect. "The twins and their mother are safe."

"Good," Kay said. She pointed to where Lily, Daniel, and Pandora stood. "Let's get back up to that platform!"

"Kay!" Lily shouted. "I warned the Muse fighting with that mechanical gremlin to defuse the bomb in the basement. They're both down there now."

"Did you reach Mayor Rio?"

"My cell phone's completely dead! Do you want me to go to him?"

"I have to have you *here* for the ceremony to work!"

"But then how can we reach him?"

Kay hugged Lily close. "We have to trust that Roy Rio will know the right thing to do, and do it."

Solstice Saturday, 4:57 P.M.

Facing a crowd of five hundred people, Roy Rio felt more alone than he ever had in his life.

The first stars had appeared overhead in an indigo sky. "Bruno and Bob Marino are both AWOL," Walter Johnson told him.

"How close are the Broadmoor Muses?"

"About two and a half blocks. They're near the Broad Street Pumping Station."

The pumping station — Lily's in there with all those creatures...

"You need anything else?" Walter asked. "I'm a little miffed you're without your warm-up acts. But you'll adjust."

"Yeah..." Roy said, "I'll... make do. I'll get rolling as soon as the Muses get here."

He was the goat, then. It was the way it had to be.

He stared up at bright Venus, the planet named for the goddess of love, and thought about the dreams and love he'd soon be throwing away.

Solstice Saturday, 5:01 P.M.

"The last of the Broadmoor Muses have passed by!" Euterpe announced an instant after re-materializing on the platform.

"They're safe — the pumps didn't explode!" Kay said. "Polyhymnia must've fixed whatever Glenn sabotaged."

"Not everything is fixed," Lily said. "Can't you feel how this platform is shaking? Those replacement pumps are still unbalanced. If we don't find a way to shut them down soon, this whole building might shake itself apart!"

As if to add an exclamation point, giant Balor tripped over Urania's celestial staff and toppled against a wall. The massive impact shook the entire station. Cracks spread along the wall's elderly bricks. "We can't wait any longer!" Kay said. "Any minute now, they're going to smash through to the outside, and we'll have no way to keep them together!"

Daniel pulled Bruno's unconscious body up the steps, out of immediate danger. Kay turned to Lily. "Bring the boxes, Lily. We're starting, whether Roy Rio is ready or not."

Solstice Saturday, 5:04 P.M.

Half the marchers had yet to make their way into the parking lot, but Roy knew he didn't dare delay any longer. He pulled the microphone close. "People of Gentilly, Muses of Broadmoor, citizens of the Ninth Ward and Mid-City — welcome to tonight's Celebration of Neighborhoods. The building you see behind me, the old Falstaff Brewery, soon to be transformed into hundreds of new homes, is a potent symbol of our city. It's a symbol of our past, when New Orleans was a regional beer capitol. It's a symbol of our present, one of thousands of otherwise sound, solid, historic structures which have been rendered temporarily uninhabitable by Antonia's flood waters. But most importantly, it's a symbol of our future..."

He paused, just long enough to listen to his pulse booming inside his ear canals. No one was going to make this easier on him. He had to take the fall. He switched scripts to the handwritten notes he'd scrawled during the past few minutes. "And... and it's a symbol of the kind of stormproof, flood-proof housing we're going to have to move toward. *Smart* housing. We have to be *smart*, people. Because despite all the swell promises coming out of Washington, Uncle Sam is *not* going to protect us from the next Antonia. We're gonna have to protect *ourselves*, because nobody's coming to our rescue next time. *Nobody*."

The crowd went quiet. This wasn't the Roy Rio they'd come to hear.

"We're going to have to change our ways of thinking and our ways of living. If we want to stay in this city — if we want to continue *having* a city — we're going to have to let go of the old ways. That's *heresy*, I know. Heresy in a town where the dearest things to our hearts are our mamas, our mama's mamas, our red beans and rice on Mondays, our churches and barber shops and all the little corner joints that make our neighborhoods *our neighborhoods*. But you know what? The rest of the country — and I don't mean to sound ungrateful for all their help — they couldn't give a *shit* about all that. You know what they care about? How their tax dollars are being spent. They look at us down here, they see our coasts and wetlands disappearing, and they ask themselves: 'Why do those people *stay* there?' And then they ask themselves: 'If they gotta stay there, why do they *insist* on rebuilding the same houses that drowned in twelve feet of water?'

"It's not that they don't have a heart, or don't wish us well. But they will *not* let their national government spend a trillion dollars to build us a flood protection fortress that can protect every New Orleans neighborhood from a Cat Five hurricane. It won't happen. That's a pipe dream. By allowing ourselves to believe it, we're killing ourselves. If we insist on rebuilding with our hearts instead of our heads... the rest of America is going to write us *off* when the next Antonia comes. And mark my words, there *will* be another Antonia, people. There will."

Solstice Saturday, 5:05 P.M.

Kay mingled her shorn hair and Euterpe's on the metal platform, then squirted lighter fluid over the pile until it looked like a drowned nutria. She lit a match and tossed it on the hair.

The pile ignited in a sudden burst of heat and dazzling radiance. She felt a tingling at the base of her spine; it climbed up her back, then pooled at the base of her skull. She looked expectantly at Euterpe and squeezed the Muse's hand. Would their fingers merge again, like they had months ago?

"What — what is supposed to happen now?" Euterpe whispered. Kay heard hoarse fear in her whisper.

"I — I don't know. Do you feel anything?"

"Only a slight tingling at the back of my neck. And that's fading away."

Oh, no, Kay thought. For she sensed her own tingling sensation also dying. She pulled Euterpe to the railing. "Can you see anything happening down there? Are they merging?"

"No, they're just fighting..."

"Nothing is happening..." Kay felt herself stumbling into a slough of despair.

It's not working!

Solstice Saturday, 5:08 P.M.

Roy heard confused whispers spread like contagion through his audience. They had every right to be confused — this wasn't who they'd come to hear, the defiant crusader who'd sworn that *every* neighborhood would be restored.

"So what do we do?" he asked his increasingly sullen audience. "What *can* we do? If you'll excuse my using another cowboys-and-Indians analogy, we circle our wagons. We shrink the footprint of New Orleans to a defensible perimeter."

A woman in the crowd's center shouted: "No!"

"Yes, ma'am," Roy answered back. "We shrink the footprint, pull our people inward to higher ground. We congregate inside a defensible border, small enough for the Corps of Engineers to realistically fortify against storm surge. We build *up*, instead of *out*. We turn parks into neighborhoods, if we have to, and low-lying neighborhoods into parks—"

"Nobody's knocking down my house!"

"You *traitor!*" another man screamed.

Roy pressed on, a small boat sailing into increasingly tempestuous seas. "If you reelect me as your mayor, I promise you I will carry out the following actions. I will use my powers of condemnation and expropriation to increase the city's inventory of blighted properties which sit on good, high land. At the same time, I will institute a land swap program, whereby the city will invite the owners of properties in severely flooded neighborhoods to trade—"

"That's *communism!*"

"Ain't *nobody* takin' my house!"

Something bounced off the front of the lectern. Roy ignored it. "I will direct my Department of Permits and Inspections to deny building or repair permits to any properties east of the Industrial Canal."

"Like *hell*, you will!"

Amazingly, Roy found his words flowed increasingly easy the more hostile the crowd grew. "For properties west of the Industrial Canal, building and repair permits will only be granted to those owners willing to raise their homes above the hundred year flood plain level."

"You'll kill New Orleans!"

"Uncle-frickin'-Tom, you'll knock down the Ninth Ward over my dead, stinkin' body!"

He looked out at the audience. He'd never seen such anger before, such wounded betrayal. "I'm a big enough man to admit I was wrong," he said. "I was wrong to promise you what you so desperately wanted to hear. Just like I was wrong to buy into the dream that a company like MuckGen could hand us utopia. I've taken a closer look at their science. They're playing with forces too dangerous to be safely harnessed. Until they can assure me their designs can be tested and produced without threatening the public safety, I must deny them use of city-owned land, and I will take them to court to prevent them from exploiting private land within the city's jurisdiction."

He cleared his throat. "That's... that's my program. No magic. No easy ways out. Just a lot of hard, back breaking work. Victory never assured, and failure always a real possibility. I wish it could be otherwise."

A white-haired black man standing in the front row threw his *Rio for Mayor* sign onto the asphalt. Roy recognized him, and the recognition made his knees go weak. It was John Wilson, whose Lower Ninth Ward home Roy had spent a blissful morning helping to rebuild.

Looking down into John Wilson's face, which trembled with hurt and disillusionment, Roy felt his heart break. He knew then that he'd accomplished what he'd needed to.

Solstice Saturday, 5:09 P.M.

Kay felt the weight of all her allies' eyes on her. *I refuse to fail. I will not accept that Owl's and Bob's deaths meant nothing. That Miriam and Amos Weintraub's deaths meant nothing.*

"Euterpe, take your clothes off," she told the Muse. Kay immediately stripped. The metal platform, heated by the still burning pile of hair, burned her bare feet. She pulled Euterpe close, then kissed her, desperately, brutally.

Remember! she told herself. *Remember how you felt when you first awoke in Felicia's bed, before the shock of seeing your melting body broke the ecstatic trance of the merging. Remember...*

The tingling returned to the base of her skull. This time, it didn't fade. It intensified until she felt a million millipedes dancing across her vertebrae. Fragmented images flashed upon the screen of her mind — she stood on a platform above a crowd, in a parking lot, and small, round, black objects, not much bigger than checkers, soared in tall arcs toward her. Then she sat at a corner table in a middle school's cafeteria — she'd never attended a middle school, never been inside one — hating the other children as they smirkingly walked past and dropped small, round, black objects on her table; yet at the same time yearning desperately for their acceptance.

She tasted something beneath her tongue. Something sweet, almost nauseatingly so. A cookie. An... Oreo?

"Kay," Lily said, her voice full of fearful excitement, "I feel something happening to me!"

"I do, too!" Daniel said. "It's like — like someone's ripping away a blanket inside my head!"

Kay felt her joints lose their suppleness. Her teeth loosened in their gums, her blood congealed as her arteries clogged with plaque. The fibers of her lungs grew coarse. The Otherness was being wrung out of her, leaving her body mortal and middle aged, a bag of weary flesh with an uncertain number of functional years left to it.

"Kay!" Lily cried. "The king of the Miasma Club and the queen of the Muses — their hands have merged to their wrists!"

Solstice Saturday, 5:12 P.M.

Roy Rio watched the small, round, black objects soar from darkness through arc lamps' beams and into darkness again. One ricocheted off his podium. Another glanced off his cheekbone, stunning him.

Sergeant Nick rushed up the platform's steps. "Mr. Mayor, get down!"

But Roy remained standing exactly where he was.

Cops rushed into the crowd, searching for the throwers. Roy grabbed the microphone. "No," he said. "No, don't try to stop them. It's just... cookies. Let them get their frustrations out. Just let them... get it all out."

He had to give Cynthia her due. None of the marchers would've brought the Oreos themselves; up until ten minutes ago, these people had been his supporters. Cynthia must've infiltrated her own people among the crowd, told them to make whatever mischief they could. And he'd given them a bigger opening than they ever could've dreamed of.

The Oreos continued falling like a storm of black hail... black hail with creamy, white filling. He protected his face with a clipboard, but refused to duck behind the podium. *Let them take it out on me; they never got a chance to take it out on Duckie Duckswitt, or the Governor, or the President. I'll show them a man can take it.* "White on the inside" or black *on the inside... a man is a man is a man. I'm just a man who tried, and failed. And, God willing, who succeeds by failing.*

At last the cookies stopped landing. People shuffled onto the buses which would take them back to the starting points of their marches. Then the buses pulled away.

Oreos lay scattered on the stage. He picked one up. *Haven't eaten one of these in more than thirty-five years. I used to like them, once.*

He slid it into his mouth.

It tasted bitter-sweet.

Solstice Saturday, 5:13 P.M.

Kay saw it was true — Calliope's and Mephistopheles's arms had merged nearly to their elbows. The more furiously they fought to disengage themselves, the faster they became entangled. *They're like tar babies*, she thought.

Clio screamed as her history tomes and hands melted into Old Scratch's concave chest. "Calliope, greatest of us all, save us from this *horror!*"

"Dear Sister!" Euterpe called down to her from the platform. "All is not horror! Remember if you can, oh Muse of history, the history of our blessed sisterhood! We cannot die, for we rise again and again! And those who come after us will eclipse even *our* radiance!"

Kay stared at Euterpe's naked feet. The flesh of her toes and ankles had begun dripping through the grating to the floor a dozen feet below, like melting wax. Droplets fell upon Ti Malice and Melpomene, Eleggua-Eshu and Thalia; close cousins, all. They lay tangled in a misshapen ball on the floor beneath the platform, limbs and torsos squished together like clumps of variously colored Play-Doe.

"Damn you, Mephistopheles!" Ti Malice shouted. "It was your weak leadership which led us to this! Had *I* been king, never would we have come to such an unmaking!"

"Oh, just shut the fuck *up*, man," Eleggua-Eshu said. "Damn, if there's one consolation in all this, it's that soon I won't have ears to hear your *crap* anymore. At least let me enjoy this urgin' to merge with these gorgeous, spirited ladies, okay?"

Kay watched Eleggua-Eshu vanish. The last remaining trace of his face, which lingered on the surface of the burbling muck like the Cheshire Cat's grin, was the glint of a gold-capped tooth.

Then Kay heard a hideous screech-hiss, the sound she imagined a cobra would spit when set afire.

"Look at Krampus!" Daniel shouted. "He's in *agony!*"

The green lizard demon had managed at last to ensnare Terpsichore with his obscenely prehensile tongue; he'd wound it around the Whirler like a living rope, binding her in a cage of glistening devil flesh. But now the living rope... *melted*. The Whirler's flesh melted, too, until Kay could no longer see where Terpsichore's body ended and Krampus's began.

The bubbling muck reached the spot where Fortuna had fallen. Kay watched her nemesis startle into wakefulness, then recoil from the touch of the gooey tide. She stared up at Kay with hatred that could melt steel. "You'll never get the best of me again, Jew bitch!" she shrieked. "Turn all of us into mud, and still I'll *drown* you in it!"

She leaped from the floor to the platform, trailing lurid ribbons of her own substance. She teetered on the railing's edge, ready to fall upon Kay. But before Fortuna could strike, Balor the Fomorian plucked her from the railing and held her tenderly in his massive arms.

She screamed in frustration. The Irish cyclops merely smiled. "Bee-you-tee-ful Fortuna," he said, "don't run away! Be with Balor! What is happening, it is *good!*"

Faebar the leprechaun kicked Balor on the nose. "Put her back on the platform, you *lummox!* Can't you see, she's our only chance to stop the Rosenblatt woman!"

Balor swatted Faebar from his shoulder. Then he squished him into the miasmatic mud, silencing his tiny tormentor forever.

He turned his sole eye on Euterpe. "Bee-you-tee-ful Muse," he said gently, "will you come join Balor, too, while he still has arms to lower you to the ground? Balor would like it so much if your face would be the last thing his eye will see."

He held out his free hand, inviting Euterpe to climb onto his arm.

Euterpe turned to Kay. "Goodbye," she said. She kissed Kay's cheek. As she withdrew, a web of slender strands hung briefly between her lips and Kay's skin, glistening like quicksilver.

"You... won't ever be forgotten," Kay said.

"I know. And I thank you." Euterpe sat upon Balor's shoulder. An instant later, her thighs and buttocks merged with his shoulder blade. The giant, sitting now in a lake of ooze, hugged Euterpe and Fortuna close. First his legs, then his pelvis, and then his torso surrendered themselves to the communal pool. Like a mastodon sinking into the La Brea tar pit, he slowly disappeared, along with his companions.

Erato the Lovely and Reynard the Fox were the last to go. With a mutual sigh, they surrendered their substance to the bubbling, greenish-brown muck — love's poetry and seduction's cruel lies, stirred together like clashing but somehow complementary ingredients, joining the earthy gumbo.

Kay descended the stairs to the pumping station's inundated floor. The miasmatic swamp rose to the middle of her calves. It felt warm and thick, a Louisiana version of the Dead Sea. "We need to return all this to the Mother," she said.

"Good heavens," Lily said from above, "*how?*"

"I spent the last few weeks familiarizing myself with this station. There's a fallback safety feature. A set of drain valves in the walls above the suction and discharge basins, to dry the station out if the pumps ever failed and flooded the building."

She waded through the muck to a control panel, then twisted three of six shuttle cocks clockwise. With a metallic grinding, the doors of the drain valves slid open in the base of the wall above the suction basin. Giant bubbles formed on the surface of the murky lake near the wall, bursting as the miasmatic mire began draining, releasing scents of cabbage and cinnamon.

"Come on down, you all," she called to her companions. She retrieved several mops and brooms from a nearby utility closet. "Help me make sure every bit of this stuff gets pushed out those drains. Once it's in the suction basin, the pumps will expel it into the outfall canals that lead to Lake Pontchartrain and Lake Manchac. It'll be spread out over hundreds of square miles, then slowly reabsorbed into the Mother."

Daniel, Lily, and Pandora descended the steps. Kay held out a push broom to Daniel. "How — how do you *feel*, darling?" she asked, almost afraid to breathe.

"I feel... *good*," he said. "Tired, but good. After I push all this glop out the drains, I want to lie down in bed for a week. Next to you."

Please, please keep feeling that way, dearest. "And what about you, Lily?"

Lily stared at Kay as though she were seeing her for the first time. Her eyes filled with tears; but she was smiling. "Kay, I... I..." She grabbed Kay's hand and pulled it to her lips, then nuzzled it against her cheek. "I had no idea, *no idea*, that *anyone* could love me the way that you do. What happened just now — you were the prism for it all, and I was able to see *inside* the prism... I'd always hoped my father loved me that way, with the kind of strength of love I saw in you. People are so cut off from each other, and it's so hard to *trust*..."

"Lily, I'm so terribly, terribly *sorry* for what I did to your parents—"

"Shhh, I *know*. I know how you've hated yourself. I know what you gave up to save us all, and to honor their memories."

Kay felt her own eyes brim over. "I'd give it up a *thousand* times, just to hear you say that." She pulled Lily close and kissed her cheeks and her nose. "Would you like a mop?"

"I would *love* a mop."

They pushed the miasmatic murk toward the drainage chutes. Kay wanted to expel it as quickly as possible so she could shut down the unbalanced pumps, which vibrated with an ominous clanging. *I can't believe it's over*, she thought, *it's* really *over...*

Her mop hit something hard beneath the surface.

"*SssKKkkeeeeeeEEEEEEE!*"

A missile exploded from out of the muck, waving its misshapen metallic arms like a deranged robot — what remained of Glenn the Gremlin. Pandora screamed. Daniel whacked Glenn with his push broom, again and again, scattering ruined circuit boards, mangled wires, and shorted-out electrodes. The disintegrating gremlin tried climbing the wall like a monstrous metal cockroach. But the muck chased after him, projecting pseudopods up the bricks, hunting him like a gigantic predatory amoeba.

Daniel tried knocking the gremlin from the wall before Kay caught his arm. "Daniel, *don't!* My God, I completely forgot! He's still got the *baby* on him!"

The pseudopods wrapped around Glenn's clawed feet, absorbing them. Glenn froze. His network of wires and coils emitted a shower of sparks, and he toppled into the muck. Kay rushed to rescue the baby, but the spot where Glenn had fallen frothed and steamed like a bed of boiling magma.

The instant the frothing subsided, she fell to her knees and swept her arms through the opaque mire. *Euterpe never realized the child was here*, she thought, *or she would've begged me to rescue it. For her sake, let me find it — but how could* anything *have survived?*

Undulant ripples disturbed the muck. The baby bobbed to the surface, surrounded by an oily membrane which popped as soon as it touched the air.

Kay picked the child up. It was a little boy. Astonishingly, he didn't cry; he stared up at Kay with large, brown eyes, curious and full of yearning. All his tiny features were perfect, from his toes to a head of luxuriant, curly hair.

He didn't drown, even though he was beneath the muck for three or four minutes. He's not mortal. She examined him carefully. *No part of him dissolved, though. So he's not fully Other, either. He's a hybrid, an amphibian, born of mother and Mother both.*

Kay hugged the baby against her chest. She swayed from side to side, rocking him. He cooed at her touch. "Daniel, honey, would you bring my clothes down, please? And Lily, call an ambulance for Bruno."

She held the baby up and looked into his eyes again. "Oh, poor little man, I can't bear to think what Glenn must've done to your mommy and daddy. But I promise you, you'll never be without a family. Isn't that right?" she said, looking at Pandora and Lily, then at Daniel.

The joy of Kay's smile was radiant enough to affect even the formerly gray-brown miasma, which shimmered like a sea of jewels.

Chapter 37

THE primary election took place on an unusually cold January Saturday marked by sleet and flurries, rare for New Orleans. That night in the Hotel Monteleone's main ballroom, Roy Rio's campaign headquarters, the mayor told the band to pack it in not long after the earliest precinct results started streaming across the room's big-screen TVs.

Only a handful of supporters and journalists lingered as the members of the Walter Payton Quartet packed their instruments. A few diehards helped themselves to lavish plates from the buffet: steamed oysters, Creole lasagna, and redfish stuffed with minced crab dressing. An awful lot of food stood to go bad if someone didn't eat it. Roy would have to make sure all this stuff got sent over to the New Orleans Mission and Ozanam Inn, the city's two main homeless shelters.

With the exception of a very junior reporter from *The Times Picayune*, the local press had decamped for the campaign headquarters of Cynthia Belvedere Hotchkiss and Van Goodfeller. A few of the foreign journalists remained, waiting for the local TV stations to officially announce the results and for the mayor to make a statement.

Kay, Pandora, Daniel, and Lily had gathered near one of the food tables. Roy went to join them. Glancing at the pans of shellfish and exotic sausage, he realized with a surge of chagrin that he hadn't provided much for three of his closest friends, all observant Jews, to eat. "Hey," he said, "y'know, I just realized virtually all this stuff is *traife*... I'm really sorry."

"Please don't worry about it, Mr. Mayor," Daniel said. "The baked macaroni and cheese was very, very good. Some of the *best* I've ever had."

"Roy," Lily asked, "are you going to be okay?"

He nodded. "Tonight will be over soon. And tomorrow, as they say, is another day. A new start." He smiled to reassure her, then took a moment to quietly appreciate the new Lily. She had undergone a sea change since the night of the Solstice. Her old discomfort with herself, the inconsolability and bitter loneliness which had never seemed that far from the surface, had vanished. It wasn't that she was happy now — not quite — but she seemed finally ready to experience happiness, to accept it whenever it chose to flutter within reach. One of the most striking changes in her was how she interacted with Kay. They'd become virtually inseparable, closer than any pair of real sisters he'd ever known.

"A new start is a wonderful thing," Kay said. She wore a floppy green velvet hat, which proved an irresistible lure for Lupé's tiny, chubby hands. "Have you thought about what you'd like to do next?"

"Actually, I have. I've been thinking about it a lot."

"Maybe I could help...?" Daniel said. He laughed. "I may not know a lot, but I'm turning into a really fast learner."

"Yes, he is," Kay said, beaming proudly at him.

"Well, I've been thinking about getting back into the entertainment software business," Roy said.

"More games?" Daniel asked.

"Kind of, but no more shoot-'em-ups. What I'd like to work on is a fantasy role-playing game, one that would revolve around people interacting with their natural and built environments. Characters would plan cities, build roads and neighborhoods and levees, drain swamps... I'd like to give players the option to move their characters from a 'man conquers his surroundings' mindset to more of a 'how can we work hand-in-hand with our environment?' mindset. Reward players who show that their thinking can evolve."

"This is a fantasy game?" Kay asked. "Will some of these role-playing characters be... bad luck spirits?"

Roy laughed. "Why not? I've got the best expert consultants a guy could ask for. Besides, wouldn't Krampus look *awesome* on the cover of a game box? That tongue..."

Lily shuddered, and Roy regretted his flippant remark. But Kay rescued the moment. "Speaking of tongues," she said, "the doctors say Bruno should regain at least eighty percent of the use of his, thanks to Daniel, who rescued it before it got washed out to sea. Bruno's surgeon is still flabbergasted that the tongue remained so well preserved before we could pack it in ice. Miasmatic mud makes a fine preservative, apparently."

"That's really great," Roy said. "Bruno is a good man."

One of the foreign journalists, an Australian, waved at Roy. "Mr. Mayor, excuse me, but they're projecting the results on the telly. Would you mind having a look, and then perhaps we could get a statement?"

Roy reluctantly shifted his attention to one of the TV screens. The final results weren't any prettier than the early returns had been. Cynthia retained a strong lead, at 38.6 percent, though not strong enough to avoid a runoff. Van Goodfeller, with 32.3 percent, had earned the right to be her opponent. A dark horse candidate, Fred "Nighthawk" Halsey, a former state representative from Algiers whom the pundits had written off months ago, had edged Roy out of third place by garnering 15.3 percent of the vote.

"Mr. Mayor," the Australian asked, "do you consider these results a repudiation of your job performance during the Antonia disaster?"

"No," Roy said. "I'd say this was more, oh, an understandable reaction on many people's parts to being told a truth they preferred not to hear."

"Would you care to elaborate on that?"

"No, I wouldn't."

"What about this, then? How does it feel to be the first New Orleans mayor in living memory to fail to either win reelection outright or be selected as a candidate for the runoff election?"

Roy tried to think of a response which wouldn't be either rude or obscene. "No comment," he said.

"Oh, *come* now! I've flown all the way from Sydney to talk with you. That's twenty hours in coach, mate. Surely you have *something* of interest to say to my readers?"

"Tell them..." He laughed. He didn't need to play this game anymore. As of tonight, he was a free man. He didn't need to upstage the Morehouses, checkmate his ex-wife, or impress anybody. "Tell them New Orleans is open for business, and we would love for them to come visit and spend lots of money."

"That's *all?*"

"That's all."

"Well, then..." The journalist stared longingly at the food table. "Do you think it would be all right if I fixed myself a couple of plates to go?"

"Be my guest, man. Knock yourself out."

When Roy returned to his friends, he saw that Nicole had joined them. She looked miserable.

"Hi, sweetheart," he said. "What's the matter? I thought your mom would want you to stick around at her shindig for a while yet."

Nicole's lower lip trembled. "Ohhh, *Daddy*..." She flung her arms around his neck and started crying.

"What's the *matter*, baby?"

"It's — it's all my *fault*. Mama — she's got no *business* being elected. She's lied, and lied, and *lied*. And I've *let* her!"

"It's okay, honey," he said, stroking her hair.

"No, it's *not*. *You* should be in the runoff. Not Mama. And if I'd been brave, if I'd told the reporters what I'd seen, you would've won, Daddy. You would've beaten her—"

"I said, it's okay, Nicole."

"Stop saying 'it's okay'! You haven't heard what I did — I mean, what I *didn't* do. You know those billboards? The ones that make Mama look like a hero? It wasn't like that at all; it was the *opposite* of what Mama says it was! I know, because I snapped the photo—"

Roy grasped his daughter's shoulders and held her at arm's length so she could see his face. "I *know*, baby. I know the whole story. Your Uncle Quincy told me weeks ago."

"He *did?* You — you *know?* But, but, but why—"

"Why didn't I pressure you to talk to reporters? Because there's no way in *hell* I'd ever put you in that position, Nicole. I would *never* force you to choose between me and your mother."

"But if you knew you were going to lose...?"

"Your mother didn't beat me, Nicole. *I* beat me. And that's a *good* thing."

"I don't understand..."

Roy looked at his other companions. "Baby, these friends can explain *everything*. But not tonight, hon. A pretty good man once said, 'I'd rather lose an election and win a war than win an election and lose a war.'" He hugged his daughter tightly. "Well, baby, I'd like to think I'm a pretty good man. A better daddy than a mayor, maybe."

"Daddy, you're the *best*."

After a moment, Nicole went to get herself a glass of punch. Lily pulled him aside. "Roy, I've been wondering about something. This game you plan to create — how does a player win?"

He turned to Kay and her tiny companion. "Why don't *you* tell us, Kay?"

"I wish I knew," she said. Lupé grew fussy, so she bounced him on her hip. "All I can say for certain is that the rules have changed since Antonia. Lupé and the twins are proof. Something changed the Mother's relationship with the people who live here."

"Maybe... it was the deaths?" Daniel suggested. "Death can bring members of a family closer. Maybe, when those hundreds of people drowned — when my father drowned — the Mother was able to see inside them for the first time. Maybe she never realized how much New Orleanians love this place... enough to risk killer hurricanes to stay here. And if they love this place that much, doesn't that mean they love *her*, too? Maybe Lupé, and the twins... maybe they're the Mother's way of saying she's sorry?"

"Like Noah's rainbow..." Lily said.

"The Lord's promise not to send the flood again," Roy said. "Wouldn't that be super?" He held his arms out toward the baby. "You mind if I hold him some?"

"Please do," Kay said. Roy discovered the baby was heavier than he looked — fifteen pounds, if an ounce. Strong, too; he squirmed when Kay handed him over and reached back for her. "The Family Services people have been very accommodating," she said. "They're letting Daniel and me keep him three hours a day, longer on weekends. We've got all our paperwork lined up, so as soon as we're married in May, we can officially become his foster parents."

"That's fantastic," Roy said. The baby felt awkward in his hands, a wiggling monkey; it had been so long since Nicole had been this size, he'd forgotten how to hold an infant. "What a big, solid fellow," he said, hoping to sound at least vaguely uncle-ish. He felt a sudden urge to sneeze. Unable to cover his nose, he looked away from the baby. The first sneeze triggered another, then a rolling tsunami of sneezes. Blindly, he passed the child back to Kay.

"Come *here*, little man," Kay said firmly as she took back Lupé. "You little troublemaker. We're going to have to work on mastering that impulse, I see. My lord, it's almost like having my aura back again." She kissed Lupé on his forehead, then set him on her shoulder and patted his back until he settled down.

"Maybe *he'll* be able to give you your answer, sweetheart, once he learns to talk," Roy told Lily after his sneezing subsided. "He and the twins, they'll sort of be our ambassadors. Maybe, with a foot in both worlds, they'll be able to figure out how we can all live in this place without killing it, and without getting killed ourselves. Hey, maybe Lupé can go to work with MuckGen, show them how to replicate the Mother's energy the *right* way. Instead of poking around in the dark, we'll have eyes to see for us and voices to talk for us. Who knows — maybe we can end up with something better than just a fifty-year truce...?"

He laughed. The easy, unforced, honest quality of his laughter surprised him — Lily, Kay, and Daniel hadn't been the only ones to experience major change, he realized. "What do I need a Muse for? I may not have figured out the end of my game, but just jawing with you guys, I've dreamed up half a dozen ways for players to get there. Ain't that a kick in the head?"

"How about we all continue the brainstorming at the Clover Grill on Bourbon Street?" Lily asked.

Roy kissed her cheek. "Babe, you've got it."

Epilogue: Seven Queens for a City Reborning

K AY had never seen the old, pre-storm Mary Queen of Vietnam church. But she was certain this new one must far outstrip the original in beauty. Not due to any architectural virtues — the new building was hardly more than a prefabricated warehouse — but because of the joyful reunion it heralded. New Orleans had taken in the Vietnamese boat people when few other communities would; now those same people returned the favor by refusing to abandon her.

Lupé clung tightly to Kay's neck as she, Lily, Pandora, and Nicole walked to the new playground next to the church for his first play date with the twins. Kay had brought a child-friendly portable music player and a set of New Orleans music CDs: traditional jazz by Sweet Emma, rhythm and blues by Professor Longhair and Clarence "Frogman" Henry, and street brass music by the Fresh Birth Brass Band. *Euterpe would appreciate what I picked out*, she thought.

"Miss Kay, may I take that bag from you?" Nicole asked.

"Are you sure you can handle more packages?"

"I'm stronger than I look."

"Yes, you are." Kay let Nicole take her bag. "I'm so proud of you, Nicole. You made a hard choice, a mature choice."

"Maybe you're giving me too much credit? I mean, what I did could've just been my way of forcing Daddy to let me move back here. 'Cause after I dropped the dime on Mama, I sure as heck couldn't stay in Houston anymore."

"Don't cut yourself short, Nicole. Maybe you had more than one motive, but no one willingly cuts their ties to their mother. It's a terrifying, awful decision to have to make. Once her anger subsides, I hope your mother realizes this. And I hope that realization will cause her to rethink some of her own decisions."

"Do you think what I did will make a difference?"

"We'll know in six days, dear, when the voters have their say. I'd like to think the people of New Orleans can make sensible judgements based on the character the candidates have displayed. We'll see."

Anh and Paul waved. They'd placed Mary and Jacob, already nicknamed Ba and Ong, in infant swings. The two babies uttered delighted gurgles as they were gently rocked. Nicole and Lily set down their packages next to the swing set.

"Oh, this is *way* too much," Anh said. "I'm so embarrassed — we only bought Lupé one little thing, and here you *bury* us in presents."

"Don't worry," Kay said, seating herself and Lupé on the recently planted grass. "These aren't gifts — they're investments in our new play group. So this stuff isn't just for the twins and Lupé to enjoy; it's also for the babies we'll discover after future equinoxes and solstices. They'll learn to love New Orleans and the people who live here, who make these wonderful things. Or, if they don't learn, it won't be for our lack of trying."

"The faster we can teach them to control themselves, the better," Anh said, laughing ruefully. "Just yesterday, while Ba was in her portable crib and Ong was in his Snugly, I nearly burned the house down with a grease fire on the stove. Thank *God* you'd warned us to have a fire extinguisher always handy!"

"And don't forget when I slipped off my ladder cleaning out our rain gutters," Paul said. "But it's worth it, it's all worth it."

"Dear, I didn't say it *wasn't!*" Anh said.

"Even though I was born here," Paul said, "I never felt like I truly *belonged* until I had my own children. And the twins don't only toss off bad fortune, you know. Three days ago, on a strange whim, I sat down at the piano in our community center. I hadn't touched a keyboard since I was eleven years old. But I felt a fresh breeze blow through my soul. It was like one of those dreams where you suspect you can fly and you leap up into the air and suddenly, you are airborne. My fingers remembered everything they'd ever been taught, and more."

"He played beautifully," Anh said. "Everyone in the room considered it a wonder."

"Those are the signs we'll watch for," Kay said. "Seemingly unexplainable phenomena of new skills spontaneously blossoming or bizarre accidents happening to parents of newborns. We'll reach out to those families and draw them into our play group."

"Does this mean we've turned the corner?" Lily asked. "The fact that, instead of the Miasma Club, we've got the... oh, I don't know, the Paranormal Play Group?"

"We'll be dealing with little human beings, so nothing can be said to be set in stone. All we can do is provide them tools to help their understanding grow, and give them reasons to learn to love. Teach them how to balance their loyalties, and how to temper their hates. The rest will be up to them."

The twins gravitated toward Pandora, reaching for her, smiling at her gentle, grandmotherly touch. Lupé had already selected her as his "nana," preferring her company to anyone's but Kay's. Nicole set up the portable music player and put on Sweet Emma.

Lily pulled Kay aside. "I've got something I need to tell you. In private."

"Nicole," Kay said, "would you mind holding Lupé for a bit?"

"Sure!" Nicole said, eagerly scooping Lupé into her arms. "C'mon, baby, let's *dance!*"

Kay followed Lily to a shady spot next to a pair of seesaws. She feared Lily would tell her the District Attorney had decided to reinstate the charges, which had been dropped when the key witness against Lily had backed out. But the news had nothing to do with the District Attorney.

"I'm seven weeks overdue for my period," Lily said. "At first, I figured, you know, this is my change of life — game over; it's time to start plucking hairs from my chin..."

"Have you taken a test?"

She sucked in a breath. "Yup. This morning. Bright, *bright* red line."

"Is it Roy's?"

"Unless this is an immaculate conception, he's the only possible candidate."

Kay smiled. "I thought so. I've suspected for weeks."

"How?"

"On the Solstice, when your Otherness flowed through me, linking us, I felt... something, another presence inside you. But I couldn't be sure. More recently, I've noticed that Lupé's been acting oddly around you."

"You mean his always wanting to put his face against my tummy?"

Kay nodded.

"But... but does that mean...?"

Kay hugged her and kissed her cheek. "I think, dear, when you find an obstetrician, you'd better let her know to block out her calendar for June twenty-first, the Summer Equinox. A good day to have a baby — she'll be an exquisite balance between light and darkness, noon and midnight."

Kay stared fondly at the young woman dancing across the grass with Lupé in her arms. "I can't wait till we tell Nicole she's going to have a very special little sister."

Acknowledgements

THE WRITER wishes to express his appreciation to the following family members and friends for invaluable suggestions they offered during this manuscript's long gestation: Dara Fox, Denise Dumars, Barry N. Malzberg, Mark McCandless, Marian Moore, Diana Rowland, Laura Joh Rowland, Peter Rubie, Lori Smith, and Fritz Ziegler.

About the Author

ANDREW FOX has been a fan of science fiction and horror since he saw *Destroy All Monsters* at the drive-in theater at the age of three. His books include *Fat White Vampire Blues*, winner of the Ruthven Award for Best Vampire Fiction of 2003; *Bride of the Fat White Vampire*; *Fat White Vampire Otaku*; *Fire on Iron*, a Civil War dark fantasy; and *The Good Humor Man, or, Calorie 3501*, selected by Booklist as one of the Ten Best SF/Fantasy Novels of the Year for 2009. In 2006, he won the *Moment* Magazine-Karma Foundation Short Fiction Award. His stories have appeared in *Scifi.com* and *Nightmare.com*, and his essays have been published in *Moment* and *Tablet* Magazine. He edited a companion volume to *Hazardous Imaginings*, the international anthology *Again, Hazardous Imaginings: More Politically Incorrect Science Fiction*, which will be available from MonstraCity Press in December 2020. His next novel, *The Bad Luck Spirits' Social Aid and Pleasure Club*, revolves around an alternate Hurricane Katrina and will be published in February 2021. He lives in Northern Virginia with his family, where he works for a federal law enforcement agency. He can be reached at http://www.fantasticalandrewfox.com.

Fat White Vampire Otaku Available April 2021 from MonstraCity Press

The third book in the Fat White Vampire Series; immediately follows the events of tie-in novel *The Bad Luck Spirits' Social Aid and Pleasure Club*. Jules Duchon and his vampiric family suffer through the ravages of Hurricane Antonia and struggle to survive in a city emptied of its population — and its sources of blood. Where will they get their meals? But salvation comes from the most unlikely source possible: a trio of Japanese superheroes called Bonsai Master, Anime Girl, and Cutie-Scary Man. However, that salvation comes with a bedeviling price. For the blood donated by the three superheroes proves to have highly unpredictable effects on Jules and his family. Chaos ensues, in the best tradition of the Fat White Vampire Series!

Available in paperback for the first time!

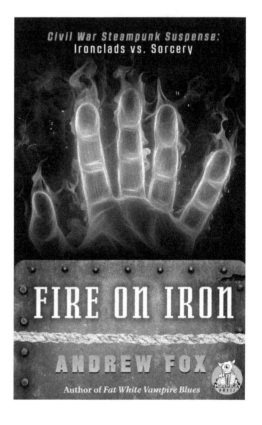

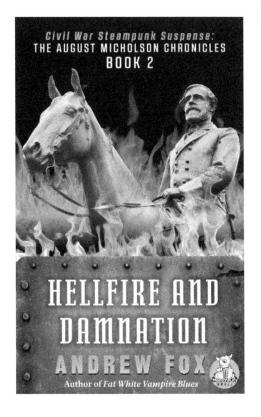

CPSIA information can be obtained
at www.ICGtesting.com
Printed in the USA
BVHW041925260221
601224BV00016B/518

9 780989 802765